WICKER GIRL

EVERYONE KNOWS... SMOKING KILLS

ELY NORTH

RED HANDED PRINT

Website: https://elynorthcrimefiction.com
To contact ely@elynorthcrimefiction.com
https://www.facebook.com/elynorthcrimefictionUK

Cover design by Cherie Chapman/Chapman & Wilder

Cover images © bilanol/ bonciutoma / Adobe Stock Photos
Disclaimer: This is a work of fiction. Names, characters, businesses, places,
events, locales, and incidents are either the products of the author's imagination
or used in a fictitious manner. Any resemblance to actual persons, living or dead,
or actual events is purely coincidental.

Published by Red Handed Print
First Edition
Kindle e-book ISBN-13: 978-1-7638413-0-7
Paperback ISBN-13: 978-1-7638413-1-4

Contact Ely North

Contact: ely@elynorthcrimefiction.com

Website: https://elynorthcrimefiction.com

Follow me on Facebook for the latest

https://facebook.com/elynorthcrimefictionUK

Sign up to my newsletter for all the latest news, releases, and discounts.

Newsletter Sign-Up below

Prologue
Sunday 4th June 1989 - North Yorkshire

She didn't want it until she did.

Twenty minutes ago, she felt the first kick.

And that changed *everything*.

Iona Jacobs exits the gloomy interior of The Crown public house located in the sleepy rural village of Ashenby.

A glorious afternoon sun is swaddled in an aqua sky, casting warmth over lush green fields.

She breathes in the pristine air. A perfume of freshly cut grass and wildflowers is carried on a warm summer breeze.

The last of the Sunday sippers drift outside: two older locals and a couple of young lads, who've only just passed the age of eighteen and seem intent on spending a huge proportion of their money, and their free time, propping up a bar.

Maybe it's a novelty that will pass? Then again... these things can linger for a lifetime.

The older men wobble off up towards the heart of the village, the lads meander across the car park towards a sorry-looking white Ford Fiesta. Grey primer and hand-brushed Hammerite scar the wheel arches and parts of the bonnet in an attempt to ward off rust. Both boys, because that is what they are, spark up cigarettes simultaneously, as if it's a rite of passage.

Iona is barely four years older than them—but mentally and emotionally she's surpassed them by a decade

Recently, she's grown up fast.

She grabs her bike propped against the sandstone wall, hitches up her knee-length skirt, and swings her leg over the saddle. It's an old-fashioned bicycle, heavy, no gears, wicker basket on the front, like the one her gran used to ride. But she likes it. And luckily, the village of Ashenby is peculiarly flat for this area of North Yorkshire. Even the five-mile ride to Ravensbane Castle only has one testing hill. Composing herself, she readjusts her ponytail and slides her sunglasses down over her eyes. The Ford Fiesta toots as it passes, the lads grinning and waving.

She returns a half-wave, smiling—slightly embarrassed—as *She Drives Me Crazy* by Fine Young Cannibals blares from the car.

———◆———

Dismounting at the entrance to St Mary's Church, she spots Reverend Hartley crouched over, filling the lawn-mower with petrol. He's still dressed in his Sunday best—smart black trousers, white shirt, and black waistcoat, his deep black hair swept back, side parting, clean shaven, athletic.

Her heart skips a beat. If she were Catherine, he'd be Heathcliff, preferably without the tragic ending, although, she reflects, too late for that now. Despite her predicament, she can't help but ogle as he wipes sweat from his brow with a muscled forearm. A twang of remorse shoots through her.

'Hello, Reverend Hartley?' she yells in her soft, Scottish lilt, waving a little too enthusiastically for a Sunday afternoon in a sleepy village. Propping the bike against the wall, she pushes open the creaky iron gate and saunters down the path, flanked by ancient gravestones and overgrown grass.

The reverend straightens from the mower, a smile spreading across his swarthy face.

'Ah, Iona. How pleasant to see you. Missed you at service this morning.'

'Sorry, I slept in. Late night at the pub. PC McGregor took his family to London for the weekend, which meant...'

He cuts her off. '... the landlord decided to extend licensing hours?'

'Yes. Something like that. Not too bad. All the stragglers were gone by midnight.' She studies him, puzzled. 'Why are you cutting grass in your good clothes?'

He laughs. 'I don't really have any old clothes. Anyway, tomorrow's washday.' Pulling a white handkerchief from his trousers, he dabs at the grime on his face. 'So, how can I help or were you just passing?'

'Just passing. Out for a gentle ride.'

'I see. Beautiful afternoon for it.'

Her smile dwindles like the setting of the winter sun. 'Yes. Well, actually. That's not true. I did want a word. In private,' she adds.

Reverend Hartley, astute to body language, frowns. 'Hmm... I see. Nothing serious, I hope?'

Her ponytail flicks back as she casts a glance around.

They're alone.

She shuffles.

Her gaze drops to the path and the orphaned gravestones, now re-purposed as paving slabs.

She makes out part of an eroded engraving.

"Departed this life aged 1 year."

The baby inside her doesn't stir.

The reverend pushes his hanky back into his pocket and extends an arm towards the church.

'Would you care to step inside and have a chat?'

A shake of the head. 'No. It's too nice a day. Maybe...' she nods towards the rear of the church where the headstones flourish like weeds.

'Of course.'

Side by side, close enough to feel each other's heat, and ardour, they meander towards the cemetery.

There's no easy way to say it.

She can't bear to look into his eyes but forces herself.

He detects her discomfort.

'I'm ready when you are,' he says with a toothy grin.

'Nicholas—I'm pregnant.'

Joy drains from his face, leaving the pallor of night.

'I see.' He sticks his hands in his pockets, then immediately withdraws them. He tries a cheery laugh, but it rings hollow. 'Well, that certainly changes things. Unlucky, weren't we? Just that once. I always imagined starting a family—just not this soon. And not out of wedlock. How far gone?'

Now she averts his gaze. 'Eighteen weeks.'

He nods, accepting of the news. 'Well, there's only one thing for it—we must do the right thing. If we get married quickly, then not many will notice the timing when the baby arrives.' He pauses. 'Eighteen weeks?' The words are full of doubt as he mentally works his way back through the calendar.

'It's not yours,' Iona murmurs.

A punch to the gut.

His face hardens to granite. 'I see. Whose?'

Iona shakes her head. 'It doesn't matter. It wasn't meant to happen. I didn't... he was... let's say I tried to resist his advances.'

'Not very successfully,' he bites back.

Hurt stings her face. 'You don't understand.'

'No, I bloody well don't. I thought we had feelings for each other?'

'We do.'

'Nice way to show it,' he snarls.

'Nicholas, you're angry and upset. I understand.'

'No, you bloody don't. If you did, you'd have kept your damn legs shut!'

She clenches her fists. 'I told you; I didn't have a choice.'

He sneers. 'Ha! What an excuse. We all have choices, Iona. But willpower is a different thing.'

'Can we at least still be friends?' she pleads, her eyes filling with tears.

He softens and nods, heartbroken but not heartless. 'Yes,' he whispers, eyes on the ground.

'I was going to get rid of it. But today I felt the first kick, and I just knew I couldn't do it. If I could get rid of his *half*, I would. But I can't. I'm going to love and cherish this child.'

'Yes, of course you will. You've made the right decision. Will I still see you in church?'

She shakes her head. 'No. It's for the best. Too painful for both of us. Anyway, I think I'll move back home.'

'Scotland?' he says, aghast.

'Don't say it like that. It's hardly the other side of the world.'

'When will you go?'

'Sooner rather than later. I'm not looking forward to breaking the news to my mother. One last hug?'

———— ◆ ————

Iona breaks away from his warm embrace.

Her eyes implore him. 'I'm so sorry, Nicholas, but please promise me, on your life, you'll never tell another soul as long as you live?'

He twitches and gazes at a patch of moss growing on a tombstone.

'I swear on Almighty God I'll never tell another living soul. But it doesn't have to be this way, Iona.'

She pecks him on the cheek. 'Yes, it does. Bye, Nicholas.'

Reverend Hartley watches, heavy-hearted, as the graceful Iona Jacobs mounts her bike and wobbles away. The handlebars skim his white Citroën 2CV. She casts one last apologetic smile over her shoulder—like it's her fault.

'All things must pass,' he whispers.

A battered red Mini Cooper roars past the church, exhaust blowing hard, followed by a white Ford Fiesta.

He doesn't notice.

The scent of rapeseed on the breeze. The warmth of the sun on his brow. The faint whine of a distant motorbike.

None of it registers.

His thoughts are full of her. His heart seethes. Blood boils. She told him enough. But not everything. No name. But he knows. He's pieced it together.

Something pure was taken. Stained. Defiled.

A dream—his dream—snuffed out.

They can never be.

His God preaches forgiveness.

But Hartley is a man. And man is not as forgiving.

And anger... well, anger acts in haste—and *repents* at leisure.

The late afternoon sunshine bathes the Yorkshire countryside in honey-gold light. Iona takes the long way back, cycling past Ferguson's meadow, where wild purple orchids and buttercups grow in abundance.

No rush.

Not today.

The baby kicks again, stronger this time. She places a hand on her belly, smiling. Despite everything, she knows she's made the right choice. As life grows within, a deadening weight lifts from her mind.

Passing Mr and Mrs Selkirk's cottage, she plucks a sprig of lavender from the overgrown garden. She won't mind—she's been sharing her lavender with village girls for years. Iona tucks it into her bicycle's handlebar grip, releasing a burst of fragrance.

An engine whines in the distance, like an angry mosquito.

A slight infraction on the tranquillity, nothing more.

An abundance of wild strawberries ripening along the mossy verge below the hedgerow catch her eye. She stops, crouches, and picks a handful. One goes straight to her mouth—sweet, sun-warmed, and early. There might just be enough to mix with apples for a crumble, something simple and fresh for the Sunday evening regulars at the pub.

Carefree, she remounts her bike and rounds the corner onto the boundary of Ravensbane Wood. An ancient oak casts a cool, dark green canopy against a watchful sun. The road ahead appears to shimmer in the heat. It's warm, but not that warm.

———◦———

Sometimes events happen so fast, it's impossible to react.

No time to scream.

No cry for help.

Just a dull clunk followed by the squeal of brakes.

A pause.

Then... the roar of an engine as it accelerates away.

The bicycle lies twisted on the warm bitumen. Back wheel buckled; frame mangled. The last thing she saw—the wicker basket, a cradle, torn from its mounting.

The front wheel spins, slowing with each rotation, marked by a mournful clickety-clack, clickety-clack, clickety... clack.

Until—it stops.

Sunglasses lie shattered on the grass verge, one lens reflecting strawberries strewn across the road.

A slender, naked foot protrudes from a grassy ditch, red-painted toenails stark against pale skin—as jarring as a discordant note in a lullaby.

The birds, momentarily startled into silence by the savagery, resume their afternoon chorus.

Sweet, melodic, idyllic.

A fat bumblebee hovers, then settles on the sprig of lavender still tucked into the handlebar, unaware that in Iona's world, everything has changed.

Forever.

1

35 years later - Sunday 30th April

Malachi Abbott sucks on the soggy stub of his rollie until it burns his calloused fingers. After fifty years of manual graft, his skin's forgotten what pain is.

He hacks out a plume of grey smoke.

Spits.

Tongue rasps against brown teeth.

He grizzles gazing upwards. 'Hrrrm...'

The Flower Moon hangs closer to Earth than it has for many a year.

A perfect night for hunting.

He tosses the tab to the ground and adjusts the twelve-bore over his shoulder until it sits snug.

The faint wisp of wood smoke visits him again.

Grimaces, like a bulldog chewing broken glass.

'Bloody heathen bastards,' he mutters... to no one.

Because no one listens to Malachi anymore—not since... *the incident.*

They believed her, not him.

Bones creak. Skin sags. Time passes.

Memories flutter by like butterflies.

But stains on a man's character are etched in stone.

He moves through Ravensbane Wood with the silent ease of a predator. Every twist, every thicket, every root-twisted oak—Malachi knows them better than he knows himself.

Removing a sturdy cosh from inside his overcoat, he clubs the terrified rabbit over the head once and loosens the snare around its foot. Placing one gnarly hand around its throat, and one around the lifeless back legs, he offers a short, sharp tug, as if pulling his own Christmas cracker. The neck snaps with a satisfying crack. With a piece of twine, he twists a loop around the feet and attaches it to his other catch, then places the pair over his shoulder like a saddlebag. Slipping out a hip flask, he takes a mouthful of whisky and gazes up at the stars.

The moon reaches its zenith—a giant white glow, close enough to touch. Scanning the horizon, he notices the reddish orange glow in the distance. The wood smoke thickens.

He slips the flask away and wipes a drop of snot from his nose onto the back of his coat sleeve.

'Hrrrm...'

The air is cool, not biting—more refreshing than debilitating, but still cold enough to make the skin prickle underneath a heavy overcoat and moth-eaten sweater.

The countryside teeters in the no-man's-land of spring and summer, not quite sure which way to lean. Warmth from the day clings to the soil, hiding from the crispness and clarity of the night. Earthy aromas of wild garlic mingle with the subtle scent of bluebells and the occasional sweet bouquet of hawthorn blossom hitchhiking on a fresh breeze.

An owl hoots. Something rustles in the undergrowth.

Malachi relaxes back into a clump of ferns and pulls out a cheese and pickle sandwich from his coat pocket. As he takes a bite, dark clouds drift across the moon, dimming the countryside in stages. A blaze of lightning zigzags across the sky, followed by deep, rolling thunder. The wind lifts, sharp with the smell of rain.

He squints northeast. 'That storm's not far off.'

With one hand still clutching his sandwich, he refocuses the binoculars on the fire near the ancient standing stones.

The sight appals him. And yet... he's entranced.

Thirty, maybe forty naked bodies dance around the fire. The women wear masks of the hunted—deer, hares, voles, rats, lambs. The men, the guise of predators—foxes, wolves, eagles, owls. Couples twist and rut like wild animals as a trio of musicians play: Celtic harp, bodhrán, tin whistle. The music flits between revelry and something darker—playful notes threaded with menace.

'Filthy pagan bastards,' he murmurs. 'An abomination against the Lord.'

And yet, he stays transfixed. Something stirs in him. Old. Feral. He swats it away with scripture, but it's buried too deep, like a splinter. Shame jousts with titillation as his devout Christian beliefs become mired in something more ancient, something animistic.

After twenty minutes, the coupling ends, and the ritual takes on a sombre mood as the gathering joins hands in a circle around the fire and chant incantations. From the shadows emerges a small figure, dressed in a black hooded cloak.

'They're all weird—but that *freak's* the worst of the lot. She's not of this world,' Malachi mutters, hate thick in his voice, before knocking back another shot of whisky.

His squint narrows, heartbeat quickening—he doesn't like what he's seeing.

'Lord have mercy,' he breathes. 'That's no child of God.'

He rubs at his eyes and takes a moment before adjusting the zoom on the glasses.

Three animal-headed silhouettes emerge, dragging a huge wicker effigy that scrapes across the forest floor. A man? A god? A monster?

The cloaked figure raises something aloft—a wooden box? A casket?—as a masked acolyte unlatches a narrow door in the effigy's chest.

The box is slotted inside. Door fastened with twine.

Malachi takes another mouthful of whisky.

'What the hell was in that box?'

A rope, slung over a tree, is attached to the wicker man. It's hoisted into the air where it swings back and forth, teasing the flames beneath.

Malachi swallows hard, his mouth bitter and dry. His night of poaching and voyeurism has taken a macabre turn for the worse. Unsure what to do, he remains rooted to the spot. The cloaked figure turns and points a staff at the moon as the worshippers chant in an ancient tongue.

'These pagans need to be stopped,' he murmurs.

The giant effigy inexorably descends into the fire. With a sudden whoosh, it erupts into flame as the chanting intensifies.

Malachi has seen enough and rises from the damp earth, his legs numb with inaction, his brain addled with confusion.

'This is witchcraft. Pure and simple,' he mutters as he stumbles over his shotgun and lands heavily in a pile of nettles. Involuntarily, he shouts and curses before extricating himself, the stinging pain exploding over his hands and face.

Unfortunately for Malachi Abbott, his profanities have attracted unwanted attention. He picks up his gun, and rabbits, and turns to slope away. As he does, he throws one last glance at the pagan ritual.

The figure in the hood—rigid as stone—is staring directly at him. Staff raised. Pointing.

His chest tightens.

Is that freak looking at me?

A shriek cuts the air. The hood drops. A raven's head. A scream of feathers and rage.

Five figures break from the circle. Sprinting. Straight at him.

He fumbles in his pocket, finds a shell, and tries to load it—but it slips from his fingers and rolls into the bracken.

Tries again, but his hands are swollen with nettle stings.

His pulse drums in time with the Bodhrán's frantic beat.

Icy sweat claws his back.

Breaths come fast and ragged as the men race through the woods.

He has only one choice.

Run!

2

Monday 1st May – May Day Bank Holiday

The cows are restless, constantly mooing.

Birds chirrup and sing.

Larger birds thud onto the caravan roof, claws scraping the metal. Sheep bleat in the distance. The dull throb of a tractor's diesel engine grows louder as it circumnavigates the field, again.

The bedroom door quietly creaks open, and Rose Topping enters carrying a cup of hot milky tea. Removing her husband's mobile phone from the bedside table, she places the beverage down.

'Chris, sweetheart, morning cuppa for you.'

Christopher Topping rolls over, plumping up his pillow. 'Christ, what bloody time is it?'

'Just gone seven.'

He groans. 'I thought the countryside was supposed to be peaceful? Cows mooing, sheep braying, a tractor going back and forth, and the bloody birds squawking and doing a clog dance on the roof.'

His wife smiles. 'Donkey's bray—not sheep. Anyway, it's nice to be up early. Best part of the day.'

He leans on one elbow and takes a slurp of tea. 'Have you got the bacon and eggs on, love?'

'Not yet. I thought we'd eat when we got back. Goebbels is waiting for his walk.'

On hearing his name, the black Labrador barges into the bedroom, wagging his tail. He makes a beeline for Chris, who gives him an affectionate pat on the head.

'How yer going, Goebbels, my little black panther?'

The dog reciprocates by eagerly licking the top of his master's hand.

Rose hangs a discarded dressing gown on a hook behind the door. 'Come on, drink your tea and get up. Let's get some of this lovely country air into our lungs.'

Rose and the dog leave the room as Chris sits up in bed.

'Country air? Bloody smell of cow manure and diesel fumes,' he grizzles, not enjoying his first foray into caravanning.

———◦———

As they lock the caravan door and head across the farmyard, Chris frowns as he eyes the tree line in the distance.

'I'm not walking through that wood again. I have a bad feeling about it. Especially after seeing... well, you know what.'

Rose half-laughs, nervously. 'You don't know what you saw. Could have been anything. Anyway, don't worry. We're not doing the wood walk. I had a chat with the farmer. If we turn right after that barn,' she says, pointing ahead, 'we can cut across the field, which will bring us onto a public bridleway. Turn right and follow the track for about a mile. When we see a broken-down wall, we clamber over it and turn right at the first farm gate we see. Then follow the wall back to the farm. It will bypass the woods. It's about an hour's steady walk, which is perfect.'

'Won't we be tramping over his crops?'

'He said not. He's growing beans for fodder. Plenty of tram lines to follow. Anyway, if he said it was okay, then it's not a problem, is it?'

'Suppose not. Better keep Goebbels on a lead though. Plenty of sheep about.'

'He won't bother the sheep.'

'You don't know dogs. They have an instinct for killing.'

'Fine. We'll keep him on the lead while we cross the fields. He can be let off once we're on the bridleway.'

—◆—

They spot the crumbling wall, clamber over the mossy stones, and emerge into a field where young plants push through the soil, reaching for the sky.

'Best put him on the lead now, love,' Chris suggests to his wife, as he takes a swig of water from a bottle.

'Nah, he'll be fine. Only beans. There's no livestock in this field.'

Chris is a little more conservative than his wife, not as carte blanche with the rules and regulations of the Countryside Code.

'Fine. Have it your way. But if he mauls a sheep to death, don't say I didn't warn you.'

After another five minutes pleasant stroll, they spot the metal farm gate that leads back home, diverting them from the wood that looms large, only a few hundred yards ahead.

Chris pulls at the mechanism to unlatch the gate as the dog waits eagerly to rush through.

As the gate swings open, Goebbels sticks his nose in the air, circles in an agitated manner, then bounds off towards the dark woods in the distance.

'Bloody hell!' Chris yells. 'I told you to put him on the lead.'

The couple takes off after him, but fifty-year-old human legs are a feeble match against the four legs of a three-year-old Labrador.

Their hearts sink as they witness the black shadow disappear deep into the woods.

———◦———

The call is loud and strident.

'Goebbels! Come on, boy!'

His wife tries a wolf whistle, but neither recall works.

'This place gives me the creeps,' Chris complains as they trudge deeper into the gloom.

'Oh, shut up. You can be such a wuss at times. We don't know what we saw. It could have been anything. A trick of the light.'

'Pig's arse. Remember what that guy in the pub said? He said to stay away from the woods. Unnatural things go on here.'

Rose, who is also spooked, rounds on him. 'Yeah? And why do you think that is? He's probably part of some drug gang growing weed, or magic mushrooms. Doesn't want outsiders stumbling over his crop.'

'He must have been seventy if he was a day. Not my idea of a drug lord.' He takes another sip of water, then calls out again. 'Goebbels! Come on boy!'

'I knew we shouldn't have named the damned dog Goebbels. It's bloody embarrassing,' Rose curses.

A series of excited barks rings out.

Chris cocks his head to one side. 'To the right, definitely to the right,' he declares, breaking into a jog as Rose follows behind.

Bashing through rough terrain, bushes, brambles, over sticks and stones, they stumble down into a hollow and a wide open space. Goebbels sniffs the scorched ground, pawing at the deep bed of ashes. He darts forward, then back again, reluctant to go any closer.

'Goebbels, get here, my boy,' Rose commands, holding the leash in her hand.

The dog drops his head, tail between legs and skulks forwards, in deliberate slow motion.

He knows he's in trouble.

Chris studies the blackened earth, his gaze drifting to the trio of weathered stones beyond the burnt circle—tall and bowed, their contours oddly human in the shifting light.

'Probably wild campers. It's all the rage these days, isn't it? You put the word—wild—in front of anything and everyone's suddenly into it. I blame social media. Complete load of rubbish.' Picking a long stick up, he flicks at the ashes. 'And another thing...'

Rose has had enough. 'Oh, shut up, and let's get back to the caravan.'

A sudden crack of a twig has the couple spinning around.

'What was that?' Chris asks, his words cloaked in fear.

Rose bends and attaches the lead to the dog. 'Probably nothing. Come on, let's go.'

Chris throws the stick into the ashes and is about to turn—until something catches his eye.

He freezes.

Stomach clenches.

His brain refuses to process what his eyes insist is true.

Rose is already striding away. 'Come on, Chris! I said, let's go!'

He doesn't speak. Doesn't look back. Just bolts.

3

DI Prisha Kumar pulls into the layby behind DS Zac Stoker's unmarked Skoda, already lined up beside a patrol car.

She exits as he approaches. 'Been here long?' she asks, noting the half dozen forensic vehicles already in attendance in the small clearing behind a wooden fence accessed by a farm gate.

'Just got here.'

They pull on protective gear and stride towards the constable standing guard in front of police barrier tape and a stile.

'Morning, Dave,' Prisha says.

He nods his reply. 'Ma'am.'

'What have we got?'

'Charred remains deep inside Ravensbane Wood,' he says, pointing towards the huge cluster of trees to the south.

'Human?'

'Apparently.'

'Who raised the alarm?'

'A married couple, Chris and Rose Topping from Newcastle. They were out walking their dog, Goebbels, and stumbled across the ashes of a fire.'

Prisha smirks. 'Goebbels—as in Dr Goebbels, Hitler's Nazi Minister of Propaganda?'

'Not sure, ma'am. I didn't take a statement from the dog, but he didn't look like an anti-Semite to me.'

She suppresses a laugh. 'But you did you get a statement from the owners?'

'Yes. They were quite agitated,' he states, retrieving his notebook and scanning the pages. 'They're staying in a caravan at Hexley Farm, owned by Mr and Mrs Baker, about a mile up the road. I told them to wait there. Said you'd want to speak with them.'

'Okay, good.'

Prisha and Zac climb the stile and follow an overgrown trail into the woods. Less than fifty yards in, they begin passing white-suited forensic officers heading back from the scene, plastic bags in hand—evidence, presumably.

The track is good, but the overhanging canopy shadows the place in a gloomy air of despondency despite the clear early morning.

'Strange there's no birdsong,' Zac notes—just as three loud caws cut through the trees, undermining him completely. 'Apart from the crow.'

'That's not a crow. It's the call of a raven,' Prisha corrects.

Zac laughs. 'Are you a closet twitcher?'

'The only time I twitch is when I'm getting a bollocking off Superintendent Banks. I'm engaged to a farmer, and farmers know everything. Don't you know that?' She stops and spins around and stares into the dense undergrowth. 'Where the hell's the crime scene?'

Zac sniffs the air. 'Can't be far. The wood smoke's getting stronger.' He spots another forensics officer emerge from behind a cluster of bushes. 'Something tells me it's that way,' he says, nodding.

'Nothing gets past you.' They continue walking. 'Much further?' she asks the officer.

'No, ma'am. Follow the trail down a dip and into a hollow.'

'Thanks.'

They push their way past bushes, follow a winding path down and emerge into a large round open space, almost like an amphitheatre, the white tent a dead giveaway for the gruesome temporary headquarters of the forensics team. A circular patch of scorched earth sits in the centre. Occasional lazy wisps of smoke spiral into the air. Adjacent to the circle are three weathered standing stones.

Prisha purses her lips. 'My initial thought was it could be a homeless person camping in the woods, but this is not the remnants of a small campfire that got out of control.'

'No. This bugger wouldn't be amiss on bonfire night,' Zac concurs.

Prisha pulls back the flap of the tent and they both enter. The aroma of charred wood still hovers in the air, along with another smell.

'Morning, Charlene,' Prisha says, her eyes the only facial feature to convey her smile.

'Ah, morning, Prisha. Morning, Zac. Fancied a stroll in the countryside, did you?'

'I heard there was a free barbecue on offer,' Zac replies.

Charlene laughs. 'Hope you brought the coleslaw.'

'So what have we got?' Prisha asks, never enamoured of Zac and Charlene's gallows humour. 'Human or animal?'

'Definitely human remains.'

'How'd you know for certain?'

Charlene picks up an extra-large evidence bag and hands it to her.

Prisha takes it gingerly and stares at the contents. 'One half burnt shoe? That doesn't mean much.'

'Take a closer look... inside the shoe.'

Prisha squints in the oppressive light, then recoils back and hands the article to Zac.

'Christ! Well, it looks like a foot. Any chance it could be a kid's prank? You know, a pig's trotter or some other animal stuffed inside?'

Charlene sucks in air through her mask. 'Highly unlikely. The ankle's built for walking upright—nothing like a pig's. And the soft tissue matches human anatomy. We'll need lab confirmation, but I'm confident it's human.'

Zac examines the seared remains of the shoe, noting its relatively intact shape—a raised heel, eyelets where the laces once were, and a distinctly narrowed toe section. Though scorched and blackened, it's still clearly recognisable.

'It's definitely a left shoe, and by the size and style, I'd say it belonged to an adult male or possibly a tall teenager. Any other remnants?'

Charlene's eyebrows rise. 'Some crime scenes yield very little... others just keep on giving.' She lifts another bag up and hands it to Zac.

'Hell! Teeth and plenty of them,' he declares in amazement, studying the contents.

'The foot was recovered from the outer edge of the fire, whereas the teeth were near the epicentre. And... there's possibly more than one body in the ashes.' Charlene picks up another bag and passes it to Prisha. 'More than two from what I can so far ascertain. The average adult human has thirty-two teeth, including four canines in total.'

Prisha grimaces and stares at the collection of blackened teeth in the bag.

'And how many canines have you found?'

'Twelve so far, and we're still sifting through. Unlike the foot, I can't yet confirm they're human. It is possible they belong to animals of some kind. Sheep, goats, pigs, deer, or even dogs, perhaps.'

Prisha places the bag aside and steps outside the tent followed by Zac and Charlene.

'Can you indicate where the foot was found?'

Charlene takes a couple of steps to her left and points at a small yellow flag attached to a spike in the ground.

'About here. We have photos and a video of the exact location.'

Prisha edges forward. 'And the teeth?'

'Closer to the epicentre of the fire.'

'And when was the fire lit?'

Charlene tilts her head. 'At first I thought it had burned the night before last, but judging by the material and residual heat, I'd say it's more recent—last night, most likely. That storm in the early hours dumped a lot of rain in a short burst. Probably helped douse the fire—or at least cooled it down fast.'

Charlene crouches and picks up a few twigs from the outer edge and hands them to Zac.

'You'll notice there are no large logs, or even large branches. Apart from the circumference, everything has completely burnt down to ash.'

'Meaning?' Zac asks studying the assortment of specimens before passing them to Prisha.

'I think the fire was built with fine combustible material, that's why there's little debris left over, and although the ground is still warm to the touch, it's not hot.'

Charlene nods at the burnt fragments in Prisha's hand.

'If I'm not mistaken, that's wicker and straw. The outer edge of the fire's littered with it. I'd say it burned hot—extremely fierce—but not for long. Maybe five, six hours tops.'

'Which means it was lit last night,' Prisha murmurs, pondering the scenario.

'Yes... although it's only conjecture at this point.'

'Could a fire of that duration have incinerated a body so quickly?'

'If it was hot enough—yes. If the rest of the body was on the fire, then we'll definitely recover bone fragments. And Dr Whipple will be able to tell you whether the foot was burnt off at the ankle or became separated by other means.'

Prisha and Zac glance at one another. 'Is Whipple on his way?' Zac enquires with an element of quiet dread.

'No. As you'll recall, the Great Doctor doesn't attend every suspicious crime scene, and definitely not one where only a foot has been found... well, not since the last time we called him out to the severed leg on Whitby Beach.'

'I remember it well,' Zac says with a chuckle. 'He was none too pleased.'

Prisha holds a strand of wicker to the light. 'Why wicker? How did it get here?'

'Old furniture?' Zac suggests.

Prisha grimaces. 'Who'd go to the trouble of dragging wicker furniture through the forest to put on a fire?'

Zac shrugs. 'It got here somehow.'

'What is wicker actually made from?' Prisha asks.

Charlene pulls her mask down and scratches her nose. 'It can be made from bamboo, rattan, reed. But this stuff,' she says, gesturing at the fragments. 'This is willow. And willow needs water—lots of it. You won't find willow trees in this patch of woods.'

Prisha scratches her cheek. 'What's the significance of wicker?'

She smiles and nods towards the three standing stones. 'Wicker was used extensively by certain ancient religions. Celts, Norse, Druids for example, and by modern pagans such as the Wicca religion—same pronunciation but spelled differently. And the three stones—they could be Druidic, then again, they could be much older. You'll need to brush up on your local history, Prisha.'

'Are you saying this may have been some sort of religious sacrifice?'

'I'm merely speculating. But it's worth bearing in mind. It is Beltane, after all.'

'Beltane?'

'Yes. The first of May.'

'What's that got to do with it?'

'May Day, my dear, was once just as important as Yule, Halloween, or the Midwinter Solstice. A turning point in the old year marking the arrival of summer and the renewal of life.'

'But May is the last month of spring.'

'Not in the Celtic calendar. They divided the year into two halves—Samhain and Beltane. The dark and the light. Christianity later absorbed bits of both, which is why Christmas and Easter line up with older festivals. But Beltane was pure paganism—polytheistic, animistic, rooted in nature. You should talk to your boss, Frank. Bit of an amateur sleuth when it comes to local religions and cults.'

'Cults?' Zac repeats.

Charlene shoots him a look. 'Yes, Zac. Cults.'

4

As the forensic team continues their painstaking work, Prisha and Zac watch on for a moment.

'Thoughts?' Prisha prompts.

Zac pulls his mask down and rubs his cropped beard. 'Early days, but it looks like we definitely have the remnants of at least one body, probably a male adult or adolescent. It appears they were incinerated in the fire, but it's also possible they died somewhere else and their body, or at least part of the body, was placed on the fire afterwards, maybe to get rid of the evidence. The amount of teeth recovered means there may be more than one body, but we can't be certain of that at the moment. The fire could have been lit last night, but if it wasn't, then definitely no longer than twenty-four hours ago, which would take us back to late Saturday night as our earliest starting point.'

Prisha spins around, taking in the wide open area. 'It's odd, isn't it?'

'What is?'

'This wood—a dense labyrinth of trees and undergrowth. And yet, here, it's clear. Flat. Like a meeting place.' Her gaze drifts to the three stones at the centre. From this new vantage point, their shape seems altered. Before, they were just weathered, and fire-blackened monoliths, six feet tall. Now, they resemble hunched figures, cloaked in black robes, like a trio of old women or ageing monks. 'And what's the significance of the stones?'

Zac shivers. 'Oh, don't go there yet, not until we have some hard facts,' he pleads.

'Go where?'

'You know—cults and sacrifices, hobgoblins, witchcraft.'

Prisha chuckles. 'For such a tall, imposing man, you can be a bit of a pussy cat sometimes.'

'Give me a thug with a shotgun over goblins and ghost stories any day. Anything supernatural puts the willies up me.'

'An unfortunate turn of phrase. Right, you go and interview the Toppings at Hexley Farm. I'm going to have a wander around the wood.'

'Aye, rather you than me. Don't get lost, and watch out for malevolent elves and pixies,' he says with a grin as he turns to head away.

After battling through the undergrowth, Prisha eventually picks up a trail and ambles deeper into the wood, unsure what she's looking for. There's not a breath of wind and the eerie silence is unsettling. Her pace slows to a stop as she has an uneasy feeling she's being watched. A flash of black in her peripheral vision has her spinning sideways.

Nothing.

A crack of a branch and another flick of black, now from behind her.

'Hello! I know someone's there. I'm a police officer. Come out and make yourself known. You're not in trouble. I just want to speak with you.'

Her voice is swallowed up by the oppressive canopy of twisted oaks and towering ash trees. The air is thick with the earthy scent of decaying leaves and damp soil. A tangle of ancient yews casts long shadows that dance menacingly, while silver birches stand ghostly pale against the gloom. The faint rustle of unseen creatures adds to her creeping dread, as if the very forest itself were a sentient being, observing an intruder in its midst.

It darkens.

Sensing someone or something behind her, she spins around.

Nothing.

She sees it again.

Something long and black fluttering like a cloak. Or hair. She's not sure.

It darts behind a drooping cluster of holly, its normally verdant leaves seem drained of colour. The landscape is a sepia montage of mordant browns and deathly greys.

'I just saw you. Now come out!'

A crackle of leaves.

The snap of a twig.

A whisper, like people talking, sniggering.

A faint giggle, or was it just the breeze?

She stares at the branches overhead.

Not a flicker of movement.

It's a mild day, but she shivers with cold.

To her left. Then to her right.

She sees something scuttling through the scrub, like a black crab.

Taking a deep breath, she breaks into a jog, weaving in and out of shrubs and bushes as she gives chase.

It's like a game of hide and seek as the black figure darts one way, then the other. Sometimes disappearing completely, other times a fleeting mirage.

Prisha leaps onto a clutch of rocks perched above a deep gully. As she navigates the boulders, her foot slips. She pitches forward, tumbling down the incline and landing with a heavy thump on the damp grass.

'Ouch!' she mutters, wincing as she stares up at the overhanging trees.

She brushes dirt and leaves from her arms, then checks herself for blood. Nothing visible—but her elbow is already swelling, and her radio and phone have been jettisoned somewhere during the fall.

'Damn it.'

The sense of being watched intensifies. A slow, primal certainty.

Someone—or something—is behind her.

Hardly daring, she swivels around on her bottom.

Her eyes drift above.

A scream erupts, sharp as a hawk's cry over an empty moor.

5

Zac accepts the offering graciously and enthusiastically.

'Thank you very much, Mrs Topping.'

'Please, call me Rose,' she says handing him a plate containing two bacon rolls. 'A tall, strapping lad like you needs to keep his strength up.'

He relaxes back into the comfortable built-in settee and takes a bite of the sandwich.

'Oh, yes,' he mumbles through a mouthful of food. 'I was ready for this. I missed out on breakfast this morning.'

Goebbels occasionally throws a morose glance at Zac's food.

The whistle from the stovetop kettle increases in volume as a plume of violent steam escapes into the confines of the warm, snug caravan.

Chris Topping enters from outside, visibly a man in a hurry.

'I've hooked the car and electrics up, love. Once we've finished here, we'll batten down the hatches and head off.

Should be home by midday,' he explains as his wife hands him a bacon roll.

Rose makes three cups of tea and passes one to Zac.

'Here you go, sergeant. It's all been a bit of a shock.'

'I can imagine.'

She takes a seat opposite him. 'There's not much else we can tell you. As I said, Goebbels got a whiff of something and took off into the woods. We searched high and low for him. He's usually good at returning to us. Eventually we heard him bark. When we found him he was at that clearing where the three stones are. It was obvious someone had lit a fire at some point.'

'Then I saw it,' Chris interrupts. 'The bloody shoe and the foot inside. Gave me the willies, I can tell you,' he adds attacking his bacon roll like a man possessed.

'Then we hightailed it out of there,' Rose adds.

'And what time was that, approximately?' Zac asks.

The couple look at one another. Rose takes a sip of tea.

'I suppose it would have been about 7:40, give or take.'

'And you didn't ring 999 until you arrived back at the caravan?'

'That's right. My phone was on charge and Chris forgot to bring his with him.'

'If someone hadn't moved it from its overnight spot, then maybe I wouldn't have forgotten it,' he grizzles.

'You said you've been here for three days?' Zac continues.

'Yes. We arrived Friday about midday.'

'I said it was a bad idea coming away on the May Day Bank holiday,' Chris states, throwing his wife a disparaging glance.

His wife snaps back. 'Don't be ridiculous. Finding that... that thing, had nothing to do with it being a bank holiday or not.'

Zac's eyes flit between them, noting the slight tension. 'Can you remember seeing, or smelling smoke in the preceding days?'

Rose shakes her head as Chris focuses on the roll.

'Nah,' he says.

'And what about people—did you notice anyone coming and going along the road or out in the fields?'

Rose gazes out of the window towards Ravensbane Wood in the distance.

'No. We've barely seen a soul apart from Mr and Mrs Baker—the farmers. It's been peaceful and idyllic up until today.'

Chris takes a slurp of tea and says, 'You're forgetting about...'

Rose shoots her husband a withering look.

There's a moment of embarrassed silence. 'You were saying, Chris?' Zac prompts.

'Oh, nothing.'

'It could help,' Zac replies in a warm but firm manner.

More nervous exchanges between husband and wife.

Rose clears her throat and clasps her hands in her lap.

'It's nothing really. But the day we arrived, Friday, once we'd set up we went for a walk in the woods with Goebbels. It would have been late afternoon. Still quite light. We both felt uneasy immediately we entered the woods.'

'Aye,' Chris concurs. 'A real weird feeling. Like we were being watched. Then I saw something.'

'What?'

He suddenly appears reticent. 'Well, I thought I saw something. Not saying I did, or I didn't.'

'What do you think you saw, Chris?' Zac says, a note of impatience in his voice as he wipes his mouth with a serviette.

'An old woman. She was wearing a black cloak with the hood pulled over her head.'

'That's quite descriptive for something you're not sure you saw, Mr Topping. Did you see the woman, Rose?'

She shakes her head. 'No... well, I say no. What I mean is I caught a glimpse of something but it was more of a shadow.'

'At the same time your husband saw the cloaked woman?'

'Yes. About the same time.'

'And your dog—did it see or smell the woman?'

Rose glances at her husband. 'No, now you come to mention it. You know what dogs are like; nose always to the ground.'

Zac nods and smiles then fixes his eyes on Chris. 'What did this woman look like?'

'Small. If she were five foot nothing I'd be exaggerating.'

'Facial features?'

'I didn't see her face.'

'But you described her as old. You must have seen something to form that impression?'

He shrugs nonchalantly. 'Just a feeling.'

'Just a feeling she was old?'

'Aye.'

'I see. And after seeing this old woman, what happened next?'

'We turned around and got out of there sharpish.'

Rose coughs, slightly embarrassed. 'It could have been our imagination playing tricks, sergeant.'

Chris appears annoyed. 'Then what about the guy in the pub?' he blurts out.

Rose shakes her head. 'Don't bring that up,' she hisses back at him.

Zac's not going to let that one go. 'What guy? Which pub? And what exactly did he say?'

Rose jumps to her feet and collects the breakfast plates. 'See! You don't know when to keep that big mouth of yours shut!' She turns to Zac, stressed. 'It was really nothing, sergeant. Not even worth mentioning.'

Zac hands her the empty plate. 'Still, all the same.'

She snaps at her husband. 'You tell him!'

Chris rolls his eyes. 'After we left the wood, we carried on walking along the road until we reached Ashenby—about two miles from the woods. We called in at the pub, The Crown. Had a quiet drink, chatting to this local at the bar. We mentioned what we'd seen in the wood, and he completely lost it.'

'He didn't lose it,' Rose contradicts. 'He was a little off, that's all.'

'He was off all right. He slammed his pint down on the bar and said if we knew what was good for us, we'd keep out of those woods, or else.'

'He didn't say—or else. You're making it up.'

'He bloody did. It was a threat. He finished his pint and stormed off.'

'Did you get his name?' Zac asks pulling out his notepad and pen.

'No.'

'Description?'

'Old, maybe eighties.'

'Mid-sixties,' Rose corrects.

'Rugged looking bugger. You know, as if he'd worked outdoors all his life.'

Rose tuts. 'He wasn't a manual worker. His hands were smooth.'

'How do you know? He was wearing fingerless gloves. Wore an old-fashioned tweed suit with a waistcoat, oh, and sported a beard.'

'He did *not* have a beard it was a bushy moustache and stubble. And he was wearing a grubby, olive trench coat.'

'His accent was broad Yorkshire,' Chris continues, unperturbed by his wife's contradictions.

'He was from Lancashire,' Rose insists.

'Smelled of...' Chris wafts his hand under his nose as if trying to recreate the scent. 'Pipe smoke. Proper old-school.'

'Stank like wet dog to me.'

Unreliable witnesses, Zac thinks as he jots down the discrepancies between husband and wife.

A scream, distant, sharp—and unmistakably human, crashes the interview.

'That came from the woods,' Zac shouts, already on his feet, bolting for the door.

6

At the top end of Ashenby, the May Day parade has begun. Painted faces, blossom crowns, and chanting children winding downhill behind a figure dressed as the Green Man, with hawthorn and twigs sprouting from his mask in a ghoulish display. The children follow behind like he's the Pied Piper, their high, bright voices weaving with the thump of drums.

The villagers have turned out in full—draped in ivy and antlers, feathers and bells—drawing curious tourists and bemused locals alike. Bright ribbons stream from the tall Maypole on the village green as young girls skip in slow, spiralling circles.

Music drifts ahead of the procession—pipes, drums, and the odd shriek of laughter. But down at the far end of the village, past the old smithy, and the Post Office, The Crown sits quiet and near-empty. The real noise hasn't reached it yet. Not quite.

The battered old Land Rover Discovery parks outside pub as Malachi Abbott surveys the decorated main streets of Ashenby and curses.

'Another bloody pagan ritual.'

Stepping from the car, he slams the door shut, pulls the collar up on his olive green trench coat and enters the pub. Inside, it's as lifeless as the Marie Celeste—no sign of crew, spirit, or trade. Not unusual for an English country pub at midday on a Monday. The aroma of beer and cooked dinners wafts under Malachi's nose like a temptress guiding him into a boudoir.

He licks his lips and leans against the bar, eyes darting left and right.

Empty.

Fidgeting inside the flap of his coat, he produces two rabbits and flops them onto the counter.

'Service,' he yells.

The landlord, Edwin Featherstone, a convivial man in his mid-fifties, with a stout frame and a ruddy complexion, emerges from behind the kitchen door. On spotting Malachi, his normally jovial demeanour devolves into a downcast expression.

'Oh, it's you Malachi. What you having—usual?'

'Aye, pint of Taylors, and give me a whisky chaser... make it a double, no, make that a treble. The cheap stuff not the expensive crap you sell to the townies.'

Edwin pushes at the optic thrice and places the shot of whisky on the bar, then stares disdainfully at the rabbits.

Malachi pulls a pouch of tobacco from his coat and rolls a skinny cigarette.

'Two rabbits for you. Call it a fiver apiece. Cheaper than Aldi.'

Edwin shakes his head. 'Not interested, Malachi. Rabbit pie is off the menu.'

'Since when?'

'Since no folk seem interested in it.'

'Tell them it's chicken. Idiots around here won't notice the difference. Majority are weekend-warriors these days, anyways.'

Edwin lowers his voice, even though there are no other customers.

'Bring me some nice fresh lamb and we can do business,' he says with a wink.

Malachi grunts from the back of his throat and throws the whisky back in one hit, wheezes, and grimaces.

'Where's the missus?'

'Out shopping. I wouldn't be serving you if she was here, would I?' he replies as he pulls at the beer pump, which spits and froths. 'Damn. Need to change the keg.' He turns to head down into the cellar. 'Oi, and don't smoke that out the front. There's a new designated smoking area in the far corner of the beer garden round the back.'

'You effing joking?'

'No, I'm not. New council bylaws.'

'Bugger the council.'

Edwin glares at him. 'Out the back. Understand?'

'Gurrrhh.'

As Edwin disappears downstairs Malachi heads out to the beer garden to smoke his rollie. He sparks up and sucks heavily on the wizened cigarette. Dislodging a rogue strand of tobacco from the gap between his front teeth, he spits it out the side of his mouth.

He's feeling pretty pleased with himself but is still figuring out how to play it.

What he witnessed last night would make a great news story for one of the more salacious tabloids. Could even lead to interest from TV. A documentary, perhaps? An exclusive interview would be far more lucrative. But if he wants to gain financially from it, he needs to not only get his story straight but also embellish and make it believable.

He returned to the fire at dawn. He regrets his warning to the Newcastle couple now. They could have come in handy. Still, sooner or later it would come to light. Maybe.

Heaving on the ciggy he pushes out a smoke ring as he contemplates his options. All he does know is he needs to act quickly before the moment passes.

'I'll give it a couple of days,' he mutters to himself. 'Drop a few hints to Edwin. He's a mouth as big as the Mersey Tunnel. It's sure to tweak the curiosity of some nosey local. Or maybe an anonymous tip-off to the rozzers? By then I'll already have sold my story.'

He saunters back inside to the bar where Edwin is busily pulling a frothing pint, before discarding half of it into the slops tray, and trying again. Finally, he presents his first customer of the day with an acceptable pint of beer.

Malachi lets it settle for a moment before taking two large, thirsty quaffs, wiping the suds from his top lip onto the back of his grimy coat sleeve.

'Any news?' Malachi asks with an air of casual indifference.

Edwin stops drying a glass and gazes at him. 'What?'

'Any news, you know, tittle-tattle or what not?'

'Not really.' His eyes narrow. 'Why, should there be?'

Malachi sniffs cockily. 'Maybe. Maybe not.'

He places the glass on the shelf. 'Okay, Malachi, out with it.'

'Don't know what you're talking about, Edwin,' he replies haughtily.

'You're not fooling anyone. You've obviously seen or heard something.'

Malachi glances around the pub as the distant strains of music filter inside.

'You know it was Beltane last night?' he says in a hushed tone.

Edwin squints and shrugs. 'Beltane?'

'Aye. Marks the beginning of summer. It's an old Gaelic word meaning bright fire. A big event in the Celtic calendar. A celebration of fertility. Union between the earth and the sky... and all that mumbo jumbo. And it was a full moon, a big one. A Flower Moon.'

'I did notice the moon when I locked up. Although, when that storm hit it was like someone had switched the lights off,' replies Edwin as he picks up another glass.

'Shenanigans going on up in those woods last night,' Malachi adds cryptically.

'Oh, aye?'

'Usual suspects. Bloody heathens.'

Edwin becomes bored with the clandestine inferences. 'Malachi, if you've something to say, then come out and say it instead of going round the houses.'

Malachi appears affronted as he takes another sup of his beer. 'Just saying, that's all.' He cracks a wide smile. 'Buggers went too far this time though. It will be the end of them and all their kind. And not before time.'

'I take it you're talking about the folk from the commune?'

Malachi looks away as if disinterested. 'Maybes I am. Maybes I aren't.'

Edwin shakes his head. 'I don't know why you can't live and let live. Why do you find it necessary to cause agitation with everyone?'

'On their side, are you?' he snarls.

'I'm not on anyone's side.'

'You were probably there yourself. There were at least forty of the buggers. Way more than live on the commune. I reckon they have half the village under their spell.'

Edwin sighs, exasperated. 'They just follow a different way of life, that's all. They're not harming anyone.'

Malachi snorts derisively. 'Ha, that's what you think. I saw them with my own two eyes. Rutting like wild animals. Naked, dancing around the fire, invoking spells and curses. And something else...' he tails off, as if he's said too much.

It's done the trick as Edwin suddenly takes an interest. 'They were having sex?' he whispers.

'Aye. At it hammer and tong. Filthy beggars.'

'You saw it?'

'Yep. Through my binoculars. Buggers nearly caught me, but no one knows those woods better than me. And that's not all.'

'Go on.'

He takes another furtive look around to make sure they're still alone, then nods at his empty whisky glass.

'I get a dry throat when I talk too much.'

Edwin purses his lips and sticks the whisky glass under the optic then places it back on the bar.

'Here you go.'

'Cheers. Witchcraft and sacrifice.'

'Get out of here!' he exclaims.

'Shush. Not a word.'

Edwin leans in closer. 'What do you mean, sacrifice?'

'They'd made this big wicker effigy in the form of a man with a goat's head. They lifted it over the fire on a rope.'

'And?'

He performs a cross over his chest. 'I swear to God there was a living soul inside that wicker man. Then, they dropped it onto the fire.'

'I don't believe you.'

'Swear to God, as true as I'm standing here.'

'Have you told the police?'

'Not yet.'

'What are you waiting for?'

'If I squeal on them lot, then next time, it might be me in the wicker man.'

Edwin takes a step back and studies him. Malachi is known for his tall stories and hatred of the commune.

Malachi slugs back the whisky in one hit. 'Right, do you want the rabbits or not?'

'No, I don't.'

Malachi turns to leave. 'Suit yourself,' he replies picking up the rabbits from the bar.

'Ahem, Malachi, aren't you forgetting something—the drinks?'

He blinks and grizzles. 'Gnnnff.' He pulls a tenner from his pocket and drops it on the counter. 'Keep the change.'

Edwin stares at the note. 'And the rest. You owe me fourteen pounds eighty, *please*.'

Malachi's top lip curls. 'Daylight robbery. I should be telling the police about you not that bunch of murdering pagans.' He pulls a wad of notes from his pocket and throws a fiver on the bar. 'Get yourself one.'

Edwin stares at the wad in his hand. 'Come into some brass, have we?'

'I get by.'

Edwin picks up the money as if he's handling a shitty stick. 'And if you happen across a nice piece of lamb, legit of course, bring it to the back door, yeah?'

Malachi nods, grunts, and trudges towards the exit. He turns.

'And not a word about what I told you. Not until I've figured out my next move. Right?'

'I never heard a word.'

Malachi steps into the cool sunshine, tired but quietly euphoric after his liquid lunch and little ruse. Slumping into the driver's seat, he fumbles for his keys, glancing up as the May Day parade spills towards the village green, the streets now thick with onlookers.

He chuckles to himself. 'I'll teach you to cross Malachi Abbott. Those pagans will be hounded out of town.'

As he reverses at an alarming rate, something on the passenger seat catches his eye.

He yanks the handbrake hard.

A small, circular object rests on the faded upholstery—slightly larger than a two-pound coin, tightly woven from thin, fawn-coloured cord. He picks it up and stares at the design: an almost complete circle, embroidered in a single piece of red twine. It's light, near weightless. The weave is tight, eerily uniform—handmade, but so precise it suggests obsession.

He turns it over and shudders.

At the centre sits a symbol—a vertical and horizontal braid, forming a cruciform shape.

He freezes.

He knows the symbol.

The Crucifix Knot.

Not a trinket. Not a charm.

A curse.

Whoever owns it is marked for death.

Suddenly, his fingers sear with pain—as if the woven threads have burst into flame. He yelps, drops it onto the seat, and jerks back against the driver's door, momentarily paralysed by the shock.

Frantically, he crosses himself.

'Sweet merciful Lord Jesus Christ,' he whispers, voice trembling. 'Deliver me from evil. Protect me from these heathen sinners.'

His gaze flicks to the windscreen.

The village outside looks unchanged. Everyone is absorbed with the festivities.

But nothing feels safe anymore.

'I've got to get out of here.'

The car roars to life as Malachi jams it into gear.

The Green Man lurches into view—towering, moss-draped, his hollow eyes slick with black pitch. Behind him trail the children, silent now, their bright faces expressionless. One wears a headdress in the shape of a raven, feathers twitching in the breeze. The drums slow to a steady, bone-deep thud. But Malachi is already gone—car speeding down the valley, the death token resting on the empty seat beside him.

7

Zac swings the car back into the farmyard of Hexley Farm.

'A goat's head?' he questions, puzzled as Prisha recounts her misadventure in Ravensbane Wood earlier.

'Yes—high up in an oak.' She swipes at her phone and thrusts it under Zac's nose.

His eyes flick quickly onto the photo. 'Was it real?'

'It looked real but as it was fifteen feet up in the air, I didn't get a chance to check. It was like it was watching me. Scared me half to death.'

'I think Frank would have heard your scream back in Whitby. And who was this mysterious caped crusader you were chasing?'

'Not sure.'

'The Toppings saw a similar figure when they first arrived. The husband said it was an old woman but when I pushed him on it, he couldn't articulate why.'

'This wasn't an old woman. Not the speed they moved. They were nimble, fleet of foot. And knew the wood extremely well.'

'How tall?'

'Not sure. I didn't get a good look.'

'You must have some idea?'

Prisha rubs at her head and slips her phone away. 'I don't know—not tall. Did you get anything else out of the Toppings?'

'They went to the pub after their first walk in the wood last Friday. Got talking to a local who warned them to stay away from the place. Their description of him was contradictory. All I know for sure is he's male, aged between sixty and eighty, and had facial hair.'

They exit the car and scrunch over gravel, gazing at the cluster of branches covered in white blossom tacked to the kitchen door.

'What type of tree has that come from?' Prisha asks.

Zac shrugs. 'Wouldn't have a clue. Botany is not my strong suit.'

Prisha knocks on the door. 'What are the farmers names, again?'

'Mr and Mrs Baker,' he replies as the rumble of a distant tractor drifts across the fields.

As Mrs Baker makes the compulsory cups of tea, Mr Baker fidgets restlessly at the kitchen table. May is one of the busiest times of year for a farmer and he doesn't have time to be sitting here discussing things that don't concern him with two police officers.

As Zac makes small talk with Mr Baker about the running of the farm, Prisha evaluates the couple and the farmhouse kitchen.

The Bakers would be early to mid-sixties perhaps. The room is a curious mix of the practical and the peculiar. It's old, maybe even a little threadbare, but immaculately clean, tidy, functional. Overhead beams support a low ceiling. The one window overlooks the back of the farm and an endless panorama of fields, some green, others yellow, some barren apart from the slate grey soil.

Amongst the many knick-knacks—vases, porcelain farm animals, and small framed tapestries hanging from the walls—Prisha also notes the oddities. Above the hearth, a sprig of dried rowan berries tied with red thread hangs like a forgotten keepsake, though its placement suggests more significance than mere decoration. She recognises the berries because Adam once pointed them out to her on a walk and said his grandmother used to make them into a jam.

On the windowsill sits a cluster of smooth river stones, each engraved with faint runes or scratches. A small bundle of dried lavender and sage wrapped tightly in twine sits alongside. A weathered iron horseshoe, blackened with age, is nailed to the wall above the kitchen door—open end facing upwards, as though catching invisible luck.

In one corner, a collection of jars line the shelf of a dresser, their labels faded or absent. The contents resemble powdered herbs or spices. A faintly sweet herbal scent wafts from the shelf, mingling with the sharper smell of fresh peppermint. Next to the jars is a roughly woven wicker circle, no larger than a dinner plate, with a small faceless figure made of twisted twigs nestled at its centre. Prisha assumes it's Mrs Baker's handiwork, an attempt at artisan bushcraft. Still, it's an odd motif.

Mrs Baker seems relaxed and affable, with a kind of permanent smile. Mr Baker is less so. He looks agitated, and who could blame him, having been called in from the fields just ten minutes ago. Prisha knows what Adam's days are like at the moment: up before dawn, home as daylight fades. Lunch from a knapsack. Two flasks of tea. Bottles of water. Then an evening meal, a half-hearted attempt to watch telly, and off to bed by nine—exhausted, but in that good, honest way.

Still—time is precious and once lost it can never be regained.

Mrs Baker places the tray on the heavy oak table, scarred with years of gainful employment and dispenses the tea into large red mugs. She hands them out, pointing at the milk, sugar, and homemade flapjack biscuits accompanying the teapot.

'It's a rum do,' Mrs Baker sighs as she takes a chair, her etched-on smile finally giving way to a grimace. 'Human remains, you say—from a person?'

Mr Baker snorts as he stuffs a piece of flapjack into his mouth. 'Of course a bloody person—woman,' he snaps. 'What part of—human remains—don't you understand?'

His wife ignores him as Zac and Prisha share an embarrassed glance.

Prisha clears her throat and addresses them both.

'We asked your campers if they'd seen any unusual activity since their arrival last Friday. They said they hadn't. What about you?'

Mrs Baker nurses her cup of tea 'No. Nothing at all, dear. Been very quiet. It always is. Nothing ever happens around these parts.'

'No strangers or unusual activity?'

'Not that I've noticed.'

Prisha makes a few notes then persists. 'Tell me about Ravensbane Woods?'

Mrs Baker raises her eyebrows, surprised.

'Well, it's a very old wood. Mentioned in the Domesday Book, though it goes back long before that. Back then it would've covered a much bigger area. I do see the odd walker, young couples now and then, but it's not exactly well known. Hardly a tourist hotspot.'

Zac sips his tea and eyeballs the farmer. 'And what about you, Mr Baker?'

He sniffs. 'As my wife said, seen nowt unusual,' he grunts belligerently.

'Of course,' Mrs Baker interrupts, 'it is a private wood.'

'Private?' Prisha questions. 'I assumed it was owned by the council, or the forestry?'

'No. Been part of the Ravensbane Estate since forever. I think that's why it doesn't attract many visitors. It won't be listed on any heritage sites or visitor information brochures. And we're well off the beaten track out here.'

'How big is the wood?' Zac asks. 'It seems to stretch on for a while.'

Mr Baker takes a gulp of tea and collects another biscuit. 'Knocking on for two-hundred-and-fifty acres. Maybe more.'

'And who owns Ravensbane Estate?'

Mr Baker averts his eyes and dunks his biscuit.

'The Hamptons,' Mrs Baker replies, a little more forthcoming.

'The Hamptons?' Prisha repeats trying to elicit more information.

'Yes. Lord and Lady Hampton. They own the estate, the land, the woods, and Ravensbane Castle. About four miles northwest from here as the crow flies.'

'So, neighbours of yours?'

Mr Baker mutters. 'Neighbours in name only.'

'You don't get along?' Prisha quizzes.

'Not saying that,' he retorts fiercely. 'You're putting words in my mouth, lass. They have their ways—we have ours, and that's the way it is.'

Prisha's attention drifts onto Mrs Baker who turns to stare out of the window, slightly embarrassed.

The silence lingers.

'Do you ever venture into the woods?' Prisha asks.

More dark looks are exchanged between husband and wife.

'Not often,' Mrs Baker replies, cryptically.

Prisha stares at Mr Baker until he offers a sharp reply. 'Nah. Why would I go in there?'

Zac edges forward on his seat. 'Your campers, the Toppings, said they went for a walk in the woods late Friday afternoon. They thought they saw an old woman, in a cloak. Do you know who she is?'

Mr Baker snorts and shoves his chair backwards—the legs screech on the stone floor. He slurps down the dregs of his tea, then fixes his flat cap with slow, exaggerated care—as if the act itself were a statement.

'I haven't got time for this *bloody* nonsense. Now, if you'll excuse me, I have proper work to do.'

Mrs Baker pulls at the kitchen door as she escorts the officers out. 'Apologies for my husband. He's a little narky at this time of year. He's tired, that's all.'

Prisha smiles warmly. 'I understand, Mrs Baker,' she says, stepping out into the sunlight of the farmyard 'Do you get many farm stays?' she asks.

'Not really. Maybe a couple of dozen a year. A bit of extra income. Every bit helps.'

Prisha eyes the branches fixed to the door. 'What type of tree is that?'

'Hawthorn.'

'It has a lovely scent.'

Mrs Baker laughs. 'Those pure of heart smell a sweet aroma. Those with a black heart smell death and decay... or so they say.'

'May Day celebrations?'

Mrs Baker nods. 'Old traditions, that's all. It wards off evil for the forthcoming year.'

Prisha throws Zac a surreptitious look. 'Hmm... about the old woman in the woods, can you shed any light on it?'

Mrs Baker scans the farmyard as if searching for strangers. 'It's nothing, really. Old wives' tales.'

'What is?'

'Folklore, that's all. Someone playing a prank by the sounds of it.'

'I'm sorry, Mrs Baker. You've lost me,' Prisha says, clearly confused.

Mrs Baker sighs and fidgets with her pinafore. 'Legend has it that in the old days, a coven of witches lived in the wood.'

'Christ. Here we go,' Zac mutters under his breath.

Mrs Baker lowers her voice. 'The Witchfinder King—he made witchcraft a death sentence.'

'The Witchfinder King?' Prisha quizzes.

'King James I of England—the Wisest Fool in all Christendom. *That* man saw witches in every shadow. Legend says the villagers rounded up three women and held their own trial. Two were found guilty and executed.'

'The third?'

'They wrapped her in metal chains and threw her into the deepest part of Ravensbane Lake. If she floated, she was guilty. If she sank, she was innocent.'

Zac grimaces. 'Either way, not great odds. Bet the local bookie took a hiding that day.'

Mrs Baker continues. 'Before she was bound in chains, the woman placed a curse on her accusers—three men. Said they'd meet the same fate and burn in hell for eternity.'

'An old superstition,' Prisha states.

Mrs Baker replies guardedly. 'Some may say.'

'But others believe it?'

'There're many things in heaven and earth that cannot be explained, inspector. It behoves one to keep an open mind but a silent tongue on these matters.'

'Right,' Prisha says, ready to leave. 'Oh, one last thing—the Hamptons. Your husband doesn't seem too fond of them. Is there a reason, a falling out at some point, perhaps?'

Mrs Baker becomes impassive. 'Not as such. My husband just doesn't agree with their practices, that's all. Each to their own.'

'Their practices?' Prisha prods and pokes again.

Mrs Baker throws her arms up, blase. 'Oh, east is east, and west is west, and never the twain shall meet,' she declares nonchalantly. 'Enjoy the rest of your day, inspector, sergeant.' She nods deferentially then closes the door.

As they saunter across the yard towards the car Prisha can't help but share her frustrations.

'I can never bloody tell with Yorkshire people,' she moans.

'Tell what?' Zac asks as he pulls the car keys from his pocket.

'Whether they're being naturally reserved, taciturn or whether they know more than they're letting on. I know you're Scottish but North Yorkshire is only a hop, skip, and a jump away. Do you understand them?'

Zac stops and grins at her. 'I've been here well over a decade and they still baffle the hell out of me. If they weren't so tight with their brass, they'd make brilliant poker players.'

'They always wrap things up in riddles and old sayings which can be interpreted in whatever way you want. Always vague and ambiguous. I mean, what did that mean—never the twain shall meet?'

Zac shrugs as he presses the fob and the car beeps and flashes its lights. 'I suppose it means—nowt as queer as folk.'

'Don't you bloody start.'

Pulling open the car door he becomes serious. 'For what it's worth, I'd say the Bakers know more about Ravensbane Woods and the Hamptons than they're letting on. And round these parts, if you don't like someone, or have a bit of dirt on them, well, you keep it close to your chest. As Frank would say—if tha's nowt nice to say about someone, then keep thy big gob shut,' he adds in a broad Yorkshire accent mimicking Frank. 'Mind you, Frank is a bit of a poet.'

Prisha laughs as she jumps into the passenger seat. 'No, I think you're right, Zac. The Bakers are hiding something. The question is—what?'

She clicks her seatbelt into place. 'Drop me back at my car. I need to inform the Hamptons about the human remains and see what they know about the fire.'

Zac starts the engine. 'And me?'

'Head back to the crime scene. Check in with Charlene, see if forensics have turned up anything new. We'll regroup at the station.'

She stares out at the sunlit fields. 'Let's see what the Hamptons know.'

8

Frank slings his jacket onto the hat stand, collapses into his seat, and rummages in the brown paper bag on his desk. He pulls out a pork pie, takes a large bite and relaxes back as he eyeballs Zac and Prisha opposite.

'What have you got then?' he asks as both officers pull out the notepads and flick through the pages. 'Hang on, before you start, it's not going to put me off my pie is it?'

'No,' Zac says with a smirk. 'Nothing too gruesome, Frank.'

'Okay, continue.'

Zac flicks through his notes. 'Chris and Rose Topping were caravanning at Hexley farm, owned by Mr and Mrs Baker, approximately a mile from Ravensbane Woods, just outside the village of Ashenby. The Toppings went for an early morning walk and as they were returning, their dog took off into the woods. After a brief search they found the dog in a clearing deep within the woods. He was sniffing around the remnants of a fire. It's also the site of three standing stones, possibly Druidic. Mr Topping spotted a half burnt shoe with what appears to be a human foot inside.'

Frank wipes crumbs from his mouth. 'Ravensbane Woods—that's part of the Ravensbane Estate isn't it?'

Prisha nods. 'Yes. A private wood. The estate is owned by Lord and Lady Hampton—Ravensbane Castle?'

'That's right. Noah Hampton. I believe he's a Viscount or Baron. Hereditary peerage. To the manor born and all that hogwash.'

'You know him?'

'Our paths have crossed occasionally. He's been to a couple of police functions over the years. Usually to give some dreary lecture about artefacts. Not a bad bloke, just a little eccentric—like a mad professor on a caffeine overdose.' He taps at his desk and calls on his powers of recall. 'If I remember rightly, there was some brouhaha to do with him.'

'You mean dodgy?'

Frank shakes his head. 'No, not dodgy. I think he may have remarried and there was a minor scandal. And in the rarefied air of high society it was frowned upon. Anyway, I take it you've informed the Hampton's of the discovery?'

'Sort of.'

'What does that bloody mean?' he grizzles.

'I called round to Ravensbane Castle and pressed the intercom on the front gates but there was no answer. I spotted a gardener inside the grounds and called him over. He said the Hampton's weren't home. Lady Hampton was due back Wednesday. I told the gardener the police were in the woods investigating suspicious activity. I wanted to keep it ambiguous for the moment. I asked him to pass the message on, and I also managed to get hold of the Hampton's landline and left a message on their voicemail. I'll call around again in a couple of days if I haven't heard anything back from them.'

'Hmm... well make sure you do. People like the Hamptons have friends in high places and love nothing more than to kick up a stink if they're not consulted over every tiny bloody thing. And don't forget to doff your cap and curtsy when you meet them. Right, where were we?'

'Ravensbane Wood and the shoe.'

'That's right.'

Prisha leans forward. 'As well as the foot, Charlene's team found quite a number of teeth, including at least twelve canines.'

Frank frowns. 'Human?'

'Possibly, but we won't know definitively until tests come back from the lab. But if they are, then it could mean at least three bodies.'

'How do you work that out?'

'Simple maths, Frank. Four canines per person, twelve canines in total.'

'Hmm... what else?'

'Charlene found strands of wicker, which she believed were made from willow. What with the standing stones, the circular nature of the fire, and the strands of wicker, it's possible we're dealing with some sort of cult or religious sacrifice.'

Frank devours the remnants of his pie, sweeps the crumbs from his desk, then steeples his fingers together contemplating the facts.

'Possibly. And let's not discount that theory just yet. But it could also be a ruse. Ritual sacrifices are as rare as hell. It may make a great TV series, or film, or enthralling reading by some wannabe author, but in reality, these so-called ceremonial killings are usually the work of sad little men who want to scare the world into thinking they have power.

'A pentagram scratched into a wall, a few candles, some half-baked symbolism—it's theatre, not theology. I've only seen two cases in over forty years where the motive was truly religious. The rest? Just killers playing dress-up, hoping we chase shadows while they get away with murder. The media, and the public, lap it up.

'Look at *The Torso in the Thames*. Ritual overtones, but the real story? Human trafficking. Or *Who Put Bella in the Wych Elm?* Rumours of witchcraft, but no real proof. People want to believe in cults and dark rituals. It's more thrilling than the alternative.'

Prisha crosses her legs and tilts her head. 'Which is?'

'The truth. Most murderers are simply selfish, brutal, opportunistic haters, dressing up their crimes in a bit of hocus-pocus to throw us off the trail. Typically men—bitter, emotionally stunted, convinced the world owes them respect. Repressed anger always manifests in one way or another.

'And remember, these little pricks think they're God's gift to creative thinking—untouchable, smarter than everyone else. In reality? They're usually as dumb as dogshit. They think they've made a pact with the Devil—but when the cuffs go on, the Devil is nowhere to be found.'

'You might change your mind when you see this, Frank,' Prisha says, handing him her phone with the photo she captured in the woods. 'After we left the crime scene I went for a wander, out of curiosity. I saw this thing high up in a tree.'

Frank frowns at the photo.

A goat's skull—wedged high in an oak, its hollow sockets gaping. He's just spent five minutes calling cult killings theatrical nonsense.

Now he's having second thoughts.

9

Tuesday 2nd May

Prisha is feeling decidedly unsure of herself as the aromatherapy diffuser bubbles away on the mantelpiece, sending wafts of lavender infused steam into the air. Her eyes drift upwards onto the dreamcatcher hung above the desk. An assortment of multicoloured feathers spins lazily around. Piped new-age music, as bland as day-old porridge, does nothing to lift her mood—quite the opposite.

Her psychologist, Donna, enters the room engrossed in the contents of a manilla folder. As usual, she's overdressed in a garish woollen jumper with two chiffon scarves around her neck. Bangles circle each wrist. A long, flowing purple skirt, with way too many pleats, swishes annoyingly above a pair of boots that may have once belonged to a Cavalier from the English Civil War.

'Prisha, I'm surprised to see you. Your next "well-being" appointment isn't for another six weeks.' Puzzlement fights with her usual pitying smile before both expressions are jettisoned, replaced by creases of concern. She slides into a seat behind the desk.

'Oh, dear. Has it suddenly happened? Has there been in a breach in the dam wall?'

Prisha screws her face up. 'Sorry?'

Donna reaches out and touches the back of Prisha's hand, which is not appreciated.

'You've been through hell these past few years. I knew something would give, eventually. PTSD doesn't always crash through the door—it waits in the wings, then ambushes you when your guard's down. You saw a colleague shot. You were shot. Hanged. Held at gunpoint. Hunted by those Russians. Locked in that lighthouse. And of course, your close call with rape,' she adds in a whisper. 'It's a lot for any woman to contend with,' she adds, as if the itinerary of life-threatening injustices were minor inconveniences like the oven packing up. 'Your mind's been trying to protect you. Bottling it all up. But trauma doesn't stay bottled forever. Sooner or later, the cork gives.'

Prisha pulls her hand away. 'No. It's nothing to do with that.'

Donna is sceptical, and a tad disappointed. 'Are you certain?'

'Positive.'

'Then why are you here?'

'It's something different entirely. This is a private visit, and I don't want it recorded on my official file.'

Donna's eyes widen as she closes the folder and pushes it aside. 'Okay. In your own time. There's no rush, although I have another appointment in thirty minutes.'

Prisha takes a deep breath, trying to overcome the feeling of foolishness and weakness.

'Ahem... it's about a recurring dream.'

Donna resorts to form and adopts her pitying smile. 'Ah, dreams. The soul's way of whispering truths the conscious mind refuses to see. They're like cosmic postcards from the universe, blending the past, present, and future into a celestial energy. A tell-tale nudge from a higher sense of self. A spiritual mirror, as it were.'

What a load of wank, Prisha thinks as she wriggles in her seat. 'Yes... well. This dream...' She pauses and checks her wristwatch, cursing herself for making the impromptu appointment.

Donna pouts and leans back in her chair. 'Go on, dear. In your own time.'

If she says that one more time, I'm going to slap that smile of hers into the middle of next bloody week.

'It's always the same... but different. I'm alone. It's dark or getting dark. In one dream, I'm walking along a narrow alleyway. Tall Victorian buildings are on either side. I'm hemmed in. The stone is black with grime. The walls are wet. There's a thin stream of dirty water in the gutter. It's cold. Deathly quiet. I inch down the alley. I can barely breathe as a sense of foreboding chokes me. But I continue. Then I see something in the gutter. I move forwards and crouch. It's a doll's head, like a doll from the past—ceramic, rosy cheeks, blond curly hair, blue eyes. It stares up at me—then blinks. I jump back. The eyes swivel until it's staring over my shoulder, watching something. I turn slowly and look up. Iron bars over a filthy window. On the window ledge, a raven. It lets out a mournful caw. Then...'

Donna appears enthralled, as if she's watching a gripping scene from her favourite soap opera. 'Yes, yes. Go on, my dear. In your own time.'

Prisha clasps her hands together in case they involuntarily lash out.

'It swoops down with huge wings. Blackness blots out everything. Then I wake up.'

'It's very specific.'

'What is?'

'That you identify the bird as a raven, not a crow or a jackdaw?'

'That's because it is a raven. They're a lot bigger.'

'Sorry. I interrupted. Carry on.'

'In another version, I'm in the countryside. I'm standing in a huge field of maize, or sweetcorn. There's a vehicle access track. It's gloomy, overcast. And yet, when I look into the adjoining fields, they're ablaze in lush green grass, swaying gently in a summer breeze. Those fields are bathed in brilliant sunshine with blue skies above. My field is in sepia. Then, I see it. The doll's head, nestled in one of the furrows, partly covered in dirt. I crouch to pick it up. It blinks. A teardrop rolls down its left cheek. I'm overcome with grief, bereavement. I sob like a child until I choke. The sense of loss is so intense it hurts, *physically* hurts. The dolls' eyes shift. I follow their gaze. Three ravens are sitting on a wire fence behind me, watching. They caw and take off into the sky until they're nothing more than three black dots. I sprint across the field, trying to reach the sunlight. I look up and see the black dots getting bigger and bigger. They swoop down. Their wings blacken out all the light. Then I wake up.'

There's a moment of silence as both women study one another.

Eventually, Donna breaks the impasse. 'And when did these dreams begin?'

Prisha pulls the hidden pendant from her blouse. 'Not long after I got this.'

Donna leans forward, eyeing the charm.

'It's jet, clearly. But what is it?'

'A wolf's claw. A clairvoyant gave it to me at the Whitby Fair—Halloween night, about eighteen months ago during the Goth Weekend. She said it can't protect me, but it will warn me if my life's in danger.'

'And has it?'

Prisha reddens, slipping the charm back beneath her blouse.

'Maybe. Or maybe it's just kidology. Or... false causation—is that a thing?'

Donna tilts her head, a smile playing on her lips.

'Post hoc ergo propter hoc.'

Prisha frowns. 'Are you feeling okay, Donna?'

'It's Latin. Means *"after this, therefore because of this."* Basically, just because one thing happens before another, doesn't mean it caused it. You had the charm, something bad nearly happened, you're still here—so now your brain's connecting the dots. Even if it's nonsense.'

'So... codswallop?'

'Pretty much,' Donna says, tapping the desk with a pink fingernail. 'We all do it—footballers with lucky socks, cricketers, and their glove rituals. Tiny illusions of control. I just didn't have you down as the superstitious sort.'

Prisha snorts. 'I'm not.'

'Then why wear the charm?'

'For my boyfriend, Adam's sake. For better or worse, he's ridiculously superstitious. A farmer, you see. He'd rather wrestle a crocodile with one hand tied behind his back than walk under a ladder. Checks his horoscope before choosing his breakfast cereal.'

'Who else have you told about this?'

'Just my partner.'

'Your boyfriend, Adam?'

'Sorry. I meant my colleague, DS Stoker.'

A raised eyebrow. 'Hmm... I see.'

'So, back to the dream. What do you think it means?'

Donna flicks a glance at the clock on the wall. 'I can give you a brief interpretation, but it'll take many follow-up sessions to get to the bottom of it.'

'You don't say.'

10

The Ashenby Post Office is typical of a rural village—blackened Yorkshire sandstone, a red pillar box hungry for letters, and a dusty window cluttered with notices: a spring dance, a sewing club drive, volunteers wanted for the village hall renovation.

Prisha pushes open the door to the tinkle of a bell and quickly assesses the layout. Small, some may say poky. Shelves line the walls offering various merchandise: notepads and pens, travel clocks, barometers, postcards of the local area, and a small rack containing artisan jewellery, the type worn by teenage girls or hippies. It's like she's time travelled back sixty years.

A shelf opposite contains a small selection of daily newspapers, monthly magazines, and stationery, the local newsagent now nothing but a distant memory.

On the counter is an electronic scale, a box of mints, and a pen attached by a chain to the counter's edge.

Prisha finds the faint smell of dust, newspapers, and mints comforting.

There's not a soul in the shop and no sign of life. She notices a small domed bell next to the pen, the type you whack with your palm to gain attention. She gives it a slap.

'Hello,' she calls out.

Spinning around, she gazes out of the cluttered window onto the main street of the village. Not a single person has she seen. No couples out walking, or children making their way to school, or pensioners venturing out for their morning read or to post a parcel. The silence is almost perfect, if peculiar. The only intruder the tick, tick, tick of the second hand from a clock on the wall. She turns back to the counter and reaches out to hit the bell again but takes a step back, startled.

A small girl, maybe eleven, stands rigid behind the counter. Jet-black hair hangs in a curtain. Her skin is alabaster white, her green eyes huge and unblinking. She appeared from nowhere. Her hands are clasped in front of her black dress like a schoolmarm from another century.

Prisha pulls her warmest smile. 'Oh, you gave me quite a shock. What's your name?'

The girl blinks and continues to stare, expressionless. The impasse feels like an age.

Prisha clears her throat. 'Ahem, my name's Detective Inspector Kumar. I'm with the police.' If she was hoping this would elicit information from the girl, she's gravely mistaken. 'Cat got your tongue?' she adds with a touch of playful banter.

Not only does the girl remain mute but her needle-like stare grows more pointed, more personal. Prisha shuffles and pulls her shoulders back. The girls' focus drops from Prisha's face onto her chest as her eyes widen to such an extent they could almost pop out.

Prisha frowns and looks down at her blouse and notices what the girl seems fascinated with.

'Ah,' she says lifting the tiny necklace up. 'My boyfriend bought me this. It's a wolf's claw.' She laughs nervously. 'Not a real wolf's claw, of course. It's made of jet, Whitby jet. It's a good luck charm, or actually, more of a talisman. It's supposed to warn me of danger.' She's rambling. And she knows it. But for some reason, she can't stop. Luckily the rattle of the bell above the door breaks the agonising stand-off.

They both turn towards Zac as he enters the shop.

'Place is like a ghost town,' he grumbles. 'None of the bloody shops are open yet.' He stops and glances at Prisha then the little girl behind the counter.

'Ah, good morning. I see you two have been getting to know one another,' he says with a mischievous wink at the girl.

'Not really,' Prisha mutters under her breath.

'And what's your name?' Zac asks, leaning forward, grinning.

The girl breaks into a wide beam, her eyes flickering rapidly. 'Morrigan,' she replies coyly, in a lilting Scottish accent giving the name a musical rise, the "Rs" rolling effortlessly off her tongue.

Zac arches his eyebrows. 'My, my, what a pretty name, Morrigan. You don't get many Morrigans these days. I'm Detective Sergeant Stoker, but between you and me,' he says, lowering his voice to a whisper, and swiftly checking over his shoulder, 'you can call me Zac.'

A giggle. 'Zac,' she repeats, now gently rocking from side to side, obviously smitten with the tall handsome officer.

'Is your mother or father home?' Prisha asks tersely, slightly miffed at the girl's reaction towards her colleague.

Morrigan's eyes reluctantly drift back to Prisha, her warm, bonny smile jettisoned at the same time. She blinks and stares but doesn't reply.

Prisha exchanges a frustrated glance with Zac.

'Morrigan, can you fetch your mother or father for us, please,' Zac asks. 'We've some important police business and we're hoping someone may be able to help us.'

Morrigan smiles. 'Sure, Zac,' she replies, turning and marching away in a rather mechanical, rigid fashion.

Zac grins at Prisha. 'Hey, some of us are just born with natural charisma. You cannae learn this stuff. It's a gift. You ken what I'm saying?'

'Shut up—smartarse,' Prisha hisses.

Their good-natured banter is interrupted as a small, white-haired, elderly woman, sporting half-rimmed spectacles, shuffles in from a side door. Her steps make no sound on the old tiles. Rotund, with a rosy complexion she wears a friendly smile, and a moth-eaten cardigan full of holes. She places her hands on the counter.

'I am sorry. I was in the back yard back hanging washing out. Going to be a warmish day so I thought I'd get it on the line early. Now, what can I do for you?' she asks, with a soft Scottish brogue.

Prisha flashes her warrant card and introduces herself, before nodding at Zac. 'And this is my colleague, DS Stoker.'

For a brief second, the woman looks concerned, before her amiable expression returns.

'Pleased to meet you. I'm Lilac Penhallow.'

Prisha stuffs her hands into her jacket pockets. 'We're investigating the discovery of human remains found in Ravensbane Woods, a few miles from here.'

'Oh, my word.'

'We're making routine enquiries to see if any locals have gone missing recently.'

'Human remains, you say?'

'Yes. That's right.'

'Are you certain?' she asks clearly shocked at the revelation.

'Yes. Quite certain. Forensics have confirmed the findings.'

'What sort of human remains?'

Zac steps forward. 'We're not at liberty to say at this juncture, Mrs Penhallow.'

'Oh, I see. And it's Miss Penhallow,' she corrects.

'Apologies, Miss Penhallow. Are you aware of any locals who haven't been seen for a while?'

She stares above their heads, deep in thought. 'Not that I've noticed, sergeant. I mean, people are free to come and go as they please.'

Prisha is already losing patience. 'Is this your Post Office?'

'It's not mine, inspector. It belongs to the community. I'm the postmistress appointed by the Co-operative to run it.'

'I see. From my experience the Post Office is usually a hotbed of local information. Not much would go on around the village without you knowing about it.'

The woman nods. 'That's true,' she replies, but doesn't offer any further information.

'What about strangers?'

'Strangers?'

'Outsiders. Have you noticed anyone you're not familiar with, say, in the last couple of days hanging around?'

'Inspector, we're in the middle of the countryside. There are always walkers, hikers, cyclists—day-trippers passing through the village. Same as all the villages round here. It is beautiful, I'll grant you that. Though once you've lived here a while, you do start to take it for granted,' she adds, almost as an afterthought.

Prisha purses her lips and shuffles as she throws Zac a disgruntled glance. She pulls a card from her pocket and places it on the counter.

'Thanks for your time, Miss Penhallow. If anything comes up, please ring me.'

The woman picks up the card and slips it into a bin under the counter.

'Of course, inspector. Always happy to help the police.'

As they turn to leave, Prisha pauses and glances back. 'The little girl, Morrigan. Is she your granddaughter?'

'That's right.'

Prisha looks at the clock on the wall—9:05 am.

'Shouldn't she be in school?'

The woman smiles benignly. 'The wee mite is ailing. Sore throat and a tummy upset. Up most of the night. I thought it best to keep her off school for a couple of days until it clears. I've rung Prudence to let her know.'

'Prudence?'

'Miss Ashcroft, the local schoolteacher.'

Prisha nods politely and follows Zac outside. 'Impressions?' she enquires as they saunter along the street.

'Typical village life,' he replies nonchalantly.

'Hmm... I don't think so.'

'Aw come on, Prisha. You don't suspect that little old lady or wee bairn of being caught up in this, do you?'

'I'm not sure but so far everyone we've spoken to has been very reticent to divulge any information. As for that wee bairn, as you call her, she's downright weird.'

'In what way?'

'Did you see the way she stared at me? It's like she was trying to steal my soul.'

Zac erupts into laughter. 'Don't be bloody paranoid. You heard what the grandmother said—she's feeling off colour, that's all.'

'There's nothing wrong with her, I know that much. And the way she interacted with you... well...'

'Well what?'

'If I didn't know better, I'd say she was flirting with you.'

Zac is appalled at the notion. 'That's sick. She's about ten years old, twelve at a push, for God's sake.'

'Didn't you notice her provocative smile and the way she fluttered her eyelashes and began to swish gently from side to side?'

'You're imagining it. She took a shine to me that's all. You can...' He stops himself and reconsiders his words.

'What?'

'Well, no offence, Prisha, but sometimes you can be a little brusque with people, especially kids. You get their backs up from the get-go. Right, where to next?'

'You check out the other shops along the high street once they're open, and I'll pay a visit to the school. I'll meet you outside the library in twenty minutes. Oh, Zac, their Scottish accent—where are they from?'

'I'd say West Highlands or Inner Hebrides. They have a soft, melodic sound to their voice, and slower-paced. Right, see you soon.'

As Zac heads off, she casts a glance back at the shop.

Morrigan stands behind the glass—just a shape in the gloom now, eyes still fixed on hers.

Unblinking.

Prisha's fingers drift to the wolf claw around her neck without realising she's gripping it.

II

The single-storey Victorian school is laid out in a U-shape, its side wings flanking the playground at the rear. The windows, tall and narrow, resemble cruciform arrow slits typically found on medieval castles. There are no railings or fences outside and one of the double doors is propped open. Above the doors, a stone lintel bears raised lettering, proudly embossed into the weathered sandstone:

ASHENBY INFANT SCHOOL 1862

As Prisha enters the vestibule, the gentle sound of children singing drifts through the air, carrying a warm, lilting melody. Ahead is a glass partition, like a booth, framed in solid, dark timber—its joints seamless, its surface still gleaming after more than a century and a half. A quiet triumph of design and craftsmanship.

She pauses. There's something humbling about the old school still standing strong—functional, elegant, and built with care. In every detail, from the architraves to the glazing, there's a sense of permanence. A belief that the building—and the children inside it—were worth the effort.

The irony isn't lost on her. She thinks of her own high school: a steel-framed, glass-walled rabbit hutch thrown up in the sixties, with all the charm of an inner-city office block. Windows ran floor to ceiling, facing north and west. Great for natural light, appalling for heat. On summer days, it became a greenhouse. Pupils wilted at their desks, stuck inside a space designed for efficiency, not comfort. Not humanity.

It was demolished ten years ago.

The rattle of a keyboard breaks her reverie as she approaches reception. She's surprised to see a young, attractive woman behind the glass—early twenties, with blonde curls and a pink bow clipped in her hair.

The woman looks up and greets her with a dazzlingly white smile.

'Good morning. Can I help you?'

Prisha flashes her card. 'DI Kumar. North Yorkshire Police. I'd like to speak with Prudence Ashcroft, please?'

'May I ask what it's concerning?'

'Routine enquiry.'

The girl nods politely and places a register on the counter. 'No problem. If you could sign in first, please, then I'll escort you to Miss Ashcroft.'

Prisha jots her name and rank in the book. 'I'd also like a quick word with the principal.'

The woman resists a chuckle. 'We don't really have a principal. Miss Ashcroft is the head teacher?'

Prisha's brow furrows. 'Okay,' she drawls slowly. 'How many teachers work here?'

'Just the one—Miss Ashcroft.'

'And how many administrative staff?'

'Just me.'

'And your name is?'

'Sally Wainwright.'

'And how many students attend school?'

'We call them pupils, and this term there are thirteen children in all.'

'I know it says infant school outside but I'm assuming this is now a primary school?'

'Similar. We take children from the ages of four to eleven.'

The penny finally drops. 'This isn't a state school, is it?'

'No. It's fully independent.'

'How's it funded?'

'Tuition fees from parents, plus financial and practical support from the Co-operative.'

'The Co-operative?'

'Yes—the Ashenby Village Co-operative.'

'The ones who own the Post Office?'

'And the library, the village hall, the pub. They're also guardians of the common, the village green, the museum, and the old cinema.'

'That's one hell of a proactive Co-operative for such a small village.'

The girl beams. 'Yes. Everyone pulls together. We are all one. And one is all.'

Christ. It's like the Three Musketeers.

The girl leads the way down a corridor towards a back door.

'Did you attend this school?' Prisha enquires.

'Yes. Some of the happiest days of my life. A child's life should be happy and carefree, don't you agree?'

'Well, yes. As long as they're getting a good education at the same time.'

'It's hard to educate an unhappy child, Inspector Kumar.'

She bangs open the door and leads Prisha into the playground where a gaggle of children are gathered around a large white circle chalked onto the bitumen.

A woman stands in the centre, a whistle poised in her hand.

'Alright, children, you know the rules. The Sun team must catch the Moon team within seven minutes. If you're tagged, you freeze. If a Moon reaches the inner circle and shouts *The Moon is bright, chase the night*, everyone's free. Otherwise, the Sun wins. Ready? When I blow the whistle, the eternal chase begins.'

The high-pitched trill of the whistle cuts through the excited shrieks and yelps of the children as the game begins. The woman steps back from the circle, watching her proteges with quiet satisfaction.

Prisha observes with bemusement.

The children wear school uniforms: green and gold tartan skirts that end just above the knee, paired with mustard-yellow blouses and matching ties. The ties aren't knotted but fastened with intricate toggles, ornate enough to seem almost ceremonial. Gold socks reach halfway up their shins, and their black shoes are simple, sturdy, and built for purpose.

The receptionist sidles up to the teacher and whispers in her ear. Miss Ashcroft glances over her shoulder at Prisha, nods once, then turns back to the game, as the receptionist drifts away.

The children dart and weave, shrieking with laughter. Some are swift and untouchable, slipping through gaps like water, while others stumble, their limbs too heavy, too slow.

The chasers lunge, arms outstretched, and each fresh tag is met with a ripple of giggles and triumphant cries.

Alas, for Team Moon, no one manages to breach the circle to free their comrades and eventually all the moons are tagged, which causes much glee and equal consternation.

Miss Ashcroft blows her whistle. 'Okay children. Take five. Fill your water bottles from the tap and catch your breath.' She saunters over towards Prisha. 'Inspector Kumar, you're no doubt here about the body parts found in Ravensbane Wood?'

Prisha's eyes narrow. 'Yes. How did you know?'

Miss Ashcroft chuckles. 'The jungle drums travel quickly through a small village. I wish I could help you, inspector, but I haven't noticed anything untoward of late. And to the best of my knowledge we are not missing any of the locals. If someone had gone missing, then I can assure you it would be all over the village in a matter of hours. May I ask how long the body has been there?'

'We can't be definite, yet. But we think it's a matter of days, not months or years.'

Prisha's eyes drift onto the girls who line up obediently in front of an old-fashioned standpipe and fill their drink bottles.

'No boys?' she notes.

'No.'

'Is this an all girls' school?'

'Not at all. It's a peculiarity of the village—a lack of the Y chromosome *in the progeny*.'

'Sorry?'

'XX equals female. XY equals male. Thank goodness the male can produce millions of sperm compared to the finite amount of female eggs.'

Prisha frowns at the turn of conversation and decides to change topic.

'That's an old-fashioned game the girls were playing. It's good to see children running free with such abandon instead of being glued to their phones or texting nasty messages to one another.'

'No mobile phones allowed on school grounds—the parents and pupils all know the rules. That's not to say we're Luddites, inspector. We have iPads for research purposes, but we mainly follow traditional values. The three Rs as a requisite, and a heavy focus on nature and renewal. And, of course, robust physical activity with an onus on fun—but fun grounded in meaning.'

'What about religious education?'

'It's all tied in with the other subjects.'

'Christianity, or do you touch on multiple religions?'

'No, just the one. We follow the Old Ways—the wisdom of those who came before us, the rhythm of the earth, the cycle of the seasons. Our children learn to listen to the land, respect all living creatures, and understand that nature is not just something to be used, but something to be honoured.'

'Paganism?' Prisha suggests.

Miss Ashcroft eyeballs her suspiciously. 'People like labels, inspector. That way they can pigeon-hole people. The building block of all racism, religious intolerance, or sexual discrimination begins with labels. Here at Ashenby we endeavour to imbue our girls with two fundamentals—tolerance and acceptance. We don't have to agree with a person's beliefs or life practices but neither should we devalue or demonise them.'

'As long as those practices are within the law,' Prisha adds pointedly.

'And who's law do you refer to, inspector? The laws made by kings a thousand years ago to consolidate their lands and power, and bestow great wealth on their lackeys? Or do you mean the universal law of nature which has been *in situ* since time began?'

'I mean the law of the land, Miss Ashcroft. The law that a civilised society follows and upholds for the benefit of all.'

A fresh-faced girl with strawberry blonde curls and freckles runs up to them.

She raises her hand and says, 'Miss Ashcroft, I'm getting that pain again in my tummy. It really hurts.'

Ashcroft smiles in a motherly way. 'I think it's your time, Poppy.'

The girl's face morphs into anguish. 'Oh no! Really?' She exclaims as Prisha studies the girl's toggle more intently.

The teacher pats her on the arm. 'I think so. And it's not something to be scared or ashamed of, Poppy. It means you're transitioning from childhood to womanhood. You once were a bud, and now you're a blossom-in-waiting. If it is your first Moon blood, then it will be time for the Triple Goddess Celebration. Run along to the toilet and I'll be there in a moment.'

Prisha raises an eyebrow as she watches the girl disappear through the door.

'Moon blood? I take it you mean her period?'

'Yes. It's no coincidence that the lunar and menstrual cycle are exactly the same length of time.'

Prisha screws her nose up. 'I'm pretty certain that's not true.'

'Menstruation is the sacred connection to the cycles of nature, inspector.'

'And what's the Triple Goddess Celebration?'

'The Triple Goddess is the combination of Maiden, Mother, Crone.'

'Crone?' Prisha questions with incredulity.

Miss Ashcroft laughs. 'Yes, unfortunately, the word has taken on negative connotations over time. People now picture a withered old woman—someone to be feared, mocked, or pitied. But in pre-Christian societies, a crone was something very different. She was a matriarch, respected for her wisdom and revered for her knowledge.'

Prisha glances at the other girls in the playground.

'Fancy toggles they're wearing. I haven't seen one since I was in the Girl Guides,' she says. 'Are they made of wicker?'

'Yes. It's called the Wicker Knot. That particular design wards off evil.'

'More superstitious nonsense?'

Miss Ashcroft shoots her a glare. 'Considering you're wearing a wolf's claw to warn you of imminent danger, I'm not sure you're in a position to sneer, inspector. Now if you'll excuse me—my girls have energy to burn before lessons begin.'

She blows her whistle and the girls flock to her like ducklings to their mother.

As Prisha exits the schoolyard, she glances down at her blouse. The wolf's claw pendant is tucked safely out of sight.

'How did she know I was wearing it?'

12

Prisha trots down the stone steps of the school and stands on the edge of the pavement. Turning right, she spots Zac sauntering across the road, a takeaway coffee in one hand and a half-devoured pasty in the other.

She turns to her left and notices the village is a lot busier than earlier. A half dozen cyclists in their brightly coloured Lycra head out of the village in a cluster, as various couples and solo hikers plod along the footpath, some studying maps, others peering at their phones.

Scurrying across the road she catches up to Zac who is now leaning against the wall of the library.

'How'd you go?' she asks as he takes another bite of his pasty.

He looks around and spots a nearby bench and nods towards it, mumbling incoherently. Prisha dutifully follows as he unloads his early morning snack onto the table.

'Here, I got you this,' he says, pulling a coffee from his jacket pocket, then a brown paper bag from inside the coat. 'Americano and a Cornish pasty.'

'Ooh, thanks. I certainly trained you well,' she says, biting into the food. Flakes scatter down her coat. Only then does she realise how ravenous she is. 'So?'

Zac takes another glug from his cup and wipes his mouth on the back of his sleeve, then retrieves his notebook.

'Bugger all to speak of, your honour. I've questioned the butcher, the baker, the...'

'Candlestick maker?' Prisha quips.

He eyeballs her with disdain. 'Sweet shop owner, the mechanic, and the grocer and greengrocer. Let's just say it wasn't an enlightening experience. What about you?'

'I had an interesting chat at the school. It's fully independent. From what I can tell, they follow their own curriculum—esoteric to say the least.'

'What do you mean?'

'Reading between the lines they seem a bit new-age hippy. Holistic. Put a big onus on nature and *the old ways,* to quote Miss Ashcroft. It's a mixed gender school and yet they have thirteen pupils, all girls. The teacher reckons it's a quirk of the village. Only one teacher and one admin staff. But the kids appear happy enough. Maybe a bit too happy.'

Zac huffs and focuses on his food. 'We're not here to debate the village school curriculum. We need to find out who that bloody foot belonged to.'

'Yeah, I know, but it could be part of the puzzle.'

Zac sighs and dabs at his mouth with a serviette. 'Why would you say that?'

Prisha places her cup on the bench. 'This village—it's odd. Who ran the bakery?'

'Henrietta Frowde. Middle-aged woman. Genial enough but knows nothing.'

'Is it Mrs or Miss Frowde?'

'Miss. Why?'

'No reason. And the grocer and greengrocer?'

Zac glances at his notebook. 'Freya Castlemain and Nora Ridge, respectively.'

'Are they a Miss or a Mrs?'

'Now you mention it—Miss.'

'Postmistress, teacher, admin staff, grocer, greengrocer, and baker all women and all Miss. Bit unusual don't you think?'

He rubs his beard and smiles. 'Ah, well, Little Miss Paranoia, the butcher is called Otis Grangewood, *Mr* Otis Grangewood.'

'Is there a Mrs Grangewood?'

'He didn't say, and I didn't ask. Was too busy trying to escape the smell of bloodied meat and loneliness. Have you ever noticed how butchers always look ill?'

'No.'

'They all have rosy cheeks, but the rest of them is deathly white, like they've come down with the bubonic plague. And they study you as if they're sizing up the space left in their freezer.'

'And you called me paranoid.'

'Look Prisha, I can see what you're driving at. You think this is the *Village of the Damned*, run by a cabal of sinister spinsters. It's probably coincidence, and even if there is a female power enclave, what has it got to do with a possible murder?'

'Secret societies are notoriously hard to breach. The code of silence.'

He finishes his snack and screws the paper bag into a ball. 'Can we at least have a few days working on Planet Normal before you start with your conspiracy theories?' he pleads.

'Fair enough,' she replies with a grin. 'Let's check out the library. By the way, the village Co-operative own most of the major civic buildings in the village including the school, pub, village hall, and library.'

'Here we go again,' he mutters under his breath.

They step into the cool hush of the library, the ornate glass doors swinging gently behind them. The earthy aromatics of outside give way to the scent of polished oak and the faint musk of ink and old paper. Prisha runs a finger along the top of an antique reading desk, worn smooth by time and touch, yet still resplendent. It feels cool and slick beneath her skin. Overhead, domed lampshades hang from a high, arched ceiling, suspended by single fabric-covered wires.

Apart from their creaking footsteps, the silence is absolute.

Prisha casts a glance around.

A trio of laptops huddle awkwardly in the corner, cast adrift in a foreign sea. They don't belong—and they to know it.

This is her happy space.

As a bookworm, her love affair with libraries runs deep—and not just for the dreams they hold... or the nightmares. For a moment, she's transported back to childhood.

She didn't just love libraries for the stories. She loved them for the sanctuary. They were her escape. Born into a world where her skin, her name, and her silence marked her as different, the library offered what life didn't: quiet acceptance. While other girls learned to smile sweetly and obey, she buried herself in myth, misfits, and murder mysteries. The library gave her a way out of a patriarchal world where girls were seen as chattels—valued only if they were pretty, hard-working, and built for childbearing.

A family asset.

Easy to marry off.

Families would queue like farmers at a cattle auction.

Of course, the opposite was also true.

Not that her own father was like that—at least not for long. It had been knocked out of him, metaphorically, by her mother and grandmother not long after she was born.

She remembers their mantra:

"Habib, we are in Britain now. We can keep our food, our culture—but we must also adapt. They don't treat girls the same here. Prisha must have her own free will. She's brighter than her brothers. Let her be free. Let her shine."

It took thirteen years of trench warfare, but Habib Kumar eventually surrendered.

Or did he?

Prisha often wonders whether her father's change of heart was down to empathy or just a bid for an easier life. She suspects the latter.

Not a surrender—an armistice.

It's a conversation they've never had. And he's not getting any younger.

'Well?'

Zac's voice yanks her back. 'What? Erm... I'll question the librarian. You search the local history section.'

'For what, exactly?'

'You tell me.'

Zac sighs, pulling a face. 'You want me to dig up some half-baked tale of witches, ritual sacrifice, and woodland mischief, don't you?'

She grins. 'Who's a clever haggis-worrier.'

He groans and walks off. 'Remind me why I put up with you.'

'Because I'm delightful,' she calls, already striding toward the front desk.

13

Prisha approaches the librarian, a mid-forties woman with black, curly hair. She's seated behind dark oak panels, not unlike the defendant's dock in a courtroom.

Before Prisha can even pull her warrant card out, the woman says, 'Ah, DI Kumar. I've been expecting you.' She taps at a keyboard, slams a book shut, and places it on top of a pile of paperbacks.

Prisha offers a passive smile. 'Jungle drums?'

'Something like that.'

'And you are?'

'Lunara Ashcroft.'

'Miss Lunara Ashcroft?'

'That's right.'

'Any relation to...'

The woman interrupts. 'The schoolteacher? Yes—Prudence is my big sister,' she adds with a grin as she scans a barcode from a book and slaps it closed. 'I'm afraid I can't help you with your investigation.'

'Which is?'

'The human remains found in Ravensbane Woods yesterday. Ashenby is a small village. If anyone was missing, I'd have noticed.'

'Any overdue books that haven't been returned?'

She pulls a tight-lipped shrug. 'No.'

Prisha picks up the contradiction between her verbal reply and body language.

'Have you checked?' The question is tantamount to calling her a liar.

It's not lost on Lunara. 'We have a computer system, inspector. Books that are overdue pop up on my screen.'

Prisha notes the shift. Defensive already. *Why?* Time for a charm offensive.

'You know what technology is like. It sometimes plays up. Would you mind having a look manually?'

Lunara huffs but acquiesces. Tapping rapidly at the keyboard her eyes dart up and down the screen. 'No. Just as I... oh, wait. Yes, there is one person who should have returned a book yesterday.'

'Who?'

'Malachi Abbott.'

'Is he usually late returning books?'

'Not usually. Comes in every Monday afternoon regular as clockwork. A creature of habit.'

'Can you give me his telephone number and address, please?'

Lunara stiffens. 'That information is confidential.'

Prisha's tired of banging her head against a wall. 'This is a possible murder investigation, Miss Ashcroft, and you could be hindering it.'

Lunara's face hardens. 'I need a formal request,' she replies, folding her arms. 'Library records are protected under data protection laws, as I'm sure you're aware. I can't simply hand personal details over.'

'You just gave me his name—Malachi Abbott—so technically, you've already breached data laws. I'm not here to report you, but if I were, it could mean fines... or worse.'

Prisha softens as a high-pitched giggle emanates from a far corner. She throws a look behind then refocuses on the recalcitrant librarian.

'Look, Lunara, I don't want the man's details for malicious reasons. I simply want to rule him out of our investigation. So, how about it?'

Lunara pouts like a teenager, then begrudgingly swivels the screen around and busies herself with more books, her back turned.

Prisha pulls out her notebook and pen and scribbles the man's address down, as a deep male voice accompanied by another giggle drifts through the air. Prisha pauses, then slips her notebook away.

'There doesn't seem to be a phone number for him.'

Lunara sniffs. 'What you see on the screen is what you see.'

'Fine. And roughly what age is Malachi Abbott?'

'Hard to say.'

'I said roughly.'

'Late sixties—at a guess.'

'And what books are overdue?'

Lunara glances at the monitor. 'Just the one—How to Disappear by Frank Ahearn. Non-fiction.'

'Thank you,' Prisha replies with a shade of insincerity. The voices distract her once more. 'Who else is in the library?'

Lunara readjusts her screen. 'Just one person excluding you and your colleague.'

'It sounds like a child.'

'It's Morrigan. This is her second home.'

Prisha raises her eyebrows. 'Morrigan from the Post Office?'

'Yes, that's right. Why?'

'No reason.'

She drifts away, her boots quiet on the polished oak floor. The voices grow clearer. Zac's soft Scottish lilt. The same giggle again—high-pitched, syrupy sweet. It's beginning to crawl under her skin.

She moves along one row, halts, and strains to catch the low murmurings drifting from behind a wall of paperbacks. Pulling a thick volume from the shelf, she peeks through.

Zac is seated, holding an open book. On his lap is Morrigan. She's draped across him like a shawl, one spindly arm curled round his neck, fingers tracing idle patterns on his collar.

Zac doesn't move. Doesn't flinch. Doesn't even seem to realise how wrong this looks. He just keeps reading.

"'She then saw that he was the most handsome Prince one could ever set eyes upon, and she fell so deeply in love with him that she thought, I cannot live if I do not kiss him this very moment. So she leaned over and kissed him, but in doing so she splashed three hot drops of tallow on his shirt, and he woke up.'"

What the fuck, Prisha thinks as she replaces the book and marches down the row and around the corner.

Zac has missed his vocation as a professional narrator.

"'Why did you look upon me? Now I must go, far away, east of the sun, west of the moon, and you will never find me again.'"

'Zac, what are you doing?' Prisha snaps.

Morrigan smirks. But her eyes—those watchful, knowing eyes—lock onto Prisha with something sharp, something not remotely childlike.

'Can we help you?' the girl asks, tone silk-soft, but there's fire and ice underneath.

Prisha glares. 'What?'

Morrigan tilts her head, feigning innocence. 'You heard me. You're spoiling the story, Inspector Kumar.'

Prisha clenches her teeth. The atmosphere tightens, charged with an unease she can't quite name—but it coils in her gut, cold and prickly.

Her patience gives. 'Zac, what the hell are you playing at?'

He looks up at her, all easy smiles, oblivious. 'What? Nothing. I mean, I'm just reading the wee bairn a Norwegian fairytale.'

Prisha doesn't miss the way Morrigan nestles closer, the way she presses against him as though she's exactly where she belongs.

Zac may be a naïve idiot, but this girl knows exactly what she's doing.

Prisha's voice is iron-hard. 'DS Stoker, a word outside. *Right now, please.*'

'Really?' he asks with all the innocence of a lobotomised village idiot.

'Yes. Really!'

Morrigan watches them leave, her lips curling—not in amusement, but in quiet satisfaction, as if the game has only just begun.

14

Dragging Zac by his sleeve she marches him down a narrow alley at the side of the library, far away from the prying eyes of the villagers. She pushes him up against a wall then paces back and forth.

Zac is genuinely baffled. 'What the hell's got into you?'

Prisha throws her hands up, struggling to keep her anger in check. She rubs at her forehead, eyes tight with disbelief.

'What was that? What were you *doing* with that girl on your knee?'

'You saw what I was doing. I was reading her a fairytale—*East of the Sun, West of the Moon*. What's the big deal?'

Prisha's eyes widen with incredulity. 'Jesus, Zac. Are you really that thick? Do you *know* how wrong that looked? You're a man. A police officer. One whisper of impropriety—no matter how innocent—and it'll explode. Social media. Complaints. Internal review. Your bloody career down the pan.'

He frowns. 'Is this what the world's come to? She's a wee girl with no father. I felt sorry for her. She handed me the book and asked me to read. That's all. And if you're implying anything else, then maybe we shouldn't be working together.'

She jabs a finger into his chest. 'Don't put words in my mouth. *I'm* not questioning your motives—I'm warning you how it looked to anyone else. A young girl, on your lap, clinging to you like you were her dad? *Christ*, Zac—it was like watching a re-run of Jim'll Fix It.'

Zac pushes his lips out and strokes his beard. 'Aye, I suppose you're right. What was I thinking?' he murmurs, more to himself than Prisha, as the enormity of the situation dawns on him. 'It's like I forgot everything.'

'What do you mean?'

'It all happened so quick. I was skimming through a book from the local history section and next minute she's right there by my side. She said something.'

'What?'

'I don't know.'

'You must bloody know what she said?'

'Erm... something foreign. A language I haven't heard before. She then handed me the book.'

'And what was that passage you read out, about the handsome prince?'

'I don't know. That's the chapter she opened for me to read.'

'Christ! She's played you like an old fiddle.'

'She's nought but a bairn. She's not even reached puberty yet, and you're making out she's Machiavelli. It was all innocent enough, but I take your point about how some people could deliberately misconstrue it.'

Prisha spins around hands on hips. 'That girl is no innocent abroad, I can tell you that much. She's been before. You didn't tell her anything about your private life, did you?'

'No, of course not.' He pauses, as a sheepish expression slips across his face. 'Well...'

'Well, what?' Prisha snaps, rounding on him.

'I told her I was married to Kelly, and that I had two boys, Tom and Sammy, and their ages, and that I lived in Whitby.'

Prisha slaps her forehead. 'Oh, you're an item you are. A real item. Anything else?'

'Ahem, I may have mentioned something about you. She asked if there was anything between us, and I said, no, we were friends and work colleagues, that's all. I think I said you were engaged to Adam.'

Prisha shakes her head in disbelief. 'I wish all our suspects were as forthcoming as you in the interview room. It would make our life so much easier. Maybe we should employ her as a freelancer? The hardest career criminal would spill their life story within minutes.' A sudden disturbing thought fights to the front of her mind. 'Please tell me you didn't mention any particulars about the investigation? You didn't say the body part was a foot in a shoe, did you?'

'No. Not a word. It never came up.'

'Good. Let's be thankful for small mercies.'

'I'm sorry. I don't know what came over me. I just experienced this sense of peace when I was near her.'

Prisha scoffs. 'You can kiss goodbye to peace if that girl mentions this to anyone or if the librarian saw it on CCTV.'

'Fuck. What am I to do? Should I write it up in my report?'

'Yes. Wait... no. We'll ride it out. Maybe I am overreacting. If it ever comes to light, then we'll both play dumb. No, let me rephrase that. *I'll* play dumb, you just be yourself. It was all totally innocent, right?'

'It was totally innocent.'

'That's not the point. Right, come on. I have the address of Malachi Abbott. He was due to return a library book yesterday but didn't. Let's see if he's home then head back to the station. I've had enough of this village for one day.'

As they hurry back to the car, something tugs at Prisha's mind

'The book?' she asks.

'The fairytale?' Zac replies sharply, tiring of the subject. 'I told you it was...'

'No. Not that one. You said you were skimming through a book from the local history section. What was it?'

'It was called *The Three Crones*. Had a photo on the front of those three stones.'

'The standing stones at the crime scene?'

'Aye.'

'And?'

'And nothing. That's when Morrigan appeared.'

15

The narrow country road dips between drystone walls, the fields beyond flickering gold and green in the morning light. Zac keeps one hand on the wheel, the other tapping on his thigh.

'I hope this Malachi Abbott bloke's home,' he mutters. 'Either to eliminate him or have him as a possible missing person. I hate it when there's no progress and we have to keep chasing our arses. What else did the librarian say about him?'

Prisha, scrolling on her phone, shrugs. 'Not much. Like getting blood from a stone. He's late sixties. The book that was overdue is called—*How To Disappear.*'

'Interesting,' Zac replies in a slow drawl.

'Or ironic.'

'I've been thinking about it.'

'What disappearing, or sex? According to a study, men think about sex nineteen times a day.'

'Bit on the low side, if you ask me. No, I was thinking about what you said earlier, that the villagers are weird.

You're right—they are. Most of them appeared friendly, like they wanted to help, but did you get a feeling?'

'Like they're putting a face on and stonewalling?'

'Yes.'

The river meanders through the distant valley, catching her eye as a triangular warning sign flashes past.

STEEP GRADIENT 1:2

'Yeah. I got the same feeling. And by the way, the librarian wasn't friendly, and neither was the teacher. Mind you, they are sisters. Obviously both born with the bitch gene.'

Zac whistles low under his breath as the road drops sharply.

'Bloody hell. Wouldn't fancy coming down here with black ice on the road. It's nearly vertical.'

At the bottom of the hill they approach a sharp bend. A police 4x4 is parked on the grass verge, lights flashing. A "DIVERSION" sign leans against the bonnet, while an officer in a high-vis jacket wrestles with another sign, planting it at the roadside.

Zac slows, winding the window down. 'Hey, Jacko. What's this, a one-man roadblock?'

PC Jackson straightens, dusting his hands off. 'Morning, sarge. Ma'am. Afraid so, sarge. Just shutting this stretch of road down for now.'

'What's happened?' Prisha asks.

Jackson jerks a thumb toward the field below, then at the collapsed drystone wall on the bend.

'Farmer spotted a section of his wall down yesterday as he drove back from Ashenby. Assumed it was subsidence. Didn't think much of it—no livestock in the field. Came out this morning to fix the wall and noticed a car in the river.'

Zac glances towards the river in the distance. 'Anyone inside?'

'No idea. I've only just arrived. We have a few officers on the scene and the farmer's down there with his tractor towing the car out now.' He nods at the incline behind them. 'Hill you just came down is Ashenby Lane—locals call it The Devil's Drop. One-in-two gradient, and a hell of a tight bend. There's broken glass all over the verge—tells its own story.'

Prisha frowns. 'You got a reg?'

Jackson shakes his head. 'Not yet. There's another patrol on its way. I'll take a wander down once it arrives.'

Zac exhales, glancing at Prisha. 'Alright, we'll leave you to it, Jacko.'

Jackson slaps a hand on the car roof. 'Okay. Drive safely.'

Zac swings the car around, watching the GPS recalculate. 'Guess we're taking the scenic route.'

Prisha folds her arms and studies the new map. 'Christ, we were only five minutes away from Abbot's place. The detour is going to take another forty bloody minutes.'

Zac smiles, accelerating away. 'Relax and enjoy the scenery.'

Behind them, the diversion sign catches the sun as they disappear back up the hill.

Prisha watches the map on the sat-nav as the car snakes along narrow lanes barely wide enough for one vehicle. The weather in Ashenby was dry and sunny, but the road ahead glistens with recent rain.

'Looks like there's been a heavy shower,' Prisha notes as she gazes out of the windscreen at the grey clouds overhead. 'Slow down, it's coming up,' she states as the sat-nav lady announces:

"In five hundred metres your destination is on the right."

Zac squeezes the brakes as they approach. He turns onto a driveway cautiously, tyres rolling over a thin slurry of mud. Puddles glisten in potholes, reflecting the skeletal branches of an ash tree that leans over a boundary wall as if trying to escape. Two small stone cottages sit side by side, squat and weathered, their facade blackened with age, roofs sagging slightly. Once built for farmhands, they seem to huddle together, isolated on the edge of Wensleydale. Fields and rising hills stretch out behind them.

'What number is Malachi's place?' Zac asks.

Prisha checks her notebook. 'Number 132. The one on the end.'

'Hell fire, what a dump,' Zac mutters, parking right outside the property.

The paint on the front door peels in curling strips, exposing bare wood beneath. A cracked windowpane is patched with masking tape, the rest dulled by grime. Behind nicotine-yellow net curtains, faded floral drapes hang limp. A rusting metal bucket, half-filled with rainwater, sits beside the threshold, next to an empty milk crate. Dozens of cigarette butts litter the ground.

They step from the car, both unsettled, though neither says it outright.

Every copper's heard the stories—officers walking into remote places and never walking out again. The countryside may be beautiful, but it has its dangers. And out here, most locals own a firearm—shotgun, hunting rifle. Not great odds when your only defence is a pair of handcuffs, an extendable baton, and a can of pepper spray.

They exchange a glance.

'It's quiet,' Prisha says.

'Aye,' Zac murmurs, scanning the landscape. 'Too quiet. No birdsong, no distant hum of a tractor, no TV.'

'Here goes nothing.' Prisha raps on the door. 'Hello? Mr Abbott, it's the police. If you're home, can you come to the door, please?'

A scuttling movement comes from next door and two wizened eyes peep through the kitchen window at them.

Prisha holds her warrant card aloft and takes a sideways step, dropping her head to look inside.

'Hello, we're police. Have you seen your neighbour recently, Mr Abbott?'

More movement followed by the rasp of a bolt thrown back and the neighbour's door cracks open. A little old woman studies them suspiciously.

'Police you say?' the woman asks in a scratchy, disbelieving voice as she wipes her hands on a tea towel.

'Yes. CID,' Prisha replies, thrusting her ID towards the woman. She tries not to wince as the faint smell of old food wafts from inside—stale cabbage, liver, and onions. 'Your neighbour, Mr Abbott, is he home?'

'His car's not here, so he can't be.'

Zac steps forward. 'Does Mr Abbott live alone, or does he have a partner?'

The woman lets out a dry, unimpressed scoff. 'Ha! Who'd have that bugger? Face like a bucket of smashed crabs. Smoking, drinking, cursing at all hours. Plays his TV too loud. I bang on the wall, but he takes no notice. Anyway, what's he done?'

Prisha notes she probably didn't win Miss Ashenby 1962 either. 'We don't think he's done anything wrong. We just wanted to ascertain his whereabouts.'

The woman squints, grinding her teeth like she's chewing toffee.

'He must have done something, otherwise you wouldn't be looking for him.'

Zac takes a breath. 'Mrs...?'

'Selkirk.'

'Mrs Selkirk. We just want to make sure he's okay, that's all. When was the last time you saw him?'

She shrugs. 'Yesterday, maybe. Or the day before. He wasn't home last night. I know that much.'

A tabby cat scurries across the sludge, sidestepping puddles, and squeezes past the woman's legs. She chuckles, opening the door a fraction more.

'He's a right bugger, that one. Only time I see him is when I'm cooking something. He loves pig's liver and kidneys.'

Prisha swallows down her nausea. 'Thanks for your time, Mrs Selkirk.' She hands over her card. 'When Mr Abbott returns, ask him to call me on this number. He's not in any trouble. It's simply a welfare check.'

Mrs Selkirk grunts, takes the card, and slams the door. The bolt slides back into place.

Their attention returns to Malachi Abbott's house.

'Welfare check?' Zac queries. 'Correct me if I'm wrong, but under Section 17 of PACE 1984, we can enter without a warrant to save life or prevent injury... amongst other things.'

'Correct, sergeant,' Prisha replies with a smile. 'Abbott hasn't been seen since yesterday morning. Could be injured inside. Reasonable grounds?'

Zac is already twisting the handle on number 132 Fellside Cottage. It gives.

'We're in luck,' he whispers.

He stops dead as the sound of a car engine approaches. They both turn to witness a patrol car sedately roll into the drive and pull up next to them.

PC Jackson steps out, pulling on his cap with a grin. 'Breaking and entering, Sarge? Didn't know CID wages were that bad.'

'Fair cop, guv,' Zac says, extending his arms like he's about to be cuffed.

Prisha frowns. 'What brings you here, Jacko?'

'Could ask you the same thing, ma'am. The car that crashed through the wall and ended up in the river?'

'Yes.'

'The driver was still inside. Name on the license—Malachi Abbott. 132 Fellside Cottage. Dead as a dodo.'

16

Miserly Joe's cafe is particularly busy, even for a Tuesday lunchtime. Frank is distracted as his hunger controls his thought process. His eyes drift from Prisha and Zac seated opposite, then flick across the room to the hustle and bustle behind the serving counter. He breathes a sigh of relief as Jenny lifts the hatch and appears carrying a tray laden with food and mugs of tea.

'Here we go,' he states rubbing his hands together with glee.

Jenny places the tray on the table. 'Toasted cheese, and tomato sandwich for Prisha. Bacon butty for Zac. And liver and onions with mash and peas for guzzle guts,' she says swiftly dispatching the plates.

'Oi, watch it,' Frank says. 'There are plenty of other caffs in Whitby. I can always take my patronage elsewhere.'

Jenny's concern is evident. 'But Frank, without you we'd have to close. You make up over half our profits,' she says before breaking out into laughter.

'She has a point, Frank,' Zac says. 'This *is* your second home.'

'Ha-bloody-ha. Surrounded by jokers,' Frank replies as he attacks the food.

Prisha stares at his plate and recoils slightly, recalling the smell drifting from Mrs Selkirk's kitchen.

'Oh yes, this is good,' Frank purrs scraping mashed potato onto a thick slice of liver dripping in onion gravy. 'Right, updates.'

Prisha takes a sip of tea. 'We're still waiting on confirmation from Whipple that the shoe from the fire contained human remains.'

Zac dollops HP sauce over his bacon and replaces the top slice of bread. 'I've done a few searches on the MISPER database. Missing persons from the last twelve months within a fifteen-mile radius of Ashenby.'

'And?' Frank prompts.

'Not a sausage. That area is sparsely populated, so hardly surprising.'

'You need to extend your search radius.'

'Already got Dinkel onto it.'

'Good. What else?'

Prisha pulls her notebook out. 'We didn't get anything from the villagers we questioned. On a hunch we called in at Ashenby Library to see if anyone had failed to return their books within the last couple of days. One name came up—a Malachi Abbot. Lived two miles outside Ashenby. Remote spot. As we were driving out there, we happened across PC Jackson and the Road Policing Unit. A car lost control on a tight bend, crashed through a wall and ended up in the river. We didn't think too much of it until forty minutes later when PC Jackson turned up at Malachi Abbott's place.'

Frank pushes back in his seat. 'Don't tell me—Malachi Abbot?'

Prisha sucks in air. 'Yes. First indications are he drowned inside the car. They found his licence—that's how Jackson knew to head to the house.'

'And what did RPU have to say?'

'Early days. They're still investigating. To the untrained eye it looks cut and dried. Car loses control on a sharp bend at the bottom of a steep hill. Crashes through a wall, ends up in the river. The field leading to the river is quite steep.'

'I can sense a—*but*, coming?'

'According to PC Jackson, the lead officer from RPU said there were no tyre marks on the road leading up to the wall.'

'Meaning the driver didn't brake?'

'Or didn't have time to brake.'

'And what about the body? Any signs of injury?'

'His vehicle was an old Land Rover Discovery—late 80s model, so it didn't have airbags, and he wasn't wearing a seatbelt. He suffered lacerations to the face and head but that's all we know so far.'

'So his head may have hit the dash or steering wheel when it impacted the wall, rendering him unconscious?'

'Possibly. Where the car was located in the river it wasn't very deep. Probably about chest high while sitting in the vehicle. But the body was slumped over onto the passenger seat, so his head would have been below the waterline.'

Frank takes a draught of tea. 'I take it this Malachi figure wasn't missing a foot?'

'No.'

'So, we can rule him out of that investigation. Sounds like an unfortunate, or possibly reckless accident.'

Zac chews on his butty and nods in agreement. 'That's what I said,' he says, throwing Prisha a desultory glance.

Frank picks up on the sign. 'But you think otherwise, Prisha?'

'I like to get to the end of a chapter before closing the book.'

Frank smirks. 'You read too many thrillers, Prisha.'

'As Zac mentioned, that area is sparsely populated. According to Wikipedia, Ashenby has a population of two hundred and thirty. Let's say the surrounding area has another sixty or so people. So, around three hundred in total. Yesterday, human remains were found in Ravensbane Wood, and today a body is found in a car in the river. And the victim just so happens to be the only lead we were investigating.'

Frank harrumphs. 'Hmm... I don't see a connection but you're right not to rule it out completely.' He becomes sterner. 'But Prisha, don't go diving down rabbit holes. Leave Malachi Abbott to the Serious Collision Investigation Unit. If they unearth anything suspicious, they'll hand it over to us, anyway.'

'Fair enough.'

'Although,' he pauses and strokes his chin.

'What?'

'While continuing the investigation into the human remains, it may be worth your while to make a few discreet inquiries into this Abbott chap. See what his story is.'

'He liked a drink, according to his neighbour,' Zac says as he picks up a serviette and wipes his mouth.

'There you go then. There's a nice country pub in Ashenby called The Crown. And landlords are a conduit for local gossip. Right, where to from here?'

Prisha shrugs. 'There's no point getting uniform to do a door knock in Ashenby, or putting out public appeals until we know for certain the foot is human.'

'Hmm... you're right. Not sure what Whipple is playing at. He's had the damned thing nearly twenty-four hours. All he has to do is take an X-ray. Listen, I have some private business to attend to over in Scarborough this afternoon. I'll pop into the pathology lab and have a word with him.'

Frank's phone buzzes in his jacket. He pulls it out and grimaces before answering.

'DCI Finnegan. Yes. Yes. Ah, I see. Hmm... yes, that is suspicious. Okay, thanks for the call. I'll send an officer over straight away.'

He hangs up and stares at the floor for a moment.

'Bad news?' Zac prompts.

'You could say that. It appears I spoke too soon. That was Terry Claymore, the Vehicle Forensic Officer with the Serious Collision Investigation Unit. They have Malachi Abbott's Land Rover at the pound and have done a preliminary investigation.'

'And?' Prisha quizzes.

'It appears the car was tampered with.'

17

Prisha steps into the forensic vehicle bay, the smell of oil, and old rubber thick in the air. Overhead fluorescent lights buzz faintly, casting a clinical glow over the workshop. The Land Rover Discovery sits in the centre, flanked by toolboxes, diagnostic computers, and a hydraulic lift that whirrs and groans as it raises the vehicle off the ground.

The Vehicle Forensic Examiner, Terry Claymore, watches the process with his arms folded. He's short—five foot five on a good day—with thinning grey hair and a light dusting of dandruff on the shoulders of his dark blue overalls. Thick-lensed spectacles, perpetually smudged, perch precariously on the bridge of his nose. He doesn't so much as glance at Prisha when she enters. He merely raises a finger in acknowledgement, flicks a button on a remote control, and the lift judders to a halt.

Claymore sniffs, adjusting his glasses.

'A 1989 Land Rover Discovery, 2.5-litre 200Tdi diesel, permanent four-wheel drive, five-speed manual, solid ladder-frame chassis, coil-sprung suspension, and a kerb weight of just over 1,800 kilos—built like a tank but about as refined as a brick on wheels. It had a recent MOT pass and was insured third-party, so technically roadworthy, but looking at it... well, it was unkempt, rough around the edges, and had seen better days. Tyres must have just crept past the legal limit. Rust creeping in. Interior like a scrapyard. The kind of motor you keep running because you've no other choice. Watch your head,' he says, voice dry as dust, as he walks under the raised car with the ease of someone who's spent a lifetime in garages.

Prisha follows, bending awkwardly to avoid smacking her forehead on the chassis. The undercarriage is coated in grime, rust nibbling at the edges of its frame. Claymore produces a torch from his pocket and clicks it on with a perfunctory snap.

'As I mentioned on the phone to DCI Finnegan,' he begins, his tone flat, methodical, like he's already testifying in court, 'we've established a significant loss of brake fluid prior to the collision. This vehicle operates on a hydraulic brake system. That system relies on pressure—fluid being pushed through these lines here.' He traces the thin metal tubing running the length of the chassis. 'To engage the callipers and press the brake pads onto the discs. You lose fluid, you lose pressure. You lose pressure, you lose braking power. Simple physics.'

Prisha nods, squinting at the piping. 'How fast would the fluid have leaked out?'

'Depends on the breach size and when the driver started braking. The cuts, which I'll show you in a second, would start a slow leak, but under braking pressure, the fluid loss would accelerate. By the time he hit that bend? Complete failure, likely within five to ten minutes of setting off, assuming he used the brakes before then.'

Prisha exhales. 'So when he approached the bend, he'd have tried to brake and... what? Nothing happened?'

Claymore shrugs, though there's nothing casual about it. 'Something happened. Just not what he expected. By the time he hit the bend, the system would have been compromised. At first, the brake pedal would have felt soft, spongy—not an immediate failure, just less response than usual. But the moment he braked hard, the master cylinder would have sucked in air. Air compresses. Brake fluid doesn't. Which means hydraulic pressure collapses. Result?'

He slaps his hand hard against the exhaust muffler causing Prisha to jump and bang her head.

'Catastrophic failure!' he shouts.

Prisha winces and rubs her head. 'No stopping power at all?'

'Not enough to slow him down before impact.'

She tilts her head. 'What about skid marks? Did you find any before he hit the wall?'

Claymore shakes his head. 'Nothing. Not even faint tyre abrasions or transfer marks, which is telling. With a failure like this, you wouldn't expect skid signatures—the wheels don't lock up because there's no hydraulic force applying the brakes.'

'And after he went through the wall? On the slope down to the river?'

'Same. No braking attempt registered. Of course, he may have been knocked unconscious by the impact with the wall. No-seat belt. Basically, he went down that slope as a passenger, not a driver.'

Prisha exhales slowly. 'You mentioned cuts?'

Claymore shifts, lifting his torch higher. The beam picks out one of the rubber hoses, the flexible section connecting the rigid brake line to the wheel calliper. He gestures with one gnarled finger.

'These,' he says, 'are your flexible brake hoses. They allow for movement between the fixed chassis and the wheels. Old vehicle like this? Not uncommon for one to degrade. Maybe even two. But...' He angles the torch around the chassis so the cut edges of each hose gleam under the artificial light. 'All four have failed in the same way. Halfway through. Same depth. Same position.'

Prisha leans in, inspecting them more closely. 'You're saying this didn't happen naturally?'

'I'm saying it would be statistically improbable for four hoses, on four separate wheels, to develop the same structural weakness at the same time,' Claymore replies. 'Wear and tear causes random failures. This? This is consistent.'

'Consistent with what?' Prisha asks, already knowing the answer.

'Tampering.' Claymore spits the word out like it's an old adversary.

Prisha rolls her shoulders, easing the pain from being bent over. 'So someone, what—used a blade? A pair of pliers?'

Claymore nods slowly. 'More likely snips. But yes, a sharp cutting tool. You can see the cut points—clean, intentional. Just enough to compromise them, not completely severed, which is important.'

'Why?' Prisha asks.

'If you cut a brake line clean through, it's immediate failure,' Claymore explains. 'Driver gets into the car, presses the brakes, realises there's an issue straight away. That's risky for the perpetrator—victim might notice and stop driving altogether. This way causes a slow leak. Brake fluid drains out while he's already on the road. By the time he hits a dangerous point—like a tight bend—the braking system is already redundant.'

Prisha exhales, processing the implications. 'So this was deliberate. Someone planned for him to crash?'

Claymore doesn't nod, doesn't shake his head—just watches her over the rim of his glasses, his face unreadable. 'That's your department, inspector,' he says. 'I just tell you how it happened.'

They both step out from under the car. 'A bit hit and miss though, isn't it?' she states.

'I don't follow, inspector?'

'If you wanted to kill someone, cutting their brake lines is leaving a lot to chance. What if Malachi had slowed on a straight, flat stretch of road and noticed the brakes were off? Or simply ran into the back of a vehicle. Whoever cut the brake lines can't possibly have known he'd approach *that* particular corner at speed. And cutting all four pipes is leaving a tell-tale sign behind. Not very professional.'

Claymore removes his spectacles and cleans them on a rag.

'Whoever it was, they had more than a rudimentary knowledge of vehicle mechanics. They knew what they were doing.'

'But not expert or clever enough to leave no trace behind.'

Claymore nods. 'True. Maybe they were in a rush.'

'You will provide me with close-up shots of the cut marks on the brake lines?'

'Of course. Next job on my list. I'll run laser scanning microscopy for ultra-high magnification and use structured light 3D scanning to create a digital model of the incision marks. That'll give you precise depth analysis and help determine the type of tool used. If you recover a suspect's tool, we can compare incision characteristics for a match. Should have them to you by first thing tomorrow. I have various personal items from the car bagged and itemised on the bench over there, if you'd care to take a look.'

Prisha gazes over at the worktop and the array of plastic bags. 'Anything of note?'

Claymore shrugs. 'Not that I can see. Spanners, a tow-rope, two cigarette lighters, a pen, a couple of magazines and a book. Old tobacco pouches. Oh, and two rabbits which have been photographed and disposed of. They were beginning to smell.'

'Rabbits? Like pet rabbits in a cage?'

'No. They'd been gutted. I'd say they were wild rabbits. Probably ready for the pot.'

Prisha ambles over to the table and takes a cursory glance at the belongings. She stares at the book in the evidence bag. It's the one from the library—*How To Disappear*, now waterlogged. Apart from that, just the usual debris from inside a car.

Something catches her attention. She pulls a pair of latex gloves from her jacket and slips them on. Carefully, she removes the item and lays it flat on the table and takes photos on her phone, intrigued.

She turns the coin-sized object over in her hand. Its braided design is disturbingly neat, soft to the eye. At the centre, woven with exacting precision, is what appears to be a Christian cross. But there's no hole for a chain to thread through, so it's not a charm to be worn or placed on a keyring. On the reverse side is a single broken circle, stitched in red twine.

'Any idea what this is?' she calls out to Claymore, who saunters over.

'Possibly a Christian symbol, or a good luck charm.'

'If it is—it didn't work.' She places the curiosity back in the bag and seals it up. 'Great, well thanks for your time, Mr Claymore.'

'Just doing my job, inspector.'

As she turns to leave, she pauses. 'One last thing. Tell me, Mr Claymore, if you wanted to kill someone by tampering with their vehicle, *and* get away with it, how would you do it?'

Claymore exhales through his nose, adjusting his spectacles.

'If you wanted to be crude, you'd cut the brake lines, sever the throttle linkage, or meddle with the steering rack—but those are easily detected. A smarter approach? Brake fluid contamination—introduce petroleum-based oil, rots the seals, causes gradual failure, and looks like poor maintenance. Or a sidewall incision on a tyre, deep enough to fail under stress, is another. All subtle, all easily dismissed as bad luck or sloppy maintenance.'

'But you have a better way?' she probes sensing he's holding back.

Claymore tilts his head, offering the faintest trace of a smile. 'The most foolproof method? Easy. Sabotage the driver... not the car.'

18

As Frank can patently see from the X-ray, the foot is undoubtedly human. Absolutely no doubt about it. But that doesn't stop Dr Bennet Whipple from extrapolating to the nth degree as he points at the image with an extendable baton like a university lecturer in full flow.

'Observe, if you will, inspector, the metatarsals—five in number—each articulating with the proximal phalanges, which, despite the thermal degradation, remain distinguishable. Note the calcaneus, the largest tarsal bone, forming the heel, with its superior articulation with the talus, allowing for dorsiflexion and plantarflexion...'

As Whipple drones on and on and on, Frank yawns as his mind wanders.

I must call in at the garden centre on the way home and buy carrot, beetroot, and turnip seeds for the allotment. Oh, and a two-kilo bag of blood and bone. But there was something else... what the hell was it?

'... the incineration has compromised the soft tissue, yet remnants of the plantar fascia suggest prior tensile integrity.'

Whipple pauses and eyeballs Frank suspiciously. 'Are you keeping up, inspector?'

'Radish seeds!' Frank yells.

Whipple blinks in slow motion. 'Radish seeds, inspector? What in the name of Jeremiah's whiskers are you talking about?'

Frank shuffles. 'Ahem, nothing. Carry on, Bennet. I'm following you like a tracer bullet.'

'Hmm... very well,' Whipple clears his throat. 'The phalanges, though charred, exhibit characteristic distal tufts. One might deduce from the skeletal robustness that our unfortunate individual engaged in habitual ambulation.'

'You mean—walking?'

Whipple peers at him above his glasses. 'Indeed. In short, Chief Inspector Finnegan, unless some heretofore undocumented species shares these precise anatomical features—this foot is, without doubt, human.'

'You don't say,' Frank replies wishing he'd had a strong cup of coffee, or maybe a shot of morphine, before entering the lab. 'And did the foot become separated from the leg due to the heat of the fire?'

Whipple's eyes light up and Frank fears the worst. 'Ah, an excellent inquiry. The separation of the foot from the lower limb was not, I posit, a consequence of the fire. Observe the clean, surgical transection of the distal tibia and fibula—entirely inconsistent with thermal disarticulation, which produces irregular charring and contraction rather than such clinical precision. This, I would surmise, was the work of an oscillating or reciprocating instrument, not flames.'

'You mean a saw?'

'Indubitably.' He leans forward and pokes the image with the tip of the baton. 'Note the straight, smooth cuts with micro-striations perpendicular to the bone axis.'

Frank takes a moment to deconstruct the words then rebuild them in English as he stares at the X-ray not really seeing anything of note.

'Ah, yes, of course, the micro-striations. Meaning the foot was cut off before it was burnt?'

Whipple takes a deep sigh and gazes wearily at Frank. 'A crude, rudimentary observation, but yes, in your vernacular, this foot was removed surgically.'

'Surgically?'

'Yes, or at least by a person with formidable skills in precision osteotomy—a veritable maestro of osseous bisection. This was not the work of brute force but of a highly adept skeletal partitionist.'

Frank strokes the stubble on his chin buying time as his brain catches up.

'I see,' he eventually replies. 'I know you're busy, Bennet. Just a few more questions and I'll leave you in peace.'

'Hmm... if only your words bore the truth of their intent,' he mumbles under his breath.

'First question: sex—male or female? And I'm not asking about your personal preferences, ha, ha, ha!'

Silence.

Not a flicker of emotion from Whipple.

Frank adjusts his tie. 'Ahem, yes, well, I was talking about the foot—male or female?'

Whipple gives him the dead-eye for a moment before replying. 'The robust proportions and phalangeal length lean toward a male origin, though I shall refrain from declaring it an incontrovertible fact.'

'Right... right...' Frank mutters scribbling into his notebook and also making a mental note not to try to be funny around Whipple. 'And shoe size?'

'Based on the proportionality of the first metatarsal and phalangeal extension, I estimate the foot would necessitate a male shoe of approximately size ten, possibly eleven.'

'Ten, possibly eleven,' he repeats jotting the facts down. 'And I can see it is the left foot. Now, what about age?'

'There are no visible epiphyseal plates, suggesting the individual had reached full skeletal maturity. While subtle indicators of wear suggest habitual ambulation over decades. I shall refrain from assigning a precise numerical age without further osteological examination.'

'But a man, not a boy or adolescent?'

'Did I not just articulate the same?' Whipple replies his impatience rising with every question.

'You did, indeed, Bennet. My apologies. Anything else of significance?'

Whipple's normally shiny, smooth bald head creases like an old chamois leather.

'Naturally, a more definitive assessment must await the delicate process of extraction,' he remarks, tapping the baton idly against his palm. He snaps the baton shut and drops it into his top pocket. 'Still... there is an unexpected residual trace—something that does not align entirely with thermal degradation. A peculiarity in the olfactory sense—subtle, yet distinct. But no doubt, all shall become crystal clear soon enough.'

I doubt that very much, Frank thinks. As he looks around the lab, he notices a tray containing the teeth removed from Ravensbane Wood.

'Ah, that's right. The teeth. Human or animal? And if human, were they from more than one body?'

Whipple's barrel chest heaves as he picks up the tray of teeth and thrusts them under Frank's nose, much to his distaste.

'At first glance, one might be forgiven for mistaking these specimens for human dentition—though only in dim lighting and with a distinct lack of scrutiny. However, radiographic analysis reveals a rather more eclectic collection.

'Observe the variance in root structure and enamel thickness. The larger molars exhibit the dense, ridged occlusal surfaces typical of ruminants—sheep and goat, I would wager—while the more compact specimens, particularly these incisors,' he says, poking them with a gloved finger, 'are distinctly those of a lagomorph origin. And these?' he says flicking at more grisly specimens. 'Swine. Possibly sus scrofa or more likely domesticus sus scrofa.'

Frank pulls at his collar, feeling decidedly hot. 'Right. And sus crofa are what exactly? Badgers?'

Whipple sighs, as though physically pained by Frank's presence. 'I just explained, inspector. Must I constantly repeat myself?'

'If you could.'

'Sus scrofa is the wild boar. Sus scrofa domesticus is the domesticated pig. As I indicated, a veritable barnyard of remains, but not a single human tooth among them.'

Frank is more than puzzled. 'Are you certain?' He immediately regrets his question as Whipple's eyeballs threaten to detach from his head.

'Inspector! I am not in the habit of indulging in speculative whimsy. I do not pluck random theories from the ether like some sideshow charlatan. If I state these remains are of the animal persuasion, you may rest assured that no amount of wishful thinking on your part will render them human.

'My conclusions are based on expert empirical observation—confirmed, I might add, by my esteemed colleague, Dr Macavity, the laboratory's forensic odontologist.'

His voice ricochets around the lab like shrapnel.

Frank winces. 'Okay, keep your wig on, Bennet. No need to shout.' Erring on the side of caution, he refrains from asking if the odontologist's first name is Phil.

Whipple turns and slams the tray down and picks up another one. 'And likewise this assortment of bones, also retrieved from your crime scene. Calcined osseous fragments—distorted by thermal trauma. Again, undoubtedly the remnants of sheep, goats, pigs and some smaller creatures, possibly lagomorphs.'

Frank scratches his head. 'Ah, yes, the old lagomorphs again. And is that some type of rodent?' he enquires, clutching at straws.

The veins in Whipple's neck visibly twitch. 'Rabbits, inspector! Rabbits! The rabbit is a lagomorph. Specifically, part of the leporidae family. And no—they are not a rodent. Rodents are omnivores, whilst lagomorphs are herbivores. Just one of many differences. Any imbecile knows that!'

Not this imbecile, obviously, Frank thinks as he composes himself. No point both men self-combusting. It would make a hell of a mess in the lab.

'I see. Of course—rabbits.'

He's got what he came for. Now it's time to make a rapid exit. But not before one last question. To be certain. For his own peace of mind.

Taking a deep breath, and pointing at the trays, he asks, 'Bennet, are you absolutely positive there are no human teeth or bones in this little lot?'

———◦———

As Frank walks back to his car, with the onset of a headache, he waggles a finger in his ear hoping his hearing may return at some point. He's certain he has a perforated eardrum.

'I really must remember to bring earplugs with me next time.'

19

The beer garden at the White House Inn is conspicuously quiet. The evening air carries the faint hint of salt and ozone from the sea, mingling with the scent of cut grass from the golf course opposite. Above, the sky, a soft wash of deepening blue, holds the retreating daylight, stretching long shadows across the wooden benches.

Frank places the drinks down on the table, a creamy head lacing the rims of the Guinness pints.

'Perfect night for it,' Zac says, lifting the pint. 'Reckon we'll get a decent summer?'

Frank takes a sip, considering. 'Doubt it. We'll get a week of sunshine, then back to business as usual.'

Prisha smirks, stirring her G&T and ice with a finger. 'Optimistic as ever.'

'Just realistic,' Frank says, slipping onto the bench seat. 'Besides, this'll do. Cool air, no rain, and a full pint in front of me. Not much more a man needs.'

Zac lifts his glass. 'One thing springs to mind, but I'll second your sentiment anyway, Frank.'

'One track mind,' Prisha comments.

They all take a sip and place their drinks down.

'Right, a quick update. I saw Dr Whipple this afternoon.'

Zac grins. 'Ah, yes. The mysterious foot. What did old Raspberry have to say about it?'

'Quite a lot, actually. I could labour the point and bamboozle you with science—but I won't. So listen up. According to the Great Doctor, the foot recovered from Ravensbane Woods is definitely human. Male, and aged at least twenty-plus but could be a lot older. The left foot was surgically removed using a saw in an expert manner—i.e. it wasn't burnt or hacked off. Which means someone who has skills in dissection.'

'A surgeon?' Prisha suggests.

'Or a butcher, or abattoir worker,' Zac adds.

Frank nods. 'Possibly. The teeth and bone fragments recovered are all animal—sheep, goat, pig, possibly some smaller animals, rabbits or such like.'

Prisha frowns and glances across at Zac then back to Frank. 'Are you sure?'

Frank takes a deep intake of breath. 'Oh, yes. I'm certain alright. I still have tinnitus and a minor brain haemorrhage to prove it.'

'Ah, yes. Doctor Whipple—you questioned his findings?' Prisha asks with a grin.

'Aye. I'm getting older but non the wiser.'

Zac rubs the condensation from his glass, clearly puzzled. 'So absolutely no other human remains?'

'Not from what's been recovered so far. Have forensics completely finished at the site?'

Prisha nods. 'Yes. I spoke with Charlene earlier. They packed up at midday.'

'Well then. There you have it. That foot was dismembered in another location and placed on the fire, which raises two questions—why? And who does it belong to?'

'Three questions, Frank—and is the owner of the foot dead or alive?' Prisha adds.

'For my money, I'd say they're long dead. Zac, did you ring around the hospitals to see if anyone had presented with a foot missing?'

Zac rolls his eyes. 'Yes. I felt like a right dickhead. Some of the nurses thought I was taking the piss. I mean, if you've had your foot cut off you don't just hop into A&E with a bandage around your stump.'

'Nevertheless, it's a process of eliminating the obvious. Let's hope the DNA results are not too far away. That may shed some light on the rightful owner.' Frank takes a hefty draught of Guinness and turns to Prisha. 'And what's the go with Malachi Abbott's Land Rover?'

'Definite sabotage. All four brake lines were partially cut.'

'Bloody great,' he sighs. 'Which means murder or manslaughter at the very least.'

'Yes. Looks that way.'

'Like we haven't got enough to do. What about next of kin?'

'Uniform have taken care of it. A distant nephew in Canada.'

'Bloody hell—is that all?'

'Yes. Bit sad really. From the state of his home and what his neighbour had to say, I get the impression Malachi was a bit of loner.'

'Anything of interest in his vehicle?'

'Not really. A couple of dead rabbits. So, he was a possibly a hunter. And some sort of small charm or keepsake. Picture of a crucifix on a braided coin. No smoking gun, as it were.'

Frank raises a finger. 'Now, that's a point. If he was a hunter, then he probably has firearms inside his house. You'll need to search the place and confiscate them. Check the firearm register as well. I take it uniform secured his property?'

'Yes. Couple of heavy-duty padlocks.'

Frank leans back deep in thought as he strokes his pint. 'Although I ruled it out earlier, we'll run the Abbott death and the missing foot concurrently as if it's part of the same investigation, until proved otherwise. The last time the sleepy hamlet of Ashenby had anything untoward happen was thirty-five years ago. And all of a sudden we have a sabotaged vehicle, a suspicious drowning, and a bloody foot turn up in a wood.'

Zac smiles. 'Wasn't much blood on it, Frank. I'd say it was well cooked, not rare.'

'Most amusing. Okay, as you know, we're short-staffed—again. Dinkel is working the car theft syndicate, and I've also given him a cold case to sink his teeth into. And with Kylie still on holiday, it means you two are it, for this investigation. I can wangle a handful of uniforms to help with a door knock in the village tomorrow but you'll only have them for the day, so make the best use of them.'

Prisha's brow creases. 'Hang on, Frank, shouldn't we conduct a full-scale search of the woods?'

'For what?'

'For a body?' she states with mild incredulity.

'A body that may not exist, and if it does exist, it could be anywhere in the country. We don't even have a missing person yet. Remember, that foot was removed with precision by someone who knew what they were doing. It's hardly likely they carried out the amputation in a wood. No, we need more to go on before we initiate a search. Anyway, with what we have so far, there's no way Superintendent Banks would ever sign off on it. Full-scale searches use up a lot of manpower, and manpower costs money.'

'But Frank...'

'The answer's still no. However, I dare say the budget will stretch to a couple of handlers and cadaver dogs giving the wood a once over. Happy?'

'Ecstatic.'

'Good. Right, I suggest one of you focus on finding the rightful owner of the foot—i.e. a missing person; the other, get some background on this Malachi Abbott bloke. We know he was aged sixty-six, unemployed. But what else? Who were his associates? Where did he used to work? How long has he been in Ashenby? Did he own his house or was he renting? Habits, haunts, past history. And Prisha, don't forget to visit to Lord and Lady Hampton—keep them in the loop about developments.'

'Should I tell them the body part was a foot?'

'Only if they press. We don't want it common knowledge.'

Prisha takes a sip of her drink. 'By the way, this cold case Dinkel's on—what is it?'

'A suspected hit and run from 1989. As it happens, a few miles outside Ashenby. That's how I knew when the last major incident occurred in the village.'

'Rather him than me. I couldn't imagine anything worse than working a cold case. You end up stuck in the office most of the day trudging through old files. I like a bit of action.'

'We've noticed.' He leans forward and lowers his voice—not that there's anyone else around apart from a pair of elderly golfers attacking the 9th hole. 'This could just be the start of it. Apparently, and keep this to yourselves, our illustrious Chief Constable is keen to reopen a whole swathe of cold cases. It's part of his mission statement.'

Zac snorts. 'Mission statement! Christ, haven't we got enough to do already with live cases?'

Frank leans back, wry smile in place. 'As Tennyson said, *"Theirs not to reason why. Theirs but to do and die."* It's just the way it is.'

Zac takes a mouthful of stout and grumbles, 'Who's this Tennyson bloke when he's at home? Some bureaucratic, pen-pushing, paper-shuffling bean-counter from HQ? Well, you can tell Tennyson from me—he's an arse.'

Prisha chuckles into her drink. Frank closes his eyes and shakes his head in despair.

'Strewth, give me strength. Did you not get an education, lad? Alfred Lord Tennyson—The Charge of the Light Brigade? The Battle of Balaclava?'

Zac shrugs and drains his pint. 'I dropped history in favour of woodwork.'

Frank groans. 'It's a bloody poem!'

'The only poems I studied were written on toilet walls. Now there's an education.'

Frank turns to Prisha. 'And you've to work with this heathen day in day out?'

'We all have our cross to bear, Frank.'

Zac picks his empty glass up and rises. 'Time for another?'

'Aye, why not. But before you get them in, let's set our stall out for tomorrow. I want to switch off for the night and enjoy my last pint talking about something other than bloody police work.'

'Shoot.'

'That photo Prisha showed me yesterday, the goats head in the oak tree. Last night I did a little research. The goat's head could represent a Baphomet.'

'A what-a-met?' Zac asks, not liking the turn in conversation.

Frank exhales, rubbing his jaw. 'Baphomet. A mystical figure—goat's head, human body, big curling horns. Eliphas Lévi drew it in the 1800s, meant it as a symbol of balance—light and dark, male and female, knowledge and mystery. Then the Satanists hijacked it, turned it into their mascot. These days, most people just see the devil. And if that's what someone, or some people wants us to think... then they're putting in a hell of a lot of effort.'

Prisha's eyebrows are in danger of migrating north. 'Frank, yesterday you were telling us most ritualistic killings are all smoke and mirrors. Now you're saying we might be dealing with Satanic nutjobs?'

'Just bear it in mind as you go about your work.' He glances up at Zac's pained expression. 'Eh, up lad, what's wrong with thee? You look like the cat's just taken a shit in your slippers.'

Zac shuffles uncomfortably. 'It's all this voodoo, hobgoblin stuff. There are a few things we maybe didn't mention to you yesterday,' he replies sheepishly.

'Such as?'

Zac places the pint glass down and rubs at the back of his neck. 'The Toppings took a walk in the woods last Friday after they'd arrived at Hexley farm. They reckon they saw an old woman in a hooded cloak watching them. It spooked them. Later, they went to the pub in Ashenby. Got talking to a local and mentioned the woman in the woods. The local guy became agitated and advised them to stay away from the woods. And the reason Prisha took that photo was because when she went off on her Easter egg hunt, she saw someone similar and gave chase and fell over. That's when she saw the goat's head in the tree.'

Frank glances at Prisha as she smirks and mouths the words "wuss" waggling her thumb in Zac's direction.

Frank's not amused. His gaze returns to Zac. 'Go on?'

'According to the Bakers—the farmers—they said three witches were tried in that wood back in 17... whatever, and were subsequently executed. Then there's the... ahem, the villagers.'

'Villagers?'

'Yeah. The villagers in Ashenby that we questioned today. They're all....' He hesitates searching for the right words.

'Come on, son, spit it out.'

'Weird.'

'In what way?'

He shrugs like an embarrassed schoolboy. 'I don't know. They were all nicey-nicey, sort of helpful but not. I just got this feeling, like...'

A moment's pause.

'Christ, this is like pulling bloody teeth. You got this feeling?' Frank prompts.

'I don't know. Like they were, you know...'

'No, I don't know! If I did bloody know I wouldn't be asking. Now, I only have a finite amount of time left on this planet, and it's rapidly ticking down, and to be honest, I'd prefer to spend it on my allotment rather than playing twenty bloody questions with you.'

'Like they were all in on it. There was an underlying smugness about them. Like they know and we don't.'

'Bugger me backwards,' Frank whispers rubbing his forehead. 'This is like trying to untangle fishing line but not as enjoyable.' He turns his attention to Prisha. 'Did you detect anything with the villagers? A sense they knew more than they were letting on?'

Prisha hesitates and gazes out towards the grey North Sea. 'Maybe,' she murmurs.

'Give me strength. Mr I Don't Know and Mrs Maybe. You're like a comedy double act with two straight men.' Frank exhales sharply, jabbing a finger at them. 'Right, listen up, Bonnie and Clyde—or should that be George and Mildred? At the moment we have a burnt shoe with a human foot inside, found in Ravensbane Wood. Now, I'm no clairvoyant, but it didn't walk onto that bloody fire by itself. Tomorrow, you get your arses back into that village and you bang some heads together. At the moment, you're acting like a pair of nervous-Nellies. Have I wasted all these years training you up to be hard-nosed detectives for nothing?

'If those villagers want to be evasive, ambiguous, and give you the runaround—the answer is simple—put the cuffs on the bastards and take them out of their comfort zone, back to the station. That interview room can be a lonely place when you've something to hide. It has a knack of loosening tongues. Do I make myself clear?' he yells, causing a golfer on the 9th hole to miss his putt.

'Yes, boss,' they both reply in unison.

Frank calms, nods, and hands Zac his empty pint glass. 'Good. Remember, we're not here to be liked. We're here to uncover the truth. Right, Zac, get the drinks in. Make mine a pint of Theakston's Best.'

Prisha shoots from her seat. 'Erm, I'll help you with that, Zac.'

'No need,' he replies. 'I can manage.'

'No *really*. I'll help.'

20

Wednesday 3rd May

The shackle of the second padlock pops open with a click. Prisha removes it, pulls back the clasp, and places the lock in her pocket. She twists the handle of the door and steps into the cottage.

The stench hits her instantly as she groans and recoils in dismay. She's been here too many times before—not this particular abode, but dozens like it over the years.

Defeat has its own perfume.

Cloying, dismal, and sour, a miasma of spilled ale, rank cigarette smoke, stale food, rancid chip fat, old sweat, and rising damp—the lingering odour of a life steeped in neglect and tarnished by misguided choices.

The gloom inside is nearly as impenetrable as the atmosphere.

The curtains, thin as shrouds, sag against the grime-streaked windows, choking out what little daylight the overcast, miserly sky outside offers.

Her boots scuff against a sticky, uneven floor, the lino peeling at the edges like decaying skin. A single lightbulb dangles overhead, its greasy pull cord swaying in the draught, but she doesn't bother switching it on.

She doubts it works.

Pulling on a pair of latex gloves she reminds herself why she's here—to search for firearms. If she finds any, she'll log the location, type, and condition, then call in an Authorised Firearms Officer to make them safe, and handle removal.

The dining room-kitchen is cluttered, but not in a way that suggests sentimentality. No framed photographs, no trinkets from a life well-lived—just piles of ancient, yellowing newspapers, slumped against a warped coffee table. On its surface, a dissected rifle, its parts cleaned but abandoned, lies next to a half-eaten plate of something grey and congealed. Empty beer cans, overflowing ashtrays, discarded crisp packets, are strewn over the floor. A sock, a pair of stained, baggy Y-fronts and what looks like an untouched hard boiled egg poke out from under a chair.

'What in all that's holy,' Prisha whispers staring at the offending articles in disbelief.

On the mantelpiece, a row of glass jars catches the weak light, their contents murky and unsettling—teeth, claws, feathers, a half-decayed rabbit's foot. An odd collection, yet something about their placement feels deliberate, ritualistic even.

The sink is an evil pool of vile water. Grey froth and scum cling to the stainless-steel edges. A pan handle pokes from the filth like the stern of a sunken frigate, lost in a futile battle, long forgotten.

Stagnant air is thick with dust motes swirling in the miserly light from the windows, coating every surface in a fine layer of neglect. The sofa, once green, is slick with age and too many comatose late nights. Cushions flattened into brittle husks. Suspicious stains dot the surface like an avant-garde splatter painting.

Prisha scratches at her forearm as a phantom itch crawls beneath her skin.

'Urrrrgh.' She expels her disgust in a long slow gasp. 'How can anyone live like this? There's no need. I don't care how poor you are, cleanliness costs nothing.'

Climbing the creaking stairs, she refrains from touching the banister.

Who knows what deadly microbes lurk unseen, waiting to strike?

Hitting the landing she uses the toe of her shoe to tap open the toilet door. She stares with distaste at the high-mounted cistern and long pull-chain dangling, as if waiting. Shuffling two steps to the left, she repeats the procedure, and kicks open the bathroom door. On the sink a grimy glass contains a tube of half-rolled up toothpaste and a forlorn toothbrush suffering from a severe case of alopecia. The avocado coloured bath reminds her of a grave, deep and cold. The roller-blind, an old man's eyelid covered in cobwebs. She wants to take a deep breath but instead, meekly takes a shallow draw of air.

Turning, she stares apprehensively at the last place in the world she wants to enter—the bedroom.

The door creaks open like it's auditioning for a horror film.

Instantly, she shudders at the state of the bed.

Pillows, brown with sweat.

Sheets that nuclear waste inspectors would refuse to examine.

A chest of drawers sit at the side of the window.

An old stand-alone wardrobe faces the bed.

Cringing, she tentatively falls to her knees on the threadbare carpet, pulls aside an overhanging sheet, and stares under the bed.

She spots it straight away—a double-barrelled shotgun. Rising, she pulls open the bedside cabinet and spots the box of cartridge shells.

'Nearly done, girl,' she murmurs, encouraging herself onwards. 'Shotgun under the bed, shells in bedside cabinet, a dismantled rifle in the living room. It matches what's on the Firearms Register. Just the drawers and wardrobe to check then I'm out of here.'

The drawers contain nothing but a few nick-knacks; a torch, a packet of unopened cigarettes, a lighter, a pen, and a well-thumbed Bible—Old Testament.

Lastly, she turns to the wardrobe and pulls it open, finally releasing the breath she's been holding onto for far too long.

One shabby suit and a few limp discoloured shirts hang from wire coat hangers. On the floor of the wardrobe, a small suitcase, the only thing that looks new, a Samsonite label hanging from a piece of string.

Puffing out air, she spins on her heels, clatters down the stairs, yanks at the front door and emerges into daylight, sucking fresh air into her aching lungs.

Scalp itches. Neck and arms too. And legs. God only knows what's going on with her back. It's like a thousand centipedes are burrowing under her skin.

She wants to rip her clothes off, burn them, then dive under a warm shower for thirty minutes.

But that's not possible.

Her day has only just begun.

Recently deceased bodies—not a problem.

Decaying corpses, blood splatter, brain matter, intestines curling from gaping stomach wounds—takes it in her stride.

But squalor and filth, and most of all, the accompanying stench, makes her dry retch.

And the thing is—those memories, those smells, always stay with you, hidden deep in the brain.

Peeling off the gloves, she drops them into the outside recycling bin, which is half-full of empty beer cans, whisky bottles, pizza boxes, and discarded fish and chip wrappers. And something peculiar—a large glass jar. Apart from the smell of stale ale, and whisky, there's also a faint chemical odour.

She shrugs and drops the lid.

Tapping at her phone, she calls the Operational Support Unit and relays her findings, telling them she'll wait for their arrival.

She pulls at the handle of the car, and grimaces at the lingering, claggy stink that has taken up residence on her clothing, skin, and deep within her nostrils.

'Christ, there must be easier ways to make a living,' she curses.

As she places one foot inside the car, she hesitates.

'Shit! The suitcase,' she mutters. 'I should have checked.'

Considering the proposition for a moment she discounts it.

'The AFO can check it when he gets here,' she reassures herself, slumping into the comfort of her seat and breathing in the refreshing artificial smell of potpourri from the car air freshener.

At last, she relaxes and closes her eyes for a moment, trying to conjure up nice thoughts.

It nearly works.

Nearly.

'Bollocks,' she whispers, as a niggling doubt returns to stomp all over her mental image of strolling through a meadow of wildflowers, hand in hand with Adam, on a warm summer's day.

'A new suitcase? The house is a bio-hazard. His car was a wreck. From impressions so far, Malachi Abbott was an unsavoury loner. Why would he have a brand-new suitcase in his wardrobe? It still had the label attached. Meaning? It was recently bought. It doesn't add up. New suitcase. No money. No family. Where was he intending to go?'

Prisha chews over every possible scenario searching for a reason *not* to go back into *that* house.

I've done my job. Leave it to someone else.

Whichever way she spins it, whatever excuse she comes up with, she knows, in her heart-of-hearts, she's missed something.

And she can't let that rest.

'Damn it!'

---◆---

The wardrobe door squeals open like a piglet being gutted.

Prisha lifts the suitcase out and lays it on the bed dreading what may be inside.

Pinching the zipper, she pulls.

Slow rasping clicks ambush the solitude of the bedroom.

Flips back the front flap.

Blinks in disbelief.

'What the hell?'

21

Zac steps out of his car as the Mercedes Sprinter police van, carrying six uniformed officers, continues up the main road. He takes a moment to study The Crown public house. The stone-built pub sits at one end of Ashenby, either the first or last building you see as you enter the village. A wooden sign, its paint peeling at the edges, creaks gently in the breeze, swinging from an iron bracket. A crowned lion, once proud and golden, now fades into ochre on a lichen-streaked green. The place has the appearance of somewhere unchanged for generations—weathered by time but still standing, still serving.

He pushes open the heavy oak door, the iron latch clanking as he steps inside. The low ceiling presses down, dark beams stretching across like the ribs of a giant whale. A faint yellow glow spills from wall sconces, their light struggling against the murk of a drizzly Yorkshire morning. The scent of beer and wood polish swirls around him, comforting in its familiarity. The floor beneath is solid—stone flags smoothed by countless feet over the years.

The place is empty. Not unusual at this time of day. The lunch crowd won't appear for another hour, if they appear at all.

A man emerges behind the bar. In his fifties, barrel-chested, with a weathered, ruddy complexion, and a belly that suggests he enjoys savouring his own stock.

He nods at Zac. 'Morning, sir. What can I get you?'

Zac steps to the bar, running a hand along the polished wood.

'Just a coffee, if you serve it,' Zac says.

The man sniffs. 'Aye, we've got coffee. It's nothing fancy, mind. Pod machine.'

'That's fine. Black, no sugar.'

The landlord vanishes into the back.

Zac's left with the low hum of a fridge, and the occasional drip from a beer tap. He glances at the array of hand pumps lined along the bar—names he recognises, local brews, the kind you don't find in the big chain pubs. He likes the place. An old-fashioned pub. No pretence, no giant TV screen, no gimmicks. Just four walls, a solid bar, and a bit of talk—if you fancied it.

The landlord returns and places the coffee on the counter.

'Thanks,' Zac says, flashing his warrant card. 'DS Stoker. North Yorkshire CID. How much?'

The man studies the badge, then places both hands on a beer towel. 'On the house. How can I help?'

'You the landlord?'

'Aye. Edwin Featherstone's the name.'

'Do you know a Malachi Abbott?'

Edwin's passive smile fades. 'Aye. What about him?'

'His vehicle was pulled from the River Ure yesterday lunchtime. He was still inside it.'

'Is he alright?'

A flicker of something—genuine or feigned, Zac can't tell. 'He's dead.'

Edwin exhales through his nose. 'Drowned?'

'Can't be certain until after the post-mortem.' Zac watches him. 'When was the last time you saw him?'

Edwin scratches his head. 'Let me think... Monday. Aye, that's right. The village was abuzz with May Day celebrations. I opened about eleven, and Malachi was the first through the door. Not unusual.'

'Liked a drink, did he?'

'Oh, aye.'

'How long did he stay?'

'Not long. Fifteen minutes. Ordered a triple whisky and a pint of bitter, then tried to flog me two rabbits in lieu of the drinks. Told him I wasn't interested.'

'Anything else you can remember?'

'Not really. The pump ran dry, so I had to go to the cellar to change barrels. Malachi was rolling a ciggy at the time. I told him to smoke it in the designated smoking area in the beer garden at the back of the pub, which he got all shirty about. If you told him water was wet, he'd argue the point.'

Zac's expression doesn't change. 'What was his demeanour like?'

'How'd yer mean?'

'Was he relaxed, agitated, depressed, happy?'

Edwin shrugs. 'Hard to tell with Malachi. I don't pry into people's private lives. They come in and I serve them drinks.'

Zac gives a slow nod. 'How long have you been a landlord?'

The question unsettles him. 'Nigh on thirty years.'

'Thirty years.' Zac lets it sit for a moment. 'Then I'd say you'd be good at reading people. Comes with the job, doesn't it? Knowing who's likely to cause trouble, who's drinking too much, who's got something on their mind?'

Edwin shifts his weight. 'Suppose.'

'So, I'll ask again—what was Malachi's state of mind?'

'Look, sergeant, I can't tell you what I don't know. He came in, had a drink, left. That's all there is to it.'

Another stonewalling bastard, Zac thinks, Frank's bollocking from the previous night still raw.

His gaze flicks out the window, towards the car park.

'You said he was first through the door.' Zac turns back to him. 'Did he drive here?'

Edwin wipes his hands on the bar towel. 'Couldn't say.'

'You didn't notice if his car was parked outside?'

A pause. 'Can't say I did.'

'Hmm... right. First customer in and you didn't notice if a car was parked outside.'

Zac tilts his head, studying him. Time to take the gloves off.

'When the post-mortem's complete, we'll have a toxicology report. If it turns out Malachi was over the limit, which he probably was, and the timing of his death lines up with leaving your pub, it's not going to look good for you.'

Edwin straightens. 'Now hang on a mo—'

'*No, you hang on, Mr Featherstone!*' He leans forward, voice low but firm. 'If you served a man a triple whisky and a pint, knowing full-well he was getting behind the wheel of a vehicle, that's negligent service. You'd be looking at a hefty fine at best, losing your license at worst.' He lets the words sink in before continuing. 'Of course, there's always the possibility of *gross negligence manslaughter* charges. That could mean a lengthy prison sentence,' he adds nonchalantly.

Edwin swallows hard. 'What?'

'You have a duty of care, Mr Featherstone. If there's a causal link between your actions and Mr Abbott's death the CPS have pursued cases like this before. Believe me, that's a world of pain.'

A sliver of a smile returns—sharp as a paper cut.

'Now, Mr Featherstone, whether Malachi Abbott was over the limit or not—that's not my primary concern. I have other avenues to investigate. However, unless you start answering my questions honestly, then I'll be looking into your actions more rigorously. Do we understand one another?'

A flicker of something—calculation, perhaps. Edwin glances around the empty pub. His fingers tap nervously against the bar.

A quiet sigh. 'Aye. We understand one another,' he mutters. 'There's a little nook round the back. We can talk there.'

Zac picks up his coffee with a satisfied smile. 'Excellent. Now we're getting somewhere.'

22

The high street bustles with hikers, cyclists, day-trippers and locals.

Prisha spots Zac emerging from the bakery, a cardboard drinks carrier in one hand with two cups, and two brown paper bags in the other. He crosses the road and takes a seat at a picnic bench on the village green. As he removes a sausage roll from a bag, he sees Prisha striding towards him.

'Ah, here at last,' he says, mockingly. 'Glad you could make it.'

'Sorry about that. Got tied up at Malachi Abbott's joint,' she replies as he slides one paper bag her way and hands her a coffee. 'Ooh, thanks. How's it going here?'

'Pretty good. Uniform are working their way from house to house. Another hour or so and they should be done. I had an interesting chat with the landlord of The Crown. He played dumb at first until I convinced him otherwise.'

Prisha takes a seat opposite and bites into the sausage roll. 'Go on.'

'He last saw Malachi Abbott on Monday, just after opening time. Served him a triple whisky and a pint of beer. Didn't stay long and took off like a bat out of hell in his Land Rover after about fifteen minutes. Oh, and he had two rabbits with him. Which indicates to me he was making his way home from the pub when he crashed through the wall and entered the river. Which would be roughly about 11:30 am give or take.'

'Makes sense. And the alcohol would have kicked in by then affecting his reactions.'

Zac takes a sip of coffee. 'When Malachi first entered the pub and ordered his drinks, the landlord began pulling a dead one.'

'Sorry?'

'The barrel ran dry mid-pull. He said Malachi was rolling a ciggy at the time. The landlord went down into the cellar to change the barrel but not before telling Malachi to smoke the cigarette in the beer garden at the back of the pub.'

'Why?'

'Some nonsense about designated smoking areas. Anyway, my point is this; Malachi's Land Rover was parked out front. There was probably about a five-minute window when the vehicle was out of sight of both men.'

'You think that's when the brake lines may have been cut?'

'Yes. I asked the landlord to show me approximately where the car was parked and guess what?'

'Brake fluid on the ground?'

'Yes,' he replies handing his phone over. 'Got a few shots of it. As you can see from the photos, it's soaked into the gravel. But brake fluid is pretty universal, and it could have come from any vehicle, but still, it fits what we know.'

She hands the phone back. 'Hmm... what about other people in the pub at the time?'

'Empty. The village was holding a big May Day event which kicked off at 11 am at the top of the village. The parade made its way down the high street and finished at the pub around 11:30.'

'Christ, they're big into their May Day celebrations around here. And what about the foot—has he noticed any of his regulars missing?'

He shakes his head and takes a large bite of sausage roll and chews for a moment.

'Apart from Malachi—no. And here's where it gets very interesting,' he teases. 'Up until a few years ago Malachi Abbott was gainfully employed.'

'As what?'

Zac grins and wipes crumbs from his lips. 'Gamekeeper for Lord Hampton.'

'Get out of here!'

'It's true. Been a faithful servant to his Lordship for over forty years.'

'Then how come he was on the dole?'

'Hampton gave him the flick.'

'Why?'

Zac frowns. 'This is where the landlord, Edwin Featherstone, became a little vague. He said a few years ago Hampton allowed a commune to set up on a few acres of his land in return for general help around the estate. That's when Malachi's job as gamekeeper became superfluous, as the members of the commune, *who are apparently "in tune" with the land,* began looking after the woods and estate.'

'That's a bit bloody ruthless after forty years.'

'That's what I said to the landlord. And that's when he became a bit shifty.'

'How'd you mean?'

'Evasive. Had enough of talking. Insisted he had to restock the bar before it got busy. I pushed him on it and eventually he said there may have been more to it than meets the eye. Apparently, Malachi had an intense dislike of the commune.' Zac scrunches the brown paper bag into a ball. 'How did you get on at Malachi's house?'

'Good. Found a shotgun under the bed, and a dismantled rifle in the dining room. Looked like he was in the process of cleaning it. I checked the firearms register. He had a licence for both. The firearm officer is there now. But, at the risk of upstaging you, I have a bigger bombshell.'

'You've always got to outdo me. Come on. Let's hear it.'

'I found a suitcase in his wardrobe.'

Zac shrugs. 'Not unusual. That's where I keep mine.'

'But this one was brand-new—Samsonite. It even had the receipt in a side pocket. Bought two weeks ago, 19th April, at 10:00 am from the Designer Outlet in York.'

'Which begs the question—why would a guy who was on his uppers splash out on a new suitcase?'

'That's the thing—he wasn't on his uppers. The suitcase contained twenty thousand pounds in used twenty-pound notes. All in neatly wrapped bundles.'

'You're shitting me?'

'Gospel.'

Zac grimaces. 'A hoarder, perhaps? You hear about folk who appear to be living on the breadline and when they cark it, turns out they're millionaires.'

'Possible. But why a new suitcase?'

'Holiday?'

'I didn't see any brochures lying around and there was no laptop, PC, or WiFi router to be found, so he certainly wouldn't have booked online.'

'Hang on,' Zac says stroking his beard. 'The landlord said he tried to pay for his drinks with the rabbits, yet he had twenty grand in his wardrobe. I know Yorkshire folk are tight, but that's fucking ridiculous.'

'It may be worth one of us having a ride out to York and speaking with the manager of the Samsonite shop.' She finishes the last morsel of her snack, collects the rubbish and drops it in a nearby bin. 'Right, what's your next plan of attack?'

Zac checks his watch. 'I'll leave uniform to it for now. Thought I might swing by the church—see if I can speak to the local vicar. Had another quick chat with Miss Penhallow at the Post Office. She reckons he'll be there today—got some workmen in doing repairs. Who knows—maybe he's noticed one of his regulars missing from communion last Sunday. You?'

'I'll head out to Ravensbane Castle and speak with Lord and Lady Hampton, if they're home. Then I'll see you back at Whitby. But first, I want to have another chat with the local, friendly, village librarian.'

'Why?'

'That book you were looking at yesterday, just before the little girl, Morrigan, approached you—what was it called—*The Three Crones*?'

'That's right.'

'You said it had a picture of the three standing stones from the wood on the cover?'

'Yes. Well, at least they looked similar. I didn't get a chance to look inside before Little Red Riding Hood interrupted me.'

'Can you remember the name of the author?'

His face creases. 'Erm... Reverend somebody or other. Why?'

'A little bedtime reading, that's all.'

23

As the swing doors clatter shut, the women lock eyes across the silent library. Like gunslingers in a dusty western, they freeze—tension crackling between them—each woman sizing up her adversary with cold scrutiny.

Prisha's right hand twitches, hovering over the trigger of an imaginary gun.

The librarian moves first, her fingers creeping towards the rubber stamp.

Prisha's eyes narrow to slits.

The clock on the back wall ticks.

The librarian grabs the rubber stamp and takes the first shot.

'Inspector Kumar, what a pleasant surprise. Back again so soon?' she snipes.

The passive-aggressive bullet glances off Prisha's skin.

'It appears so, Miss Ashcroft. Your powers of observation are acute.'

She strides over to the counter, slaps her hands down on the wood and performs a rat-a-tat-tat just to annoy the hell out of her.

Lunara Ashcroft stares at the hands as if it's something stuck to the bottom of her shoe. Finally, she lifts her head.

'And what can I do for you today? Or have you returned to intimidate and harangue me again?'

Prisha cackles, holds a hand to her heart, and flutters her eyelashes.

'Intimidate and harangue—moi? As if.'

'Then what is it? I am rather busy.'

Prisha slowly scans the empty library. 'Yes, I can see you're rushed off your feet. It's about the book—*How To Disappear*—I've found it.' She winks at her. 'Bit of wordplay there, in case you didn't notice.'

Lunara blinks, showing no emotion. 'I wasn't aware the book *was* lost.'

'Well, it is, and it isn't. If you get my meaning.'

'I don't.'

'It was retrieved from Malachi Abbott's car yesterday afternoon. A car that was pulled from the river with Mr Abbott in it.'

'I see.'

'Aren't you going to ask how Mr Abbott is?'

A slight flinch. 'Very well. How is Mr Abbott?'

'He's dead. But I'm sure you know that already. As you mentioned yesterday, you know everything that goes on around the village. As for the book... water damaged, I'm afraid. Once the investigation is over, I'll ensure it's returned to you.'

'That won't be necessary. I'll flag it on the system and make a note.'

'I'd also cancel Mr Abbott's membership while you're at it.'

Lunara drops her head to one side, as if waiting. 'Anything else, inspector? Only it's nearly my lunch break.'

'Yes, there is actually. I'm after a book for myself.'

'Are you a member of the Ashenby Library?'

'You know very well I'm not.'

Lunara pulls a self-satisfied smile, finally landing a punch. 'Ah, well then. You'll have to fill out a form, then I'll need to enter you into the system.'

'Not a problem.'

'It takes seventy-two hours to process. Once you've received your library card, by post, only then will you be able to borrow books.'

'Three days to enter my name and address into a computer!'

'Due process, I'm afraid.'

'Very well. I'll read the book here. And if I don't finish it, I'll come in tomorrow, and the next day and the day after that until I have finished it.'

Lunara pouts, hung by her own petard. 'Title of the book,' she snaps.

'*The Three Crones.*'

'It doesn't ring a bell. Author?'

'Reverend somebody.'

She stops hammering at the keyboard and eyeballs Prisha. 'Reverend somebody?'

'I can't remember the surname.'

She continues typing before emitting a huff. 'Sorry. We don't have the book.'

'You mean it's out? Someone borrowed it?'

'No. I mean, we don't own a copy.'

'Yes, you do. My partner who was in here yesterday was flicking through it.'

'Then he must have got the title wrong. There's definitely no book with that title logged into the system. And the only book by a reverend is—*Fly Fishing Knots and Lures* by Reverend Shankly.'

Prisha taps a fingernail on the counter. 'It was in the local history section. Mind if I have a look?'

'Be my guest, but I'm locking up in five minutes.'

Prisha navigates the aisles and finally finds the local history shelf, which contains a rather meagre selection. Tracing a finger along the spines, she quickly eliminates all the titles. She stares into the distance and ponders. Pulling each book from the shelf, she examines the cover, looking for the three standing stones.

She comes up blank.

'That's bloody odd.'

Striding back to the counter, Lunara spots her and makes a grab for her coat and handbag.

'I really need to lock up now, inspector.'

'It's not there,' Prisha states.

'I know. I told you that a moment ago.'

'But my colleague had it in his hand yesterday.'

'As I said, he must have got the title wrong.'

'No. I've pulled every book from the shelf. He described the front cover, and it's not there. Has anyone taken a book out that has three standing stones on the front cover?'

'No. Maybe your partner was confused.'

'Confused? He's a detective sergeant in CID, not an octogenarian in a care home.'

Lunara shrugs. 'Well, I can't help you. Now I really must...'

'Yes, yes, yes! Lock up, it's your lunchtime. Well, thanks for nothing.'

'Likewise.'

Prisha throws her one last dismissive look. 'We must do this more often.'

The shootout is a stalemate.

Both women walk away with minor battle scars, ready to fight another day.

Prisha takes a deep breath as she emerges from the library. Glancing left, she spots the girl, Morrigan, marching briskly along the pavement.

'Hmm...' Prisha breaks into a jog. 'Morrigan, wait up!' she calls.

The girl keeps walking in her peculiar, mechanical fashion.

'Morrigan, wait!'

She catches up and taps her lightly on the shoulder.

'Morrigan, I just wanted to see—'

The girl whirls round and screams in her face. '*Don't touch me!*'

She boots Prisha hard in the shin and tears off like a bat down the street.

Prisha grits her teeth and groans, dropping to her haunches.

'Ooh, you bloody little madam,' she mutters, rubbing her leg. She hauls herself upright, wincing, as Morrigan vanishes down a side alley.

Sensing a presence behind her, she wheels around.

'What are you doing here?' she snaps. 'I thought you were speaking to the vicar?'

Zac grins. 'Had to take a call of nature. On my way now. Anyway, what the hell's wrong with you?' He pauses, a wicked gleam in his eye. 'Oh no, don't tell me—you farted and followed through?'

'No. It's that little shit, Morrigan,' she mutters. 'I only wanted to ask if she was feeling better.'

'And?'

'The bloody little cow kicked me in the leg.'

Zac chuckles and saunters off. 'Told you, Prisha—some of us are born with natural charisma, and others... well, you work it out.'

'Wanker,' she mutters under her breath.

24

Zac steps through a side door into the dim, cool interior of St Mary's Church. The nave is silent, the air laced with the scent of old stone and wax. Not unpleasant.

Sunlight filters through stained-glass windows, casting fractured patterns onto the flagged floor. Somewhere high above, muffled voices carry down, interspersed with the occasional clunk of footsteps on floorboards.

He moves towards the far end of the church, where a small, arched door stands ajar. Beyond is the base of the bell tower—a cramped chamber with a tall, narrow window. To the right, a door bears a simple brass plaque: 'Office'.

Against the back wall, a ladder of ancient iron stretches upwards, bolted into the stonework, ninety-degrees to the floor.

Zac cranes his neck, squinting at the opening at least thirty feet above. A wooden hatch is open, allowing the echo of voices to drift down.

He exhales sharply.

Heights have never been his strong suit.

'Reverend Hartley, are you up there?' he bellows, hands cupped around his mouth, his voice bouncing off the cold walls.

'Who is it?' a male voice replies.

'DS Stoker from North Yorkshire CID.'

'Who?'

'Christ,' he murmurs. 'DS... it's the police!' Louder this time.

'Oh.' The reply is barely audible. A head appears above the hatch. 'What is it?'

'Are you Reverend Hartley, vicar of St Mary's?'

'Yes. Why?'

'I'd like a word. Just a few questions.'

'Really?' A touch of annoyance.

'Of course bloody really,' Zac curses softly. 'It won't take long. Can you come down, please?'

A shake of the head. 'I'm afraid not. You'll have to come up, we're just finishing off.'

Zac eyes the ladder with foreboding.

It looks solid enough, but the thought of climbing it makes his stomach lurch. He grips the sides, testing its stability before hoisting himself up. Each rung is worn smooth, the iron railings cold against his palms. He tries not to think about how high he's climbing, focusing instead on the hatch above.

As he hauls himself into the belfry, the space opens up around him. A high, pointed ceiling soars above. Wooden beams crisscross the rafters, thick with centuries of dust. Louvres in the stonework allow in shafts of daylight, along with a slow drift of cool, fresh air. Above him, the great bell looms, suspended in its wooden frame. The figure of an indistinguishable man teeters on the top of another ladder.

The vicar—sixties, dog-collar, grey-haired, and quietly handsome—is standing beside a workman in faded dungarees, sporting a flat cap. He's stocky, middle-aged, slightly paunchy, and less handsome. He's footing an extension ladder and peering up at his colleague, twenty feet above. Zac spots an assortment of tools scattered on the wooden floor.

'Bit of a predicament,' Reverend Hartley explains, wiping his brow. 'The sally's perished. Natural wear and tear over the years. To be expected. Of course, it means replacing the entire rope. We're just threading a new one through the garter hole.'

'The sally?' Zac asks, brow raised.

'Yes, it's the part the bell-ringer holds. The colourful striped section,' he explains. 'Old Tom's just about to attach the top end now.'

Zac gazes up at the man leaning out towards the giant bell at an alarming angle.

'Exactly what age is Old Tom?'

'Not sure. He's always been known as Old Tom, even during my first tenure.' The vicar pulls a quizzical look and turns to the workman. 'Norm, how old is Old Tom?'

Norm, the workman, rubs his chin. 'Old Tom? Not sure, Rev. Hey, Old Tom, how old are you?' he shouts up.

'Turning eighty-three next b'thday,' the brittle disembodied voice replies. 'Not that it's any of your bloody business,' he grumbles as an afterthought.

'There you go,' Norm says. 'Nowt but a spring chicken. Ha, ha, ha.'

Zac watches on as the man on the ladder—Old Tom—fumbles with the thick new rope, his grip precarious. Below, his mate, Norm, steadies the ladder with a foot, seemingly unconcerned, whilst he sparks up a cigarette one handed.

The whole setup is a recipe for disaster.

'Shouldn't you have safety equipment?' Zac suggests.

The vicar shakes his head. 'Too expensive. We received one quote for ten thousand pounds. Most of it was on erecting a scaffold. Norm and Old Tom only charge two hundred pounds. That's more within the church budget.'

'It looks extremely dangerous,' Zac states, incredulous.

'Oh, we've done it this way for years,' the vicar reassures him. 'Old Tom's got a good head for heights.'

'Yeah,' Norm mutters, puffing out a plume of smoke, confident he's safely grounded on a solid floor. 'Safe as houses... if his dicky knee holds up.'

Zac shifts his weight. 'Old Tom should be wearing a harness at the very least.'

Norm scoffs. 'A harness! We'll be fine. Won't take but a minute. Like Reverend said, been doing it this way for donkey's years.'

Zac swallows, watching on as Old Tom loops the new rope through the garter with jerky, irregular movements. The whole ladder sways with each shift in his body weight.

'So, what is this about...erm... sorry, didn't catch your name,' the vicar prompts

'Sergeant Stoker—CID.'

'Is it about the remains discovered in Ravensbane Wood on Monday?' he asks carefully watching Old Tom.

'Yes. News travels fast.'

'Bad news does. It was in the Ashenby Gazette this morning.'

'I didn't even know there was an Ashenby Gazette. Have you noticed anyone from your parish missing recently?'

'No. Sorry. I can't help. We're a small parish, and if someone misses Sunday service, I always make a point of checking on their welfare.'

Norm takes another drag on his smoke. 'Ow yer going up there, Old Tom?'

'A lot better if you lot stopped asking silly bloody questions. Job'll be done when it's done.'

Zac realises it's been a wasted climb, but something he'll put in the memory bank. The vicar, unlike the rest of the villagers, appears forthcoming and honest. No artifice.

He glances down at the huge drop below, and girds his loins, then decides to have one last shake of the dice.

'Reverend Hartley, what can you tell me about Malachi Abbott?'

The vicar's whole persona changes. His face hardens, eyes narrow, body stiffens.

'What about him?' he almost spits.

Zac studies him for a moment. The edge in the reverend's voice is hard to ignore.

'You can't have heard yet. We pulled his vehicle from the river yesterday with Mr Abbott still inside. He's dead.'

The reverend's eyes glaze over for a moment as Norm pulls the cigarette stub from his mouth, drops it onto the wooden floor, and uses the toe of his boot to grind it out.

Reverend Hartley takes a deep breath. 'Norm, can you manage without me up here?'

'Aye. Job's a good 'un, Rev.'

'Right, Sergeant Stoker, if you'd care to lead the way, we can talk in my office.'

'Ahem,' Norm says accompanied by a cough. 'Reverend, we did say cash on the day?'

'Yes, yes. I have it waiting for you in my office,' he replies with an air of impatience.

Norm beams. 'Ah, good. Only me and Norm have worked up a bit of a thirst.'

The reverend stares at him. 'Yes. It must be exhausting work footing the ladder.'

Norm chuckles. 'Dirty job but someone's gotta do it. We'll finish off here and give the bell a ring, make sure it's firing on all cylinders, then we'll be down.'

'Excellent. Thanks.'

Zac teeters at the edge of the hatch, legs like jelly.

Reverend Hartley extends an arm. 'Come, come, Sergeant Stoker. You first, that way if I slip, you'll break my fall.'

As Zac painstakingly navigates down the iron rungs, his whole body shaking, Norm's dulcet tones ring out.

'Hey, Old Tom?'

'What now for God's sake?'

'Did you hear that?'

'What?'

'Copper said they pulled Malachi Abbott out of the river. Dead as a doorknob.'

'Aye? Well good riddance to bad baggage is what I say. Long time coming. Right, I'm done. I'm coming down.'

'About bloody time. You need to lift your game, otherwise I'll be looking for a new apprentice.'

25

With great relief Zac places a foot on solid ground and takes a deep breath. The vicar clatters down above him and lands with a thump on the floor. Zac has one last look up at the hatch and shakes his head at the height, then gazes around the small room.

'Is this where the bell-ringer rings the bell?'

Reverend Hartley dusts his hands off and nods. 'Yes. The ringing chamber. Thankfully we don't need to change the rope that often. I dare say the new rope will outlast me.'

'How long before you retire?'

'Five years. Come, let's talk in my office,' he says leading the way to a side door.

Zac follows him into his office containing a desk, a bookcase groaning with books, and an antique bureau nestled in the corner. A small oval-shaped window offers a view out onto the graveyard at the back of the church. Reverend Hartley quietly closes the door, runs a hand through his swept-back grey hair then makes his way to the bureau and pulls the lid down.

'Care for a sherry, sergeant?' he asks swiftly filling a small sherry glass from a crystal decanter.

'Not while I'm on duty. But thanks,' he replies throwing a sly glance at his wristwatch—12:15.

'Please, take a seat,' he says nodding towards a swivel chair behind the desk.

Zac sits down and pulls out his notebook. 'So, Malachi Abbott?'

The vicar flops down on the other side of the desk and takes a sip of sherry, clearly savouring the moment.

'Malachi Abbott,' he murmurs. Peering out of the window at the blackened gravestones he momentarily slips into a trance as a carriage clock on top of the bookcase ticks away at time.

The pause lasts too long and unsettles Zac.

He clears his throat. 'Ahem...'

The vicar slowly shakes his head, as though turning a riddle over in his mind.

'Time is a trick we play on ourselves, sergeant. We carve it into hours, days, years—pretend it moves forward in a straight line. But does it? The past clings to us long after it's gone. The future's a fog of fear and wishful thinking. And the present? An illusion.

'This church has stood for five hundred years. The bell above us has tolled for births, deaths, victories, tragedies—most now forgotten. What once felt urgent is dust. And still, we live as though time is ours to spend or save. But time doesn't pass. We do. Time stays where it is. We're the ones moving through it. And when we're gone, the bell will keep ringing, and someone else will sit here, asking the same question: *Where did time go?*'

Zac, not known for abstract thinking, finds himself unsettled by the words. His mind drifts to his wife and sons, an unexpected pang of homesickness tightening his chest.

What is he doing here, chasing yet another mystery? He solves crimes, puts bad people behind bars—but it's like trying to hold back the tide. No matter how hard he works, how many hours he gives to the job, the tide still rolls in. Day in, day out.

And in the grand scheme of things, what does it matter? What difference is he really making? If he didn't exist, if he simply stopped—would the world even notice?

The vicar breaks his existential reflection. 'I'm sorry, sergeant. Don't mind me. As I get older, I have a tendency for maudlin introspection. You want to know about Malachi Abbott?'

'Yes.'

He leans back in his chair and runs a finger around the top of his sherry glass.

'If you cut out Malachi's heart, it would be blacker than pitch. He was a thoroughly odious man without a single redeeming quality. He revelled in others' misfortune. Where there was peace, he brought chaos. Where there was kindness, he sowed bitterness. He held grudges like a miser hoards gold, nursing them, feeding them, taking pleasure in their weight. He thrived on division, whispering poison into open ears, turning friend against friend, brother against brother.

'And yet, I am a man of God. I have spent my life preaching forgiveness, believing in redemption. But as the years wear on, I find it harder to summon that grace. Some men commit sins in ignorance, in weakness. Malachi did so with joy. There was no remorse in him, no regret, no flicker of doubt. He lived as if absolution were a fairytale meant for other men. And I...' He sighs, rubbing a weary hand over his face. 'I fear that, in my old age, my ability to forgive such men has deserted me.'

'I take it the village won't be in a state of mourning at his demise?'

The vicar offers a wry smile and takes a sip of sherry. 'The villagers are a conservative lot. And while they won't show any outward display of pleasure at his passing, I dare say, between close friends, and behind closed doors, there will be an element of schadenfreude.'

'What made him that way?'

The vicar's eyes widen. 'I don't know. I tried with him; I really did but in the end he defeated me. I can only assume his twisted, malevolent spirit was borne in the cradle. Maybe a horrific childhood trauma but who knows.'

'When you said you tried with him, was that recently?'

The vicar is startled. 'Good Lord, no. It was during my first stint as vicar of St Mary's. It was my first posting back in 1987. Fresh-faced and eager to make a difference.'

'I see. You haven't had any contact with him recently?'

'No. I saw him around. It's a small parish. Drove like a maniac. Hardly surprising he ended up killing himself.' He glances out of the window again, reflective. 'And yet, he was a devoutly religious man. Some may say a fundamentalist at heart.'

'A Christian?'

'Yes.' He chuckles. 'Not a church goer, although he used to be. I think he favoured the fire and brimstone of the Old Testament.'

'You said he *defeated* you. Was there one particular incident or was it an accumulation of events?'

The vicar drops his eyes for a second, before staring out of the window again.

'There was an incident, many years ago. We had a confrontation. Accusations were made. It ended in a brawl. I was quite fit and active back then.'

Zac chuckles. 'You had a fight with him, a physical fight?'

'Yes. I should be ashamed of myself but I'm not.'

He smiles at his honesty. 'Who won?'

'Let's just say I was the last man standing. But I was bloodied and battered. Malachi was bigger, stronger, but I had rage on my side.'

'What was the pivotal incident that led to the fight?'

The vicar pauses and casts a cryptic gaze at Zac. 'Some sins can never be washed clean, sergeant. *Remember not our sins* is a plea to God for forgiveness, no matter what we have done. God may forgive, but man doesn't.'

'What sins exactly are you talking about?'

Hartley offers a resigned, thin smile. 'As I said earlier, the bell above us will continue to ring long after we're both gone, Sergeant Stoker.'

Zac waits, hoping he might elaborate, but he doesn't. 'Okay, well—thanks for your time, Reverend Hartley.' He pushes back in his seat, then stops. 'It's strange.'

'What is?'

'Malachi Abbott—according to you he was universally hated or at least disliked. And yet Lord Hampton kept him on as gamekeeper for all those years. I don't know Hampton from a bar of soap, but I assume he has standing, and respect, around here. Why employ a man so despised?'

The vicar rises and opens the office door. 'In this village, sergeant, the gentry get to choose their monsters. And better to keep the monster chained to you than let it wander free.'

Zac frowns. 'And yet Lord Hampton let him go a few years ago?'

Hartley chuckles softly. 'Which brings us full circle—back to time. When enough years pass, people feel safe. Safe that secrets will stay buried. That old sins no longer have voices to reveal them.'

He follows the vicar out into the ringing chamber as voices from the workers drift down from the belfry.

Norm yells out from above. 'Watch out below!'

The reverend pushes Zac against the wall as a swishing sound is accompanied by the bell rope cascading down through the belfry hatch.

'Christ, those two don't believe in occupational health and safety, do they?' Zac groans as the rope swings back and forth in front of him.

The reverend chuckles. 'Old-school.'

'Right, well good luck with the bell,' Zac offers. As he turns to leave, he has one last thought. 'Reverend Hartley, know anything about cars?'

He frowns. 'Cars?'

'Yes. The car I'm driving loses power going up hills.'

He shakes his head. 'Sorry. Don't know the first damn thing about them. But there's a good mechanic in town—Yardleys. It's down a side alley behind the butcher's shop.'

Zac nods. 'Thanks. I may pay them a visit.'

Outside, he pauses a moment to take in the tranquillity of the churchyard.

'Hello, Zac.'

The voice startles him. He jumps, spinning round. 'Bloody hell, Morrigan, you scared the life out of me. Where did you come from?'

The girl stares up at him, a thin smile on her lips. 'Sorry. What you up to?' she asks, her melodious Scottish brogue as delicate as a butterfly wing.

He shifts, uneasy. 'Oh, nothing. Just police business. Anyway, why aren't you in school?'

She kicks at the path, head down. 'I'm too old for school.'

He chuckles. There's something endearing about her.

'You might *think* you're too old, but you're not. A good education's the foundation for a good life.' His smile slips. 'That wasn't very nice, what you did earlier; kicking Inspector Kumar in the shin.'

The girl gives him a fierce glare, eyes ablaze. 'She grabbed me. That's assault. I was defending myself.'

He sighs. 'She only wanted to ask if you were feeling better. She's actually very nice if you gave her a chance.'

'Pah,' she snorts, scornful but not for long.

Her upper body sways from side to side, hands clasped primly behind her back.

'Do you want to go for a walk? There's a lovely field not far from here called Gallows Meadow,' she asks, all demure. 'It's lovely at this time of year. It's not really a meadow anymore. They grow maize there now. Cattle feed. But it's still enchanting.' Her voice lowers slightly. 'Got a creepy scarecrow too,' she adds as an enticement.

'What? Erm... it sounds lovely. But I can't, I'm afraid. Too much to do.'

Her smile retreats like a weary battalion from the battlefield. She breathes in, slow, deep.

'Shame. Maybe another time.' She steps closer. 'Here, I made this for you,' she says, holding her arm out.

Zac takes the object and turns it over in his palm. About the size of a large coin, light but solid, woven from pale golden braid that catches the light like dried grass in late summer. In the centre, fine as a whisper, is the outline of a faceless girl's head, her hair spiralling outward, threading into the braided edge as if the whole thing had grown naturally, not been made.

'That's beautiful, but you shouldn't be spending your money on me. Where did you buy it?'

'I didn't. I made it.'

Zac scoffs. 'Yeah, right.'

She pouts. 'I'm not *lying*.' She kicks at the ground again. 'Lying's for sinners.'

He scratches his head. 'You really made this?'

Face softens. 'Yes.'

'You've certainly got a talent. And who's this in the middle?' he asks, brushing a finger over the raised centre.

'The Wicker Girl.'

Zac frowns. 'And who's she when she's at home?'

'I'm the Wicker Girl.'

A tightness slithers up his spine. 'Right. I see.'

'It will protect you. Not like that stupid wolf claw *she* wears.'

Uneasy, he takes a step back. 'I'd better keep moving. Thanks for the... this,' he says, holding the coin up.

Turning, he strides towards the gate, a prickle rising along the back of his neck.

The church bell tolls once, echoing out over the valley, the sound flat and hollow.

As the gate clanks shut behind him, he glances back.

The churchyard is empty.
She's gone.

26

The car pulls off the narrow road into a semi-circular forecourt, the entrance to Ravensbane Castle. Imposing wrought-iron gates wet with rain, guard the entrance. Security cameras perch high, dark and watchful. Wipers drag across the windscreen, rubber squealing. The sky is low and grey, drizzle spitting against the glass.

The car window rolls down as damp, cool air wafts inside. The intercom on the nearest gate pillar glows under a weak LED. Prisha presses the button.

'Good afternoon. DI Kumar, from CID. I'm here to see Lord or Lady Hampton. I called earlier.'

Silence. Then, a low mechanical hum. The gates fold open, slow and deliberate. She shifts into gear and drives through, tyres crunching over gravel. Behind her, the gates seal shut with an ominous clank.

'And a good afternoon to you, too,' she murmurs sarcastically.

The driveway to Ravensbane Castle is exactly what you'd expect—grand, sweeping, and just a bit self-important.

It winds majestically in undulating curves passing through a thick, dark wood, which thins out to reveal manicured lawns and ornamental gardens. A large lake, dotted with weeping willows resides on the right with a boat house and a few outbuildings in the distance. A series of large glasshouses and a walled cottage garden appear on the left as the car purrs along.

As the imposing castle grows larger, she spots a group of people to the side of the lake. They appear, at first glance, to be a motley crew. The men have long bushy beards and are dressed in dungarees, and t-shirts. Some have tattoos and various body piercings on their face. At first count, Prisha spots five of them; two with spades, two with wheelbarrows. A woman, early thirties, with long, dirty-blonde dreadlocks, directs proceedings.

The car slows as it nears.

All the men are tall, not muscular as such, but lithe, fit, a picture of health. They all stop whatever they're doing and turn to gaze inquiringly at Prisha.

'Afternoon,' Prisha says, with a welcome smile.

The men flash their pearly whites as the dreadlock woman approaches and half bends towards the open window.

'Can I help?' she asks, a hint of suspicion in her voice.

'I'm here to see Lord and Lady Hampton.'

'Oh, I see. Well, I take it you know where to find them?'

'The castle dead ahead?' Prisha replies, half-jokingly.

The woman grins. 'Yes.'

Prisha throws a quick glance at the works in progress. 'Hard at it, I see.'

The woman looks over her shoulder as the men resume work, two removing soil from the bank of the lake as the others carefully unload large oblong stones from a trailer attached to a quad bike.

'Yes. A minor leak in the lake wall. Running repairs,' she explains. 'There's always something to do,' she adds with a slight chuckle.

Prisha's instincts kick in.

They don't look like your average workers engaged in manual labour. In fact, they look more like prisoners on a working party supervised by a prison officer, although the woman most definitely is not employed by HMP Service.

'Right, well good luck with it all. I'm DI Prisha Kumar, by the way.'

The woman's face darkens for a split second before a warm smile pushes it aside.

'Violet. Pleased to meet you.'

Prisha hesitates on noticing the round token dangling from the woman's neck. It's of a similar size and material as the one discovered in Malachi Abbott's car. The motif is different, a female face, with long hair.

The woman slips the amulet down her shirt front and turns back to the workers.

'All right you lot, come on, get on with it. We haven't got all day!'

Prisha puts the car into gear and drives on. In the rear-view mirror, she catches Violet watching, her warm smile already fading.

27

It may call itself a castle, but Prisha isn't fooled. No turrets, no moat—just a grand Georgian manor with the kind of façade that suggests money, and a lot of it. Harewood House with delusions of grandeur.

Prisha rings the bell and stares back at the crew of workers halfway down the driveway. The woman in charge is barking orders. Not aggressive, but definitely a rigorous taskmaster.

She turns as the door opens. A woman in her forties appears—refined features, porcelain skin, elegant but understated dress. Prisha assumes it's the housekeeper.

The woman offers her hand.

'Abigail Hampton. Pleased to meet you, Inspector Kumar.'

'Likewise,' she says shaking hands and masking her surprise. She'd pictured the Hamptons to be doddery and grey.

'Please, come in. I'm afraid my husband isn't home.'

Inside, the hallway is vast and echoing. Without pausing, Lady Hampton leads her deeper into the house.

'My gardener mentioned your visit, and I listened to your voicemail. What a ghastly business. We can talk in the study. It's a little cramped but I find it homely. I'll have the housemaid bring tea and biscuits. Or would you prefer coffee?'

'Tea's fine, thanks.'

Lady Hampton pushes open a heavy oak door and strides in. Prisha follows, inhaling the scent of leather and a soft, sweet trace of jasmine or rose—barely there, but unmistakable.

Yeah, very cramped, she thinks.

The study is larger than her flat and dormer bedroom combined. But it's the view beyond that arrests her.

French windows open onto a wide stone terrace. Beyond the balustrade, Wensleydale stretches wide, a mottled spread of green pasture, yellow rapeseed, and tilled earth stitched together by winding walls. In the distance, Ravensbane Wood marks the horizon, dark and dense.

A fountain tinkles into a wide stone basin. Carp flash gold beneath the surface.

A gentle knock. The maid enters.

Lady Hampton scowls at the young woman—olive skin, jet-black hair, exquisite almond eyes.

'Magdalena, how many times must I tell you? You knock and wait to be invited in. Otherwise, what's the point in knocking?'

'Sorry, madam,' she replies in a soft Eastern European accent.

'Tea and biscuits for two, please.'

The maid pulls a quizzical look. 'Tea and...'

Lady Hampton mimes eating a biscuit. 'BIS-CUITS,' she states slowly, enunciating each syllable.

The maid smiles. 'Ah, kraker?'

'Yes, yes. Now run along.'

Prisha feels slightly awkward with the interaction, not warming to Lady Hampton's manner with the maid.

As the door clicks shut, Lady Hampton sighs. 'I apologise, inspector. Magdalena is Polish and relatively new. I try to employ British people, preferably English. But they're either too lazy to work or they expect to be paid a small fortune. Magdalena is a work in progress. She's cheap but her grasp of the English language is pitiful.'

'And I take it your Polish is not up to scratch?' Prisha replies, deadpan.

Lady Hampton's expression hardens, unsure if it's a jab or a joke.

'I'm hoping you're here to tell me the bones you found are ancient? Ravensbane Wood is thousands of years old. My husband and his ancestors have discovered many relics over time.'

Prisha remains impassive. 'We believe they're recent.'

Lady Hampton stands with her back to a large, open fireplace a deep crease across her forehead, hands clasped in front of her.

'How recent? Days? Weeks? Months?'

'Too early to say. We're waiting on the forensic report.'

Lady Hampton radiates impatience, and sharp intelligence.

'You must have *some* idea?'

'Off the record? I'd say less than a month.'

'How can you deduce that from bare bones?'

Prisha cocks her head. 'I didn't say they were bones.'

Lady Hampton's face twitches. 'Good grief. You mean... flesh?'

'Yes. Flesh on bone.'

Prisha sits and opens her notebook. 'Just to confirm, Ravensbane Wood is part of your estate?'

'Yes. That's correct. You were gazing upon it a moment ago from the window. Where exactly were the remains discovered?'

'A mile south of Hexley Farm, owned by the Bakers. The remains were found about a half-mile walk into the woods, near three standing stones.'

Lady Hampton tilts her head back as if she's detected an unpleasant odour.

'Ah, yes. Noah once took me there many years ago to show me the stones.'

'Noah?'

'My husband—Lord Hampton.'

'May I ask where he is?'

'Overseas. Syria, to be precise.'

Prisha blinks. 'Syria?'

'Yes. On a dig.' Lady Hampton detects Prisha's befuddlement. 'My husband is an archaeologist, inspector,' she explains sweeping an arm around the room at various artefacts mounted on stands and encased in glass.

Prisha studies a faded photo: men and women squinting into the sun, digging trenches under makeshift canopies.

'And when are you expecting him back?'

She rolls her eyes. 'Early July, depending how things go. The political situation is very febrile over there. They've had guarantees of their safety. Even so, it only takes one despot to oust another and the whole thing could change. The Middle East is a basketcase. Always has been, always will be.'

'And how long has he been over there?'

'He left the early hours of Monday morning.'

'May first?'

'Yes.'

Prisha hesitates.

The same day the remains were found.

28

'Have you heard from him since his arrival in Syria?' Prisha asks, careful not to telegraph her suspicions.

'No. But that's not unusual. They're in a remote location and due to security, they must keep a low digital presence. There's always the fear a renegade group could detect their whereabouts and take them as hostages.'

'So the last time you saw him was?'

'Late Sunday afternoon. I had dinner with a friend that evening. When I got home, I went straight to bed. He was up early to leave by three. His flight was at seven.'

There's a slight intermission as the maid arrives with a tea tray, then departs.

Lady Hampton takes a seat and pours the tea before her eyes settle on the plate.

'*Good heavens!* The stupid girl's brought cream crackers,' she states, as if she's just opened an eviction notice. 'Do they even *drink* tea in Poland?'

'I think tea is universal,' Prisha replies equally amused and appalled at Lady Hampton's sense of entitlement. She clears her throat. 'Your husband...'

Lady Hampton takes a genteel sip from the cup. 'I know what you're thinking, inspector, but I can assure you the remains are not my husband. His bags have gone, his car's not here. He'll be happily foraging in some dreadful desert right now, oblivious to everything apart from his precious artefacts.'

Prisha nods. 'That's good to know.'

Lady Hampton smiles—briefly, then frowns. 'Although... no, no. That's silly.'

'What is?'

'He was invited to the Beltane festival but declined because of his early start.'

'Beltane festival?'

'A celebration the commune holds in the woods. May Day. Sunrise and moonrise rituals.'

Prisha recalls her conversation with Zac. 'Ah, yes, the commune. Can you tell me about them?'

'A few years ago, my husband let a group live rent-free on five acres. In return they look after the grounds.'

'And the people working by the lake?'

'That's them. Hard workers. English, thank God. Odd little quirks, but they've been a blessing.'

'Quirks?'

'Their peculiar belief system. They're pagans, inspector. Followers of the Wicca religion.' Her eyes narrow. 'I thought you were here to tell me about the remains?'

Prisha softens. 'Sorry. Habit of mine to dig. Just a couple more things.'

'Very well.'

'What can you tell me about Malachi Abbott, your former gamekeeper?'

She straightens. 'Well, I heard he tragically died yesterday. Is it true he drowned, trapped in his car in the river?'

'We're not certain yet. He worked for your husband for many years I believe?'

'It was a long time, yes. My husband inherited the estate young, and Mr Abbott was with him from the start.'

'Why did your husband let him go?'

Her gaze drifts back to the window before she turns, hesitant. 'The truth? Mr Abbott had a serious drinking problem. His work suffered. My husband tolerated it for years, gave him warnings, but it didn't improve. Then—' she stops, her eyes fixed on the far wall.

'Then?' Prisha prompts.

'There was an incident. Not long after the Wicca community moved onto the estate.'

'What kind of incident?'

'He... he touched someone.'

'A sexual assault?'

'Yes. A young girl from the commune. He touched her inappropriately on the...' Her index finger briefly points downwards.

'On the vagina?'

She reddens. 'Ahem, yes,' she replies, barely a whisper.

'Was it reported to the police?'

'No. We dealt with it in-house. It was one person's word against another. No witnesses. But the girl had no reason to lie.'

Prisha's tone sharpens. 'What did her parents say?'

She almost laughs. 'Parents? The commune doesn't believe in the nuclear family. The children don't know who their fathers are. They're raised collectively by the women until they're adults.'

'Did your husband confront Abbott about it?'

'Yes. He denied it. Said it was a misunderstanding, then claimed he couldn't remember—hardly surprising. He was sozzled most of the time. I told Noah it was time to cut him loose before he brought scandal upon us. My husband was generous—paid him four months' wages and let him go.'

'After forty years slog, four months' wages doesn't seem generous,' Prisha says before she can stop herself.

Lady Hampton cocks her head and sniffs. 'Inspector, I'm a busy woman. I don't have time to rake over old coals. I'm genuinely sorry Mr Abbott has passed on, but he was not a likeable individual. Now, have you any further questions?'

'Just a couple. Did you or your husband have any interaction with Abbott after he was sacked?'

'None. Though he still poached rabbits. My husband turned a blind eye.'

'Almost done, Lady Hampton. I'll just need your details, along with your husband's, and I'll be on my way.'

'Details?'

'Yes. Full name, address, date of birth. It's for the report. Purely routine.'

Prisha drives through the gates, slams the brakes, snatches up her phone, and taps Dinkel's face on the screen—then waits.

'Ma'am?'

'Listen, Dinkel, what are you doing right now?'

'Speaking to you.'

A roll of the eyes, a shake of the head, a silent curse. 'No! I meant before that.'

'Oh. I've got my nose in this cold case DCI Finnegan gave me. It's fascinating stuff. I've just...'

'Shut up and take your nose out of it. I need a favour.'

'Sure.'

'Get onto Border Force and run a check for me. Name: Noah Jermaine Hampton. Sixty-five. Supposedly flew out May 1st. Check a day either side. Flight to Syria, possibly indirect, maybe bumped to another airport. Manchester was the original plan.'

'Got it. Roger Daltrey that.'

Prisha winces. 'And Dinkel, call me the second you know. I don't care what time.'

She ends the call and glances up. A camera blinks red, then turns toward her.

Watching. Recording.

29

With a grunt, Frank drops onto a bench on Whitby's West Pier, facing the harbour.

He likes to get out of the office occasionally. Reminds him there's a world beyond forms, briefings, and endless emails.

He wrestles with the butcher's paper until he uncovers a healthy portion of freshly fried chips—or an unhealthy portion, depending on your inclination. They are liberally, some may say recklessly, doused in hefty doses of salt and vinegar.

Prisha and Zac take a seat either side of him.

'Okay, boys and girls, tuck in. A little afternoon snack. Plenty for all,' he says, spreading the paper between them. His fingers grab a portion and drop them into his mouth. 'Oh yes,' he murmurs, as if having an orgasm, 'they taste good. Done in beef dripping as well.'

Prisha takes a chip and nibbles at it. 'Christ, Frank!'

'What?' he replies, his voice muffled as he chews.

'What did you ask for—salt and vinegar with a side of chips? There's enough salt on them to cause liver failure.'

'Nonsense.'

Zac picks up a handful. Though the condiments are excessive, it doesn't stop him from devouring them.

'She's right,' he says, grabbing another fingerful. 'Just because you've had a stent put in doesn't give you a free licence to eat whatever you want, when you want.'

'Bollocks,' comes the mumbled reply. He chews, swallows, wipes his lips on the back of his hand. 'Do you know what's on the menu at Finnegan Mansion tonight? Bloody salmon steak and quinoa with in-season garden greens.'

'Sounds lovely,' Prisha says.

'Aye. You try having salmon steak three times a week, every week, then you'd change your tune. Salmon's alreet—a couple of times a year. More than that, it's overkill. I can't remember the last time I had any proper meat.'

Zac takes another chip. 'Yesterday, Miserly Joe's. Liver and onions,' he reminds him. 'Oh, and this morning. Didn't I see you with a sausage and bacon butty?'

Frank stops chomping and glares at him. 'Listen, Jamie Oliver—are you going to give me an update on the Ashenby case or lecture me on healthy eating?'

'Just trying to extend your life, Frank. I'll be sad to see you go. For a day or two at least. Then, life carries on, doesn't it?'

'Smartarse. Prisha, I can't get any sense from yon idiot, so you may as well give me the brief.'

'Okay.' Prisha wipes her hand on a tissue and takes a swig of water from a bottle.

After a brisk ten-minute download from Prisha and Zac, Frank scratches his chin and scrunches up the butcher's paper.

'So, we've a dead gamekeeper with a suspicious twenty grand in a new suitcase and enemies on all sides. Brake lines cut on his car, last seen at The Crown. A bunch of hippies living rent-free on Ravensbane Estate. And we're unsure where Lord Hampton is until Border Force get back to us. Oh, and not forgetting Reverend Hartley, who hinted Malachi—or possibly Lord Hampton—may have a skeleton or two in the cupboard.'

Prisha nods. 'That's about the size of it.'

'Another straightforward case, then,' he mutters, pure sarcasm. 'If you're overloaded, I can pull Dinkel from whatever rabbit hole he's burrowed into and assign him to the case.'

Zac groans. 'No. For fuck's sake, Frank. Let him stay put.'

'Come on, Zac. Even you've got to admit he's getting better.'

'Like a triple heart bypass patient. Very slowly.'

Frank sighs. 'It's horses for courses, Zac. You, me, Prisha—we like boots on the ground. Scenes of crime, local colour, a bit of gut instinct. We prod, we poke, we rattle cages. But Dinkel? He's more... cerebral.'

'Aye. Like a fucking catastrophic stroke.'

Frank ignores him. 'Stick him behind a desk with a laptop and a pile of dusty files and he comes alive.'

'Alive?' Zac scoffs. 'I've seen more life in a mausoleum. His idea of a good time is rearranging his crockery cupboard. He's not cut out for the job, Frank. It takes a proper pair of bollocks. Prisha's got a bigger set than him—no offence intended, Prisha.'

'None taken.'

'The job's changing, Zac,' Frank shrugs. 'Even I can see that. Digital forensics, facial rec, financial trails, DNA. The days of leaning on people to cough up a bit of info, and banging heads together are dead and buried.'

Zac is incensed. 'Hang on a mo... it was only last night you told us to bang a few heads together!'

'I never said that.'

'You bloody well did! And what was your old motto—*you can't make an omelette without kicking the shite out of someone?*'

Frank raises an eyebrow. 'Nay, lad. You're thinking of someone else.'

'You've a very convenient memory.'

Frank rises and checks his watch. 'Right. I better get back to the station. I've a hook up with Herr Gruppenführer of Internal Misery.'

Zac smirks. 'Superintendent Banks?'

'Aye. She wants to discuss some new integrated benchmark KPI reporting software they're rolling out. I get an erection just thinking about it.'

'Rather you than me. The day that woman cracks a smile I'll alert the Pope and tell him I've witnessed a miracle.'

Frank glances at Prisha. 'The money in the suitcase—how was it bundled?'

'Twenty stacks of twenty-pound notes with a rubber band around them.'

'And where is it now?'

'With forensics. Asked them to check the bottom and top notes for recurring fingerprints.'

'Good. I think we can safely say Malachi didn't acquire twenty grand from flogging dead rabbits, and from what you've told me he doesn't come across as an international safe-cracker. So, where did he get the money from, or more importantly, who from? Answer that riddle and you might be on your way to solving this little mystery.'

30

Thursday 4th May

The silence is almost perfect.

Prisha's eyes flicker, threatening to open, but the anaesthesia of sleep pulls her back under. She floats in that delicious space between consciousness and dreams, savouring the weightless drift. It reminds her of lazy Sunday mornings as a teenager, cocooned in warmth, the world kept at bay.

But then, the noise again. A faint, insistent niggle at the edge of her awareness. A clunk—something dropped, or knocked over.

Reluctantly, she peels back the shroud of slumber, dragging herself upright on her elbows. The effort is monumental, her limbs leaden, thoughts sluggish.

Her mouth is dry. She turns her head, blinking at the travel clock on the bedside table.

5:03 am.

She grabs her phone and slips it into her dressing gown pocket then pads down the stairs from the bedroom and hovers outside the bathroom door, listening to the water cascading from the shower. She cracks the door open and stares.

Adam is rinsing suds from his hair. She studies him for a moment, his physique, the way he moves in a determined energised way.

Motivated, focused.

It stirs something in her.

She takes a step forward as he turns the tap off, grabs a towel slung over the glass door, and steps out onto a bathmat, oblivious of her presence.

'Morning, sexy,' she says, releasing the belt from her robe revealing her nakedness beneath.

He rubs his face dry then looks at her and grins. 'Prisha, I'd really like to but I'm running late.'

'It's just gone five.'

'I know. I should have been off twenty minutes ago. Big day on the farm. The vet's arriving in two hours and I need to round up the bullocks and get them into the stockyards. Today's the day they kiss goodbye to their two veg.'

'They're being castrated?'

'Yes.'

She leans in and drops her hand down below and massages. 'Poor little bullocks,' she whispers provocatively.

'Prisha, I mean it! I haven't got...'

She falls to her knees.

It's too late for Adam.

Logical thought, reasoning, and any modicum of self-discipline are instantly jettisoned in favour of carnal lust. A pack of wild horses could not drag him back from the precipice now.

He sighs and places his hands on her head as if anointing her.

A violent muffled buzz echoes out. Prisha fumbles in her pocket and pulls out the phone.

'Shit! It's Dinkel,' she says rising to her feet. Holding her palm to Adam she says, 'Stay right there, I'll be back in a minute.' She rushes from the bathroom to the kitchen, flicks the kettle on then accepts the call.

'Dinkel, this better be good otherwise there could be another castration in the offing today.'

'Ma'am?'

'Nothing. What is it?'

'You told me to contact you as soon as I heard. Well, I've just heard.'

'About what?'

'The man you asked me to check on yesterday. Just got a call from Border Force. Noah Hampton did not leave the country on Monday.'

A pause.

'Or any other day, for that matter.'

'Then where the hell is he?' Prisha murmurs to herself, just as Adam shouts goodbye and the front door slams shut.

31

The Polish housemaid opens the door to the study and ushers Frank and Prisha inside before departing.

'Lady Hampton?' Frank asks.

She lowers her phone, a flicker of concern crossing her face. 'Yes?'

'My name's DCI Finnegan. You met my colleague yesterday, DI Kumar.'

'Yes, of course. Please, take a seat. Have you more news on the human remains?'

Frank and Prisha settle into armchairs as Lady Hampton takes a seat opposite, hands cupped in her lap.

Frank smiles. 'I've had the pleasure of meeting your husband a number of times,' he begins, easing into the conversation with a touch of warmth.

'Really?'

'Yes. I've attended some of his lectures over the years. A very knowledgeable man.'

Lady Hampton relaxes a little, a faint smile appearing. 'Oh yes. Ask him anything about the ancient pyramids of Egypt or classic cars and he's lost in a world of his own. Ask him to make a simple pot roast for dinner and he's all at sea.'

Frank chuckles. 'I must confess, my culinary skills are somewhat lacking. Though I do make a wicked cheese on toast. You have to use hearty bread and Red Leicester cheese. Then top it off with a smear of Dijon mustard and a few drops of Worcestershire sauce. It's to die for.'

Lady Hampton tilts her head. 'You're making me quite ravenous, Inspector Finnegan.'

Frank nods, his smile fading. Fingertips tap together as he leans forward. 'Lady Hampton, it's important not to overreact, but we need to be thorough.'

'I'm sorry, inspector, you've lost me. Are you talking about the remains?'

'Yes and no. Yesterday, DI Kumar took your husband's details.'

'That's correct. Routine, she said.'

'We passed them on to Border Force, the agency that tracks who enters and leaves the country. I'm afraid your husband didn't board a plane from Manchester Airport on Monday morning. Nor at any other time.'

Her brow furrows. 'No... what? That can't be right. There must be a mistake. His bags and car weren't here when I woke up.'

'There's no mistake, Lady Hampton. Passport control systems are extremely robust, as they must be in this day and age.'

Her voice drops. 'Then where is he?'

Prisha leans forward. 'That's what we hope to find out—with your help. We'll need a list of his friends, business associates, and close family members, and his phone number. And the make, model, and registration of his car. We'll also need a contact for the archaeological dig he was supposed to be attending in Syria.'

'I understand.'

'And we'd like your permission to conduct a thorough search of the house and grounds. We'll also need to question and take statements from yourself, your staff, and the community that live on your estate. We'll need access to your CCTV from the front gate and from the cameras mounted on the walls outside.'

'Yes, of course. You have my full blessing. There has to be a logical explanation for all this.' She hesitates, cogs turning. 'The hospitals—have you checked the hospitals? He may have had an accident on the way to the airport. Maybe he's still unconscious.'

Frank and Prisha exchange a glance before Prisha answers.

'We've already checked, Lady Hampton. No one matching your husband's description has been admitted.'

'But... without being disparaging, my husband is a rather nondescript-looking man. How would they know?'

'If he was involved in a traffic accident, officers at the scene would have recovered personal ID. If he was admitted to a hospital, we'd know.'

She rises and walks to the glass frontage overlooking the estate. Her voice is quieter now, more to herself than to them.

'If he disappeared Monday, then today's Thursday. That means he's been gone for over three days.'

Frank stands and moves to her side. 'I understand this is a shock. And I won't lie to you, losing three days in an investigation is never good. That makes it all the more important to get ahead of things now. We need to know if he had any enemies, recent or past. If he was in dispute with anyone. And we'll need an overview of your financial situation. I know it sounds invasive, but it could be crucial. At the very least, we need to start ruling things out.'

Prisha joins them at the windows. In the car on the way over, Frank suggested the next question would be better coming from her.

'Lady Hampton, this is a delicate matter, but it needs to be asked. Was your husband having an affair?'

She wheels around, stunned. 'Noah? An affair? Good Lord, no.'

'You've never had any reason to suspect him?' Prisha presses gently.

'No. Why would I? The only love affair my husband has ever had is with his precious artefacts and damn classic cars.'

She turns back to the view outside.

Frank draws a slow breath, bracing himself for the next part of the conversation.

'We'll also need to take some personal items belonging to your husband,' he says, voice measured.

'Such as?'

'A toothbrush, hairbrush, comb. Something that will yield a DNA sample.'

'Oh, I see. Yes, of course. I'll escort you to his bedroom in a moment.'

'We'll also need something that has only been handled by your husband, Lady Hampton,' Prisha adds. 'So we can obtain a clean fingerprint. The sooner we get these things onto the system the better.'

Lady Hampton nods, deep in thought. 'Wait, let me think. Ah, yes, I know. I bought him a bottle of expensive aftershave for Christmas—Creed Aventus. It was in a box so the only person who will have touched it is Noah. It will be in his bathroom cabinet.'

'Excellent,' Prisha says. 'Do you have children?'

Lady Hampton glazes over. 'No. I'm afraid we weren't blessed in that department. I...' she hesitates. 'Well, what I mean to say is, I can't have children.'

'So, who stands to inherit... I mean, forgive me. That was inappropriate.'

Frank scowls at her.

Lady Hampton doesn't flinch. Instead, she offers a faint, sad smile. 'It's a fair question. One we've been asked before. We've spoken to the National Trust about preserving the estate, but... nothing's final. And I am a lot younger than my husband.'

Frank clears his throat. 'Lady Hampton, there's one line of enquiry we need to prioritise. Let's call it the elephant in the room.'

She turns slowly, as if the nightmare couldn't get any worse. Her voice barely above a murmur.

'I'm not stupid. The remains in the wood?'

'Yes. It hasn't been made public yet, but what we recovered was just the one item—a badly burnt foot of an adult male inside a charred shoe. Nothing else. We believe the foot was removed elsewhere and deposited on the fire later.'

Her eyes widen. 'What side?'

Frank exchanges a worrying glance with Prisha. 'Sorry?'

'What side, inspector? Was it the left foot or the right foot?'

Frank hesitates. 'It was a left foot.'

She closes her eyes and emits a slow, shuddering sigh. Her hand reaches out, unconsciously resting briefly on Frank's lapel before she pulls it away, mildly embarrassed at her show of emotion.

'Thank God,' she breathes. 'Then it cannot belong to my husband.'

Frank stiffens. 'Why?'

She turns to face them fully, voice steady, laced with a newfound conviction

'Because my husband lost his foot in a traffic accident a long time ago. It was his left foot.'

32

Reverend Hartley enters the bell chamber whistling happily. It's his favourite hymn, Jerusalem. A little obvious, but you like what you like. He places his briefcase down outside the office door and fumbles for his bunch of keys, the metal chinking softly. From the school grounds, the distant strain of shrieking children drifts in—laughter in the wind, light as birdsong. It brings him comfort.

He flicks through the keys, then pauses, catching something in his peripheral vision.

He turns and frowns.

'What in God's name?'

The end of the bell rope—the *sally*—is lying curled at the base of the wall, limp and severed like a snapped tendon. He walks over, kneels, and picks it up.

From high above, a faint creak breaks the silence. He swivels to his right, eyes narrowing.

'And where's the bloody bell rope gone?' he mutters, dropping the sally.

Tilting his head back, he peers up through the gloom to the belfry hatch. The rope still descends from the bell above—but it doesn't make it through the hatch.

'Old Tom? Norm?' he calls. 'Are you up there?'

No reply. Another creak.

Floorboards.

Light but distinct.

He strains to listen, squinting at the hatch.

Footsteps? Possibly.

But way too soft for Norm or Old Tom.

'What the bloody hell's going on? I don't need this today,' he mutters, the chill of unease sliding down his spine like a bead of sweat.

He grips the iron ladder and begins to climb, each rung biting into his palms. As he ascends, his thoughts race—*kids, maybe, messing about inside the church. But why cut the bottom off a new rope? A prank? An act of vandalism? Possibly Norm and Old Tom back again, not happy with their work yesterday. Hoping to extract a few more quid from me.*

He steps from the ladder into the belfry and straightens. Dust particles drift in the shaft of sunlight that filters through the louvres.

The coil of rope lies beside the hatch, cleanly severed.

He stoops to examine it, fingers brushing the stiff, frayed end.

From behind him—another creak.

He turns sharply.

The space is empty.

There's a scent in the air. Not dust, not damp. Something else. Slightly sweet. Perfumed—faint and fleeting.

'Hello? Who's up here?'

Sudden movement.

He throws up his hands in panic, shielding his face.

A pigeon flutters to the louvres and coos, watching him with a glassy eye.

He sighs and half-smiles.

'Bloody old fool,' he chastises himself with a chuckle.

Something catches his eye on the floorboards. Lying in the dust, a small, braided disc. He crouches and lifts it carefully. One side bears an inverted crucifix, the other a red twine circle, almost complete, but not quite. His heart gives a frantic, broken flutter, like a bird trapped in a box, then lurches hard against his chest as the meaning slams home.

'*The Cru... Crucifix Knot,*' he stammers.

He hears it before he sees it.

A slithering drag across the boards.

He looks down.

The rope writhes against the floorboards.

33

The officers stand in two tight rows, boots firm on the gravel of Ravensbane Castle's forecourt. In the distance, a peacock calls—beautiful, haunting—a sound that belongs to a different era. Ducks quack lazily on the lake, where a small boat drifts. A police diver perches on the edge, fitting his facemask, while his assistant lowers a submersible camera into the water.

DS Zac Stoker rolls his shoulders, scanning the group of officers in front of him

'Right, listen up. Lord Hampton was last seen Sunday afternoon. It's now Thursday. That's four days of bugger all, which means we're already on the back foot. So—stay sharp, be thorough, and don't assume anything.'

His tone is brisk, but there's a thread of dry humour undercutting the tension. The officers know him well. They like him and respect him.

'PC Malone, Carter, Knowles—you're inside where DCI Finnegan will be leading the search. Top to bottom, every room, every corridor, every locked drawer. I don't care if it's a linen cupboard or a dumbwaiter—if it's large enough to contain a body, or a husband hiding from his missus—then search it. And you'll be pleased to know that the DCI has left his grumpy head at home today.'

Muted chuckles ripple through the group, though no one's taking it lightly. Lord Hampton's absence isn't a joke.

'Anything out of place, log it.'

PC Knowles raises a hand. 'That include the cellars and loft, sarge?'

'Yes, Knowles, of course it does. In fact, at the risk of stealing DCI Finnegan's thunder, I'd suggest that's where you start.' Zac shifts his attention to the other officers. 'Nine of you—gardens, outbuildings, hedgerows, entrance, driveway. If he left, he might've dropped something. If he didn't leave, then where is he?' His gaze lands on the dog handlers. 'You've got Lord Hampton's scarf. Let them have a good sniff before you start. Once I'm done here, I want them working for their dinner.'

The handlers nod and tighten their grips on the leashes. The dogs, ears pricked, tails twitching, already sense the job ahead.

Zac claps his hands, sharp and brisk. 'Right, let's get moving. Chop chop! And remember—anything that appears odd, out of place, make a note of it!'

The officers stride off with purpose, splitting into their teams without hesitation.

Zac exhales, glancing back at Prisha, who stands a step behind, arms folded, watching the team disperse.

'How's Lady Hampton?' he asks.

'Suitably distraught. Nothing of any use on the CCTV. It shows Hampton's car leaving the gates at 3:05 am on Monday and turning left but it has tinted windows. Impossible to see inside. No one entered the gates before then, apart from Lady Hampton arriving home Sunday evening.'

'So if we know his car left the grounds then why the hell are we searching for him here?'

'Just because his car left doesn't mean he did—does it? It's called being thorough. We have a couple of patrol cars scouting the countryside to see if he went off the road.'

Zac puffs out air, slightly deflated. 'And what about those cameras?' he says nodding up at the castle.

'Nothing. It was a full moon on Sunday night but that storm rolled in about 2 am. Pitch black.'

'Security lighting?'

She shrugs. 'Either they weren't working, or they'd been manually switched off.'

'All very convenient,' Zac notes pulling on a pair of rubber gloves. 'Gut feeling?'

Her gaze tracks an officer disappearing into the trees. 'Something's off.'

Zac follows her line of sight, then looks back at the imposing castle.

'Yeah, that's what worries me.'

After two hours of fruitless searching Zac and Prisha move onto the final outbuilding. A cavernous shed with mountain blue aluminium cladding. It's at odds with the other buildings on the estate that are built from rustic bricks, stone, and timber with slate roofs.

Zac jingles a huge set of keys from his coat pocket and holds them up.

'Christ, I feel like a jailer from some ancient fairytale,' he notes, picking through the assortment of keys.

'This is the classic car shed,' Prisha says as she cradles the oversized padlock in her palm. 'After our search here, we'll take a walk down to the Wicca commune and see what they know.'

Zac tries the largest key first. The padlock clicks open with a satisfying snap. He slides the door along its squealing runner. Prisha steps inside, flicks on the lights, and taps the security code into the alarm panel. High overhead the fluorescents flicker on, revealing a strangely eerie sight. Three rows of six vehicles, perfectly spaced, each hidden beneath a white dust sheet.

Prisha shakes her head, and chuckles. 'Normal people collect porcelain pigs or seashells from the beach, but not the aristocracy. I wonder what this little lot is worth?'

Zac studies the layout hoping to spot a dishevelled sheet which may indicate a car that has recently been uncovered. He sees none.

Prisha takes a deep breath. 'Right, nothing for it but to remove every sheet, check the interior and boot, then replace the sheets.'

Zac approaches the first car and removes the dust cover, then groans in awe.

'Take a look at this little beauty,' he whispers in sycophantic reverence as he runs his gloved hand over the roof. 'A 1937 SS Jaguar 100.' The silver bodywork shimmers under the light. The car's sweeping fenders and low-slung stance exude elegance. 'A beauty like this could easily fetch over £300,000 today.'

'Are you all right?' Prisha enquires, worried her partner may have suffered a paralysing stroke.

'What? Oh, aye. It's just... well, it's hard to express.' Reluctantly he moves on to the next car and delicately pulls back the sheet. 'Oh, I don't believe it.'

'What?' Prisha asks, hoping he's spotted a clue.

'A 1959 Bristol 406 Zagato. See how the deep blue paintwork contrasts with the chrome accents. Oh, and that distinctive grille is like a big set of grinning teeth. This is as rare as an honest MP. Only a handful were ever made,' he says, running a hand along the curved bonnet. 'In pristine condition like this, it'd be worth around £200,000.'

Prisha is already striding forward with impatience. She approaches each car, grabs a corner of the sheet, and with scant regard for their majesty, yanks the covers violently away.

Zac is appalled at the action. 'Whoa, whoa, steady on there, Prisha. Remember, these are classic cars you're dealing with. The slightest scratch could devalue them.'

She points at her face. 'See this? Does it look like I give a shit? We're here to do a job—make sure Lord Hampton's body is not hidden in one of them. Now, put your erection away, and focus on the job. Once we're done, you can take photos. That way you can pleasure yourself in your own time.'

'Christ, you have no soul,' he murmurs.

Prisha is ruthlessly efficient.

Sheet back. Door opened. Check inside.

Boot opened. Check inside.

A quick peer underneath.

Next car.

Unlike her partner. 'No, get out of here!' Zac exclaims. 'You're toying with me now.'

'Zac, I'm warning you!' Prisha yells from the back of the shed.

'You don't understand. It's a 1964 Aston Martin DB5. This is what James Bond drove in Goldfinger. It wouldnae surprise me if it was the actual one. Could easily fetch half a million or more at auction. If only I had the money,' he laments.

'Does it have a body inside?'

'What? I hope not. Could ruin the upholstery.'

'Check it and move on!' Her yell echoes around the harsh interior.

As Zac continues his slow, near-reverential circuit of the cars, Prisha moves along the workbench, eyes scanning the meticulously arranged tools and supplies. The side wall is a shrine to maintenance and preservation. The long bench is a masterclass in order—rows of engine oils, coolants, and transmission fluids stand in neat formation, their labels facing outward. Spark plugs, light bulbs, waxes, and polishes are arranged with military precision. A section of the shelves is devoted entirely to ratchet sets, spanners, torque wrenches, and precision screwdrivers. A tyre pump and pressure gauge hang beside a pair of heavy-duty work gloves, as though waiting for Lord Hampton's return.

Above the bench, Prisha pauses by a series of framed photographs. Lord Hampton beams in each one, always with a car at his side—a 1950s rally event, a smoky hill climb in his vintage Aston Martin. His face is alive with enthusiasm, shaking hands with fellow enthusiasts, laughing beside his prized machines. On the bench below the photographs is a small hacksaw, and a pair of snips the only things without a home in the carefully curated workspace. Prisha's gaze lingers on them for a moment.

'Christ,' Zac murmurs, admiring a Jaguar E-Type. 'This lot—conservatively? Three million pounds. Maybe more, depending on the market. Wait till Frank sees it.'

Prisha rolls her eyes and lets out a short, unimpressed breath. 'Boys and their toys. What a bloody waste. All this money tucked away in a dusty old shed.'

Zac straightens, glancing around at the pristine space, the carefully calibrated equipment, the obsessive care in every detail. He gestures towards the humidifiers and air filtration units humming softly in the background.

'This isn't some damp old barn, Prisha. He's got air control systems to stop rust, extraction fans to clear out fumes.' He nods at the cars. 'Battery trickle chargers on half of them—means they're ready to run at a moment's notice. This isn't a shed. It's a bloody museum. I've never seen a garage kept in such meticulous order. Maybe Lord H suffers from OCD?'

Unimpressed and frustrated, Prisha slowly spins around taking one last look at the space. 'I take it you didn't find anything of note?' she queries as her eyes fall onto something of interest tucked away in a far corner.

Zac falls back to earth. 'Erm, no,' he mutters, realising his search for clues was ambushed by his overzealous admiration of the cars.

Prisha strides across the cavernous room, followed by Zac. She slides a bolt back and tugs open the flimsy garden storage shed—the kind typically used to house lawnmowers and bags of compost.

Inside, something large sits under yet another white dust sheet, its shape awkward in the confined space.

She pulls the cover back.

A motorbike. Wedged in, barely enough room to stand beside it.

'What do you make of this?' she asks.

Zac pokes his head inside. 'It's a late 80s Honda GB500. Japanese-built, styled like an old British cafe racer. Had a bit of swagger back in the day.' He pauses, frowning. 'Not that it's worth bugger all now.' He crouches, running a hand over the smashed headlight and bent handlebar. 'Took a hit at some point.' His fingers skim the cracked front fender, then pause on dark stains on the petrol tank. He rubs at one with his thumb, but the mark has long dried in.

'What is it?'

'Could be mud. Could be blood,' he mutters. 'Probably ran over roadkill. Upward splatter.'

Prisha folds her arms. 'When was the damage done?'

Zac straightens, eyeing the machine. 'Rust in the cracks, perished tyres, chain's seized. This thing hasn't been ridden in many a long year.'

Prisha stares at the broken headlight spider-webbed with cracks, like a frozen scream. She exhales and pulls the sheet back into place.

She doesn't know why it niggles. Just that it does.

A relic among relics, too damaged to shine, too personal to discard. In a collection worth millions why keep a knackered old motorbike? Sentimental reasons, perhaps?

The thought dissipates as quickly as it was born as Zac pulls at her sleeve, grinning.

'Eh, get your phone out, Prisha. I want some photos of me sitting in the Aston Martin. I'll be Bond—Connery era. You can be Pussy Galore draped over the bonnet.'

'In your dreams, man-boy,' she snorts, swinging the door shut and ramming the bolt home. She stares at the shed for a moment, then follows Zac as he hurries towards the Bond car, as excited as a child on Christmas morning.

34

As Peggy Thornton pulls her front door shut, the erratic chime of the church bell rings out across the village rooftops.

She pauses, craning her neck toward the belfry in the distance, lips pursed in mild confusion.

'Why is the vicar ringing the bell at 9:15, and on a Thursday?' she muses aloud. Then, with a small tut, she shakes her head. 'Oh, that's right. They were replacing the rope. He must be giving it a test.'

The thought dissipates as she sets off on her usual route, a pleasant ten-minute walk to the outskirts of the village. She admires the bursts of colour in the gardens she passes, tulips and bluebells beginning to bloom, the morning air crisp with the promise of a fine day.

It's peaceful. It's *always* peaceful in Ashenby.

As she reaches the churchyard gate, she pushes it open with a familiar creak, the rusted iron cold beneath her fingers. A flutter of butterflies stirs in the overgrown grass, their pale wings flickering between the leaning gravestones.

The air carries a delicate waft of sweet hawthorn blossom and honeyed cowslip, laced with the damp earthiness of morning dew. She breathes it in, smiling, the scene as familiar and comforting as an old hymn.

The main doors to the church stand open, and she counts her blessings. She's heard that in some places, churches keep their doors locked out of hours—too much crime these days. Would never have happened in the old days.

She steps inside. A hush wraps around her like an old shawl. The scent of candle wax and a million unanswered prayers lingers in the cool air.

Retrieving the mop and bucket from the storage cupboard, she fills it with hot water from the small laundry room, steam swirling like breath in winter. As she flicks the kettle on, the quiet click feels like a starting bell for the day ahead.

Peggy Thornton likes routine.

First, she wipes down all the pews and ledges. Then, she has a brew.

Then, she mops the floor.

Another brew and a Bourbon biscuit.

Next, she starts on the choir stalls and altar.

Two therapeutic hours of voluntary work. It doesn't feel like work. Not really. There's a rhythm to it, a quiet pleasure in keeping God's house clean.

It gives her a sense of purpose, and she's doing her bit for the community she's lived in all her life.

It's another ordinary morning in Ashenby.

⸻◈⸻

Peggy fills the bucket for the last time. Only the vicar's office and the bell chamber to do, then she's done for the day. Both easy jobs. The vicar can be a bit messy, leaving books strewn about, but he keeps his office relatively tidy.

She checks her watch—11:08 am.

Usually by now, the vicar has made an appearance. A quick hello, maybe a cup of tea and a natter. But not today. She assumes he's busy in his office, maybe on the phone with the bishop or checking on one of his parishioners. He's like that—a good man.

As she ambles towards the closed door of the bell chamber, a niggle visits her.

The workmen. Norm and Old Tom.

They've probably left a hell of a mess. They always do. No matter the job—replacing tiles, fixing pews, clearing gutters—there's always something left behind. Old cement, wood shavings, screws. Like it's not their mess.

Pushing open the door, she scans the floor.

'Well, I'll be.' A pleasant surprise. The only thing left behind is a length of rope in the corner. From the cloth stitched around it, she recognises it—the sally.

That'll be why they replaced it.

She turns towards the office door.

That's when she sees it.

A puddle.

Dead centre of the room.

She frowns.

Gapes.

'Where the hell has that come from?' she mutters as her eyes spot another oddity. A small braided disc near the office door.

The unnerving feeling creeps up on her, like a predator stalking prey.

Her skin prickles. Breath falters.

Fear blooms, sudden and senseless.

A drip.

A soft splat as it lands in the shallow puddle.

Peggy sets the mop and bucket down, her fingers trembling against the handle.

She doesn't want to look up.

Every fibre of her being screams against it.

But she does.

And what she sees will haunt her until her dying days.

35

Prisha and Zac follow the dirt track down from Ravensbane Castle, their boots squelching on damp ground. The sky hangs low, a slate lid pressing on the surrounding countryside. Beyond a copse of gnarled oaks, the Wicca commune appears—six log cabins clustered in a loose circle, smoke rising from a central fire pit, the air thick with woodsmoke and something sweetly herbal.

People move between the cabins, slow and deliberate, some feeding scraps to chickens, others weaving baskets or fixing tools. A few children dart between them, playing a chasing game, laughing in bursts before disappearing behind the buildings.

Prisha stops and turns to Zac. 'We question their spokesperson or leader firstly about Lord Hampton, see what they have to say. Then, as we're about to leave, we'll quiz them about their Beltane festival and the foot found in the ashes.'

Zac's eyes wander. 'Okay,' he replies slowly, hesitant. 'Why in that order?'

'Reverse psychology. If they know anything about the foot, they'll expect us to open with that. Throw them off their game.'

'Okay. You're the boss.'

As they enter the encampment, a woman steps forward—the same woman with dreadlocks Prisha encountered the day before supervising the lake repairs. Her eyes are sharp but unreadable, and today she wears a flowing skirt and loose-knit top that does little to conceal the outline of her body. She moves with a quiet confidence.

Prisha flashes her warrant card. 'Hello again. DI Kumar and this is my colleague, DS Stoker.'

'Greetings. I'm Violet Fox,' she says, her voice even and calm. 'I take it you're here about the disappearance of Lord Hampton?'

Prisha nods. 'Yes. Who told you?'

'One of your officers searching the grounds.'

'I see. Who's in charge here?'

Violet tilts her head slightly. 'No one and everyone. We don't follow leaders, but I am one of the Council Elders, which means I can speak on the commune's behalf.'

Prisha has already taken a dislike to her and forces a smile. 'How very democratic. And this place? It's a Wicca commune, yes?' she says, slowly taking in the surrounds.

Violet offers a patient smile. 'We follow the old ways, but we're not bound by doctrine. We respect the land, the seasons. Nature provides, if you watch, look, and listen.'

Prisha's gaze flicks to the solar panels and the four e-bikes propped against a cabin wall. 'Seems nature's providing lithium batteries as well.'

Violet's smile doesn't falter. 'We balance tradition with practicality. The world moves forward. We move with it.'

A group of children play near the fire pit, drawing symbols in the dirt with sticks.

Zac studies them. 'What's the game the kiddies are playing?'

'It's an old game. Teaching them about the cycles of life,' Violet replies smoothly.

Prisha folds her arms. 'Tell me about your setup?'

'We're a matriarchal, self-sufficient community with a net-zero carbon footprint.'

'You mean the women are in charge?'

'Yes.'

Prisha nods at the open fire. 'Net carbon?'

'We regrow more than we burn.'

Prisha spots a young man to the side of a cabin chopping wood. 'And what do the men do?'

Violet follows her gaze. 'The men have two primary roles—manual labour. They're physiologically designed for heavy work.'

'And their other role?'

Violet smirks. 'Isn't that obvious, inspector? The species needs to survive.'

Prisha shakes her head. 'Hard labour and sex. Sounds like servitude.'

Zac grins. 'Oh, I don't know. I reckon it's a good pay-off.'

Violet's eyelids flicker as she teases him with a playful smile. 'We don't fight against the laws of nature, inspector, we embrace them.'

'And how many of you are in the commune?' Prisha asks, slightly irked at the way she's sizing up Zac.

'Thirteen women, nine men, seven children.'

'Why aren't the children in school?'

'They're home taught.'

'What if they get ill?'

'Exceedingly rare and we have our own natural medicines. Also, our group come from all walks of life. A school principal, doctor, maternity nurse, mechanic, carpenter, baker, and even a butcher. Comes in very handy for the goats and pigs.'

'And do any of you work?'

Violet smirks. 'If you mean work in the conventional sense, i.e. labour from nine-to-five in a job we hate, for a narcissistic, incompetent, idiot—usually male—and are paid in money to feed the insatiable capitalist system, then no. But if you mean do we perform industrious, fulfilling duties throughout the day, and find comfort in our collective creative endeavours, and sleep soundly on a night—then yes, we work—very hard.'

'Really?' Prisha says her irritation with the woman growing.

Zac detects the brewing discontent and intervenes. 'Did you build the log cabins yourselves? They're very impressive.'

'Yes, as I said, every single person here has a life skill, something useful to bring to the group.' She nods towards the cabins. 'We have the women's, men's, and children's sleeping quarters, schoolroom, kitchen, and utility room.'

'Can't have been cheap,' Prisha notes. 'Log cabins, solar panels, e-bikes. How do you pay for it all?'

'Many of our group came from well-paid jobs, some with a substantial inheritance. When we accept a new member into the community, we pool our resources.'

'When you say resources, you mean money?'

'Yes.'

'So, you're actually pooling *their* resources?'

'Everything is shared.'

'And these resources are kept where?'

'In a bank. We're hardly likely to keep it under the mattress,' Violet adds, with a laugh.

'And let me guess—only the Council Elders can access the money?'

Violet stiffens. 'You're a very cynical person, inspector. I suspect your chakras are blocked.'

'My chakras are fine, thank you very much.'

'You seem to think we're freeloaders. We're not. As I said we work hard. We have extensive organic vegetable plots in the walled garden, along with various fruit trees, and numerous hothouses, so we produce food all year round. We keep chickens and goats, and a small pig farm on the edge of the woods. We also forage for food and medicines, and there's a natural spring. The vegetable garden alone provides way too much for our community and the occupants of the castle. Any surplus is donated to charity or sold at Sunday markets.'

'Bit hypocritical though, isn't it,' Prisha notes, getting into her stride.

'What?'

'All this,' she says pointing at the camp. 'If it wasn't for the benevolence of Lord Hampton, an aristocrat who epitomises the capitalist system, then you wouldn't be able to sustain any of it.'

Prisha knows she's letting her personal feelings slip—again—but something about Violet's smug serenity makes her itch.

Zac shuffles uneasily. 'Ahem, anyway, we seem to have ventured off-topic,' he interrupts throwing Prisha a glare. 'The *main* reason we're here is to ask you about Lord Hampton. When was the last time you saw him?'

'Sunday afternoon. He called around to tell us about the slight breach in the lake wall and asked if we could fix it. We invited him to our Beltane festival on Sunday night. He said he'd like to attend but that he probably wouldn't because of the early start he had. He was flying out to Syria on an archaeological dig.'

'And did he attend your festival?'

'No.'

'And you, nor any of your commune have seen him since?'

'I'm afraid not. Later tonight we'll gather around the circle and invoke the earth spirits to guide us to where he is.'

Prisha's eyes screw into a knot but before she can open her mouth Zac steps in.

'You believe he's still alive?'

'Oh, yes. Our spiritual leader cast runes earlier which confirmed he's alive.'

'I thought you didn't have leaders?' Prisha snipes.

Violet tightens her lips and glares back. 'Not in the conventional sense.'

'And where is your spiritual leader as I'd like a word?'

'She left for the village twenty minutes ago.'

'How convenient,' Prisha mutters under her breath.

As the sun breaks through Zac undoes a button on his shirt. 'And would you say your relationship with Lord Hampton is good?'

'Yes. In perfect harmony. He's a kindred spirit.'

Prisha scoffs. 'A multi-millionaire aristocrat a kindred spirit.'

Violet tilts her head. 'You assume money corrupts the soul, inspector?'

Prisha steps closer, voice sharpening. 'Isn't money the root of all evil?'

'Ahem, right,' Zac says. 'Just a few more questions and we'll leave you in peace, Violet. I'm sure you've heard about the death of Lord Hampton's former gamekeeper, Malachi Abbott—when was the last time you saw him and what was he like?'

Violet frowns. 'It seems like an unfortunate accident from what we've heard.'

'And what have you heard?' Prisha interjects.

'That he crashed his car in the river and drowned.'

'And the last time you saw him?' Zac prompts trying to keep the questioning on track.

Violet shrugs. 'Not sure. Maybe a week or so ago. Just around the village. Occasionally one of us saw him in the woods, hunting rabbits.'

Prisha has the bit between her teeth. 'He was sacked by Lord Hampton not long after your commune was established on Ravensbane Estate. He was accused of sexually assaulting a young girl.'

Violet glances over her shoulder at the children who are now vociferous and playing tig. Her gaze eventually returns to Prisha.

'Sorry, was that a question or a statement?'

'It was a question,' she says with some force.

'The girl was alone in the woods, searching for wild mushrooms. Malachi touched her. She ran back here and told us what happened. I naturally informed Lord Hampton who was mortified. Mr Abbott was not a pleasant man, neither in appearance nor in his heart.'

'And why didn't you inform the police?'

She sniggers. 'I think that's obvious from your own hostile reaction to our lifestyle. I don't judge you, inspector, so why do you think it fair game to judge us?'

Zac offers a warm smile and intervenes again. 'Well, that will do for now. Thanks for your time, Violet.'

'My pleasure,' she replies gazing admiringly at him. 'You know, sergeant, the commune is always looking for fresh seed. It invigorates the stock. Cross-pollination.'

Zac smiles appreciatively. 'Sorry, never had green thumbs. I only have to look at a pot plant and it withers and dies.'

Prisha rolls her eyes. 'She wasn't talking about your gardening skills. She's after your sperm.'

Zac freezes. 'What!'

Violet winks at him. 'We only select men who are strong in mind, body, and spirit.'

'Sounds like selective breeding,' Prisha scoffs.

Violet throws her the dead-eye. 'We aim to build a strong and robust society, inspector. There's not one person here who suffers from diabetes, cancer, heart-disease or any of the curses of the modern age. We believe it's down to the organic food we eat, our spiritual fulfilment, and our love of the life we lead. But yes, you're right. Genetics is crucial in building a stronger race, not just for our small commune but for the survival of humanity.'

Prisha snorts her distaste. 'Sounds familiar. Wasn't there a guy in the 1930s with a funny little moustache who had similar ideas? I believe he was German.'

'Austrian, actually. I used to be a history professor.'

'I bet that comes in handy around here.'

Violet leans forward, and whispers, 'You really do need to unblock your chakras, inspector. Your aura is very faint. Repressed anger blocks the third eye. Now, if you'll excuse me, I have a *pig* to prepare for slaughter.'

The pig reference is not lost on Prisha, but she doesn't rise to the bait.

'Mrs Fox, one last question,' she says with the utmost politeness.

'It's Ms, actually.'

'My apologies, *Ms* Fox. You said you held a Beltane festival in the woods Sunday night to welcome in summer, yes?'

For the first time she appears apprehensive. 'Yes. It's private land. It's not illegal. We had Lord Hampton's blessing.'

'What time was that?'

'We lit the fire about 11 pm. Why?'

'And how long did this festival last?'

'Until about 2 am. That's when the storm hit.'

'Any rituals, sacrifices?'

She folds her arms. 'There were offerings made to the wood spirits, yes.'

'Offerings?'

'Sick animals—rabbits with myxomatosis, a lame goat, a deer that died naturally. All humanely dispatched beforehand.'

'And this festival was held where, exactly?'

'In a clearing close to the Three Crones.'

'The standing stones?'

'Yes.'

'On Monday morning we were called to the scene of your fire. A member of the public stumbled upon it by accident. They spotted a shoe. A shoe with a human foot inside it.'

Violet's mouth parts in silence before she finds her voice. 'What? No, that cannot be.'

'*It is be,*' Prisha replies, deadpan, resisting a smirk.

She's flustered. 'Then... it must have been placed on the fire after we departed. Maybe someone is trying to set us up.'

Prisha, Zac, and Frank have already formed the same conclusion, but Prisha is not going to confirm Violet's assumption

'Maybe. We'll be back at some point to question you further about it. Happy *pig* slaughtering.'

She turns and marches away as Zac offers an apologetic shrug, then follows her.

36

As they head back to the castle Zac can barely control his anger.

'What the hell's got into you?' he finally barks as Prisha walks ahead.

She spins around. 'What?'

'Your attitude. At best you were downright rude, at worst, openly hostile. Just because they're hippies and follow a different religion doesn't mean you don't show them the same respect as everyone else.'

'Oh, do me a favour. The Wicca religion isn't some ancient pagan theology. It was invented by a guy named Gerald Gardner, a well-to-do British civil servant, in the 1950s. Don't you see? It's all a game, a sham. Self-satisfied, sanctimonious, holier-than-thou, dippy-hippy hogwash. And who does she think she is? Building a stronger race, for the saviour of mankind. Give me strength. They're nothing but a cult. And she's no better than your run-of-the-mill con-artist, just with better skin.'

Zac stops dead, his fingers flexing at his sides before he plants his hands on his hips.

'I've noticed this about you before. Normally, you're on the ball, sharp as a tack. You're forthright, sometimes blunt, but that's your style, I get it. But whenever you question someone who has an alternative lifestyle, it's like the red mist comes down.'

'It's the pretentiousness of it. At least with drug dealers, thieves, and killers there's no pretence. What you see is what you get. They're out to feather their own nests or settle a score. They don't sugar coat it and make out they have an altruistic reason. That lot back there, they're all fake. Spoilt middle-class tossers who have the time and money to take five years out and play at saving the planet. And when they tire of it, they'll simply melt back into the folds of decent society and probably write a book about finding themselves.'

'You can't let your personal views colour your judgement. It's unprofessional.'

Prisha throws her arms in the air. 'Unprofessional! And what about you?'

'What about me?' he yells.

'Something I've also noticed—whenever an attractive woman flirts with you, your brain migrates south and takes up residence in the end of your dick!'

'That's bullshit!'

'It's true. Vanity is not a good look, Zac. You can be such a walkover, a naïve fool. A flutter of the eyelashes and you're like a puppy dog drooling over a bowl of raw liver.'

'Take that back,' he thunders.

'Like hell I will!'

Silence descends briefly during the cessation of hostilities—until... Zac starts laughing.

'What's so funny,' Prisha snaps.

'You. I've figured it out. Now I understand.'

'What are you rambling about?'

'You talk about pretence but it's you who's the hypocrite.'

'Don't try to be clever, Zac. It doesn't suit you.'

He ignores the barb and slowly circles her. 'You see, with me, at least I'm honest. I admit the truth. I hate anything to do with the occult, satanists, off-beat religions, mystics. And do you know why?'

'Enlighten me, Plato.'

'Because even though logic tells me it's all nonsense, deep down a little part of me isn't sure. What if there is something to it? What if there's some force of nature we don't yet understand? And that scares me—the unknown, the dark side. But you, DI Prisha Kumar, aren't scared of anyone or anything—or so you say. That's why you get all shitty. If you were true to yourself, you'd admit it scares the merry bejeezus out of you too, but you can't admit that, not to the outside world, not even to yourself.'

Prisha flinches. Doesn't meet his eyes. Something hits home, but she'll never admit it.

'You've even been paying a shrink to psychoanalyse you about the ravens and doll's head in your dreams. You're fearful, and that fear manifests as belligerence. It's your shield. It's true, isn't it?'

Prisha hesitates, then snaps and lunges at him. 'Don't you dare to try to understand me. You don't have the brain cells for it!'

She raises her hand as if to slap him, but he spots it coming and grabs her wrist.

The wind picks up, as the clouds open.

Rain falls.

A drop lands on Prisha's top lip and slowly meanders down.

Eyes lock.

The air between them crackles

He yanks her forward.

His mouth crashes into hers—angry, hungry.

The kiss is passionate... from both.

Hot. Torrid. Lustful—completely wrong, and all the more delightful.

They part just as violently and stand breathing heavily staring at each other, as the drizzle intensifies, and dark clouds gather momentum.

Prisha folds her arms and stomps towards the distant castle, head down, cocooned.

Zac gazes after her, his heart thumping against his chest.

'Damn it,' he whispers, lifting a hand to wipe his mouth and erase her scent.

He stops himself, and takes a moment to regain his composure, unaware of eyes watching him.

As he walks away, keeping a safe distance behind Prisha, Morrigan emerges from behind a bush. Her face remains passive, but in her eyes, something flickers.

Calculation? Jealousy? Or something darker?

37

Frank closes the heavy door behind him and saunters down the steps of Ravensbane Castle, eyes on his phone.

'Where the hell are they?' he murmurs to himself.

Footsteps distract him.

He looks up and sees Prisha marching towards him, arms firmly folded, with Zac following a good ten feet behind.

'Ah, Cagney and Lacey. About bloody time. I've been trying to get hold of you,' he calls out.

Zac glances at his phone. 'Sorry, boss. Your missed calls have just dropped in. Must have been in a signal black spot. The commune's in a bit of a hollow.'

'Aye, well, never mind that now. I had a call ten minutes ago from HQ. A body's been found at St Mary's Church in Ashenby.'

'Who?' Prisha asks.

'Not sure. Details were scant. Paramedics are there now. I want you both over there, pronto. It's probably nothing to do with our investigation but let's make sure.'

Prisha is already pulling open her car door.

The engine roars alarmingly, giving the oil seals a proper workout. She takes off at breakneck speed, sending a shower of gravel into the air.

Frank and Zac take a frantic step back to avoid the airborne grit.

'What the bloody hell's got into her?' Frank demands, watching the car slew along the winding driveway and disappear around a bend.

Zac shrugs, sheepish. 'Not sure, boss,' he murmurs.

Frank turns to him, scratching his head. 'Not sure, boss,' he repeats, the words dripping with cynicism. 'You look like the blind butcher's dog—guilty as sin. Anything to confess?'

'Ahem.... no.'

'Very well. You heard me. What are you waiting for? Get in your car and get your arse over to Ashenby.'

'But...'

'There *but* for the grace of God go I. Now move it!'

As Zac's car pulls away at a more sedate speed, Frank exhales, shakes his head, and scratches his chin. He's seen this film before—one storming off, the other trailing in shame.

Something's happened.

'I don't like the smell of this one little bit. If I'm correct, *and I think I am,* I see trouble ahead. Big trouble. Stupid, *young* buggers.'

38

Prisha and Zac pull up outside St Mary's Church almost simultaneously, parking on opposite sides of the narrow lane beside the old stone wall. Without speaking, they climb out and fall into step, passing an ambulance idling at the kerb.

Zac touches her arm. She stops.

He exhales, raking a hand through his hair. 'Look... about earlier.'

She meets his gaze—tense, unreadable.

He fidgets. 'I shouldn't have said what I said. Or done what I did. It was—out of line. I don't know what came over me. I'm sorry. If it makes things easier, I'll put in for a transfer.'

Prisha blinks, caught off guard. 'Don't be daft. Uproot everything—and for what? A lapse? We were both out of line,' she says. 'An aberration. It won't happen again.'

They hold eye contact—long enough for the air between them to settle. Tense, but no longer volatile.

'Alright,' Zac nods. 'We move on?'

'Yes. And stay focused.'

'Aye. Focused.' A flicker of a grin.

She turns, but he touches her arm again. Hesitates.

'What?'

He winces. 'I think Frank might've twigged.'

She winces. 'Of course he did. He notices everything.'

'He won't say anything... except maybe to Meera.'

Prisha sighs. 'Meera wouldn't gossip.'

'No—but Whitby's small, and she knows everyone. She's like the Town Cryer.'

Her jaw tightens. 'The only people who know what happened are you and me. If anyone asks, we deny it. End of.'

Zac nods. 'Yeah, you're right. End of.'

She steps away, voice crisp now. 'Let's get to work,' she says pulling a pair of latex gloves from her pocket.

'It's good to see old Frank back on the beat, as it were,' he says, changing the subject.

Prisha riles. 'Not by choice. Superintendent Banks insisted. The moment she heard the missing man was Lord Hampton, a member of the aristocracy, she demanded Frank head up the case. "It will give it more gravitas," in her words. Like I can't be trusted to possibly search for a missing Lord of the fucking Manor.'

Zac sighs as he pushes open the iron gate into the church grounds.

'Nothing changes in this country, Prisha. The old guard still call the tune, and we still pay the piper. If the missing person was a local drug pusher or an elderly woman with dementia, Banks would've let Dinkel handle it alone. But slap a title on someone, and suddenly, it's all hands on deck.' He stutters mid-stride and groans. 'Oh, no.'

'What?'

'The paramedic standing outside the church.' Zac jerks his chin towards the large man in a hi-vis jacket. 'Blair Kilpatrick.'

'What's wrong with him?'

'He's a regal pain in the rusty bullet hole. Fancies himself as an amateur sleuth. A right know-it-all.'

'Sounds charming.'

'He'll already have deduced the how, the why, the who, and the wherefore. If he wasn't built like a brick shithouse, had an Irish accent, and smelled of Parmesan cheese... you'd swear he was Hercule Poirot—minus the silly moustache.'

As they approach, Zac plasters on a false smile. 'Ah, Blair, how's it going? Long time no see.'

'Sergeant Stoker.' The paramedic nods, his beady eyes lingering too long on Prisha.

Zac steps slightly in front of her. 'This is my gaffer, Detective Inspector Kumar.'

'Inspector,' Blair says, all wet lips and smarm. 'Must be nice to work under a female boss,' he sniggers, winking at Zac.

Prisha ignores the smutty inference. 'Were you first on the scene?'

His posture straightens, suddenly serious. 'Aye. Me and my partner, Bob. He's in the bell chamber now, with the body. We arrived ten minutes after the call came in. Just happened to be in the area, dropping off an old dear from surgery. There was nothing we could do to save him. Been dead a while, I'd say.'

'Who is it?'

'The vicar. A Reverend Nicholas Hartley, according to the old biddy who found him.'

'What else can you tell us?'

He offers an arrogant smile. 'I always find it best to relate events at the actual scene of death, inspector. If you'd care to follow me.'

Zac swivels his eyeballs towards Prisha, who barely suppresses a sigh.

Inside the church, a uniformed officer stands over Peggy Thornton, who is huddled on a pew, her shoulders trembling. An older man sits beside her, arm wrapped around her for support.

The constable spots them and hurries over.

'Inspector. Sergeant. Constable Mike Dodd.'

'Mike,' Prisha nods. 'Give me a quick rundown.'

Dodd flicks back through his notepad. 'The woman on the bench is sixty-nine-year-old Peggy Thornton, an Ashenby local. Cleans the church twice a week. Arrived at approximately 9:20 and discovered the deceased, Reverend Hartley, at approximately—' he glances at his notes, '—11:10 am.'

'Was she alone?'

'Yes.'

'Who's the man sitting with her?'

'Her brother. She called him after she dialled 999. Neither of them are married, they share a house in the village. She's in a bad way, ma'am. Pretty shaken up.'

'I can tell. Have you finished taking her statement?'

'Yes.'

'Good. Make her a cup of tea. We'll speak to her in a few minutes, then she can go home.'

'Ma'am.'

Prisha and Zac trail Blair into the bell chamber.

Inside, the second paramedic stands near the vicar's body, which lies in one corner, shrouded beneath a white sheet.

'I need some air,' he says thankful for his partner's return as he exits the room.

Blair chuckles. 'Newbie. Not cut out for the job if you ask me. You need an iron constitution.'

Zac crouches next to the body and peels the sheet back.

'A deep red furrow around the neck, indicative of hanging. The tongue's not protruding, which usually occurs if the body's been hanging for several hours.' He lifts each arm of the body up. 'No markings around the wrists.' He stares at the face of Reverend Hartley for a moment before replacing the sheet. 'Almost looks peaceful,' he says, rising.

'Tell me what you saw when you first entered the room, Blair?' Prisha asks.

'Well, it was obvious.' Blair leans back, nodding up towards the hatchway, thirty feet above, the entrance to the belfry. 'Peggy pointed us in here, but she was too shaken to explain. So me and Bob rushed in and there he was—the vicar swinging from a rope. Right above us.'

Prisha follows his gaze. A length of thick rope still swings gently, ten feet above.

Blair continues. 'Goes up another forty or fifty feet and attaches to the bell.'

Prisha takes photos on her phone. 'There's no noose.'

'No. The rope was looped around his neck twice. We climbed the wall ladder. I took his weight, creating some slack, while Bob unravelled the rope. Then I held the body while Bob climbed back down. Then I lowered the body to him. Took his vitals but it was too late. Cool to the touch. *Long gone.*'

Zac's gaze drops to the puddle on the floor.

'Piss?'

Blair nods. 'Aye. Be grateful for small mercies.'

Prisha turns, spotting the discarded rope in the corner. She walks over, takes a few photos, crouches to examine it.

'This looks like the end of the bell rope?'

Zac nods. 'Aye. When I was here yesterday, the vicar explained that the cloth-wrapped handle—the bit the bell-ringer grips—is called a sally. Cushioned for comfort.'

Prisha frowns. 'Then why has it been cut off?'

Blair puffs out his chest. 'I think I can explain, inspector.'

Prisha smiles. 'Really?'

Blair visibly grows. 'I'm a bit of a crime buff enthusiast in my spare time. I watch all the shows—Wire in the Blood, Midsomer Murders, Death in Paradise, Line of Duty, Happy Valley.'

'A solid grounding,' Prisha says dryly. 'Go on.'

Blair launches in, animated. 'The vicar comes in about nineish—we know that because Peggy heard the church bell at 9:10. He gives the rope a tug, it snaps off—that's why it's discarded in the corner. He decides to check the belfry, climbs up, pulls the rope up with him, gets in a right tangle, loses his footing, drops through the hatch. The rope snags around his neck. And it's Goodnight Vienna.'

Prisha and Zac exchange a glance, nodding as if in acknowledgement of his genius.

Zac mumbles in Prisha's ear. *'That's one theory. Shame it's bollocks.'*

'Sorry?' Blair asks. 'Did you say something sergeant?'

'Excellent hypothesis, Blair,' Zac declares. 'Apart from the fact the rope in the corner hasn't snapped. Look at it. It's been cut.'

Prisha steps closer. 'And what are the chances of a rope magically looping around his neck twice as he fell?'

Blair shrinks. 'Erm... okay. My other thought was... suicide?' he suggests as a get-out-of-jail card.

Prisha nods. 'Thanks, Blair. We'll bear that in mind. You can stand down. We'll take it from here.'

As he leaves, Zac folds his arms. 'Well?'

Prisha exhales. 'You were right. He's a knobjockey. Shall we get down to business?'

39

The end of the discarded rope is illuminated by the daylight as Zac holds it aloft.

'I know for a fact—this is a new rope. There's fraying, but it's too uniform—every fibre cut clean at the same angle. If it had snapped from wear, you'd get an uneven break, strands separating at different points. This was sliced or cut deliberately, not weakened over time.'

Prisha shoves her hands deep into her pockets, frowning.

'What was the vicar's state of mind when you spoke to him yesterday?'

'Perfectly normal. A decent bloke. His mind was sharp, reflective. Fit and healthy. Climbed down those ladders like a twenty-year-old. He said he was due to retire in five years. I think the Church keeps their vicars going until seventy, barring ill health—so I'd say he was about sixty-five—but ten years younger in mind and body, if you know what I mean.'

Prisha stares up at the hatch. 'Who's going up?'

Zac holds his hands aloft. 'I did my duty yesterday. Your turn.'

'Who said chivalry's dead? While you're doing nothing, ring the coroner's office and forensics and get them down here.'

With an effortless grace that baffles Zac, Prisha scales the ladder and hauls herself into the belfry. She studiously navigates the room, Zac's muted voice drifting up to her. After five minutes, and none the wiser, she hovers at the edge of the hatch. There's nothing to indicate how the vicar came to be swinging from a rope, apart from the obvious.

'Anything?' Zac calls up.

'No.'

She shimmies down the ladder, jumping the last four rungs.

'We have three possible scenarios,' Zac states. 'Suicide, accidental death, or foul play.'

Prisha's lips harden. 'Okay, let's go through them. You know the stats—almost all hangings are suicide unless it's a child, where it's usually accidental. Normally this would be straightforward, but two things give me cause for concern.'

'The fact the vicar hanged himself in the church?'

'Yes. Wouldn't that be sacrilege or something?'

'It's definitely odd. And what else is bothering you?'

'No noose. If people have passed the point of no-return, they want to make damn sure they're successful. A noose, a self-tightening knot, is a lot more foolproof than wrapping the rope around your neck twice.'

'True. And he didn't appear depressed.'

Prisha wriggles her nose. 'Yeah, but people can be masters at hiding it.'

'Okay, accidental death—as Blair hypothesised, the vicar climbed into the belfry for some reason, maybe pulled the rope up, got in a tangle and fell. The rope becomes wrapped around his neck—twice.'

'Possible but improbable,' Prisha says. 'Which leaves foul play, which is also unlikely.'

'Why?'

'Leaving motive aside for now, it'd mean someone either waiting up there to lure him, or forcing him up. Then what? They overpower him, wrap the rope round his neck twice, and shove him through the hatch. High-risk strategy for one person. And why bother with the rope? A straight fall would have killed him.'

'So we're both agreed—suicide.'

'Not so fast, big boy. There's the other puzzle.'

'The discarded piece of rope?'

'Exactly. Newly installed bell rope, deliberately cut. Why would anyone cut it? Come on, let's look inside his office.'

Zac pushes open the door, and they enter the quiet room. 'Looks like it did when I was here yesterday. No sign of a struggle.' He strides to the bureau and pulls the lid down. 'He told the workmen he had money for them in his office, so maybe there's a petty-cash tin.'

He rummages through the bureau without luck as Prisha scrutinises the bookcase.

'Here,' she says, retrieving a small metal box.

Zac moves to the desk and pulls open the top drawer, and spots a key. He takes the box, inserts the key, lifts the lid and removes the handful of notes.

'Sixty-five quid,' he states, replacing the money and locking the box. 'So no robbery.'

'Do you think they're related?' Prisha asks as she peruses the contents of the bookshelf.

'The vicar's death, Malachi Abbott, the foot, and the disappearance of Lord Hampton?'

'Yes.'

Zac drags a hand through his hair. 'Apart from geography? Not really.'

'Odd though, isn't it? Ashenby has virtually zero crime, and within the space of a few days we have two suspicious deaths, human remains, and a missing person.'

'True, but despite Frank's mantra, sometimes coincidences do happen. And you know from experience—killers tend to stick to a method. The two deaths couldn't be more different: a drowning and a hanging.'

Prisha freezes as her gaze rests upon the spine of a book. She lifts it from the shelf and flicks through the pages.

'I don't believe it,' she murmurs.

'What?' Zac asks, still rummaging through the desk drawers.

She turns and holds the book aloft. '*The Three Crones*. Is this the book you saw in the library?'

Zac peers at it. 'Aye, it is.'

Prisha taps at the name printed on the bottom of the cover. 'The author is Reverend Hartley,' she whispers. She flicks a page back. 'First published in 1985 by Black Bank Books. Probably a local press.'

Zac shrugs. 'It doesn't help though, does it? Just muddies the waters further.'

As Zac continues searching and trawling over the abstract aspects of the deaths, Prisha zones out, absorbed in the first chapter of the book. 'And I mean, the foot, what's that got to do with either the vicar or Malachi? Okay, it was found in the wood where Malachi used to be a gamekeeper, but so what? It's a big wood. Then there's Lord Hampton; he could be anywhere. We don't know what's happened to him. For all we know, he may have run off with a fancy woman.'

'Shut up.'

'I beg your pardon?' Zac replies, affronted.

'I said shut up.'

'Bloody charming.'

'There may be a link,' she whispers, still reading.

'What are you talking about?'

'The standing stones are called The Three Crones. They used to be a meeting place for pagan rituals. Remember when we questioned the farmers, Mr and Mrs Baker, from Hexley farm?'

'Aye.'

'And Mrs Baker mentioned three witches lived in the woods and were executed during the witch trials?'

'Yes.'

'And they put a curse on their accusers?'

'And?'

'Guess who the three main perpetrators of the witch trials were?'

Zac shifts uneasily. 'Not sure I want to know.'

'Lord Richard Hampton, 7th Baron of Ravensbane. Local magistrate. Ruthless in persecuting witches. Confiscated their lands for himself. Thirteenth great-grandfather of our missing Lord Hampton.'

Zac stands tall and puffs out air. 'Thanks for the local history lesson. You said *three* perpetrators?'

'The second was Lord Hampton's sergeant at arms—his gamekeeper—Tobias Crompton.'

'And the third?' Zac asks wearily.

'Reverend Ezekiel Harrow. Vicar of St Mary's.'

'I don't like where this is heading.'

'You haven't heard the worst,' Prisha murmurs, eyes still glued to the page. 'Guess how the witches were executed?'

'We know one was drowned. Mrs Baker told us that.'

'Another was hanged.'

Zac shakes his head. 'And the third?'

Prisha meets his gaze. *'Buried alive.'*

40

The clack-clack of Prisha's marker pen against the interactive whiteboard is the only sound in the room.

The scent of stale coffee lingers, mingling with the faint chemical tang of dry-wipe pens. Outside, the sky over Whitby is bruised with the fading light of the day, casting a grey pall over the office.

Frank sits at the head of the table, arms folded, expression grim.

Zac shifts in his chair next to him, absentmindedly flipping the braided coin Morrigan gave him in and out of his fingers, a muscle in his jaw twitching.

Superintendent Anne Banks sits directly in front of the whiteboard, silent and watchful, her habitual scowl deepening.

Prisha finishes writing and steps back, surveying the evidence board, checking she's listed everything.

OPERATION WITCH HUNT
CASE OVERVIEW

- **Unidentified Male Foot** – Surgically removed. Found in fire ashes near standing stones. Beltane celebration by Wicca commune.

- **Malachi Abbott** – Deceased – Possibly drowned in Land Rover, River Ure. Brake lines cut. Lord H former gamekeeper. £20,000 in suitcase.

- **Reverend Nicholas Hartley** – Deceased – Found hanged in bell chamber. No bindings. Suicide? Author of The Three Crones.

- **Lord Hampton** – Missing – Last seen Sunday 30 April. No departure record. No sightings.

- **Possible Links** – Two deaths mirror witch executions: Drowning / Hanging.

- **Immediate Actions** – Search Ravensbane Woods. Investigate commune. Trace money. Re-interview villagers.

Anne Banks taps the table with a bony finger. 'I'll tell you one thing you can get rid of right away, inspector,' she snaps. 'The investigation name—Witch Hunt. You're well aware of the connotations—a baseless, often hysterical campaign to persecute or blame individuals without proper evidence. If the media got hold of it, they'd have a field day.'

Frank sighs. 'It's just a working title, Anne, plucked out of thin air.'

'Yes, sounds like it. Pluck another one out of thin air.'

'Very well,' he says glancing first at Zac then Prisha. 'Ideas?'

Zac twiddles the coin. 'How about Operation Ravensbane? That's where the foot was found in the woods, and it's only a mile away from Ashenby and two miles from where Malachi Abbott was dragged from the river?'

Anne shakes her head. 'No. That wood is part of Lord Hampton's Estate. The last thing we need is sightseers descending upon the place. Lady Hampton has enough to contend with. I suggest Operation Raven. Lose the bane.'

'If only we could,' Frank mutters under his breath.

'Sorry, Frank, did you say something?'

'Good choice, Anne. Operation Raven it is.'

Prisha reddens. 'I'm not sure Operation Raven is...'

Anne cuts her off. 'It's just a name. Get on with it, inspector. I have a media briefing in less than an hour and I want to be confident of all the facts in advance. So, please continue, and be succinct. You have a tendency to over-explain.' She turns to Zac. 'In fact, Zac, why don't you give me a quick rundown? You're forthright and to the point.'

Zac glances at Prisha who is in danger of self-combusting, then at Frank, who offers him a weary nod of the head.

'Okay,' he replies joining Prisha at the whiteboard. 'Monday morning, a severed adult male foot was found in the ashes of a fire in Ravensbane Wood near three standing stones known as The Three Crones. The Wicca commune living on Lord Hampton's land held a Beltane celebration there the night before. They left about 2 am. Foot was discovered around 7:40 am by a couple staying at Hexley Farm. One of the Wicca leaders, Violet Fox, admits to them burning dead animals as an offering to the spirits but denies any knowledge of the foot.'

'Who found the foot?' Banks queries.

'Mr and Mrs Topping, from Newcastle.'

'Have you checked them out?'

'Yes. They seem legit. Genuinely shocked. Were eager to get out of there sharpish. Lady Hampton was told about the human remains. She said her husband left for Syria early Monday. But Border Force has no record of departure.

Last phone use was Sunday evening. His car is still missing. CCTV at the castle was of no use.'

'Could the foot be his?'

'No. Lady Hampton says he lost his left foot years ago. We're waiting on DNA.'

'Okay. Go on.'

'Malachi Abbott, Lord Hampton's former gamekeeper. Got the sack a few years back for his fondness of the drink and an *alleged* sexual assault of a young girl from the Wicca commune. It was all kept hush-hush. His body was found in his car in the river Tuesday. Brake lines cut. Last seen Monday at The Crown. Twenty grand in cash at his house. No current job, history of alcohol abuse. Pathology report pending.'

'And today's death?'

'Reverend Hartley vicar of St Mary's in Ashenby. Hanged in the bell tower. Rope looped twice around his neck—no noose, no bindings. Looks like suicide but there are a few disconcerting aspects to it.'

Banks leans back. 'Such as?'

'I spoke to him yesterday about Malachi, and to see if he'd noticed any of his parishioners missing. He was in fine spirits if a little reflective. Was keen to get the new rope attached to the bell, which to me would not indicate someone who was contemplating suicide. Also, the new rope had been cut off at the bottom. Why? We don't know. And lastly, a vicar hanging himself in his own church seems...' He hesitates.

'Seems what, sergeant?'

'Unlikely. Killing yourself inside a consecrated building could be considered sacrilege.'

'I'm assuming St Mary's is Church of England not Catholic?'

'Yes, ma'am.'

'Catholics still view suicide as a mortal sin. The Church of England has more moderate views. I don't think where the vicar was found has any bearing on the matter.'

Zac dips his head. 'Ma'am.'

Banks muses. 'A foot. A drowning. A hanging, and a missing Lord. Lovely. Have the next of kin been informed?'

'Yes, ma'am.'

She glances at Frank. 'So, the million-dollar question; are they connected?'

Prisha steps forward clutching the book. 'I think they are, ma'am. *The Three Crones*, written by Reverend Hartley. It describes three witches who were tried near the standing stones. They were found guilty of witchcraft by the ancestor of the current Lord Hampton, his gamekeeper, and the local vicar of St Mary's at the time.'

'Witches. When exactly was this?'

'They were executed in 1647. One drowned, one hanged, and one buried alive. The book includes a photo—an old drift mine in Ravensbane Woods. Hartley believed it was where the third woman was buried. It's possible that's where Lord Hampton is.'

'Do you have an exact location?'

'No. Just a photo in the book.'

'How old's that book?'

'From 1985.'

Banks purses her lips. 'And that's your connection and theory? A forty-year-old book about local folklore from 1647. I suggest you focus your efforts on facts, evidence, and forensics, inspector, instead of these flights of fancy. Until we confirm the cause of death, we don't even know if these are homicides. At the moment one looks like an accident and the other as someone who'd had enough.'

'But Hampton *is* missing ma'am. He could be in that mine.'

'Ninety-six thousand adults go missing every year. Most are found quickly.'

'And some end up dead.'

Superintendent Bank's leaps from her chair and slaps a palm on the table.

'Inspector Kumar! Why do you always have to lock horns with me on every major investigation? We have systems and protocols in place. We not only follow the book, but we must be *seen* to follow the book.' She turns to Frank. 'I believe you questioned Lady Hampton today?'

'Yes, along with Prisha.'

'Any threats? Blackmail? Suspicious activity at the castle?'

'No, Anne.'

'And did you find anything to arouse your suspicion during the search of the castle and the grounds?'

'No.'

She takes a deep breath composing herself. 'Then it seems obvious. Lord Hampton has either had a medical episode or accident whilst driving and gone over an edge, or he's driven to a remote spot and regrettably taken his own life. It's way too early to start assuming foul play. And as for the nonsense about witches and standing stones... well, it may make a great horror film but I prefer my officers to stay grounded in reality.' Her eyes dart from Prisha, to Zac, finally resting on Frank. 'Right, keep me updated on any major developments, Frank.'

'Yes, Anne.'

'Oh, and we need to set aside some time next week to discuss proposed budget cuts for the next fiscal year, and possibly some re-adjustment of personnel.'

Frank grimaces, wondering why she needed to mention it in front of his officers.

'Right, I see. Well, you have access to my calendar.'

She sweeps a glance around the room, her gaze landing on Dinkel in the far corner wearing headphones. 'What's that lad up to? He's not listening to music I hope?'

'He's not. I've given him a cold case to work on. He's listening to a police interview recording.'

'Ah, I see. Well keep up the good work everyone.' As she heads away, she touches Frank on the arm and leads him to the far end of the room. Leaning in, she lowers her voice. 'I want you to keep a tight leash on Calamity Jane. I don't want her gallivanting around the countryside like a lone wild west sheriff. This is a sensitive case. Lord Hampton has influence. I want this investigation to run like clockwork. Tick all the boxes. By the book. We need to control the situation, not let the situation control us.'

'I think you're being a little unfair on Prisha, Anne. Her track record at solving tough cases is unparalleled.'

'And the devastation she leaves behind is also unparalleled. She's like a bloody tornado, and sooner or later, her luck will run out.'

She strides out. The door clicks shut.

Prisha hurls the whiteboard marker across the room. It ricochets off a wall and hits Dinkel in the back of the head nearly dislodging his eyeballs.

'Aaaaargh! That woman,' she screams, fists clenched.

Zac shakes his head. 'I bet she needs a checklist to take a shit.'

Frank steps forward and gently takes Prisha's fists. 'It's been a long tiring day. Tempers are frayed. I suggest a relaxing drink at the White House. Zac's shout.'

His smile is warm, steady, fatherly.

41

Meera stares at Frank's reflection in the bathroom mirror and stops rubbing moisturiser into her face.

'What do you mean by shenanigans?' she asks, seeking clarification

Frank peels off his jocks and drops them into the laundry basket. 'You know, Tomfoolery.'

'Tomfoolery?'

'Yes, jiggery-pokery, how's yer father,' he replies, staring at the shower suspiciously.

Meera turns to him. 'You're talking about Prisha and Zac, yes?'

'Do you ever listen to a bloody word I say?'

'If you could speak in plain English, it may help.'

Frank abandons the thought of a shower and stares at his wife. 'They want their bread buttered both sides.'

'What does that mean?'

Frank harrumphs and grabs his toothbrush. 'What I'm trying to say is that something's going on.'

Meera frowns and asks a tentative question. 'You mean… in a sexual way?'

'Aye, shenanigans.'

Meera is shocked as Frank squirts an overzealous amount of toothpaste onto his brush, losing half of it in the sink.

'But Zac is happily married with two gorgeous boys, and Prisha's engaged to that lovely farmer—what's his name again—Adam?'

'Aye, well. The grass is always greener in Farmer Boddington's field.'

Meera shakes her head, refusing to go down that rabbit hole. 'And what evidence do you have to make such an accusation?'

The foam from the toothpaste is rapidly multiplying like an alien virus as it slithers from Frank's mouth, down his chin, and onto the bathroom floor.

'I'm a bloody detective. I notice things.'

'What things?'

'Things!' he shouts sending a fine splatter of spray onto the bathroom mirror.

'It doesn't make sense,' Meera replies as she washes her hands under the warm tap.

'It happens in this job, Meera. There's always a great weight above, pressing down. Danger. Confined spaces. A disaster around the corner.'

'You make them sound like coal miners. Surely they wouldn't be that reckless with other people's hearts?'

'Not everyone's like us, love. Different vibes today. When we wed, it was for better or for worse.'

Meera reflects, wistfully. 'Yes, I remember.'

'Young ones today, they don't know what commitment means. They're not willing to do the hard, monotonous slog, year in, year out. Like pushing a boulder up a never-ending hill. Relentless.'

'Is that how you see our marriage?'

'Nay, I wasn't talking about us, love,' he says, quickly backtracking.

'Then who were you talking about?'

'Other folk.' He rinses his brush under the cold water, taps it on the enamel basin and drops it back in the tumbler. 'By the way,' he adds, changing the subject, 'where are all my underpants? I've none in the drawer and there's none on the line or in the tumble dryer.'

'I don't know.'

'Bloody champion! That means I'll have to walk into work tomorrow, commando fashion.'

Meera glances down. 'I think that tackle needs at least two layers of fabric between you and the unsuspecting public, Frank. During my lunch hour tomorrow, I'll buy you a new set. Until then, you can wear a pair of mine.'

'Yours! Like hell! I'll turn over in my grave before I wear women's knickers!' he bellows.

'They're not knickers. They're trunks. Not much different to mens, apart from a slightly higher hip line. I only have them in pink though.'

'What if something should happen to me? I can hear Whipple now. *My conclusion, the chief inspector was a sexual deviant, indubitably.*'

'You plan on dying tomorrow, Frank?'

'That's not the point. I had seven pairs, and now there's one in the basket. They can't just vanish.'

'Oh.'

'What do you mean, "oh"?'

Meera appears contrite. 'Over the last few months, as your underwear makes it through the washing cycle, I've been discarding a few.'

'Why?'

'Some had holes in them, others, the elastic was gone. Then there were the ones that... well, let's not go there.'

'Wonderful. Sabotaged by my own wife.'

'Anyway, shut up about your damned underpants. It's not important.'

'It bloody is to me.'

She follows him into the bedroom and throws the sheets back. 'This thing about Prisha and Zac is really upsetting me. Are you one hundred per cent certain?'

Frank climbs into bed, slips his spectacles on, and picks up his nighttime reading—Dunkirk.

'When you know, you know.'

'If this gets out, then it's going to be…'

'… a right shit fight.'

'I was going to say—a disaster for a lot of people. You need to have a word. Make them see sense.'

He frowns at her. 'And what am I supposed to say? They're not kids. They won't appreciate me interfering.'

'Just make them realise they're playing with fire and it's not worth it. Please Frank, for me, speak to them?'

He can't resist her pleading eyes. 'Okay, love. I'll have a quiet word. But when it comes to affairs of the heart, logic flies out of the window.'

He kisses her on the forehead, and she rolls onto her side as he opens his book and settles back.

Meera yawns and snuggles into her pillow as a long weary day finally ends.

'I mean, we've all made silly mistakes, haven't we,' she murmurs as her eyes close.

'Aye,' Frank replies, already engrossed in his book. His focus dissipates as Meera's words float around his mind. He lowers the book. 'Hang on a minute, what the hell's that supposed to mean?'

'What?'

'We've all made silly mistakes?'

'Nothing. Go to sleep.'

42

Friday 5th May

Frank hangs his jacket on the coat rack, slumps into his chair, then pulls the bacon and egg butty from the paper bag. Taking a bite, he closes his eyes and relaxes in the early morning tranquillity. The serenity doesn't last long as the door to the incident room bangs shut. He glances out of his office window as Zac enters, appearing slightly bedraggled, not his usual neatly groomed self. Frank holds his hand in the air and motions him forward.

Zac enters, yawning. 'Morning, Frank.'

'Morning, Zac. Take a seat.'

He sits down. 'Any developments?'

Frank shrugs. 'Don't know. I haven't even lifted the lid on my laptop yet. I like to start the day with a bite to eat and a cup of tea before I let the real world in.'

Zac stares at him, slightly bemused. 'Right. So, what do you want to talk to me about?'

Frank takes another bite of his roll and washes it down with a slurp of tea, before carefully dabbing at his mouth with a serviette.

'Oh, nothing in particular. Just wanted to see how you're travelling, you know, in general.'

Zac relaxes back. 'I'm fine.'

A pause ensues.

'Good, good. And the family, how are they doing?'

'Yeah, all good. Thanks for asking.'

'The boys?'

'They're a handful, as boys are at their age, but no, they're both good lads. No problems.'

'That's great to hear. And Kelly?'

'Yeah, she's fine.'

'No problems?'

Zac frowns. 'No. Should there be?'

Frank emits a chuckle. 'Oh, you know. Marriage is never a walk in the park, is it? It's always a work in progress.'

'Suppose.' He shuffles in his seat. 'Look, Frank, what's all this about?'

Frank pulls his most innocent hurt look, which, to be honest, is not very convincing.

'I just worry about you. As your boss, I have a duty to ensure the welfare of all my officers. It's not all about nabbing villains. I care.'

Zac is even more suspicious. 'You *care*?'

Frank clears his throat. 'Aye, that's right, *care*.'

Zac tires of the conversation and rises. 'Right, I better crack on. Hopefully, the post-mortem results will be in on Malachi Abbott and Reverend Hartley. It will make things a little clearer if we know the exact cause of death.'

'Okay. And think on.'

As he pulls at the door, he stops and stares back. 'Think on about what?'

'Our little chat about family. Cherish it.'

'Cherish our chat?'

'No! Not the bloody chat. Cherish your family. They're important. Number one, always.'

'Right, got it.'

As Zac meanders across the incident room to his desk, Frank relaxes back, pleased with a job well done.

'Let's hope the bugger sees sense. I couldn't have made it any clearer. He'll thank me for it one day.' Finishing off his butty, he notices Prisha arrive. He waves and beckons her forward.

She enters his office, yawning. 'Morning, Frank.'

'Morning, Prisha. Now, how are you travelling, and how's that fella of yours going—Adam? Take a seat.'

Prisha makes a cup of coffee and ambles over to Zac, her brow furrowed in a puzzled expression.

'Hey Zac, have you spoken with Frank this morning?'

'Aye, just before you arrived,' he replies, as his laptop flickers into life.

'What was he like?'

'Rambling like a dementia patient in a wheelie bin. Mind you, he is at that age. He's turning into the mad uncle no one wants to sit next to at a wedding reception.'

'Yeah, he was like that with me. Wanted to know how I was getting on with Adam. Asked if we were still courting, and if we planned to live *over-the-brush*. After I'd asked for a translation, he waffled on about how we need to cherish, honour, and be faithful to those we love. Wanted to know if we'd set a date for the wedding.'

'And have you?' Zac asks, as he swiftly scans the mountain of unopened emails awaiting him.

'No. Then he ended by saying that...' She pauses. *'That he cared.* I have to say, it quite unnerved me.'

Zac pulls his gaze away from the screen and looks up at her.

'Odd. He was asking me about the family and...' He freezes, then groans. 'Oh, I get it. This is about yesterday and you taking off in a huff. I told you he noticed something was wrong. His fatherly chat was a friendly warning shot across our bows.' He pauses and chuckles. 'Maybe a new career beckons. I can see him as a marriage guidance counsellor. Aunty Frank—the listening ear.'

Prisha winces. 'Christ. The divorce rates would skyrocket.'

The conversation is interrupted as Dinkel enters, smiling way too broadly for such a godforsaken hour.

'Morning chaps,' he shouts cheerfully as he joins them.

'What are you looking so happy about, Dinkel?' Zac grizzles.

'Nothing,' he says, suddenly feeling guilty. He hangs around like a bad smell before finally saying, 'I watched a fascinating programme on YouTube last night.'

'Really,' Zac replies as he refocuses on his emails. 'Well, don't let us keep you.'

Dinkel, naturally immune to social cues, continues. 'It was about this American girl. Well, I say girl, she's actually a woman but...'

Frank appears in his doorway and cuts him off. 'Oi, bug-a-lugs, when you have a minute, you can give me an update on the carjacking case you're working.'

'Right, yes sir.' Dinkel scuttles off to his desk to retrieve a folder.

Zac throws Dinkel a dismissive glance. 'Which just goes to prove—dementia can affect the young as well as the old.' He turns back to his screen. 'Here we go, the interim post-mortem reports from pathology. Looks like Whipple's been busy.'

Prisha leans over his shoulder a little too closely, but neither adjusts their positions.

'What do they say?'

'Hang on, give me a minute. I'll read Reverend Hartley's first. I'm an expert at deciphering Whipple's tech-speak. Okay—death's consistent with hanging. Compression of the carotid arteries, cutting off blood flow to the brain, and asphyxia from airway compression. Cervical vertebrae intact, which means he didn't fall far — otherwise his neck would've snapped. No other signs of injury. Hypoxia and vagal reflex would've knocked him unconscious within a couple of minutes, if not sooner, followed by full cardiac arrest not long after.' He turns and looks up at Prisha. 'And apart from being dead, he was fit and healthy.'

She leans in closer. 'But he also notes there was no self-tightening knot, which is often the case in suicide hangings. Okay, it confirms what we knew; he died from hanging but it doesn't answer our questions as to why.'

'And you know Whipple's reply to that? *The post-mortem establishes the cause of death, inspector, not the mechanism by which it occurred. I believe that falls within your remit,'* he rumbles in a deep, plodding baritone.

Prisha smiles. 'That's very good. Okay, what about Malachi Abbott?'

Zac opens the next email. 'Cause of death is listed as drowning. Lungs were full of water, so he was still alive when the car entered the river. There's a sizeable bump on the forehead, just above the right eye—likely from hitting the dashboard or windscreen when he went through the wall.'

'No seatbelt, so that figures.'

'No other injuries noted. Blood alcohol level came in at twice the legal limit. So definitely under the influence. Matches what we know.'

Prisha nods in agreement. 'He was a heavy drinker, so that much booze probably wouldn't have flattened him like it would a moderate drinker.'

'True. But here's the interesting bit. Toxicology picked up traces of an unidentified compound in his blood and stomach contents. Described as a plant-based alkaloid. They've flagged it for further testing. Might be nothing, but they're not ruling it out. Said it's unusual enough to warrant further investigation.'

Prisha takes a step back, deep in thought. 'Likely scenario; three shots of whisky and a pint at the pub, jumps in his car, encounters the steep hill and sharp bend, hits the brakes which don't work, slams through the wall, knocks himself out, car rolls into the river, he drowns.'

'Pretty much,' Zac says.

'But the tox screen raises a question mark. Could be something in his system that made him more drowsy or disoriented than just the alcohol alone. We won't know for sure until the full report's in.'

'Hang on,' Zac says, opening another email. 'We're on a roll today. This one's from forensics.'

Prisha straightens. 'What is it?'

'The money in Malachi's suitcase. They've tested the top and bottom notes of each bundle, like we asked.' He grins. 'Bingo.'

'Go on,' she urges.

'Lord Hampton's fingerprints. Clear as day on every note.'

'Okay, now we're getting somewhere, Zac. Malachi was living hand to mouth, yet he's sitting on twenty grand in cash, covered in Hampton's prints.'

'Looks like a pay-off to me.'

'Exactly. Right, I want you at the Designer Outlet in York as soon as they open. See if they have CCTV of who bought that suitcase.'

Zac nods. 'What about you?'

'I'm heading to Ravensbane Castle. I want another word with the Wicca lot—and Lady Hampton, and if I can summon up the courage, revisit Malachi's cottage, see if I missed anything.'

He hesitates. 'You think Lady Hampton might be involved?'

Prisha pauses, chewing her lower lip. 'Not sure. She's been helpful so far. Doesn't come across like someone wrapped up in murder or secret cash drops.'

'But?'

She meets his eye. 'Some people wear a very convincing mask.'

43

Zac eyes the shopping centre with disdain. A gleaming, soulless glass edifice, already teeming with shoppers. The place is too bright, too loud, too full of people moving in slow, aimless clumps, dragging bags stuffed with overpriced junk. He hates shopping at the best of times. Shopping centres? A special circle of hell.

He parks up, wishing he was somewhere else, when something catches his eye. A flash of polished chrome, red trim, and curved fenders—like a Cadillac fresh off the showroom floor. The van gleams under artificial lighting, its sleek metallic body a perfect replica of a 1950s American diner on wheels. A neon sign flickers above the serving hatch: Gourmet Hotdogs & Fries.

Then the aroma hits him.

Not the greasy tang of bog-standard fairground hotdogs but something richer, smokier. Spiced sausage, slow-grilled onions, maybe even truffle oil. The kind of thing food bloggers queue an hour for.

His stomach tightens in anticipation.

'Every cloud...' he mutters. He makes a mental note to grab one on the way out—something to look forward to after the air-conditioned nightmare.

With that sliver of optimism banked, he squares his shoulders and pushes through the glass doors.

Inside, the air is thick with artificial perfume, a blend of expensive candles and cheap aftershave. He passes a dozen shops flogging designer gear at eye-watering prices. A row of mannequins gawk at him from a high-end fashion boutique, dressed in outfits that cost more than his fortnightly mortgage payment. A cosmetics counter blasts out some chirpy pop tune, the sales assistant grinning with the hollow enthusiasm of someone forced to flog fifty quid face creams for a living.

He hates places like this. The sterile polish. The fake smiles. The music, a constant looping drone of inoffensive chart hits that regurgitate the three-chord trick until you want to vomit.

Whatever happened to music? he thinks.

Luckily, the Samsonite luggage store isn't far.

He clocks it on the left, bright and clinical, rows of pristine suitcases arranged like an art display. He exhales slowly, relieved to see only two customers inside—a couple in their sixties, leisurely browsing the hard-shell suitcases. No queue, no hassle. Should be quick.

Behind the counter, an older woman in thick-framed glasses is hunched over a sheaf of papers, oblivious to his arrival.

'Excuse me,' he says, flashing his ID. 'DS Stoker, CID. Are you the manager?'

She looks up sharply. A flicker of something crosses her face—not quite fear, but close. No one likes a copper turning up unannounced.

'I am. What's it about?'

He slides a crumpled receipt across the counter. 'I'm investigating a serious crime. A suitcase was purchased here recently. I need to confirm who bought it. Do you remember the customer, or would your CCTV still have the footage?'

She picks up the receipt, adjusting her glasses as she studies the date and time. 'Hmm. I was working that day, and at ten o'clock I'd have been on the floor, but... I don't recall selling this particular case.'

Zac pulls a dog-eared photo from his jacket—a grainy copy of Malachi Abbott's driver licence photo, enlarged and reprinted to the point of blur.

'This is the man who we think purchased the suitcase. Apologies for the quality.'

The manager studies it, frowning slightly, then shakes her head.

'No, I don't recognise him at all. Not our typical customer. But if you'd like to check the CCTV, follow me.'

She leads him into a back office, a cramped little box reeking of stale coffee and printer toner. The only furniture is a desk, a battered old laptop, and a chair that looks like it was nicked from a school. A tiny, wall-mounted safe sits above the desk, the keypad worn shiny from use. The place has the impersonal air of every back office he's ever been in—functional, cluttered, and somehow very depressing.

The manager drops into the chair and clicks open a programme. The laptop screen flickers, then loads a series of time-stamped files.

'We keep footage for thirty days before it resets. Shoplifters. They're getting more frequent and brazen. Work in gangs now. Of course, your lot are no good. By the time you turn up, if you do at all, then they're long gone,' she explains, scanning the dates. 'Right... here we go. This is from the day on your receipt.'

She skips forward to 9:55 am. Zac leans over her shoulder, eyes fixed on the grainy feed. The camera captures a wide shot of the store, four customers visible. Two women—who he instantly discounts. One man—too young, and the last man is black.

'Keep it rolling,' he says, frowning slightly as he checks the time-stamp again.

At exactly 10:00 am, a figure moves towards the till, placing a compact suitcase on the counter.

'Oh, it wasn't me who served them,' the manager murmurs. 'That's my assistant.'

Zac watches closely. The footage is grainy but clear enough to make out the small details—the flick of a credit card, the assistant tapping at the till, the slow rhythm of a transaction playing out.

Something's not right.

'Wait. Freeze it. Can you get closer on that?'

The manager double-clicks. The screen blurs, then refocuses on a section of the footage.

Zac frowns. 'Are you sure about the date, April 19th?'

She nods, pointing to the time-stamp in the top-right corner. 'See for yourself.'

He exhales slowly. 'Alright. Keep it rolling.'

The figure turns.

Zac stiffens.

It's not Malachi Abbott.

Not even close.

The manager lets out a quiet chuckle. 'Well, that's not your man, sergeant.'

His jaw tightens as the investigation takes a sinister turn.

'Not even the right sex,' he mutters.

A leaden weight settles in his gut. They'd been sure Malachi had bought the suitcase. The ride out here had been solely to confirm the fact. Tick another box. Now he's left with more questions than when he arrived.

44

The car slows as a magnificent peacock struts across the gravel driveway—each step a display of effortless arrogance, its electric-blue chest gleaming in the morning sun. It halts near a drab peahen and shudders its opulent tail into a shimmering fan of emerald and bronze, each 'eye' a hypnotic swirl of cobalt and gold—an unapologetic overture, impossible to ignore.

The peahen appears to be playing 'hard-to-get', offering nothing but indifference.

If it could yawn, Prisha is fairly sure it would.

Still, she smiles—partly at the absurdity of it all, partly at how often nature mirrors human behaviour. She waits patiently until the bird crosses onto the manicured lawn, its pride unbruised.

Exiting the car, she skips up the steps to the castle as her phone rings.

'Zac, that was fast work. Have you confirmed what we thought?'

'Not quite. Where are you?'

'Just arrived at Ravensbane. What do you mean, "not quite"? Did Malachi buy the suitcase or not?'

'He didn't. Guess who did?'

Prisha's mind kicks into gear. 'Lord Hampton?'

'Wrong again. One more guess.'

'Zac, stop pissing about. Who bought the suitcase?'

'Lady Hampton.'

'You're shitting me?'

'I shit ye not. Footage was a bit grainy, but it was definitely her.'

'Did you get a copy?'

'Of course.'

'Right, I want you back here as soon as. I'm about to quiz Lady Hampton again, then I'll pay another visit to the commune. What's that noise?' she asks as a muffled, disgusting sound drifts into her ear.

'Just munching on a gourmet sausage outside the shopping centre. A chilli-dog, loaded with fried onions, swimming in mustard, in a soft white roll. I'm in heaven. Might get another.'

'Greedy sod. Right, call me when you're a couple of miles away.'

———◆———

When Prisha first met Lady Hampton, she exuded calm confidence. Today, she looks older—fine lines hugging the corners of her eyes. The sparkle dimmed. Her hands clasped close to her chest instead of resting, assured, at her waist.

This time, she doesn't offer refreshments. Not even a nod towards a seat.

Her mouth tightens. 'Good news, bad news, or no news, Inspector Kumar?' she asks, bracing for the worst.

Prisha offers a sympathetic half-smile. 'No news, I'm afraid.'

A sigh of relief and a composed nod. 'Well, they say no news is good news, so I'll take that as a positive.' She turns to the large French windows. 'Is it true about the vicar, Reverend Hartley? That he's... dead.'

Prisha shuffles and sighs. 'I'm afraid so. Yesterday. His body was found inside the church. Do you and your husband attend the church?'

'What? Erm, no. We did up until about three years ago, when Reverend Hartley returned. Noah and the reverend didn't exactly see eye to eye.'

'Why?'

Lady Hampton slips quietly into a high armchair and cradles her hands.

'My husband is an enlightened man, but when it comes to the church, he's a traditionalist. He doesn't have much time for the "Rainbow Collared Clergy" as he refers to the new generation of woke vicars. He thinks the church should be preaching the word of the Gospel, not gender politics. Still, I always liked Reverend Hartley. A quiet, gentle man, if a troubled soul.'

Prisha's ears prick up. 'A troubled soul?'

'Oh, I'm sorry. I'm speaking out of turn. That was purely my impression of him. As though he carried a burden.'

'I believe this was his second stint at Ashenby?'

'Yes. He was here in the late eighties, before my time. I met Noah some years after the reverend had moved on.'

Prisha checks her watch. 'You may have seen the news last night. Superintendent Banks gave a media briefing on your husband's disappearance, and we've released details to the social media sites. However, it's a double-edged sword. It may yield results. Sightings, hopefully. But on the downside, as it's a high-profile case, you can expect the media to turn up outside your front gates. I'd strongly advise that you don't engage with them at the moment. And I'd also warn your staff to do the same.'

An intensely private woman, Lady Hampton deflates like a burst balloon.

'Oh, dear,' she murmurs.

Prisha gives her a moment to digest the news. 'Did you manage to sleep last night?'

She turns towards the window, gazing out over the rolling countryside and the dark swathe of Ravensbane Wood.

'A little. Restless. My mind won't stop. Where is he, inspector?' she pleads. 'None of it makes sense. He didn't catch his flight. You said his car wasn't recorded on any major roads. He's not in hospital. You've searched the grounds. All I can think is that he's gone off the road somewhere. The lanes around here are narrow, winding—sharp bends, steep hills.'

'We've conducted multiple patrols looking for any signs. So far, nothing. But we'll keep searching.'

'Yes, of course. It wasn't a criticism, inspector. I know how much effort is being put into this, and I appreciate it.'

Time for the harder questions.

'Yesterday you told DCI Finnegan and myself that there are no financial worries.'

'That's correct.'

'And you're quite certain your husband isn't or wasn't having an affair?'

'Absolutely positive. The very notion is ridiculous.'

'And you haven't received any calls or letters?'

She spins around, puzzled. 'From?'

'Blackmail or threats, Lady Hampton.'

Her head jolts back. 'No. I explained all this to you and Mr Finnegan yesterday.'

Prisha watches her carefully. 'Just one final thing, Lady Hampton.'

'Yes?'

'Have you been to the Designer Outlet in York recently?'

Her eyebrows lift, wary. 'Yes, why?'

'On April 19th, you bought a suitcase from the Samsonite store. Is that correct?'

A pause. Then, 'Yes. But how do you know?'

'Can you tell me where it is now?'

A moment of silence.

'I can't say for certain. But I can make an educated guess.'

'Go on.'

'It's probably still in the back of my husband's Mercedes.'

45

Frank descends into Grimscar Quarry on foot, the path narrow and treacherous, half-eaten by gorse and nettle. His boots slip once on the wet shale, sending a clatter of stone into the hollow below. He steadies himself with a muttered curse. Grimscar lives up to its name—a dark wound in the land, silent and desolate, the kind of place that swallows things.

PC Jackson waits near the wreck, high-vis jacket dulled by the sepia-coloured landscape, shoulders hunched against the wind. He nods a greeting as Frank approaches.

'An old lass out walking her dog called it in a couple of hours ago, Frank.'

The Mercedes sits half-crushed at the base of the cliff, its shell warped and blackened, long since cold. No heat, no smoke—just tangled metal. The windows are gone. The roof buckled inward. Whatever fire gutted it did its job days ago.

Frank takes it in slowly. The air smells faintly of char and moss, oil and damp stone. Burn patterns radiate from the boot, which gapes open at an awkward angle.

He leans over for a closer look. Melted handles, twisted zips, an ash pile of what used to be clothes.

'Numberplate and engine number?' Frank asks.

'Hampton's, sir. Confirmed on the system.'

Frank squats beside the wreck and peers into the driver's side. No blood. No bones. No scorched silhouette. The interior's empty, save for seat springs and warped plastic. He runs a hand across his mouth, thinking, as he turns to take in the layout of the quarry.

'No direct vehicle access,' he says, looking up. 'Probably set alight at the top and pushed over the edge.'

Jackson gestures vaguely upwards. 'There's a break in the fence up there. Tyre tracks on the grass, but nothing useful. Been too long. Rain's washed most of it out.'

The cliff's edge looms above them, jagged and overgrown. Fifty feet, sheer in places. The rock face shows fresh gouges where something heavy scraped its way down.

'So... was it dumped here early Monday morning, or is it more recent?' Frank mutters.

'Doesn't look recent,' Jackson replies.

Frank nods, gaze fixed on the wreck. He doesn't like how quiet it is down here.

'I'll get forensics down here, and a couple of uniforms to grid-search the area, cliff edge too. Until then, I want this site manned. Can you stay put until they arrive, Jacko?'

Jackson nods. 'Yes, Frank.'

Frank turns to leave, then pauses. He casts one last look at the ruin of the car—its blackened carcass, boot yawning like a mouth mid-scream.

'Either someone's done away with Hampton before dumping his car,' he mutters, 'or a certain person's playing silly buggers.'

Jackson frowns. 'Frank?'

Frank smiles without humour. 'Never mind, Jacko. Just thinking aloud. Good work.'

He sets off back up the path, coat flapping behind him. The quarry closes in at his back, quiet as a sealed crypt.

46

Prisha makes her way down the gravel track towards the Wicca commune, leaving the castle behind. Wood smoke hangs on the breeze, earthy and sweet. She can smell it before she sees the cabins through the thinning trees. From this angle, the place looks deserted.

It's warm for the time of year. A faint sheen on her neck, sunlight dancing off greenery. She slows her pace, taking it in. To the south, dark woods stretch far and silent. To the west, the fields rise and fall like gentle waves. The walled vegetable garden is to her right, and inside, a handful of people move between raised beds with quiet purpose.

It looks... ideal. Too ideal. A bubble. Self-contained. A place where time folds in on itself and refuses to budge. For a moment—just a flicker—she feels the tug of something.

Jealousy, maybe.

As she steps through the open gate, the silence deepens. No chatter, no kids playing, no one. Just the low crackle of the fire pit and a strange floral scent drifting in and out like a memory.

A dull clang echoes from behind one of the cabins. She heads over, keeping her tread light.

Around the back, a young man kneels by a bank of tangled wiring, screwdriver between his teeth.

'Hello,' she says.

The tool drops from his mouth with a muffled thud as he startles. He looks up, wide-eyed.

'Bloody hell. You gave me a right fright.'

'Sorry.' She holds up her ID. 'DI Kumar, CID.'

He rises, brushes down his trousers. Early twenties, lanky build, hands nicked and grimy.

'Right. I heard someone say the police'd been by. Any word on Noah?'

First-name terms. Interesting.

'I'm afraid not. Still ongoing. Where is everyone?'

He shrugs, easing into something close to friendly. 'Kids are in the schoolhouse. Men off doing jobs—veggie garden, goats, pigs, fencing.'

'And the women?'

A flicker. Small crease at the corner of his eye. 'They're in witan.'

'What?'

'A meeting.'

'Oh, I see. What's your name?'

'Birch.'

She lifts an eyebrow. 'Unusual name.'

He grins. 'Name I was given when I joined.'

'I see. What was your name before?'

His grin fades. Just for a second. He steps back half a pace. 'Am I under arrest?'

She chuckles. 'No, of course not. Just curious.'

He nods slowly. 'We give that stuff up when we join. Names, possessions. Old baggage. Everyone does. Males are named after native trees and shrubs. Females after flowers.'

She gives a non-committal nod. 'And what did you do before you joined the commune?'

'Auto electrician.'

'Bit of a leap from that to this.'

He shrugs, gestures at the cabling. 'Still get to tinker. Solar panels have been playing up. Conduit had a perforation, moisture got in, connector rusted out. Just fixing it up.'

She looks at the narrow box mounted to the cabin wall.

'Battery bank?'

'Aye. Solar and battery banks—way cheaper than the grid in the long run. More reliable, too. We only need it for lighting in the cabins, and the hot water.'

She runs her eye over him. 'Most of the people I've seen here are early thirties, to early forties. You're younger. What, twenty-five?'

'Twenty-four.'

'So, why'd you pack it all in?'

He shifts, eyes focus on the far fence line. 'Long story cut short; was engaged. House, joint mortgage, overtime up to my eyeballs. Two weeks before the wedding, I find out she'd been shagging someone behind my back for eighteen months. I flipped.'

She doesn't interrupt. Just watches on.

'We sold the house. I quit work. Bought a Kombi, drove round the country for a bit. Did some thinking. Realised I was living someone else's life. One night I was in The Crown in Ashenby, having a pint, feeling sorry for myself. Got chatting to Oak.'

'Oak?'

'He oversees the men. Sort of like a gaffer. Makes sure jobs are getting done, that kind of thing.'

'So, you joined up?'

'Eventually. Had to show I was serious. They don't take just anyone. No room for freeloaders. You join because you believe there's a better way.'

'How long have you been here?'

'Six months.'

'Do you enjoy it?'

He smiles, genuine this time. 'I love it. Quiet. Honest work. No bollocks. No one breathing down my neck. I wake up to birdsong. I sleep under stars. No commute. No banks robbing you blind. I wish I'd joined years ago.'

'And your family? Parents? Mates?'

He lifts his chin. 'We're not locked in here, if that's what you're asking. We can visit, call, whatever. We're free to leave whenever.' His jaw tightens. 'This isn't a cult. I know that's what people think. But it's not. We live by mutual respect. If you do your bit, you're welcome. That's all there is to it.'

'And if someone doesn't *do* their bit?'

He shrugs. 'The women hold counsel. If they all agree, the person's banished into the wilderness.'

She raises an eyebrow and sniggers 'Banished into the wilderness? You make it sound biblical. This is North Yorkshire, not the Sinai Desert.'

He scowls. 'The wilderness is that mess out there. The place where you still live.'

'Apologies. I meant no offence.' She realises she's put him offside and gazes around, her eyes falling onto a spread of vibrant green plants budding with beautiful hues of purple and violet, sheltered behind the cabin. 'Looks like a lovely plant,' she adds, trying to get him back onside.

He glances over his shoulder, then smiles. 'Devil's Helmet.'

'Sorry?'

'Monkshood. Starting to bud early this year due to the warm spring, according to Oak.'

She nods slowly. Monkshood. The name rings a bell, but she can't recall why. She files it away. Just in case.

'It'll look stunning when it flowers.'

She turns to go. Birch crouches again, picks up his screwdriver. 'Was there anything in particular you wanted, inspector? I can pass it on to counsel.'

She hesitates a second.

'No. Just a courtesy call. No developments on Lord Hampton yet, but we're still looking. Good luck with the battery bank.'

'Cheers.'

She's already heading back towards the path when his voice calls out behind her.

'By the way. My name's Kelvin. Kelvin Potter,' he says with a wide, cheeky grin.

She stops. Turns halfway.

'Bye, Kelvin.'

As he disappears around the back of the cabin, she notices a flurry of activity from the far lodge and garbled female voices. She takes a step sideways into the shadow of a large Hawthorn bush bedecked in white flowers, offering a sweet scent. She takes care to avoid the prickly thorns. The commune leader, Violet, leads a procession of women down the wooden steps as they all chatter independently.

Prisha squints against the morning sun as she sees an older woman. 'That's the postmistress, Lilac Penhallow. What's she doing here?' She's even more surprised when she notices the librarian and teacher emerge. 'Lunara and Prudence Ashcroft. Why are those three part of the commune's meetings?'

Puzzled, she slinks away and follows the path back to Ravensbane Castle.

47

Prisha dry retches as she opens the fridge door. She pulls out a tissue and clamps it over her nose. No human body parts—just a couple of whole rabbits, fur and all, staring back at her with dead, glassy eyes, long past their use-by date. A conga-line of maggots wriggle around their mouths and in other foodstuffs too gruesome to identify. She slams the door shut feeling her breakfast lurch in her stomach.

The itchiness returns with a vengeance as she tiptoes around Malachi's house and picks up various items with the outermost tips of her finger and thumb, arm outstretched.

'Oh, yuk. I think even the rats have moved out,' she mutters. Despite her professionalism, she point-blank refuses to go upstairs and take another step into the bedroom. From her first inspection, and confirmed by forensics, it was pretty barren.

She inspects an ancient bureau in the corner which yields nothing apart from bank statements and some very old letters from Malachi's mother, and an unsent one from

Malachi. A few have date stamps on them, the last being from 1989.

Closing the front door behind her, she padlocks it shut, and heaves in the sweet, fresh air, but the smell lingers on her clothes, hair, and skin.

'Oh gawd,' she moans quietly.

'Back again, I see,' the croaky voice of an elderly woman calls out.

She spins around and offers a smile to the woman standing on her doorstep, pinafore on, arms folded.

'Hello, Mrs Selkirk. How are you doing?'

'Better than that bugger next door,' she says, breaking out into a cackle. 'I didn't think he'd be pushing up daisies before me. I'm ninety-five, you know. Mind you,' she reflects, downcast, 'I've stayed too long. Seen both of me own bairns pass away, and my husband, and five brothers, and my little sister. There's only me left now.' She hesitates, then brightens. 'Would you like a cuppa? I've got the kettle on and a nice fruit cake on the go.'

Prisha swallows hard.

Every sinew and fibre in her body screams no.

Every molecule in her brain retreats in fear.

She peers into the old lady's eyes. That hopeful, expectant glint, still there even after all the sorrow she must have endured, and now, completely and utterly alone.

Something stirs inside. Images of her own grandmother come flooding back. She hasn't visited for over eight months, even though they talk on the phone once a week.

Mrs Selkirk's smile begins to fade, anticipating the usual answer to her usual question.

Prisha girds her loins. 'Why not. I'd love a cuppa. I can spare ten minutes.'

If smiles could be captured and sold, Mrs Selkirk's would be worth a million pounds.

As Mrs Selkirk teeters back inside, Prisha makes the sign of the cross. A reflex, despite her lack of faith.

'I deserve the King's Gallantry Medal for this,' she mutters.

Stepping over the threshold into the kitchen-living room, she expects the worst.

Her fears are unfounded.

It's humble, true. Well-worn, from a different era, but it's immaculately clean and tidy.

She takes a seat in a faded high-backed armchair.

'Would you like a hand?'

'No. I'm quite capable of making a cuppa tea, love. Now, milk and sugar?'

'No. Just black.'

'Just black?' she replies, astounded. 'Nowt as queer as folk,' she mumbles to herself.

The promised ten minutes quietly stretch into forty as Prisha is shown dozens of faded photographs chronicling Eileen Selkirk's life, loves, and heartaches—a condensed tale of ninety-five years on planet earth, most of it spent within five miles of Ashenby village.

The tea is clean, refined, like it's been poured through silk. The fruitcake, moist and succulent, although Prisha is still confused why it was served with a slice of crumbly Wensleydale cheese. She doesn't have the heart to ask.

Rising from the chair, she places her cup and plate on the kitchen counter.

'Thanks, Eileen. I think that might have been one of the most refreshing cups of tea I've ever had.'

She chuckles. 'Get on wi, yer. Tha's trying to put butter on t'bacon, now lass.'

Prisha hasn't the foggiest idea what she means.

As she steps over the threshold, she says, 'The cake and cheese were delicious too.'

'Yer welcome, lass. Anytime. If you're ever passing again, please feel free to drop in. I like a natter now and again. Don't get many visitors apart from Mrs Baker.'

Prisha halts in her tracks and spins around. 'Mrs Baker from Hexley Farm?'

'Aye. She comes once a week to do a bit of cleaning for me. Doesn't charge. Has a heart of gold, that one. A true Christian.' She hits her forehead with her palm. 'Damn and blast. I'd forget my head if it wasn't screwed on.'

'What's the matter?'

'It's the reason I came out to speak to you in the first place.'

'What is?'

'I have something for you. Wait there.'

Prisha checks her watch as her impatience resurfaces.

The old lady returns a moment later with an envelope and hands it to her.

'What's this?' she asks, studying the faded white envelope, which is well-thumbed.

'Malachi give it to me. Said if anything should happen to him, untoward like, then I should hand it to police.'

'When did he give you this?'

Mrs Selkirk looks to the heavens. 'eeeh, now yer asking. Maybe a few weeks back... or months. Hard to say. I 'ave me good days and me bad.'

'I assume there's a note or letter inside. What does it say?'

'Couldn't tell yer, lass. He said it was never to be opened by no one, bar police.' She glances over her shoulder into the house, quickly losing interest. 'Right, I don't want to be rude but the Archers is starting in a minute. I never miss it.

By the way, there's some in the village saying Malachi was done in. Is it true?'

Prisha slips the envelope into her pocket. 'It's an ongoing investigation, Eileen.'

The old woman chuckles. 'You're just like that Vera off TV.'

'Who?'

'You know, the detective series, Vera. The old lass with the hat. Mind you, if I had a hat like hers, I'd burn the bugger.' She turns and closes the door.

As Prisha steps into the car, she pulls on protective gloves, then delicately removes the letter from the envelope, opens the folds, and reads.

> *If anything untoward should happen to me, then*
> *only two other people know the truth about that*
> *young lass.*
> *N.H.*
> *So hear me God.*
> *Malachi Abbott*

None of it makes sense.

48

Saturday 6th May

The bacon sizzles and spits in the pan, the sliced rounds of tomato rest quietly alongside as they soak up the fat, a nice blackened crust forming on the bottom. A handful of button mushrooms are pushed up along one side. The microwave pings and Frank removes the small bowl of baked beans as the toaster ejects four slices of well-done toast.

He glances at the dog under the table. It stares up at him with imploring eyes.

'No point looking like that, Foxtrot, you little bugger. You've had your breakfast.'

The dog whimpers and rubs a paw over its eye, in a "woe is me" display.

Frank sighs. 'Look, I tell you what; I'll save you a scrap of bacon and egg. How does that sound?'

The dog's tongue darts out, licking its lips as Meera bustles into the kitchen and eyeballs her husband with a severe scowl.

'Frank, what are you doing?'

'I'm knitting a sweater... what does it bloody look like?'

'And what about the diet? We agreed on only one fried breakfast a month.'

'Yes, I know.'

'You made a fry-up last weekend.'

'True. But that was April. We are now in May. It's a new month.'

She shakes her head despairingly. 'So, you're having your fry-ups back to back?'

'Yes. There was nothing in the rulebook about that. Your rulebook, may I add,' he mutters under his breath as he pulls two eggs from the carton. 'Now, one egg or two?'

Meera shuffles over to the kettle and flicks it on. 'One, please.'

'I tell you what, I'll do you two. If you can't manage it, Foxtrot can have it as a treat.'

Meera shoots a look at the dog. 'It's a toss up as to who's going to die of a heart attack first, you or the dog.'

'Stop mithering. Make the tea, butter the toast, and don't be miserly with the butter. There's no shortage. And don't forget the HP sauce.'

'Yes, chef,' she mumbles.

As Frank cracks an egg on the side of the pan, his phone buzzes violently on the countertop.

'See who that is, love?'

Meera lifts the phone. 'It's Prisha.'

Frank grimaces. 'Damn it. Ask her what she wants?' he says, cracking another egg into the pan.

Meera taps at the phone. 'Morning, Prisha. Frank's a little busy at the moment trying to kill us both. Can I take a message?' Her face, impassive at first, slowly creases as she listens. 'Right, right. I see. I'll pass you over. What? A shower? Okay, I'll get him to call you back in ten.'

Frank tilts the pan and spoons bacon fat over the eggs. 'Don't tell me it's bloody work?' he grizzles.

'No. She was ringing you up for a date. Of course it's work.'

'Go on. What is it?'

'Your missing person—Lord Hampton. He's back at Ravensbane Castle. Alive and well, apparently.'

49

The maid ushers Frank and Prisha into the study, their arrival barely noticed by the occupants—Lord and Lady Hampton, and a gentleman with a stethoscope around his neck.

Frank glances around. The study smells of vanilla and sandalwood from a scented candle flickering on the desk. A small wood fire crackles in the hearth, unnecessary on such a mild morning but releasing a steady, comforting heat. Sunlight floods through the tall windows, casting long rectangles across the parquet floor.

Lord Hampton is slumped in a leather armchair, dressed in a navy blue dressing gown and leather slippers, the picture of faded dignity. Silver hair, neatly parted, sweeps back from a face more lined than the press photos suggest. He's thinner, too—not gaunt, but diminished ever so slightly. One leg rests crookedly over the other. Frank notices the prosthetic foot protruding from the bottom of his pyjama bottoms.

The faint welts on his wrists, the scratch on his cheek, the slight hollowness beneath his eyes—none of it detracts from his air of quiet defiance.

He barely glances up as Frank and Prisha edge forwards, feeling like intruders. Lady Hampton stands beside him, one hand on the back of his chair, the other lightly skimming the pearls at her throat.

She eventually acknowledges the officers. 'Oh, Noah, this is DCI Finnegan and DI Kumar from CID.'

Hampton throws them a cursory glance and nods.

'Ahem, this is our local physician, Dr Julian Brant,' Lady Hampton continues, holding a hand towards the doctor.

'Officers,' the doctor nods as he peels off the blood pressure cuff from around Lord Hampton's arm.

'Prognosis, Doc?' Frank enquires regarding the doctor's flamboyant dress sense with a raised eyebrow.

Immaculately attired, he carries himself with the ease of a man accustomed to private clientele. His dogtooth-patterned suit is sharply tailored, his bow tie—a deep purple flecked with gold—a flamboyant contrast. His cologne subtle but undeniably expensive. A shock of brown curly hair gives him the appearance of a mad scientist who's just discovered a way to blow up the world.

He removes the stethoscope and drops it into his medical bag and clasps it shut. He sports a wry, almost exasperated expression as he stares at his patient.

'I advised His Lordship to go to hospital,' Brant says, tone smooth, almost amused. 'Dehydration, minor cuts—nothing serious, but still, a precautionary stay would be wise.' He casts a glance at Hampton. 'Naturally, he refused.'

Lord Hampton's mouth twitches. 'I'm not an invalid, Julian.'

'No, but you are bloody stubborn,' Brant mutters as he picks up his coat. 'Physically, he'll be fine. A good meal, plenty of water, and rest. Mentally...' He shrugs. 'It's been an ordeal. Right, I'll leave you to it. I'll call around again in the morning.'

'Thank you, doctor,' Lady Hampton says.

He strides past them, giving Frank and Prisha a slight nod as he leaves.

Lady Hampton lets out a breath, straightening. 'I'll make tea.'

Her fingers trail lightly over her husband's shoulder before she moves towards the door, heels tapping against the wooden floor.

Frank watches her go, then steps forward, lowering himself into the chair opposite Lord Hampton. Prisha follows, flipping open her notebook.

'Well,' Frank says, fixing the man with a steady gaze. 'Shall we begin?'

50

Lord Hampton rises and ambles over to the ornate marble fire surround. From the mantelpiece, he lifts the lid on a small silver box, and selects a cigarette with the care of a man choosing a vintage port.

Frank studies him as he makes his way back to the chair. The limp is almost imperceptible.

'You move well, considering,' Frank says. 'I wouldn't have guessed about the prosthetic.'

Hampton glances over his shoulder with a wry smile. 'Lost the foot over thirty years ago. I've had plenty of time to adjust. These days, they make them lighter, quieter, and far more forgiving than in the old days. Better than the real thing. Still aches in the cold, mind. Ghost limb, they call it. Bloody poetic for something so annoying. Oh, please,' he says, nodding at the cigarette box on the shelf. 'Help yourself.'

'Thanks, but we don't,' Frank replies—though he's sorely tempted—as Hampton flops into his seat, sparks up, and takes a lusty drag.

'Been gagging for one of these widow-makers for days. Thought it prudent not to light up in front of the quack. You know their dogma—no smoking, no booze, no fat, no sugar, more greens, more exercise. I ask you—what's the point in bloody living?' He wheezes out a cough.

Frank smirks. 'A man after my own heart.'

A pause.

'Now, let's start from the beginning.'

Hampton exhales smoke, eyes half-lidded. 'Early Monday morning. My alarm went off at 2:45. I showered, dressed, grabbed my suitcase and holdall—already packed—and headed downstairs.' He glances up. 'I assume my wife told you about my planned trip to Syria?'

Frank nods. 'An archaeological dig, yes.'

'Quite. I opened the front door and went down the steps. My car was parked out front. I'd just put my luggage in the boot when I heard footsteps on the gravel behind me. I turned—and a second figure grabbed me from behind. Clamped a rag over my nose and mouth. Sweet chemical smell. I tried not to breathe, struggled, but then the other man joined in. I blacked out.'

He pauses to flick ash into an ashtray.

'When I came to, I was lying on my side. Pitch black. My hands were cable-tied behind my back, and the ground was rough. After a while, my eyes adjusted. It was some kind of tunnel—natural rock. Eventually, I saw a shaft of light in the distance. I shuffled towards it. The way out had been boarded up—planks of wood. Through a crack, I could see trees. I had a rough idea where I was.'

Frank tilts his head. 'Where?'

'An old mineshaft in Ravensbane Wood. Locals used to call it Maggie's Tomb. I played there as a boy.'

Frank throws a look at Prisha, who draws a slow breath, vindicated.

'Go on,' Frank says.

'It's well off the beaten path—dense terrain, barely a track. No one would ever stumble across it. I waited, dozed, woke again in darkness. I was thirsty. An owl hooted now and then, but that was it. Once daylight returned, I began to explore. I remembered a sheer drop at one end of the tunnel. Then—my foot kicked something. Bottled water.'

Prisha leans forward, pen tightening in her hand. 'Someone left water for you?'

'Yes. Two bottles. Which puzzled me. Either someone else used the place... or my captors left them. But why? Maybe they planned to come back. Then I found something else—a metal tool. Could've been a blade or a chisel. Not sharp, but enough to work at the cable ties. I lost track of time. A day? Two?'

'Understandable,' Frank says with a nod.

'Eventually I cut myself free, drank a bottle in one go, and passed out again. I rationed the second one and explored as far as I dared. No other exit. I waited, hoping they'd come back. But by what I guessed was day three or four, I knew they weren't.'

He pauses to drag on his cigarette. Smoke hangs in the air like a veil.

'That's when the anger hit. It galvanised me. They meant to leave me for dead, and I had no idea why. The shaft of light returned. I chipped away at the wood, slowly. Got one board loose using the chisel. Kicked it free with the heel of my good foot. But the gap was too narrow, so I started on the next. Darkness came again. I rested. Next dawn, I went at it again. Removed three planks. Just enough to wriggle through.'

He sips his water. 'Had to crawl about twenty feet. Roof had collapsed in places. Then I stood. I was outside. Alive! Took me a few minutes to get my bearings, but I knew where I was—about three miles from the castle. Walked to the gates, buzzed the intercom. Spoke to my wife.'

Frank glances at his watch. 'What time was this?'

'Roughly, 6:30—7:00 am.'

Frank checks his watch 'About three hours ago?'

'Yes. My wife rang the doctor. Then Inspector Kumar. And that's the long, tall, and short of it.'

Prisha closes her notebook. 'We'll need to bag your clothes for analysis. Could be critical—hair, fibres, DNA from you abductors.'

Hampton winces. 'Ah. I'm afraid my wife put them through a hot wash while I showered.'

Prisha stiffens. 'A hot wash?'

'Yes.'

Frank drums his fingers on the chair arm. The wash isn't damning—but the timing raises questions.

'Lord Hampton,' he says, 'you've been through a hell of an ordeal, but we'll need to ask a few more questions while it's fresh.'

'By all means.'

'When you turned and saw the first figure approach—can you describe them?'

'By the build, I assumed male. Five ten, five eleven. Broad. Wearing black. Ski mask. I only saw the eyes.'

Prisha leans in. 'Did he speak?'

'No.'

'And the rag—how long did the struggle last?'

'Twenty, thirty seconds. Maybe less.'

'You didn't see the person holding the rag?'

'No.'

Frank scratches his cheek. 'Any other details? Scent, body ticks, a weapon?'

'Not that I recall.'

'Do you know how you were transported to the mine?'

'No, I was unconscious.'

Prisha flips a page. 'Could you draw us a map of the tunnel's location?'

'No need. There's an old estate map from the 1700s in the bookcase. Shows it precisely.'

Frank shifts forward. 'By the way—we found your car.'

Hampton raises an eyebrow. 'Ah, yes. Meant to ask about that. Where?'

'Grimscar Quarry. About ten miles from here. Burnt out. Nothing left inside.'

'Damn,' he says, but the timing's off—like he's reading from a script.

He rises, cigarette dangling. 'Well, that's what insurance is for. Now... where's that damn map?'

51

Prisha skips down the steps outside Ravensbane Castle, while Frank ambles after her—slow, awkward, with an unnatural gait.

She glances back, concerned. 'You alright there, Frank?'

He grimaces, eyes watery. 'I'm fine, lass. The wife bought me new underpants. Says extra-large on the label, but I swear she got them from the boys' department. I'm all bunched up. Twisted. Me tackle can't breathe. They need air—freedom to swing. Right now, it's like they're in a straightjacket in solitary confinement.'

Prisha pulls a pained expression like she's been tasked with cleaning the male toilets in a homeless shelter after a long weekend.

'Too much information, Frank.'

'You bloody asked,' he growls as they climb into the car.

The seat belts clunk into place.

Prisha turns to him. 'Thoughts?'

Frank sighs and pulls a packet of jelly babies from his pocket and drops one in his mouth.

'I think Lord Hampton should be nominated for the Booker Prize. Hans Christian Andersen would be proud of that tale. A kidnap, a daring escape, a conveniently placed chisel—it's got all the makings of a bestseller. Just needs a dragon to round it off,' he explains, offering her a sweet.

She declines, shaking her head. 'I agree. As tall stories go, it gave me vertigo.'

Frank chuckles. 'That's what I like about you; naturally suspicious. Go on then. Let's hear it.'

'Okay, first thing, he gave a generic description of the mystery man who walked up behind him. Five ten, dressed in black, ski mask. No distinguishing features. And yet...' she pauses and cranes her neck, staring out at the castle.

Frank squints up at the walls. 'Security lighting. The forecourt *should* have been lit up like a bloody Christmas tree the second Hampton stepped outside. Yet it didn't come on, otherwise CCTV would have picked up Hampton and his abductors.'

'Exactly. Secondly, the chemical rag placed over his nose. He said it smelled sweet, which indicates chloroform. Despite how it's portrayed in TV and film, we both know chloroform is a poor way to anaesthetise someone. It can take at least two minutes to take effect and is notoriously dangerous unless handled by an expert.'

Frank nods in agreement. 'And he said he struggled for about thirty seconds before blacking out.'

'Yeah, that doesn't ring true. And the bottles of water. Why? If his captors planned to kill him, why leave two bottles of water? And how fortuitous that an old chisel was discovered in the tunnel.'

Frank purses his lips. 'He was taken in the early hours of Monday morning. Escaped the early hours of today, Saturday. That's five days. Apart from a few superficial scratches and red marks around his wrist, he appears remarkably lucid and fighting fit.'

'Then there's the shower and the clothes.'

Frank holds his hands up. 'I'll let the shower thing pass. Understandable a person would want to immediately rinse the dirt, grime, and sweat from themselves after such a trial... but the washing of the clothes?'

'And by Lady Hampton? She doesn't strike me as the doting OCD wife ready to throw dirty washing into the front-loader immediately her husband disrobes.'

'Which means any DNA, hair, or fibres from his captors will have been eradicated.' Frank takes another Jelly Baby. 'And for a car lover, he didn't seem too concerned about his Mercedes.'

Prisha's face hardens in concentration. 'No, that's right. More evidence destroyed. But it's the amount of days which puzzles me. If he *has* fabricated his capture and incarceration, why wait this long to materialise? Not that there's a strong connection yet, but Malachi Abbott perished in the river on Monday. The vicar died on Thursday.'

'And Lord Hampton resurfaces today.'

Prisha taps at the steering wheel, then grins. 'Of course. It's the perfect alibi, Frank. Whilst he's imprisoned, Malachi drowns, and the vicar is hanged. Nothing to do with me—your honour.'

'It's a theory, but the question we need to answer is this; if Lord Hampton is the killer of Malachi and the vicar—why?'

Prisha throws her hands up. 'Malachi had twenty grand in his wardrobe containing Hampton's fingerprints. We know the suitcase was purchased by Lady Hampton, who said she bought it for her husband's trip to Syria. That's a definite connection. Maybe Malachi was blackmailing one of them?'

'And the vicar?'

She ponders. 'There was something Zac mentioned when he spoke to the vicar the day before he died.'

'What?'

'The vicar said Malachi was a bad egg, detested by everyone in the village. Zac asked why Lord Hampton would employ him for so long.'

'And his reply?'

'The vicar mentioned something about secrets staying buried and old sins.' Prisha brightens. 'How about this; Malachi was blackmailing Lord Hampton, hence the money. Whatever he was blackmailing him about, the vicar was also privy to it.'

'Kill two birds with one stone?'

'Yes. Pretend you've been abducted. While you're "supposedly" incarcerated, you bump off the two people who have something over you. Perfect.'

Frank considers the implications carefully as his years of experience kick in.

'Hmm... possible. But Prisha, let's not put the blinkers on.'

'What do you mean?'

'Despite our suspicions, we've got to consider the alternative. Maybe, *just* maybe, Hampton really was left to die in that tunnel. And if that's the case, then someone else is out there running amok.'

52

Prisha studies the natural rise in the woods, map in hand. She taps it, nodding to Zac.

'I reckon that's it, dead ahead—the old mine.'

Zac eyes the overgrown mound, then glances at the map.

'I think you're right.'

Ahead, a narrow gravel track slides into the earth before narrowing into a trench. Prisha pulls on gloves and bootees, tucks the map away, and flicks on her torch.

'I'm not sure I'll fit down there,' Zac says.

Prisha throws him a look. 'No. This mine wasn't built for men over six feet,' she says, grinning. 'I'll go and check it out.'

She drops into the trench, her head just visible above the top as Zac trails her from higher ground.

'Take it easy,' he calls. 'Old bloody mines can collapse at any moment.'

'Didn't know you cared.'

'You don't know the half of it,' he mutters to himself.

Prisha picks her way along, the torchlight skimming over damp stone and tree roots. Ahead, the trench narrows further, swallowed by a dark entrance.

'Stop!' Zac bellows, voice sharp.

Prisha freezes, heart lurching. 'What?'

Zac leans over, grinning. 'Massive spider's web about a foot in front of you.'

Prisha tilts her head, catching a shimmer of silk strands stretched across the trench.

'Ooh, yes. That's huge. Christ, I wonder how big the spider is?'

'More importantly—where is it?' Zac adds with a chuckle.

'Shut up. You're not helping.'

'Just knock it away with your torch. The spider's more scared of you than you are of it. It's what I tell my kids, anyway. Not that they believe me.'

Prisha raises the torch, then hesitates. She peers closer at the web.

'What are you waiting for?' Zac calls down.

'Odd, isn't it?'

'What is?'

'A perfectly formed spider's web,' she says, pulling out her phone to take a few shots.

Zac glances around at the gloomy wood. 'Not really. We're in the wild and woolly arse-end of nowhere.'

'Know anyone who's an expert on spiders?'

Zac scratches his beard. 'As it happens, I do. Yours and mine's favourite pathologist.'

Prisha groans. 'Not Whipple?'

'Aye. Old Raspberry has more outside interests than a serial bigamist on Viagra. Why?'

Prisha smiles faintly, torch beam steady on the gossamer strands.

'Because if Lord Hampton really escaped through here four hours ago,' she says quietly, 'then why's the spider's web still perfectly intact?'

53

Frank knocks on the door with a loud rat-a-tat-tat. A mumbled curse emanates from inside.

'Enter,' Bennet Whipple's voice booms out.

Frank walks in and glances around the study. Towering shelves containing medical journals and archaic tomes adorn one wall. An old wooden desk, with a leather inlay top, stands in the middle of the room, strewn with papers.

A rank cocktail of smells catches the back of Frank's throat—formaldehyde and antiseptic, certainly, but layered with something earthier: peat-rich soil, the loamy scent of damp moss, like the underbelly of a forest floor.

Along one wall, three glass cabinets stand like eerie exhibits.

Each is subtly distinct. Different soil depths, climbing branches, silk threads clinging to rocks. Within, something stirs, slow, deliberate.

'Ah, Bennet, the lass on reception said I'd find you here,' Frank states, still taking in the rather shambolic room as

Whipple bends ungainly over a microscope. 'This is a cosy little bolt-hole you have.'

'Detective Chief Inspector Finnegan.' His response is weary, as if dealing with a hyperactive child after a long, tiring day. 'In our professional capacity, do we not spend enough time in one another's company? Must you now hound me in my free time?' he asks, not bothering to look up from his work.

'No need to be like that, Bennet. I was hoping to pick your brain, actually.' Frank idly walks over to him. 'What are you looking at?'

'Lysergic acid diethylamide.'

'LSD? The old fly-me-to the-moon stuff. You realise that's a Class A drug? I could arrest you for possession under the Misuse of Drugs Act 1971.'

'I have all the necessary exemptions and paperwork to be in legal possession. It's for research purposes, inspector,' he replies in a lethargic, bored tone.

'Aye, that's what they all say,' Frank retorts spying a plate of biscuits on the table. 'Ooh, chocolate digestives. My favourite. Do you mind?'

'Help yourself.' Whipple reluctantly pulls himself away from the microscope and plods over to the bookcase where he lifts a large book from the shelf and languidly flicks through the pages.

'So, what's the research?' Frank asks, taking a bite of the biscuit, unwittingly sending a spray of crumbs everywhere.

'In controlled micro-doses, LSD has shown potential in alleviating severe pain associated with cluster headaches, also known as "suicide headaches" due to their intensity. The alkaloids derived from LSD interact with serotonin receptors in the brain, which could modulate the neural pathways involved in pain perception.'

'Easy for you to say.'

Whipple ignores him. Head down, engrossed in the book, he heads back to the table.

'The challenge lies in isolating the beneficial compounds while mitigating the psychoactive effects. My research aims to synthesise a derivative that retains the analgesic properties without inducing hallucinations. It's a delicate balance, but one that could revolutionise pain management for sufferers of this excruciating condition. It would need to be a slow release, maybe contained within a lozenge. It's a side project of mine, to stave off the banality of examining cadavers.'

Frank picks up a petri dish and gives it a shake. 'Aye, well, we all need a hobby to keep us out of trouble. And if this wonder-drug goes into production, would it be named after you? Maybe Bennetomol, or what about Whipplegesic?' he says with a wry chuckle. 'I can hear the jingle on the TV adverts now—*Got a niggle? Suck a Whipple.*' Frank coughs, slightly embarrassed. 'Ahem...then again—that catchphrase could conjure up disturbing mental images for those with a sordid disposition.'

Whipple places the book down and snatches the petri dish from Frank's hand.

'Don't be asinine, inspector. And please refrain from tampering with the samples. The slightest contamination could waste months of painstaking work.'

With both eyes fixed disapprovingly on Frank, Whipple hunches over the microscope again but misjudges the proximity and pokes himself in the eye with the top of the scope.

'Sweet jumping juniper berries! Confounded contraption,' he yells, blinking rapidly.

Frank smirks. 'Aye, aye. You want to watch yourself with that thing, Bennet. You could have your eye out. I may have to rush you down to the Ophthalmology Department. Mind you, we're in the right place for it.'

Whipple takes a pristine white handkerchief from his pocket and dabs at the red, watery eye.

'Could you please expedite the primary motive for your visit, inspector,' he snaps, becoming increasingly irritated by Frank's presence. 'You said you were here to elicit information.'

'Oh, yes. That's right,' he replies as he wanders over to the glass cases, not dissimilar to fish tanks, lining the back wall. He bends and stares through the glass at a particularly large specimen of spider. 'Look at the size of that bugger,' he mutters. 'What do you call this one, Boris?' he says pulling a pen from his pocket and tapping the glass trying to instigate a response from the brutish-looking spider. He chuckles. 'You wouldn't want to find that bugger in your underpants first thing on a Monday morning. You'd never whistle *Moon River* again.'

Whipple strides over. 'Inspector, please refrain from tormenting the specimens! They are not playground pets. That is the Phoneutria nigriventer, or Brazilian wandering spider. The venom is highly neurotoxic, affecting the nervous system, and in high enough doses can cause respiratory paralysis, loss of muscle control, asphyxiation, and even—agonising death.'

'Nasty,' Frank says, nodding in respect as he moves onto the next case. 'Eh up, Bennet,' he says squinting inside, 'This cage is empty. I think one of your insects may have done a runner.'

Whipple's barrel chest expands to an enormous degree. 'Contrary to common misconceptions, spiders are not insects. They are arachnids—a separate class within the arthropod species. And that specimen is the Cyriopagopus albostriatus or zebra tarantula. It's a burrower and has built its nest in the substrate of loam and coconut fibre.' He pulls the handkerchief from his pocket and dabs his forehead. 'Now, inspector, the reason for your visit?' he demands, his voice booming.

Frank looks up. 'Ah yes,' he replies, pulling an envelope from his pocket and handing it to Whipple. 'I'd like you to look at these two photos of a spider's web, photographed not far from here, and see if you can identify the spider.'

Whipple slides the photos out and picks up a magnifying glass from the desk. His face becomes a mask of intrigue.

'Hmm...' He angles the photograph towards the light, his mouth twitching into something close to reverence. 'A sublime piece of arachnid engineering. Not some slapdash corner cobweb. This is Metellina merianae, the cave orb-weaver. Native to Europe, though rarely spotted unless one pokes about in places dark, damp, and generally considered inhospitable to the civilised foot.'

Frank leans forward slightly. 'Any idea about its habits? Web-building routine, that sort of thing?'

Whipple lowers the glass and peers at him. 'Unlike her more excitable cousins, Metellina merianae is a creature of remarkable patience and nocturnal discipline. She constructs her web under cover of darkness—usually once the temperature drops and the air grows still. When the web is *in situ*, she refrains from constant renovations unlike others of her ilk. Her web remains intact for a good forty-eight hours, sometimes longer, untouched and unaltered.'

Frank taps the photo with his pen. 'The geometry suggests this web was undisturbed when photographed. What does that tell you?'

Whipple considers the implications of the question like a professor of mathematics.

'It tells me two things: the spider is active and nearby, and—more intriguingly—no one has passed through this entrance for at least a full night. Possibly two, otherwise the web would have been irrevocably disrupted.'

Frank gives a low whistle. 'A sort of time-stamp?'

Whipple nods. 'In a sense, yes.' He hands the photos back. 'I assume your line of questioning is based on some logical extrapolation, inspector?'

Frank frowns and slides the photos back into the envelope and drops them into his pocket.

'Yes. An ongoing investigation. A person of interest said they emerged from the tunnel behind the web early this morning. From what you've said, that's nigh on impossible.'

Whipple shrugs. 'Is it not conceivable this person of interest simply crawled beneath the web?'

'The web sits about six inch off the ground and stretches the full width of the trench.'

'Then you have your answer, inspector,' Whipple replies rapidly losing interest in the subject, as he lumbers back to his microscope.

Frank rubs thoughtfully at his chin before he's distracted by the venomous spiders again.

'I take it these spiders have something to do with your mad scientist experiment?' he says, peering down into the spider enclosure.

'It's cutting-edge research, actually, but yes, indeed they do, inspector,' Whipple replies as he bends over the eyepiece of his microscope with a little more care this time. 'Nestled within the biochemical chaos of their venom lies a pharmacological blueprint—specific peptide toxins that bind with exquisite precision to nociceptive ion channels, effectively blocking the transmission of pain without the soporific or addictive side-effects associated with your garden-variety opiates.'

'Really,' Frank replies, already zoning out as he slides open the tiny feeding hatch on the enclosure. He sticks his biro inside and waggles it around trying to antagonise the spider. It remains completely still.

Whipple waffles on. 'Nature has, through several hundred million years of elegant trial and error, engineered compounds capable of modulating neural activity at a molecular level we're only just beginning to comprehend.'

'You don't say,' Frank murmurs. 'Come on little fella, let's see those fangs,' he whispers, grinning as he twiddles the pen back and forth.

With no warning, the spider explodes forward—legs flaring, fangs bared, a blur of brown fury.

It strikes the pen with a sickening crack, so fast Frank barely sees it move.

'Sweet Jesus on a trike!'

He jerks back instinctively, releasing the biro from his fingers. It clatters into the tank, bouncing once before landing beside the spider with a soft, accusatory tink.

He gasps, stumbling back. 'Vicious little bastard!' he hisses.

Whipple lifts his head. 'Something the matter, inspector?'

'Ahem... what, no, nothing's the matter, Bennet. Just admiring the majesty of these insects, I mean arachnids,' he replies as nonchalantly as possible with a heartbeat in the cardiac arrest zone. He hastily makes his way to the door.

'Well, thanks for your time, Bennet. I'll leave you to it. I never like to outstay my welcome.'

Whipple watches him go, exhales deeply, then shakes his head. 'An encumbrance,' he murmurs as he ambles over to the fridge and extracts a bottle of water. As he takes a gulp, his eye detects the alien object in the spider's habitat. His throaty groan resembles a grizzly bear with a severe hangover. He picks up a notebook and pen from the desk and scribbles into it.

> *Reinforce feeding hatch on enclosures. Or install inspector-proof barrier.*

He returns to his experiment, bends over the microscope and resumes his research, adjusting the dial on the scope as something catches his attention.

'What in blue blazes,' he murmurs, perplexed.

Using a pair of tweezers, he removes the glass slide from below the scope and studies it intently. Carefully, deliberately, he uses the tweezers to extricate a foreign body from the sample of LSD. He holds the contaminant up to the light to see it clearly.

'Hmm... a biscuit crumb,' he growls. He glances out of the window and notices Frank striding happily across the car park munching on a Cornish pastie.

'That man could test the patience of a saint.'

54

Gentle spring rain peppers the windows of the incident room—dull, persistent. Prisha steps inside, clutching a takeaway cup, steam rising in the air as she takes a cautious sip.

She saunters over to Zac, who is engrossed with his laptop.

'Had a call from Frank twenty minutes ago,' she begins.

'Oh, aye?'

'Whipple identified the spider and said it builds its web during the night. He also confirmed the web was untouched.'

'Hmm...'

Prisha picks up on his lack of enthusiasm. 'What?'

'I get it, I really do. We'll need a damn sight more than that. Your theory would be torn to shreds in court.'

'Not if we find an expert in native spiders to confirm what Whipple has said.'

Zac leans back in his seat and sighs. 'Prisha, no spider expert on the planet is going to stand up in court—especially not in a high-profile murder trial—and swear, one hundred per cent, that species only builds webs at night.' He turns back to the images on his screen.

'What are you looking at?' she asks.

He barely glances up from his screen. 'Reports just came through from Charlene's crew and Vehicle Forensics. Photos too.'

'And?'

He exhales, shifts in his chair. 'What we suspected, mostly. The bell rope was cut clean, not snapped—fine-toothed blade, Charlene reckons. Brake lines the same—sharp shear marks, plus a consistent crescent-shaped flaw. Could be from a damaged snip jaw.'

'Almost like a fingerprint,' she murmurs.

Zac nods. 'Exactly. Snips are easy to pocket. Slide under a car, snip the lines, done in sixty seconds. *If* you know what you're doing.'

Prisha's brow furrows. 'If we find the snips—and the indentation matches—we've got a link.' She takes another gulp of coffee, eyes narrowing as something floats back. 'Christ. I don't believe it.'

Zac turns to her. 'What?'

'When we searched Hampton's car shed, I noticed something on the workbench—there was a hacksaw, and a pair of snips. They were the only things not stored away.'

Zac rubs his chin. 'And it's safe to say Lord Hampton knows his way around a car. But what about his alibi?'

Prisha shakes her head. 'It's not an alibi though, is it? We only have his word he was in the tunnel.'

'But we have his fingerprints from the chisel and water bottles we found.'

'Yes, but that only proves he was there—not when.'

'You really believe he staged the whole abduction thing?'

'I'm certain. We need a warrant as soon as.'

'Whoa! Hold your galloping majors, Prisha. Don't you think you're rushing it? At the moment, Hampton doesn't have a clue we suspect him of murder. If we barge in there with a search warrant, he's going to be straight onto his brief. And it won't be a local solicitor. It will be a high-profile barrister, a Silk.'

'And if we falter now, how long before he goes to his car shed and spots the tools on the bench? It may already be too late.'

As she strides towards the exit, Frank enters—his face a puzzle of unreadable lines.

'Frank, some important developments...' She trails off, noticing his distant, faraway gaze. 'Are you okay?' she asks, flicking a glance at Zac.

Frank stares at the carpet before lifting his head and rubbing a hand through his grey locks.

Zac steps forward. 'Boss, what is it?' His voice tightens, sensing bad news.

He blinks, still in a fog. 'I had a call from forensics a moment ago.'

Prisha swallows. 'And?'

'It's the damnedest thing,' he mutters, as if trying to convince himself. 'The foot recovered from the fire. They've got a DNA match.'

'Who's it belong to?' Zac asks.

Frank gazes at him, mouth open.

'Lord Hampton.'

55

The three officers, seated in Frank's office, talk non-stop for thirty minutes—covering the two deaths, the foot, and Lord Hampton's vanishing act. Evidence, theories, what-ifs—they go over it all, but in the end, no consensus is reached.

Frank eventually brings the discussion to an end and rubs wearily at his face.

'Right, enough. There's a time for talk and there's a time for action. First of all, let's park Reverend Hartley's death. Whether it was murder, suicide, or misadventure, no one can be certain yet. I can't see a man of God, who's served the church for forty years, taking his own life in a church—but stranger things have happened at sea. And let's put that damned foot aside for the moment, along with Malachi's cryptic note he handed to his neighbour. All they're doing is muddying the waters. The only thing we *all* agree on is we're certain Malachi Abbott's car was sabotaged, which ultimately led to his demise—agreed?'

Prisha and Zac nod and mumble, 'Yes,' in unison.

'Now, Prisha, lay out your case.'

'Malachi was Hampton's gamekeeper for decades—we have a connection. He was dismissed over his drinking and the incident with the young girl from the commune. Paid a measly four month's wages—grievance right there. The suitcase bought by Lady Hampton was found in his house—fact. The money inside the suitcase contains Lord Hampton's fingerprints—fact. Which leads me to the hypothesis that Malachi had dirt on Hampton and was blackmailing him. Which in turn gives Hampton motive.'

'Then why not kill Malachi *before* handing the money over?'

She shrugs. 'Let's say Hampton felt remorse for Malachi and paid him twenty grand to keep him quiet *and* to assuage his own guilt for how he'd treated him. Then Malachi comes back for more. Hampton realises this thing will never end and Malachi will keep coming back, over and over.'

Frank nods thoughtfully. 'It's got legs. And with Malachi being fond of the drink, then how long before he blurted out Hampton's secret? Again, back to supposition, but at least you have two solid facts. Zac?'

He breathes deeply. 'I'm not convinced, boss. I'm not disputing the suitcase or the money—that leads right back to Hampton.'

'Then let's hear your qualms.'

'He's sixty-five, Frank. With a prosthetic foot. You really think he hid out near the pub, shimmied under a car and cut brake lines like it was Mission Impossible? It doesn't ring true to me.'

'He's a fit and active sixty-five-year-old, Zac. It's not like when I was a lad, when most over sixty were infirm and ailing. Times have changed. And as for his foot—he barely has a limp.' His gaze returns to Prisha. 'You've made it quite clear you think his abduction story is a ruse to paint him out of the picture.'

'Yep. Way too many holes in it.'

'Zac?'

'I'm not as certain. Prisha's spider web theory doesn't fill me full of confidence. And if he wasn't in the tunnel for five days, then where the hell was he?'

Prisha snorts. 'Don't be naïve, Zac. He could have hidden anywhere, gone anywhere.'

Frank raises his hand. 'Okay, let's not get into a heated debate. We're all on the same side. Prisha, get onto the magistrate and obtain a search warrant. Then you and Zac head to Ravensbane and try to locate the snips and hacksaw. If you find them, bring them back to the station, hand them over to the desk sergeant and tell him to get them over to Forensics, *tonight*, my orders. Meanwhile, I'll ring Charlene and ask her to expedite the examination and get the results to us by Monday. Then we'll have a clearer picture of where we're at. And don't mention anything about the DNA results from the foot yet to the Hamptons. We'll save that little chestnut until we bring Hampton in for questioning. Once you've done that, knock off for the night, and enjoy a day of rest tomorrow. Switch off. Understood?'

'Yes, Frank,' they both agree.

He rises lethargically. 'Right, I have a meat and tatty pie waiting for my attention at home and a few refreshing ales. I'll see thee Monday morning, bright and early and Bristol fashion.'

56

The sun is rapidly sinking behind the hills.

Zac is behind the wheel as they park up outside Ravensbane Castle. The engine idles as he looks at Prisha.

'How are we going to play this?' he asks, doubt in his words.

Prisha fixes him with a determined gaze. 'There's only one way to play it. Matter-of-fact. We have a search warrant. If we're bombarded with questions, we reply like a politician.'

'What?'

'We prevaricate, obfuscate, change the subject.'

'You mean lie?'

'No... well, yes. Anyway, we're not dealing with low-level drug-dealers who know their rights and automatically detest the police. We're dealing with His Lord and Ladyship. They'll be all of a quiver, but ultimately, they'll let us get on with our job.'

Zac stares out of the windscreen at the imposing house. 'Still, they're no slouches. Lord Hampton will be straight on the blower to his lawyer.'

Prisha tires of the conversation, and the fact he's not fully convinced of Hampton's subterfuge.

'Let's call it a day then.'

Zac frowns. 'What?'

'He is a Lord. Can't possibly be guilty of anything.'

Zac's lips curl. 'Okay, smartarse. Let's do it. But for the record, I'm not thrilled.'

She's already out the door. 'Liar. You love every minute of it.'

Zac slams the door shut behind him. 'Oh, aye? And why would I love every minute of it?'

'Obvious reasons.'

Lady Hampton opens the door and stares down her nose at them. Tired and with a food stain on her chiffon blouse, she takes a deep sigh.

'What now, inspector? If you wish to speak with my husband, then you'll have to come back tomorrow. He's in a deep sleep and I refuse to wake him. It's been a very long and trying week. Can you not respect our privacy?'

'We don't wish to speak to him or you, Lady Hampton,' Prisha says. She pulls the search warrant from her jacket and hands it over.

'What's this?' she says with a scowl.

'A search warrant.'

She appears momentarily stunned. 'A search... but I don't understand. What does this mean?'

'It means we've been granted authority to conduct a search on your property to look for items we believe may have been used in a serious crime. Any such items we find can be legally seized for further forensic analysis.'

Lady Hampton throws the warrant back in Prisha's face. It flutters softly to the ground.

'Poppycock! Who the hell do you think you are? You've just got off the boat and now you're strutting around the place like a colonial governor.'

Zac bristles and takes a step forward. 'Lady Hampton, that's deeply offensive and uncalled for.'

'Well, it's true. Can't you recruit British police officers anymore?'

Prisha swallows hard, but remains unmoved. 'I am British. I was born here,' she replies calmly.

Lady Hampton scoffs. 'Ha! If a cat has kittens in a kipper box, it doesn't make them kippers.'

Prisha forces a smile. 'I haven't heard that one before.'

'You've opened a can of worms, inspector. I'll be taking this up immediately with my legal representation.'

'As you're entitled to do.' She bends and retrieves the search warrant. 'We don't need to come inside. We'll be searching Lord Hampton's car shed.'

'I hope you realise my husband is on first-name terms with Baroness Willoughby. She sits on three ethics committees and the Lords Select Panel on Policing Standards, I'll have you know.'

Zac smiles. 'Be sure to give her our regards.'

The bang from the door reverberates around the grounds.

<hr />

Zac drops the plastic evidence bags containing the snips and hacksaw into the boot, then slams it shut. He casts one last look around as the sun slips below the horizon, leaving only an orange glow behind.

He jumps into the passenger seat next to Prisha.

'Well, that went down about as well as a turd in a Jacuzzi.'

Prisha laughs as the car moves off. 'She certainly showed her true colours,' she replies as the car glides along the driveway towards the entrance.

He turns to her. 'I'm sorry.'

She throws him a puzzled glance. 'For what?'

'I forget how hard it must be for you sometimes, you know, with the racist stuff.'

A slight shrug. 'Don't let it worry you. I don't. What's the point of using up my nervous energy on people who mean less than zero to me?'

He nods. 'Yeah, still. I'm not sure I'd be as forgiving.'

'I didn't say I was forgiving. That's for saints. I never forgive. Anyway, I always put my big girl knickers on before work.'

He chuckles. 'You've a spine of steel.' He checks his watch. 'Right, we've officially knocked off. Come on, let's get out of this place. There are some nice country pubs on the way back and I could murder a pint.'

'Yeah, me too. My shout.'

57

Frank's Day

Sunday 7th May

Although situated high up on the east cliff of Whitby behind the Abbey, the allotments have protection in the form of corrugated sheeting that encircles the area. It's not exactly state-of-the-art—in fact, to the untrained eye, it looks more like the start of a shantytown. But it serves its main purpose: shielding the vegetables and fruit from the harsh elements and salty sea air.

Frank bends over and groans.

'Jeepers bloody creepers,' he mutters. 'These bones aren't getting any younger.'

He pulls a radish from the ground and admires the vibrant red skin that fades to white near the root. Fishing out a handkerchief, he gives it a perfunctory wipe-down before taking a bite. Sweet at first, followed by a peppery sting that brings tears to his eyes as he gazes out towards the Abbey ruins, where seagulls drift lazily on the thermals.

'Hell, that's got a kick. Just how I like 'em.'

He yanks out another handful and drops them into a plastic carrier bag. Placing his hands on his hips, he stretches backwards and winces. Two plots along, a shed door clatters open and muttered cursing drifts through the air.

'What's that old bugger up to now?'

His attention shifts to the oversized rhubarb plant growing like a triffid. Taking out his paring knife, he slices a bunch clean through and adds it to the bag as Arthur emerges from his hut and beckons.

'Eh up, Frank. Got a minute?'

Frank studies the old man, stooped with arthritis.

'Aye, what do you want?'

'Last year's rhubarb wine. I think she's ready. I'm about to pop the cork. Fancy a snifter?'

Frank checks his watch. 'Well, it is nearly twelve, give or take an hour. Why not?'

He ambles over and steps inside Arthur's gloomy shed, a shrine to rusted tools and the ghosts of summers past. Most of the gear would be too old even for a museum.

Arthur grabs two glasses and hands one over. Frank squints at the grubby, stained interior.

'No need to get the cut crystal out on my account, Arthur.'

Arthur pulls a gurney of a face and snatches the glass back.

'Fussy bugger,' he mutters, producing a handkerchief that is a bio-hazard to humanity. He wipes the inside of the glass and hands it back.

'Thanks. That's... a lot better,' Frank mumbles, staring at the glass with a curled lip.

Arthur twists in a corkscrew and, with a grunt of effort, pops the cork.

'How'd you go with the rhubarb wine I gave you last year?' Arthur asks.

'Managed one bottle. Was temporarily blind for twenty-four hours but I came good in the end.'

'Bit on the strong side?'

'Just a tad.'

'What did you do with the other three bottles?'

Frank takes a seat as Arthur pours. 'I was redecorating the house. Used them as paint stripper on the doors. They came up a treat.'

'Ungrateful sod,' Arthur chuckles. He fills his own glass. 'It wasn't that strong.'

'Arthur, I'm surprised NASA didn't contact you. They could've fuelled the Space Shuttle with it.'

'Shut up yer miserable old twannock. Take a sip.'

'Now, the elderflower wine you gave me—that was perfection in a bottle. Like drowning in the tears of a virgin.'

They clink glasses and drink.

Silence follows.

Frank puckers his lips and pulls a face like he's had electrodes attached to his testicles. He lets out a gust of air and erupts into a violent cough.

'Sweet hairy bollocks!'

Arthur barely flinches, savouring his own glass.

'Hmm. Robust. Nice bouquet. A hint of blackcurrant, a whisper of cinnamon, and an underlying note of pork knuckle.'

'Christ, you need your taste buds checking out. Or taking out.'

'Get it down. You only live once.'

'I might not be living at all in a minute.'

He knocks back the rest and Arthur tops him up. The alcohol hits fast, a warm wave that glows beneath his ribs. Frank smacks his lips together.

'You know what, Arthur... it's growing on me. A bit like a puss filled abscess, but growing all the same. Cheers.'

Arthur cackles. 'Plenty more where that came from, Frank.'

58

Prisha's Day

Prisha drizzles maple syrup over the pancakes, followed by a dollop of double whipped cream.

Adam leans across the table and plants a kiss on her lips. 'You know the way to a man's heart.'

She takes a seat and picks up a fork, smiling. 'What do you fancy doing today?'

He shrugs as he tucks into his food like a hungry farmer. 'Whatever you like.'

'We could go for a long walk on the moors, or drive out to a nice pub and have a long lunch.'

He wipes his lips on a tissue then slurps on coffee. 'I'm easy. You choose.'

'Okay, well how about...'

The ping from his phone cuts her off. He frowns at her, then reads the text message. His face clouds.

'What is it?' she asks, already guessing the answer.

'Message from Jack.'

'Your farmhand?'

'Yes. A fence line is down. I have cattle out on the road. Bugger it!' He's already reaching for his jacket. He hurriedly wolfs down the remaining pancake, washes it down with two glugs of coffee and once again leans across the table and plants a kiss, this time on her forehead.

'When will you be back?'

He shrugs. 'Hard to say. Rounding up the cattle up could take a while, then I'll have to fix the fence.'

'I thought that's what you paid Jack for?'

'Catching cattle is a two-man job. Need someone in a vehicle with hazards to warn oncoming traffic. You could come over later and stay the night.'

She tries not to sulk but fails miserably. 'No. I need an early start tomorrow.'

He walks around the table, pulls her to her feet and hugs her. 'Hey, I'll make it up to you, honest.'

'Yeah, sure.'

'What are you going to do all day?'

She pushes him away without much conviction. 'I have plenty to do. I did survive before you came along, you know. I'll go for a run. Have a browse in a bookshop. Pick up a man at a bar. Have debauched sex all afternoon, then watch Call The Midwife. The world's my oyster.'

Another peck, this time to the top of her head, like a mother placating a child.

'Okay, have fun. I'll call you later, promise. Love you.'

As the door slams shut, she picks and prods at her pancake, then slumps back in her chair, arms firmly crossed.

'Yeah... love you too. Bloody farmers.'

On the return leg of her run, she bypasses the overcrowded 199 steps that lead to and from the Abbey and St Mary's Church. Instead, she takes the rather precipitous adjoining cobbled street—a Grade I listed pathway known as Donkey Road. It's become her favoured route in and out of town, away from the hordes of day-trippers.

Slowing to a brisk walk as Church Street bottlenecks with tourists, she ducks into a side hatch selling hot chocolate and emerges with a steaming cup. The scent follows her into the creaky hush of the Whitby Bookshop.

Inside, it's cooler, quieter, the street noise muffled by old timber and paper. She browses the ground floor aimlessly, fingers grazing the spines, before the spiral staircase catches her eye.

Upstairs, the air shifts—faint incense, something woody and herbal. The shelves here lean darker: folklore, witchcraft, Gothic fiction, the occult.

She scans the shelves without intent until one name stops her:

James Frazer.

She pulls the book free—*The Golden Bough*. A title she's heard quoted a dozen times by academics and crackpots alike but never read. A sweeping exploration of ancient myths, magic, and religious rituals, tracing how human belief evolved from superstition to organised religion.

A flick through the index, curiosity piqued, her decision is made.

Seems the day job follows her even on Sundays.

59

Zac's Day

Sunday morning at the park and every blade of grass is spoken for—dozens of pitches marked out in chalk, echoing with whistles, thudding boots and high-pitched shouts. Parents line the touchlines like prison officers, coffees in hand—some cheering, some seething, some scrolling their phones. To most, it's just a game. To others, it's life and death.

As the whistle blows for the start of the match, Zac yells through cupped hands from the sideline.

'Come on, Sammy! Let's have a good game!'

Kelly saunters up, holding two takeaway coffees. She hands him a cup.

'Black, no sugar.'

'Lovely,' he says, taking the drink.

'Let's not forget we have to pick Tom up from his sleepover in Scarborough after the game.'

Zac shuffles, agitated. 'No. Won't forget. That's the fifth time you've mentioned it now.'

'The party was at Kyle's. They live near the castle, on Castle Road, opposite the church.'

'Yep. Got it.'

'Lovely place. They used to be holiday flats, but they've converted it back into a single house.'

'Really.'

'Huge inside. Must have cost a fortune. How do people afford it?'

'Not sure.'

'The father's a solicitor and the mum's a dental assistant. Nice couple. Do you think we'll ever be able to afford something as grand as that?'

'No.' His reply ends the conversation. 'Come on Sammy, watch the ball!' he bellows.

'How long've they been playing?' she asks, nodding at the boys tearing round after the football.

'They've just kicked off. Did you nay hear the whistle?' he replies, bemused as ever by her lack of sporting awareness.

'There are whistles going off left, right and centre,' she says, glancing at the neighbouring pitches. 'Who's winning?'

'Okay, you're taking the piss now.'

'Sorry I spoke. Where's Sammy?'

Zac points. 'There, in the middle—big number six on his back.'

'Doesn't look like him. Do you think he's warm enough?'

She's already getting on his wick.

'Is that your phone I heard ringing, love?'

'Nope. Left it in the car.'

Thwarted.

Sammy makes a clean tackle and threads the ball down the left wing. A rotund lad pelts after it with grim determination and a hell of a lot of optimism.

A voice bellows from the touchline.

'Aw come on, ref! Foul! He's been doing it all game!'

Zac peers along the white line at the man. 'What a knobhead,' he murmurs.

'Who?'

'That muppet in the Man United shirt.'

Kelly stares at her husband. 'Zac, you're not going to get all argumentative again, are you? The coach has warned you on two occasions. One more incident and you're banned for the rest of the season.'

He sniffs, carefree. 'Doesnae matter now. Only two games left.'

'That's not the point.'

'Offside, ref! Bloody offside! Are you blind or what?' the United fan shouts.

Zac breathes deep. 'Oh, give me strength,' he mutters. 'Touchline referees.'

Kelly's attention span wanes. 'Ooh, I've spotted Becca behind the goal. I'll just go and have a chat. Her mum had a hysterectomy recently. I heard there were complications. I better see how she's doing.'

'All right, love. Don't rush back,' he adds under his breath.

'Get a grip, referee! You need bloody glasses. That number six should be sent off! He's been niggling from the start.'

Zac clenches his jaw, a low growl slipping out.

Kelly marches towards the car, arms swinging.

'Well, that was bloody embarrassing,' she snaps, stabbing the fob.

Headlights flash. Doors click open.

'Calm down, Kell,' Zac says, trudging behind as Sammy races up.

'Dad, Dad!' the boy yells.

Zac keeps walking, but glances back. 'Good game, Sammy. You played a blinder. Ran rings round their midfield. Bit more shape up front and we'd've had six, not two.'

The boy beams, breathless. 'Is it true?'

'Is what true?' Zac asks, as Kelly climbs into the driver's seat, steam billowing from her ears.

'Did you punch that gobby bloke in the Man United shirt on the touchline?'

'No. Of course I didn't punch him.'

'Danny Dwyer said you did.'

'Aye, well, Danny Dwyer's got the eyesight of a bat—that's why they stick him in goal.'

'He said you had him in a headlock.'

Zac pulls open the back door. 'Hop in. It may be true his head somehow ended up wedged under my armpit, but that's all.'

'Nice one, dad!' the lad grins. 'He deserved it.'

'No, he bloody didn't!' Kelly yells, fastening her seatbelt. 'What sort of example is that you're setting? You're a police officer! You're supposed to uphold the law, not get into fights at a kids' football match!'

'You're overreacting, Kell. I just had a quiet word. Motormouths like that need putting in their place.'

'And picking him up off the ground by his throat is putting him in his place, is it?'

Sammy laughs. 'Cool, Dad.'

'No, it's not bloody cool!' Kelly barks. 'Your dad's a disgrace. I wanted the ground to open up and swallow me alive. You'll probably be banned for life now. Well done.'

'Take a chill pill, love. No harm done. Anyway, it shut the gobshite up, didn't it?'

'Yes—only because he passed out after that chokehold you put him in!'

'It wasn't a chokehold. The bloke obviously suffers from asthma. Hardly surprising. He never stops to draw breath. Yap yap fucking yap. Like one of those little dogs that barks till it passes out and keels over.'

'I'm not coming again. That's it. You can take the boys to football by yourself. I'll stay home and have a relaxing Sunday morning at home like normal people.'

'But mum, you'll miss all the action!' Sammy protests.

'Action I can do without.'

Zac throws an arm around her shoulder and plants a big, wet kiss on her lips.

'Aw, come on, Kell. You can't help but love me.'

She pummels his chest but can't hide the smile. 'You bastard,' she mutters.

Zac claps his hands together. 'Right, we'll collect Tom, then who fancies a sit down pizza at Gianni's?'

60

Monday 8th May

There's an air of anti-climax in the incident room.

Last week had been full-on—go, go, go—with two suspicious deaths, a missing Lord, and his miraculous return five days later. Not to mention the peculiar villagers of Ashenby, the pagan commune, and the thoroughly racist Lady Hampton.

Right now? Tumbleweed. Just the occasional buzzing fly and the hum of malfunctioning radiators.

Prisha shoots a look across at Zac. 'Heard anything?'

He stares back wearily. 'I could swear to God you asked me that five minutes ago. Look, the moment we get anything from forensics, it'll hit your inbox same time as mine.'

'And you definitely chased them up yesterday? Asked them to fast-track the snips and hacksaw?'

'Yes, after football. I spoke with Jake—Charlene's number two. He said Charlene already flagged it. But I don't see the rush. It's not like Hampton's going to do a bunk.'

'How do you know? He's got money. Probably got contacts. Could pull a Lord Lucan.'

Zac swivels in his chair. 'Prisha, I've been thinking.'

'A first time for everything.'

'I'm being serious.'

'Sorry. Go on.'

'If forensics match those snips to Malachi's brake lines—fine. That pins it. I can accept your theory. Malachi had dirt on Hampton. Blackmail. Motive. But in your rush to the gallows, there's something else you've not considered.'

'What?'

'You said it yourself—Hampton's car shed was immaculate. Tools labelled, ordered, locked away. Why would a man that particular leave incriminating tools lying around like a novice? It's sloppy. Doesn't fit. It doesn't pass the pub test.'

She squints. 'What the hell's the pub test?'

'What people say down the Dog and Duck over a pint. If it sounds implausible to them, it won't convince a jury either.'

Prisha gives a slow nod, conceding the logic—then steps in with her counter.

'Maybe he thought his plan was so watertight he didn't think we'd come looking. Or he was rattled and screwed up. No one's infallible. Who else on our radar knows how to cut brake lines? And don't forget about the suitcase, money, and fingerprints. The only person that connects all the dots is Hampton.'

He exhales slowly, unsure. 'Hmm... still doesn't sit right.'

Frank is nursing a cracking hangover, the malevolent type that, instead of slowly fading, seems to increase in severity as the morning progresses. At present, it feels like someone has taken an angle grinder to slice through his brain.

'That bloody Arthur,' he grumbles as he slowly swishes his signature across another sheet of paper. 'I should have learnt my lesson by now—keep away from his rhubarb wine. It's like embalming fluid.'

The door is nearly taken off its hinges as Prisha bursts in.

'Boss!' she shouts, holding a printout in her hand and a clutch of photos. 'Just came in from forensics.' She throws the papers onto his desk.

Normally, she'd receive a severe bollocking for bursting into his office that way. But not today. He winces in excruciating pain and merely waggles his hand up and down, indicating for her to take a seat, then puts a finger to his lips.

'A little quieter if you don't mind, Prisha. I have a migraine,' he says, barely audible as he pours water into a glass and extracts a Beroca from his desk drawer.

'Sorry, boss. Didn't know you suffered from migraines.'

As the water fizzes purple, Zac saunters in. 'He doesn't. Normal people call it a hangover,' he says with a grin. 'What was it this time, Frank?'

Frank doesn't wait for the tablet to fully dissolve and instead throws the fizzy water down in one, tablet and all.

'Arthur's rhubarb wine,' he mumbles.

'Ah, I thought once bitten twice shy. What did Meera have to say?' he enquires with a wry chuckle.

Frank eyeballs him. 'You've been wed long enough now, lad. You know not to give away your position to the enemy. If I'd shown even a sliver of weakness I'd be eating "I told you so pie" for the next two days.' He picks up Prisha's papers. 'Right, let the dog see the rabbit.'

He studies them intently for a moment, along with photo prints.

'Okay, the indentation on the snips match the marks on the brake fluid lines. The microscopic fibres on the hacksaw match the rope from the bell tower. And Hampton's fingerprints are on both handles. Highly suspicious. Not enough for a conviction, I wager, but enough to bring him in for questioning and progress the investigation.'

Prisha clenches her fists. 'Yes!'

'Steady, Prisha. A long way to go yet before celebrations are in order. We need to tread softly. I suggest you and Zac take a trip to Ravensbane Castle and politely ask Lord

Hampton to voluntarily accompany you to the station. If he refuses, then arrest him and bring him back for questioning. And be discreet.'

Prisha scowls. 'Why? Because he's a Lord?'

'No. Because at the moment, he's innocent—until and if we charge him. And as such, he should be treated the same way as every other member of the public—with dignity. We can get it wrong, you know.'

Prisha is already out of the door as Zac hovers in front of Frank's desk.

'Something to say, Zac?'

He glances over his shoulder as Prisha throws her jacket on in the incident room.

He shuffles from foot to foot. 'It's, well, just...'

'Come on lad, spit it out. It's not like you to be all of a dither. You're acting like the blushing bride on her wedding night.'

'I'm not convinced about any of it. It doesn't feel right. The tools were too obvious, like they'd been planted.'

Frank reclines back. 'We're not sending him to the electric chair, Zac. We're bringing him in for questioning. To shake the tree. Now, are you going with Prisha, or shall I assign you to Dinkel's cold case?'

'On my way, boss.'

61

Frank's eyes flit between Prisha and Zac as he speaks to the desk sergeant on the phone.

'Okay, thanks, Bill. They'll be down in five minutes. Cheers.' He hangs up, his gaze lingering.

'Hampton's legal rep has arrived.'

Zac shifts in his seat. 'I'm guessing it's not a local duty brief.'

'Your guess is right. It's Bernard Ogilvy KC.'

'Shiiiite,' Zac says, deflating like a souffle.

Prisha frowns. 'Bernard Ogilvy... doesn't ring a bell.'

'Nicknamed The Scalpel,' Zac says. 'Mostly defence. Permanent fixture in York and Durham Crown Court for the last twenty years.'

Frank taps a finger against the desk. 'Wily bastard. Has no time for the police. Twists everything you say until you forget what day it is. Full of his own self-importance.'

Prisha raises an eyebrow. 'You've dealt with him before?'

Frank nods. 'Last time was just before you joined us. Young lad, found dead in the River Wharfe near the Strid at Bolton Abbey. He suffered from aquaphobia. We were certain he'd been pushed in. Ogilvy carved the case to pieces. Defendant walked. We've not forgotten it.'

He leans back in his chair.

'Right. Thinking heads on. Let's hear what Hampton has to say. Start off with your weakest evidence first. Build the pressure. I can't wait to hear how his amputated foot ended up on that bloody fire. And remember—he's attending voluntarily, so play the long game.'

62

The interview room is a sterile, windowless box, but the air inside is anything but neutral.

Lord Hampton sits motionless, stone-faced. Impeccably dressed: three-piece charcoal suit, monogrammed cuffs, a lapel pin that whispers old money. He radiates the composure of a man who's spent his life unchallenged. His hands rest lightly on the table, though one thumb taps, barely perceptible.

As Prisha and Zac enter, Bernard Ogilvy rises, smoothing the line of his tailored jacket and offering a faint smile of surprise.

'Ah, Sergeant Stoker. Been a while. Two, three years, is it?'

Zac places his folder on the table and drops into a chair opposite.

'Aye, something like that.'

Ogilvy's smile widens. 'Don't tell me... I have excellent recall.' He taps his chin theatrically. 'Ah yes—Crown versus Loretta Shackleton?'

'That's right.'

'A satisfying outcome. Justice served, I thought.'

'Not for the lad who drowned in the river. Suffered from aquaphobia, if you remember. His final moments would have been terrifying.'

Ogilvy frowns, mildly inconvenienced. 'Yes... I forget the young man's name.'

'Luke Bretton. Twenty-five years old.'

'That's right. Unfortunate. The prosecution's case was—shall we say—structurally unsound?'

He resumes his seat beside Hampton, who hasn't moved.

Prisha takes her seat. 'I'm Detective Inspector Kumar, this is Detective Sergeant Stoker. For the recording, this is a voluntary interview under caution. Mr Hampton, you're not under arrest and are free to leave at any time.'

She opens her notebook and reads the caution aloud—measured, precise—then glances at Ogilvy.

'You've had time to review the written summary outlining the nature of our enquiries. I trust it was thorough?'

Ogilvy nods. 'Indeed. Though I'd hesitate to call it thorough,' he says, letting the word hang like a challenge.

Prisha taps the table lightly. 'Shall we begin?'

Ogilvy smooths his tie and offers a gracious nod. 'Inspector, I've advised my client to be forthright and cooperative. He has nothing to hide and every reason to assist you in resolving this unfortunate misunderstanding. As you know, he's still recovering from an extremely traumatic ordeal.'

Hampton says nothing. Eyes fixed on the table, but there's a tremor in his fingers.

Prisha nods, well aware Ogilvy's aim is to control the situation.

'Good to know.' She adjusts the manila folder slightly, then focuses on Hampton. 'Mr Hampton, Malachi Abbott was your gamekeeper for forty years, correct?'

'I can't recall exactly how long. But yes, roughly.'

'And you dismissed him three years ago?'

'I let him go, yes.'

'Can you tell me why?'

'You know why. My wife has already told you.'

'For the recording, please.'

'His drinking had worsened and was affecting his duties. I warned him repeatedly, but it made no difference.'

'An alcoholic?'

'I believe so, yes.'

'Was there another reason?'

'Yes. The final straw. Three years ago, I allowed a small commune to stay on my land—free of charge—in exchange for helping manage the estate grounds.'

'The Wicca commune, located about a mile from the castle?'

'That's right. Malachi was accused of interfering with a young girl from the commune.'

'And that's when you dismissed him?'

'Yes.'

'But you didn't alert the police?'

'No. Neither my wife and I nor the elders from the commune wanted the authorities involved.'

'To avoid a scandal?'

His shoulders stiffen. 'No. We didn't want to put the girl through police interviews or a trial. It wasn't what you'd call serious. He touched her—once.'

'She told you this?'

'No. It came from the commune leader. I never spoke to the girl.'

'I see. And how did Mr Abbott react to being dismissed?'

Hampton gazes past Prisha. 'He was contrite. Claimed not to remember the incident. Apologised. I felt sorry for him, but I had no choice.'

'Was he compensated?'

'I paid him four months' wages.'

'And have your paths crossed since?'

'Occasionally. In the village, mostly. It's a small place.'

'And the interactions?'

'Brief. Cordial.'

'Not heated?'

'No, of course not. Despite his faults, we went back a long time.'

'Before his dismissal—would you call your relationship a friendship?'

'Not friendship. Mutual respect.'

Ogilvy flicks through his own notebook. 'Inspector, if I may?'

Normally Prisha would shut him down. But it's a voluntary interview, so she lets it go.

'Go ahead.'

'Just to clarify—you've brought my client in because you suspect him in the death of Malachi Abbott?'

'Correct.'

'According to your summary, Mr Abbott died on Monday, May the 1st, shortly after leaving The Crown pub in Ashenby. His car crashed through a stone wall into the River Ure, where he drowned?'

'Yes.'

'He left the pub around 11:20 am and was found roughly ten minutes' drive away?'

'Correct.'

'Vehicle forensics confirm the brake fluid lines were cut. You believe this was done while he was in The Crown?'

'Yes.'

Ogilvy places his notebook on the table, slow, deliberate, then laces his fingers.

'As you're aware, my client was abducted from Ravensbane Castle at 3 am that same day and imprisoned in a tunnel for five days. So how could he possibly have been at The Crown around 11 am?'

Prisha leans back, her signal to Zac.

He opens his folder. 'Mr Hampton, let's revisit your account of the abduction. You say you woke at around 2: 45 am on Monday. Showered, dressed, and stepped outside Ravensbane Castle with your bags, intending to drive to Manchester Airport for a 7 am flight. You heard a noise, turned, saw a figure, then were grabbed from behind and had a rag pressed to your face—smelling of chloroform or ether. The next thing you recall is waking, bound, in a sealed mineshaft. Correct?'

Hampton nods. 'That's about the gist of it, yes.'

'The front gate CCTV recorded your car leaving at 3:05 am but there was no footage of the intruders entering before that?'

He shrugs. 'Then they didn't use the gates. The castle sits on a hundred acres. They could have entered by foot from any direction.'

'And the CCTV on the castle itself—it captured nothing because the security lights were off.'

'Yes. My fault. I turned them off before leaving.'

'Why?'

'They're motion-sensitive. Flood the whole grounds. I didn't want to wake my wife.'

Zac nods slowly. 'Let's move to the tunnel—Maggie's Tomb. Inspector Kumar and I inspected it around four hours after your return. Forensics examined it in detail. We found your prints on a pair of one litre water bottles inside. And footprints matching your shoes. But no trace of anyone else. How do you explain that?'

A shrug. 'Maybe they wore gloves. Protective gear. And five days had passed—maybe the weather played a part. I can't say.'

'You don't find it odd they left you water? If they meant for you to die in there, why leave anything? And if they planned to return—why wait five days?'

Ogilvy smirks, reclining. 'Sergeant, this is beginning to feel like a fishing expedition. My client isn't required to explain the motives of his abductors or your lack of evidence. Perhaps we can skip to the point?'

Prisha leans forward. Her voice cool.

'The point is—we're not convinced your client was abducted at all.'

'Ah. So you believe he invented the entire ordeal as an alibi?'

'Yes.'

'Fascinating. He only needed an alibi for Monday. Why not return Tuesday morning? Do you have any actual evidence? Because so far, I've seen none.'

Prisha opens the folder and removes four photographs.

'For the recording, I'm showing the suspect four images. One is of a cave spider. The other three show its web—photographed at the scene of Mr Hampton's alleged imprisonment.'

Ogilvy exhales sharply, smirking wider. 'Spiders and webs? Inspector, really?'

'I'll explain.'

'Please do. This ought to be entertaining.'

Prisha ignores him, tapping the first photo.

'This is the European cave spider—Meta menardi. It favours tunnels, culverts, and disused shafts. Spins large orb webs, up to a foot across. Only spins in total darkness.'

She taps the next image.

'Its repair cycle is unique. It doesn't rebuild its web straight away. It waits—a minimum of forty-eight hours. And only works at night.'

She holds his gaze. 'According to your statement, you escaped the tunnel in daylight. Crawled through the exit on your knees, then stood up. You're what—five-foot-ten?'

She slides forward the final image.

'The web was stretched across the exit trench—intact. Photographed just hours after your return to the castle. So, tell me—if you really came out that way, how is the web untouched?'

Lord Hampton adjusts his cufflinks glares at her. 'Are you seriously accusing me of murder because of a cobweb?'

It's his first sign of emotion.

Bernard Ogilvy barks a theatrical laugh. 'My client's right. You're staking your case on a spider's web? I'll have no trouble finding an arachnologist to destroy your theory in court.'

Zac leans in. 'Mr Ogilvy, you're not in court. You're here to advise your client—not cross-examine. You'll have plenty of time to display your brilliance if this reaches trial.'

Ogilvy shifts in his seat.

Prisha sets aside the spider photos and pushes another photograph across the table.

'Recognise this suitcase, Mr Hampton? Bought by your wife in York. She gave it to you for your Syria trip. We have the receipt. CCTV of the purchase. We found it in Malachi

Abbott's wardrobe. Inside—£20,000 in used notes. Many of them bearing your fingerprints. Would you care to explain?'

Hampton stares at the image. His lips tighten. Eyes blink rapidly.

'Ahem... Excuse me, I'd like a break. I want to speak to my barrister. Alone.'

Prisha stands, folding her notebook.

'Of course. It's nearly lunchtime. Shall we say one hour?'

63

They collect their takeaway from Mr Chips and grab the first empty bench near Battery Parade. The smell of vinegar and chip fat fills the air, accentuated by the warmth of the midday sun. A stiff breeze whips off the water, enough to stir Zac's napkin and threaten the integrity of his mushy peas.

Seagulls wheel above them, ever hopeful, while holidaymakers spill along the harbour path—sunhats, buggies, ice creams. A toddler screeches as a gull swoops too close. Somewhere down below the pier wall, a boat coughs into life, sending a puff of blue smoke into the air.

'Not bad, is it?' Zac says with a grin, easing back with a chip already halfway to his mouth.

Prisha shields her eyes from the sun, taking in the soft glint from the sea.

'Worse places to be,' she replies with a shy smile, capturing the moment and placing it in her memory bank.

They sit in silence for a few minutes, elbows brushing lightly as they leisurely eat. The fish is hot, crisp, flaky. The batter cracks like glass. The chips are firm on the outside, soft and fluffy inside.

'So,' Zac says eventually, wiping a thumb on his jeans. 'Hampton, what do you reckon so far?'

'He's nervous.'

'Hmm... I'm still not convinced.'

'I know.'

'If he did kill Malachi by sabotaging his car, why not immediately go to his house and retrieve the suitcase and cash?'

Prisha shrugs. 'Loads of reasons. The chances of being seen. Or he might have assumed Malachi would have already hidden the money. Remember, Hampton would have been in a high emotional state, not even certain whether his plan was going to work or not. Critical thinking can desert you in those situations. Or maybe he didn't intend to kill him, just injure him. A warning.'

'Maybe. Either way, letting him stew for an hour's not a bad move.' He scrunches the butcher's paper into a ball. 'If we carry on eating like this, we'll end up looking like Frank in twenty years.'

She laughs, but it's soft, almost wistful. 'Twenty years,' she murmurs. 'I wonder where we'll be and what we'll be doing?'

'You'll be Chief Constable and I'll be...'

'Deputy Chief Constable?' she interrupts with a sparkle in her eye.

'No. I was going to say, I'll still be a DS.'

'Don't say that. You'll go far.'

He rises and takes her fish and chip wrapper. 'I'm not sure I want to go far. Honestly, Prisha... I'd be happy if things stayed exactly the way they are now. Forever. But... they can't.'

She watches him walk towards the nearest bin, a wave of guilt *and* want washing through her like saltwater—harsh, unforgiving. She feels sick to her stomach at the thought of what can never be.

64

Bernard Ogilvy isn't quite as arrogant as when he first arrived. Not rattled, but the smarmy confidence has been replaced by something more workmanlike. A barrister who just wants to get the job done and get out of there.

Lord Hampton has composed himself—likely after a stern word in his ear.

Prisha and Zac take their seats. She presses the record button.

'It's now 13:32. Interview recommencing after a break requested by Mr Noah Hampton to consult with his legal representative. Also present are Detective Sergeant Zac Stoker and Mr Bernard Ogilvy KC.'

She glances at Hampton. 'Before we continue, I must remind you—you are still under caution. Do you understand?'

Hampton nods faintly. 'Yes.'

She rubs her hands together. 'Let's return to the suitcase and the money.'

Hampton glances at Ogilvy, a flash of guilt in his eyes.

'I can explain.' He coughs into his hand. 'Malachi had been asking for money for about a year. At first it was small amounts—fifty, a hundred pounds. Said he was struggling to find work at his age. Then the amounts crept up. Always some excuse—car trouble, roof leak. I suppose I felt partly responsible. Then, about three weeks ago, he stopped me in Ashenby high street. Insisted we go for a drink at The Crown. I sensed it was for more than a friendly chat. We sat in a quiet corner, and he said he needed twenty thousand. He was planning to move to Scotland. Said it'd be the last time. He swore he'd never ask again. So... I agreed.'

'And the suitcase?'

'My wife bought it for my trip abroad. It was too small, so I used it for the money. I dropped it off at Malachi's one night. That was the last time I saw him.'

Prisha lets a long pause settle as she scribbles notes.

'Where did the cash come from? Did you withdraw it from the bank?'

'No. I keep cash in a safe at the castle—thirty grand or so. For emergencies. Tradesmen prefer cash. Sometimes it saves me money.'

Zac leans forward. 'Who served you at the pub?'

'Sorry?'

'You said you had a drink with Malachi. Who served you? Was it the landlord, Mr Featherstone?'

'Er... yes. Yes, I believe it was.'

'So he can verify that?'

'I imagine so.'

'And when you dropped off the money, did Malachi's neighbour—Mrs Selkirk—see you?'

'I can't say.'

'She lives next door in a one-up one-down cottage. It would have been nigh on impossible for her not to see you.'

'I... I can't speak for Mrs Selkirk. And from what little I've seen of her, I'm not sure she's entirely compos mentis.'

Prisha reaches into the folder. 'Oh, she's very much compos mentis. I had a long chat with her last week.'

She slides a photocopy across the table. 'Recognise this? Malachi gave it to Mrs Selkirk, with instructions to hand it to the police if something happened to him.'

Hampton and Ogilvy lean forward, scanning the handwritten note:

If anything untoward should happen to me, then only two other people know the truth about that young lass.

N.H.

So hear me God.
Malachi Abbott

Prisha's tone is calm. 'Who's the young lass, Mr Hampton?'

The colour drains from his face. 'I... I've no idea. Perhaps he meant the girl from the commune.'

'The initials N.H. could stand for Noah Hampton.'

'Well—yes. Possibly. I'm not denying I knew about the incident. I've already explained that.'

Prisha studies him. 'He says only two people knew the truth about the girl. What truth?'

He shrugs. 'I don't know.'

'And why would he say—if anything untoward should happen to me—like he was expecting something bad to happen?'

'I really can't help you. Maybe he'd been drinking when he wrote the note.'

Prisha's eyes drop onto the wording. 'Clearly legible. I'd say he was stone cold sober when he wrote it. Another oddity; he says two people knew. But only writes down one set of initials. N.H.'

'Yes. I see that.'

Prisha shifts tack. 'You're aware that Reverend Hartley—vicar of St Mary's—died early Thursday morning?'

'Yes. Suicide, I believe.'

'Who told you that?'

'It's what I heard.'

'We're treating it as suspicious. Do you know Reverend Hartley's full name?'

There's a pause. A flicker of unease.

'Erm... yes. Nicholas Hartley.'

'N.H.' Prisha says slowly.

Ogilvy's patience snaps. 'Inspector Kumar, I think we've had enough fishing for one day. As you stated earlier, my client is here voluntarily. He's free to leave. I suggest we conclude the interview now.'

He stands and brushes down his jacket.

Hampton looks up at him sharply. 'No, Bernard. Wait. I want to get this sorted. I don't want it hanging over me. I'm innocent.'

Ogilvy sighs, then lowers himself back into the chair. 'As you wish.'

Zac breathes deep. 'Let's go back to the money.'

'I've already explained,' Hampton snaps becoming agitated.

'You don't strike me as the kind of man who's easily manipulated. You're shrewd. Sharp. So why hand over twenty grand? What did Malachi have on you?'

'Nothing. There were no threats. I just felt responsible for his situation.'

'I can understand fifty quid here and there. But twenty thousand is a stretch. So what was it he knew? Was it this?' He taps the note. 'The girl?'

Hampton shakes his head. 'No. Definitely not.'

Prisha catches something in his manner. Whatever the truth is behind the cryptic note, it's rattled him.

'Definitely not the girl... but definitely something?' she asks.

Hampton rubs his face and turns to Ogilvy. 'I may as well tell them, Bernard. It doesn't affect my innocence.'

Ogilvy's voice is flat. 'I'd advise against that, Noah.'

65

Hampton faces Prisha directly.

'Very well. The whole truth, inspector. Yes, Malachi was blackmailing me. But not at first. What I said before—about him asking for small handouts—that's true. But when he asked for twenty thousand, I lost patience. Told him he was off his bloody rocker. I wanted nothing more to do with him.'

He falters. Lost in the memory.

'Go on,' Prisha says gently.

'He said... if I didn't give him the money, he'd tell my wife about an affair I'd had.'

Zac and Prisha exchange a look.

'An affair?' she prompts.

'Yes. Five years ago. Brief and foolish. With a married woman. Malachi caught us... in flagrante, shall we say. In the back seat of a car in my shed. He saw the door ajar and came to investigate. My wife was away for the weekend. None of us ever spoke of it again. Then, two weeks ago, he stopped me in the village. Said he needed twenty grand. If I didn't pay up, he'd be paying a visit to my wife.'

Prisha notes it down, then looks up. 'What's the woman's name and address?'

'What?'

'The woman's name you had an affair with. We'll need to speak with her to verify your account.'

'Absolutely not. You'll have to take my word for it,' he declares, adamant.

'That's not how murder investigations work, Mr Hampton. I can assure you, we'll be discreet. Is she married?'

'Yes. But I'm not giving you her name. It's dishonourable. A woman's reputation is at stake.'

Zac can't help a smirk. 'Maybe you should've thought of that before you took her into the back seat.'

Prisha stays focused. 'If you won't name her, it casts doubt on your story. It begins to sound like a convenient invention.'

He folds his arms. 'Then so be it.'

A long pause ensues, like a chess game between two masters.

Prisha breaks the silence. 'The Wicca commune held a Beltane Festival the night before your alleged abduction. It was held near the standing stones in Ravensbane Wood. I believe they're called the Three Crones.'

'Yes. And the commune had my blessing. They hold a number of celebrations throughout the year. I can assure you, there's no ritual sacrifices, inspector,' he adds with a forced chuckle, trying to break the oppressive atmosphere.

'Mr Hampton, you have a prosthetic left foot, I believe?' Prisha quizzes.

He hesitates, baffled by the question, before finally replying, 'Yes, but what has...'

'When did you lose it?'

'Erm, many years ago. The late eighties.'

'How?'

'In a... in a car accident. My own fault. Young and foolish. Too much testosterone. It had been raining, and I took a corner too fast. Slammed into a wall. No one else involved. The engine was shunted forward and completely mangled my left foot. It was amputated in hospital.'

Ogilvy harrumphs. 'Inspector, where exactly are you going with this?'

She fixes him with a steely glare. 'Mr Ogilvy, this is a police interview. *We* ask the questions.'

'And may I remind you my client is here voluntarily,' he retorts, voice rising in frustration.

'Being here voluntarily does not exempt your client from answering questions, otherwise, the process would be pointless. May I continue?'

Ogilvy shares a disgruntled glance with Hampton, then nods.

She pulls two more photos from her folder and drops them on the table.

Hampton stares at the gruesome images. At first, his eyes don't appear to recognise what they are. Then a slow realisation dawns as both he and Ogilvy curl their mouths up.

'A shoe and a badly burnt foot,' Hampton murmurs.

'The charred remains of the shoe and foot were found in the ashes of fire held by the Wicca commune early Monday morning.'

Hampton is clearly befuddled. 'I... why are you showing me this? I don't understand.'

'DNA tests confirm it's your foot.'

He shakes his head vehemently. 'Impossible!'

'DNA doesn't lie. Also, forensic analysis indicates it had been preserved in formaldehyde for quite some time.'

'But that's...' His eyelids flicker as he rubs nervously at his mouth. He seems to deflate like a balloon with a slow leak. 'Malachi,' he murmurs.

'Malachi?'

He throws back in his seat and sighs. 'The foot—I kept it after I left hospital. It was housed in a large glass jar in a formaldehyde solution.'

Prisha and Zac swap baffled looks.

'Why?' Prisha continues, hiding her own confusion.

'As a reminder as to how close I'd come to losing my life. Up until the accident, I'd been wild and reckless in everything I did. It gave me pause for thought. The foot was a sort of prick to the conscience. I'd been given a second chance, and I wasn't about to waste it.'

Prisha rolls a pen around in her fingers. 'So how did it end up on the fire in *your* woods?'

His lips vibrate like a horse. 'I kept the jar in a cupboard in my study. I'd occasionally bring it out to show friends and visitors, as a sort of sick joke, to shock them. My first wife tolerated it, but after her passing, I remarried to Abigail. She insisted I get rid of it.'

'When?'

'Maybe eight years ago.'

'And why did you say the word—Malachi—a moment ago?'

'I asked him to dispose of it. Obviously, he didn't. God knows why. As to how it ended up on the fire, I've no idea. Unless Malachi put it there as some sort of gruesome payback, or possibly to bring suspicion upon the Wicca commune.'

Ogilvy makes a note in his diary. 'I suggest a ten-minute recess, inspector.'

66

Frank's jaw is in danger of suffering a carpet burn.

'He kept his foot in a jar?' he bellows.

Prisha grins 'Yes. Preserved. Reckons the current Lady Hampton wasn't too enamoured of it and told him to get rid. He asked Malachi to dispose of it about eight years back.'

Frank fidgets with a pen. 'That's right, he was married previously. Can't remember how his first wife died, but there were a few raised eyebrows when he wed the current Lady Hampton. A lot younger than him.'

Zac snacks on a chocolate bar. 'It kinda adds up, Frank. Malachi had no time for the Wicca commune. He could have placed the foot on the fire to bring unwanted attention their way.'

'Hmm... so, a bit of a red herring,' Frank mumbles. 'And what about Malachi's cryptic letter he left with Mrs Selkirk?'

Prisha shrugs. 'Hampton played dumb, but it definitely unnerved him.'

'How's he holding up?'

'Composed, initially. But with the foot and note evidence, it's definitely flustered him. Would help if that arsehole barrister wound his neck in.'

Frank chuckles. 'Aye, that's Ogilvy. A legend in his own underpants,' he says, gazing out onto the harbour. 'And you haven't confronted him with the evidence of the snips yet?'

Zac rises and drops the chocolate wrapper in a bin. 'No. We'll go back in and have a friendly chat about his classic car collection. Then—blam—Prisha hits him with the snips. Not literally, of course.'

'Sounds good. Offer the hand of friendship, then snatch it away. Right, well keep at him. He's not the type to break down and confess, but I think we have enough.'

67

Back in the interview room things have calmed somewhat.

Bernard Ogilvy now looks thoroughly cheesed off. Like a man who has been drip fed information from his client.

After Prisha finishes the preamble, Zac slides into his spiel.

'I have to say, Mr Hampton, I was very impressed with your collection of classic cars. Especially the Aston Martin.'

Hampton blinks, caught off guard. He can't resist a smile. 'Yes. A lifetime's work. The Aston is *my* personal favourite too.'

'Must be worth a small fortune?'

'The insurance alone is a small fortune. Of course, most of the vehicles were in a terrible state when I got them.'

'Oh, I see. You fix them up yourself?'

'Yes. No formal training. Just tinkering over the years. It's a labour of love,' he says with an element of pride. 'My wife says I care more about the cars than I do about her.'

Zac nods along. 'So, it's fair to say you know your way around a vehicle?'

'Yes. I suppose I do.' His expression darkens as he realises he's being led. 'Is the interview over?'

'Not quite,' Zac says, sliding a series of photographs across the table. 'Take a look at these. The top ones show the cut marks on the brake lines of Malachi's Land Rover. The ones beneath are enhanced close-ups. You'll notice all four lines have a distinctive indentation—a small nick left by the tool used. These final images show a pair of snips. The same imperfection appears on the blade. Forensics recreated the cuts using those snips. The marks matched exactly. They also found traces of brake fluid in the hinge.'

Hampton studies the photos closely. 'Yes, well... I see all that. But what's it got to do with me?'

'Because those snips were seized from your shed on Saturday. They have your fingerprints on the handles.'

His eyes widen. 'No. That can't... it...'

Prisha folds her arms. Her voice hardens.

'Malachi Abbott was murdered, Mr Hampton. You've admitted he was blackmailing you—that's motive. We don't believe a word of your abduction story. You went to that tunnel to plant your prints, not to suffer imprisonment. The undisturbed spider's web proves you didn't leave when you claimed. And now we have the tool that cut the brake lines—found in your shed, bearing your fingerprints, and a forensic match.'

'No. You've got this all wrong, inspector. I can assure...'

'You've lied to us from the beginning. First you said Malachi wasn't blackmailing you. When presented with the suitcase and money evidence, you quickly changed your story and said he was blackmailing you. Then fabricated a story about a mystery woman you were having an affair with but refuse to name. Malachi left a note behind with your initials on, the same initials as the dead vicar.'

Hampton reddens, shoves his chair back and stands up.

'Come on, Bernard. You were right. I should've kept my mouth shut. I was here to help the police as a responsible citizen but obviously they're trying to fit me up.' He glares at Prisha. 'Inspector, this interview is now over. I'm going home.'

Prisha rises too.

'You're right, Mr Hampton. It is over. But the only place you're going is into police custody.'

'What?'

She inches forward, voice clear, firm.

'Noah Hampton, I'm arresting you on suspicion of the murder of Malachi Abbott. You do not have to say anything, but it may harm your defence if you do not mention when questioned something you later rely on in court. Anything you do say may be given in evidence.'

68

Prisha and Zac climb the stairs in a jubilant mood, each congratulating one another on their performance. They amble into the interview room and spot Superintendent Banks in Frank's office.

'Shit,' Prisha curses. 'I could have done without her today.'

'Or any day for that matter. Come on, let's front up and get it over with.'

'I hope she's in a better mood than last week.'

As they enter Frank's office Banks rises and offers a warm smile, which immediately puts them on guard.

'Ah, Prisha, Zac, Frank's just been giving me the latest on the Malachi Abbott murder. I take it you've arrested Lord Hampton?'

Prisha's eyes swivel onto Frank. 'Erm, yes, ma'am. A moment ago. We'll let him stew overnight, then question him again tomorrow and formally charge him.'

'Excellent. If it hadn't been for the damning evidence of the snips, and the money in the suitcase then I'm not sure you really had a case. So the blackmail story's his official motive. Do you buy it?'

'Not for a second. He's hiding the real reason.'

'Which is?'

She takes a sideways step. 'Not certain yet, ma'am.'

Her eyes narrow. 'Hmm… well you need to wheedle it out of him. Jurors like a good motive. I don't suppose he confessed to the actual murder?'

'No,' Zac says. 'Not with Bernard Ogilvy riding shotgun.'

Frank regards his officers with a flicker of quiet pride. 'And what about the cryptic message from Malachi? Did Hampton shed any light on it?'

Banks frowns. 'What cryptic message?'

Prisha looks at her. 'Malachi left an envelope with his neighbour to be handed over to police if he should die in unusual circumstances. It said there were only two people who knew the truth about the young lass. Then there was an initial—N.H.'

'And who was the young girl he was referring to?'

She shrugs. 'Not sure.'

'And if he said two people, then why only one initial?'

'Well, pure speculation but the vicar who was found hanged shared the same initials—Nicholas Hartley.'

'Hmm… and Frank said fibres from the bell rope matched fibres on the hacksaw also recovered from Hampton's shed.'

'Yes.'

'So you believe he had a hand in that too?'

Prisha takes a sharp intake of breath. 'The forensics suggest so, but we're far from finding out how and why. We haven't confronted him with that yet. Frank wanted us to focus on Malachi's murder first—the evidence was stronger.'

Banks slips her jacket on. 'Yes, good advice. The vicar's death is an ongoing investigation, and as Hampton's a suspect in that case also, it should prevent him from getting bail. Spend the rest of the week collating a watertight case before handing it over to the CPS. I'm sure they'll run with it. And again, well done to all involved. That includes you, Frank.'

'I did bugger all, Anne,' he says with a chuckle.

'Nonsense. A team needs strong leadership.'

She heads towards the door then stops and peers at Prisha. 'I did say last week to focus on forensics and not superstition and hocus-pocus. I'm glad you heeded my advice. Have a nice evening.'

They wait in stunned silence until she disappears out of the far door.

'Hell, what's got into her?' Prisha asks.

'I don't like it,' Zac states, with a concerned expression. 'Her being pleasant upsets the whole equilibrium of my existence. The world spins around the sun. Night follows day. Newcastle will never win the league, and Anne Banks is never nice. That's how things work. That's how they've always worked.'

'Daft bugger.' Frank undoes his top button and loosens his tie. 'I tell you what, how about we have a little celebration tonight. A sit down curry and a few drinks? Partners included.'

Prisha looks at Zac, and smiles. 'Okay, sounds good. I'll call Adam. You up for it, Zac?'

'If Frank's paying, I'm not going to miss out. I'll ring Kelly now.'

Frank is alarmed. 'Hang on a bloody minute! I never said owt about paying.'

The door slams shut as they make a quick exit.

Epilogue

Tuesday 9th May

Frank enters the incident room carrying breakfast. He dumps a carrier bag on the table and gingerly places a cardboard cup holder next to it containing three coffees. He stares knowingly at Prisha and Zac, who are looking worse for wear.

'You may look and feel like crap, but at least you made it in on time. Ten out of ten for dedication to duty. I've got you both a coffee and a bacon and egg butty. It will either kill you or cure your hangover.'

Zac tries a grin but aborts it as a stabbing pain pummels his head.

'Cheers, Frank. Just what the doctor ordered.'

'Whose idea was it to kick on to the pubs after the curry?' Prisha grumbles as she takes a delicate sip of strong black coffee.

Frank chuckles. 'If my memory serves correctly, it was your idea. Just the one you said.'

'Wasn't my idea to go onto Sambuca shots and Baby Guinness. Christ, what's even in Baby Guinness?' she asks as Zac attacks his breakfast roll.

He chews and wipes his mouth on his sleeve. 'It's coffee liqueur topped off with Bailey's Irish Cream. Meera's idea, if I recall.'

Prisha groans, eyeing the rolls suspiciously. 'She's a bad influence, Frank.'

He chortles. 'Tell me about it. I haven't seen her let her hair down like that for many a year. I knew it was time to call it a night when she started dancing on the table to Abba. Lucky for her she has a rostered day off.' A frown spreads across his face as he recalls something. 'Forgot to mention it yesterday because of all the excitement, but while you were interviewing Hampton, I had a call from Charlene.'

'About?' Zac mumbles, chewing like he's not eaten in a week.

'Toxicology report on Malachi Abbott. Remember the traces of the unknown substance they found in his blood—well, they identified it as aconite.'

'Which is?'

'A botanical alkaloid toxin obtained from wolfsbane or monkshood. They're both types of plant, Zac.'

'Ha, ha. Very funny. And what effects does it produce?'

'A whole host of symptoms. Low blood pressure, slow heart rate, irregular heartbeat, muscle weakness, disorientation. Anyway, enough talking shop.' He focuses back on Prisha, who has fallen silent. 'How did Adam pull up?'

'What?' she says, her addled brain trying to digest the information.

'Adam—was he suffering from a hangover?'

'No. He was fine. Smarmy get. He was up and off at five, heading back to the farm full of the joys of spring. He never seems to get a hangover. It's bloody annoying. Why should I suffer alone?'

'He stuck to beer, that's why,' Zac comments with a muffled laugh.

Prisha looks at him and nods at a large dollop of egg yolk nesting in his beard.

'Oops, sorry.' He fumbles in his trouser pocket and pulls out a scrunched up tissue along with a number of coins that fall onto the table with a clatter.

Prisha stares at the coins. 'What's that?' she asks, pointing.

'What?' he replies, daubing at the yolk.

'That round charm?'

He picks it up and hands it to her. 'It's what that young lass gave me last week. Said she'd made it. Not that I believe her.'

'What young lass? The weird one, Morrigan?' she asks, turning it over in her fingers.

'Aye.'

Prisha examines the exquisitely made fabric coin. 'Hang on... when did she give you this?'

'Last Wednesday afternoon after speaking with Reverend Hartley.'

'The day before his death,' she mutters. 'What exactly did she say?'

Zac reddens and drops the tissue into a bin as Frank's eyes dart between his officers.

'Erm, she asked if I wanted to go for a walk to some place called Gallows Field. I declined. Said I was busy. Then she handed me the coin. Said it was for me. I asked who the face on the coin was, and she said it's the Wicker Girl. I asked who that was.'

'And?'

He shuffles, embarrassed. 'Ahem, said she was the Wicker Girl.'

Frank's eyes screw into knots. 'Does someone mind telling me what you're bloody talking about?'

The conversation is rudely interrupted as the door clanks open and Dinkel strides in, his usual ebullient self.

'Morning chaps!'

'Keep it down, Dinks,' Zac advises.

Dinkel stops in his tracks, assessing the sorry-looking trio. Finally, the penny drops.

'Oh, I see. You must have solved the case you were working on. Big night out, was it?'

Frank pats him on the shoulder. 'We'll make a copper out of you yet. Sorry, I didn't get you any breakfast.'

'Don't apologise, sir. I had a kipper and a cup of bone broth when I got up. It's a new diet I'm trying.'

Prisha holds back a dry retch. 'Urgh, please. Kipper for breakfast,' she murmurs.

Dinkel saunters past them and casually glances at the whiteboard, which is still emblazoned with Prisha's scribblings from the previous day. He drops his backpack by the side of his desk and picks up an empty cup.

'Time for a green tea.'

He shoots another look at the whiteboard as he passes, moves on a few steps, then halts as if he's walked into a brick wall. Still facing the same way, he takes three steps backwards, as if moonwalking, then stares at the board again. He points at it.

'The names,' he mutters. 'I've seen them before. It's this... this cold case Mr Finnegan gave me.' He rushes back to his desk and picks up a folder, and flicks through it like a man on a mission.

Prisha experiences another moment of disquiet. 'What names exactly?' she asks in a hushed tone. 'Lord Hampton?'

'No, no. The victims.'

Frank straightens, his brow furrowing. 'Malachi Abbott and Reverend Hartley?'

'Yes. That's them, sir. Ah, yes, here we are.'

Prisha's sense of foreboding increases a notch. 'Dinkel, what exactly *is* this cold case you've been tasked with?'

Dinkel rubs at his hair. 'The death of Iona Jacobs in 1989. Classified as a hit and run. Perpetrator never caught.'

'And?'

He flicks back a page. 'Sunday 4th June 1989. Iona Jacobs worked as a barmaid and helped in the kitchen at The Crown pub. She also lodged there.'

'In Ashenby, near Masham?' Zac asks, his interest also piqued.

'Yeah, that's right. She finished her shift at 2:15 pm, then cycled to the outskirts of the village—to the church, St Mary's, about a fifteen-minute ride. There, she spoke with

Reverend Hartley for about thirty minutes before leaving. Instead of heading straight back to the pub, she took the scenic route, skirting the boundary of Ravensbane Wood. She never made it back to the pub.

'Her body was found at around 4 pm by a Mr Malachi Abbott, who was the gamekeeper for Ravensbane Estate at the time. He recognised her straight away because she'd once worked at Ravensbane Castle as a maid.'

Prisha steps forward, her face flushed. 'Was she dead?'

'No. She was alive, but never regained consciousness. And...' he pauses. 'She was eighteen weeks pregnant.'

'Christ,' Zac mutters, rubbing a hand through his beard.

Dinkel skim-reads further. 'She and the baby were kept alive on life support for twelve weeks. But Iona started to deteriorate—something to do with the placenta breaking down. They delivered the baby via C-section, put it in an incubator, and switched off Iona's life support.'

Silence grips the room for a moment.

Dinkel keeps reading. 'The baby was adopted by Iona's mother, a Mrs Lilac Jacobs, the grandmother, who I've been trying to trace. Yesterday, I found out that in 1994, she reverted to her maiden name—Miss Lilac Penhallow.'

Prisha instantly feels woozy, her mind unable to process, her mouth unwilling to form words.

Dinkel is oblivious to her plight, still caught up in the file. 'I'm not one for conspiracy theories, but don't you think it's a bit odd the last person to speak to Iona Jacobs was Reverend Hartley, and the person who found her was Malachi Abbott? Both of them now victims of a suspected murder. I know it was a long time ago, but what are the chances of that?'

Prisha stares out of the window, her eyes focusing on a trawler chugging between the Whitby piers as it heads out to wide, open waters.

Animated cross examination ensues between Frank, Zac, and Dinkel, but to Prisha, their words are a jumbled alphabet.

Eventually she composes herself and whispers, 'Dinkel, what was the baby's name?'

Dinkel checks the file. 'Erm... Morrigan. Morrigan Penhallow.'

'That would make Morrigan at least thirty-five years old.'

'Yes, that's correct.'

'No, you've made a mistake. That can't be right.' She turns to Zac for support. 'The girl... Morrigan, she's... eleven, twelve... it doesn't make any...' Her voice dries up as the room begins to spin. She places a hand on the table to steady herself and drops onto a chair.

Fragments of memories, observations, conversations, half-chewed theories bounce around inside her head.

Zac's braided coin, similar to the one found in Malachi's car. Lilac Penhallow, the librarian, and schoolteacher at the Wicca lodges. Monkshood growing at the commune. The Wicker Girl—Morrigan Penhallow. Something Dinkel said.

She stares at him. 'Last week you mentioned a reality TV Show on YouTube. Something about a girl, then you said woman?'

Dinkel's eyes roll heavenwards in recollection. 'Oh, yes. An American woman called Shauna Rae. Fascinating viewing. Aged twenty-nine, but to look at her you'd swear she was aged about twelve. Something to do with her pituitary gland not developing.' Hesitation as his face turns into a question mark. 'But why are you bringing that up?'

The room stills.

Prisha's head swivels until her gaze locks onto Zac.

He's computing the same information.

He doesn't say anything. Doesn't have to. His eyes say it all.

I said you were rushing things. I was never convinced. You wouldn't listen.

Frank is increasingly concerned. So much so, he abandons his bacon butty.

'What is it, Prisha? None of this is making bloody sense, but I have a bad feeling about it. A very bad feeling.'

She tries to lick her lips, but her mouth is dry.

'Frank... I think we've...'

She falters.

Swallows hard trying to suppress the rising bile.

'I think I've arrested the wrong man.'

Frank scowls, his face thunder. 'What the bloody hell are you saying, Prisha?'

'Lord Hampton didn't kill Malachi Abbott or Reverend Hartley. He's been set up. We've *all* been set up.'

<hr/>

Outside, a girl in a black cloak lingers across the street from the station.

Stares up at the windows.

She turns.

A thin smile on her lips.

Then skips away, giggling like she was never there at all.

THE END... FOR NOW.

Author Notes

You made it to the end. And by now, you're probably thinking one of two things:

"Ooh, I can't wait for the next book,"

or

"He's left it on a cliffhanger*! The bastard*!"

If it's the latter, then I offer my sincere apologies.

I promise, it wasn't some cheap marketing ploy to force you into buying the next book.

Scout's honour.

I realised before the halfway mark that the story I wanted to tell was simply too broad for one novel.

I wrestled with it. Truly. It kept me awake some nights.

I know all too well the sting of a cliffhanger.

I've seen the reviews. I know the frustration.

I suppose I could've condensed the plot, trimmed the layers, raced to the finish.

But then I'd have had to cut back on the quiet scenes that show Frank, Prisha, and Zac off the clock—their quirks, habits, vulnerabilities.

And those are the bits I love most. The moments where they feel like real people, not one-dimensional cardboard cut-outs in a play.

Alternatively, I could've written it all. Every twist, every revelation.

But that would've taken twice as long to finish, and cost twice as much to buy.

And I figured you'd prefer half the wait.

That's my excuse. And I'm sticking to it.

But just think what's still to come in the follow-up book, **Crucifix Knot.**

Who killed Malachi Abbott?

What's really going on in the strange village of Ashenby?

Are the Wicca commune innocent bystanders—or something much darker?

What's the truth behind Reverend Hartley's death?

Is Lord Hampton guilty—or the perfect fall guy?

Lady Hampton—refinement behind a teacup, or rotten at the core?

Morrigan Penhallow—The Wicker Girl—is she a malevolent force or a guardian angel in disguise watching over Zac?

And talking of Zac—like a moth drawn to the flame, is he flying too close to Prisha's burning candle?

Will Dinkel ever solve the cold case about the hit and run of Iona Jacobs?

And more importantly...

Will Meera finally catch Frank red-handed with a bacon butty breaking his strict diet regime?

As I write this, even I don't know.

Or maybe I do...

All will be revealed in Book 11 – Crucifix Knot.

Thank you for reading.

***Ely North* - May 2025**

Keep In Touch

Thank you for reading. I hope you enjoyed this latest case in the DCI Finnegan series. Your support means the world to me.

If you're ready for the next investigation, **Crucifix Knot** — Book 11 in the series — is due for release in **August 2025.**

It will be available in paperback and ebook from **Amazon**, and can also be ordered from your **local bookshop** or requested through your **library** (distributor – IngramSpark).

If you enjoyed the story, I'd love it if you left a quick review on **Amazon**, **Goodreads**, or gave it a mention in your favourite **Facebook** group. *Please, no spoilers, especially the ending.* You can even leave a rating straight from your **Kindle**—or better still, tell a friend, or if you've just finished the paperback, lend them the book. Word of mouth remains the best recommendation.

Thanks again for your time, a precious and finite commodity.

All the best,
Ely North

Join the Ely North Newsletter

If you'd like to keep informed of imminent release dates, and lot's more, then why not join my free newsletter? It's where I share crime news, my top ten Unsolved Mysteries, behind-the-scenes writing insights, plus occasional special offers. It's a bit of fun.

When you sign up, I'll send you a free ebook copy of Aquaphobia — the prequel novella to Black Nab. Simply scan the QR code below.

Also By Ely North – DCI Finnegan Series

Book 1: **Black Nab**

Book 2: **Jawbone Walk**

Book 3: **Vertigo Alley**

Book 4: **Whitby Toll**

Book 5: **House Arrest**

Book 6: **Gothic Fog**

Book 7: **Happy Camp**

Book 8: **Harbour Secrets**

Book 9: **Murder Mystery**

Book 10: **Wicker Girl**

Book 11: **Crucifix Knot** – Pre-order

DCI Finnegan Series Boxset #1: **Books 1 − 3**

DCI Finnegan Series Boxset #2: **Books 4 − 6**

Prequel: **Aquaphobia** (Free ebook for newsletter subscribers)

*Note: All books are available from Amazon in ebook, paperback, and in **Kindle Unlimited** (Aquaphobia not in KU). Audiobooks Books 1-5 available from Audible, Spotify. Paperbacks can be ordered from all good bookshops.

Boxset print editions are one book compiled from three books. They do not come in a box.

*** Pre-orders only apply to ebooks.

Printed in Great Britain
by Amazon